# THE GRANDFATHER CLAUSE

Philip A. Genovese, Jr.

authorHOUSE®

AuthorHouse™
1663 Liberty Drive, Suite 200
Bloomington, IN 47403
www.authorhouse.com
Phone: 1-800-839-8640

This book is a work of fiction. People, places, events, and situations are the product of the author's imagination. Any resemblance to actual persons, living or dead, or historical events, is purely coincidental, unintentional, or a fictionalized version created solely for entertainment value.

First published by AuthorHouse 10/10/2007

ISBN: 978-1-4343-3428-2 (e)
ISBN: 978-1-4343-3426-8 (sc)
ISBN: 978-1-4343-3427-5 (hc)

Printed in the United States of America
Bloomington, Indiana

This book is printed on acid-free paper.

For my wife, MaryAnn, and our children - Taylor, Melissa, and Tommy


And, in remembrance of my grandfathers, Tom and Vito.

# ACKNOWLEDGMENTS

It has been said that writing is a lonely pursuit. But thanks to all the many early readers of my manuscript and their kind words, I was rarely alone and always encouraged. You are too many to mention but too few to forget. I never will. Thank you.

When I announced to my parents my sophomore year in college that I no longer thought I would be a doctor and had switched my major to English Literature, they bought me an electric typewriter. I'm still not sure that was a good idea, but I love them for their support of my dreams, their wonderful grand-parenting, and darn good proofreading.

If you have a demanding day job and decide to write a book, you better plan to have five years worth of missed weekends and vacations with your laptop. It is also best to have great friends and good neighbors who excuse your absences and tolerate your book funk way longer than reasonably necessary. The 'hood rules.

Mostly, though, you need a wonderful family that forgives each others' weakest moments and celebrates the best. There would be no book without their peace, love, and understanding.

**GRANDFATHER CLAUSE** - A provision exempting persons or other entities already engaged in an activity from rules or legislation affecting that activity. Grandfather clauses sometimes are added to legislation in order to avoid antagonizing groups with established interests in the activities affected.

lectlaw.com

People may be "grandfathered" to receive new benefits they are not otherwise entitled to.

wikipedia.org

# Prologue
**Sunday, March 1963**
**Red Bank, New Jersey**

What I remember about Sundays back then was that they were always the same. Even knowing that our memories play conveniently with the truth and most often live longest the closer they reside to the boundaries of comfort and sorrow, I think this is mostly correct. Certainly, it was God's day and, I guessed, it was by His design that Sundays were meant to be a mix of pain and pleasure, punishment and reward. Week after week, I'd find my hidden pleasures amid a strange brew of uneasiness, resignations, and small wonders, one of which being that Sundays were always the same. That is, of course, until this Sunday.

The day began at seven-thirty with a glass of orange juice. In those days, the Catholic Church decreed a three-hour fast prior to receiving the Holy Sacrament. However, to ease the suffering of the faithful, liquids were allowed up to one hour before. My brother and sister were younger and having not yet made their First Holy Communion, they were exempt from fasting. As I sipped my juice, they would taunt me with delicious moans and closed-eyed groans as they ate their cereal. I remember this as one of the early signals that being the oldest was not simply a chronological fact but also carried with it some weight.

My parents woke up cranky on Sundays. We were not morning people, and I suspect that their mood was in anticipation of the mad dash to get everyone ready for the glorious peace and light awaiting us at the nine-fifteen at St. James. Tension draped the house from the moment my mother came into our rooms and snapped up the shades. I went about my morning routine carefully, the way you walk through a minefield. God forbid you were caught

xi

lingering or engaged in anything not directly related to the grand preparation. This is not to say that my parents were mean or ugly people, quite the opposite. They were simply victims of the angst born of the prescribed routines and responsibilities of young family life, which occasionally can suck the breath out of living.

A benefit of the being the oldest was that I had learned the program. I knew when the tempest was nearing its end. I would close my eyes and breathe in the sweet powdery smell of my father's aftershave as he bent to tie the Windsor knot under my chin. And when he would overdose me with enough Odell's Hair Trainer to stiffen the wind, and comb my hair so roughly that the tines felt they would leave bloody tracks across my scalp, I would smile to myself and wait for the command we heard every Sunday. "You three just sit on the couch. Don't talk. Don't touch. Don't even look at each other. Just sit there until your mother and I are ready."

For me, this was the true beginning of Mass. And the only part in English.

Receiving Holy Communion was the best part of Mass. I was starving by then so I savored the thin wafer, letting it dissolve slowly in my mouth, imagining it was a warm cinnamon bun, the ones from Freiman's Bakery that my father would buy on the way home. It also signaled that Mass was almost over. A few more mumbles in Latin and my family would earn another week of Sanctifying Grace. Thank God. I reckoned that religion was another one of those things that only adults could understand, even if they couldn't speak Latin.

After Mass, my family ate a big breakfast at our big dining room table. My mother liked it that way and that's how most things were decided around our house. She would say, as long as it was her house to keep, it would be kept her way. After breakfast, I would secretly watch her clear the dishes and simultaneously reset the table for dinner. She did this with such grace and economy that I wondered if she practiced it during the week. This Sunday, she didn't speak until she was done.

"Mike, are your father's *friends* coming again today?" she called to my father in the living room.

"Of course, nothing's changed. Things are still unsettled. You know that," he answered from behind the newspaper. Lowering the paper. "Let's not start this. Just set them a place in the kitchen like he wants and pretend they're not here."

"Pretend they're not here? You've got to be kidding. We need to talk."

My father crumbled the newspaper and walked deliberately into the kitchen. I strained to listen, but they argued quietly. Even so, I knew what the problem was. My mother didn't like my grandfather or his friends, Mario and Nico. I couldn't understand then why she felt that way. Sure, he was a very serious man, but there was something else about him. Something special - there had to be. If not, how could he have been friends with my favorite Yankees, Mickey Mantle and Whitey Ford? One Sunday, he brought me a baseball they both had signed and it wasn't even my birthday or Christmas. I was more surprised to hear my mother say under her breath, "I wonder how he got that?"

My grandfather's friends, Mario and Nico, were always very polite to my family. They dressed in suits and always did whatever my grandfather asked. They were a lot younger than my grandfather, maybe around my father's age. But Pop Pop Carmine had a lot of friends of all ages, which made it more difficult for me to understand why my mother couldn't love him, too. But I was just eight years old and my attentions turned quickly, unencumbered by the unresolved, looking forward to the best part of every Sunday.

Just before one o'clock, I began to watch for him through the living room draperies. Soon I'd see my Pop Pop Carmine's sky blue Chrysler Imperial rolling to a stop in front of the house. I remember thinking how nice it was of my grandfather to let Mario drive his new car and Nico sit up front while he rode in back. I watched Nico and Mario get out and look up the road and behind the towering elms and sycamores that lined our street before they opened my grandfather's door. They even carried all the boxes of pastries and fruit and the warm loaves of bread for him. Nico and Mario couldn't speak English very well but they sure knew their manners. It was a mystery to me why my mother couldn't recognize that Pop Pop was lucky to have such good friends.

However, soon the aromas of Pop Pop Carmine's meat sauce would fill the kitchen and displace my disappointment. All the ingredients - the garlic and olive oil, canned plum tomatoes and paste, the sausage and pork, cheeses, seasonings, pasta and wine were carefully arranged beside the stove. Like the priest's Sunday altar, everything had been set out in advance by my mother. After lifting his grandchildren one by one high over his head and following quick pleasantries with my parents, which my mother dutifully endured, Pop Pop Carmine would take me by the hand into the kitchen. Shortly after, the heavy incense of sizzled garlic and the sweet smell of the thick red sauce would waft to very corner of our house, rendering it redolent and warmed.

I remember one Sunday the garlic wasn't fresh.

My grandfather had cursed, "Mannaggia, Michael, this garlic is stale. You can't cook with this. I don't ask for much. My grandchildren and fresh garlic once a week. My son can't give his father that?"

"Dad, calm down. I'll get you some fresh garlic," my father called from the other room.

"Your wife can't do that?"

My mother hurried to the kitchen and handed my grandfather another clove. He took the clove and without a word drove her from the kitchen, her eyes red and pooled.

But this Sunday everything seemed to be just fine. Pop Pop Carmine carefully prepared the sauce while I sat close by on a stool and watched and listened. Like the altar boys at Mass, I had learned to hand over each of the ingredients without being asked. I would sit patiently waiting for my grandfather's outstretched hand, the right moment to tender the next offering. Then I'd hold my breath for the faint nod, the signal I had done well. This was my church.

We sat and stirred the sauce for hours. Mario and Nico played pinochle at the kitchen table and talked Italian to each other and to my grandfather. I couldn't understand the Italian any better than the Latin at Mass but I could somehow feel the words. Their cadence created a rhythm that beat deeply and naturally in my core. Normal conversation lulled me like soft music. I had even come to sense a certain buoyancy in the meter before they would laugh and I'd smile along with them. But, if the words came quickly, clipped and sharp, I'd pretend I wasn't listening and concentrate on stirring the sauce slowly and evenly as I had been taught.

And, as always, while the meat sauce simmered, my Pop Pop Carmine told me long stories about great Italians. These might be gospels about the adventures of Marco Polo, Cristoforo Colombo, and Amerigo Vespucci; or testaments to the genius of Brunelleschi, Da Vinci and Michelangelo, Virgil and Dante, or Galileo, Fermi, and Marconi. By my grandfather's telling, it was the Italians who had single-handedly discovered America, created all the world's masterpieces, and laid the foundation for modern science. In fact, he would conclude that without the Italians the world would not be what it is today - certainly, it would be devoid of culture and true civilization. I sat enthralled by these homilies and begged for another when each would end. This Sunday, the sermon was in praise of Puccini, which my grandfather punctuated by closing his eyes and humming the defining arias.

Finally, when my grandfather tore the heel off the loaf of bread, like a good altar boy, I tilted my head back and opened my mouth to receive the holiest of communions. The bread dunked in the hot sauce burned my mouth and watered my eyes. My grandfather dipped a piece for himself, swallowed slowly, and wiped his chin with the dishcloth. I waited while he neatly refolded the towel and sipped his wine.

After a moment, he patted my head and smiled, "It's ready, Joseph. Tell your father."

There was no mystery to making a good meat sauce.

After dinner, my mother and sister washed the dishes in the kitchen. My brother and I ate pastries and fresh figs at the dining room table with my father and grandfather. The two men smoked cigars, drank espresso and poured Strega into tiny glasses. We picked from a bowl of nuts, finding fun in cracking walnuts and pecans for the older men. Mario and Nico smoked cigarettes on the back porch. My mother insisted on that. And she always made a lot of noise banging the pots and pans on Sundays. I had come to know that this was no accident. No matter the weather, Mario and Nico knew to stay on the back porch until the racket stopped.

When the last shiny pot was put away and the kitchen was quiet, my father called, "Are you girls all done in there? Come and join us for dessert."

Little Annie came but never my mother. Not until the doorbell rang. As usual, some of Pop Pop Carmine's other friends had come to visit. Only then did my mother come into the dining room and only to take Tommy and Annie upstairs for their baths. My father and I moved into the den to watch television. Mario and Nico joined Pop Pop Carmine in the living room.

The Wonderful World of Disney was on by that time and I pretended to watch. I had learned to position myself just right. Davy Crocket was one of my favorite movies but through the half-opened doorway was the real show.

The first to arrive were two men dressed in suits. Mario opened the door for them and Nico took their coats and hats. They must teach you a lot of manners in Italy, I thought. The visitors walked softly to where my grandfather sat and stood there until he motioned them to the sofa. They spoke quietly and sometimes leaned forward to whisper in Pop Pop Carmine's ear. When my grandfather raised his voice for a moment his friends became very quiet and still. But soon they were all talking again. When they were ready to leave, Nico helped them on with their coats and Mario held the door for them.

Soon more men came and left. This Sunday three groups of friends came over to talk with him. Every visit was more or less the same. The visitors were polite and respectful. They seemed very thankful to have Pop Pop Carmine as their friend. One man even kissed his hand, which almost made me laugh out loud. And, they all called him by his nickname, Don Carmine.

Just as Davy Crocket was ending, Mario and Nico leaned into the doorway to say good-bye. My grandfather came in wearing his coat and hat.

He winked at me and said, "Hey, Joseph, I need some help finding something in my car. How about getting your jacket and helping your old Pop Pop?"

This was the way every Sunday ended. Mario and Nico would go out and start the car. Rain or shine they'd stand on either side of the Chrysler and wait for my grandfather and me to come out. When we reached the car, my grandfather would say, "Some change fell out of my pocket today. You can keep whatever you find if you share it with your brother and sister."

But this Sunday was unlike all the Sundays before. Mario and Nico were not standing by the car and the trunk was open. It was dark, but as we got closer we saw Mario bent over into the trunk. We didn't see Nico.

My grandfather called out, "Mario, abbiamo una ruota sconfiata?" *We have a flat tire?*

Mario didn't answer. He didn't even move.

"Mario!" Louder this time. "Nico!"

In the silence I felt my grandfather stiffen. He put his hand across my chest and motioned for me to stay behind. As he walked around to the rear of the car, I followed instinctively.

My grandfather stopped suddenly. "Figlio di puttana!" *Son of a bitch!*

I saw what caused my grandfather to swear. Mario's right cheek was pressed against the floor of the trunk in a pool of blood. His eyes were wide open and brain tissue blossomed from his forehead. My grandfather reached down to touch Mario's shoulder as if he could somehow still feel.

I was mesmerized by the horror of the moment. My grandfather's voice hissing through clenched teeth startled me.

"Nico. Tu!"

I looked up to see Nico pointing a large pistol at my grandfather. It was the type soldiers used in World War II movies but it had a black pipe extending from the barrel. Nico looked past my grandfather at me.

"I sorry for you, Joey," he said.

"Nooo!" my grandfather screamed and swung up wildly from the trunk.

Nico never saw the cross-shaped tire iron fisted in my grandfather hands. It struck diagonally across his face, knocking him hard to pavement. I heard Nico's gun clatter on the street.

With the quickness of a much younger man, my grandfather stepped across and stood astride Nico's chest. He leaned forward and, holding the arms of the iron cross, shoved one end into Nico's mouth until he started to gag and grab at my grandfather's arms.

My grandfather looked over his shoulder at me. "Go, behind that tree."

I heard his voice but the face was one I had never seen before. The mouth seemed smaller and thinned under flared nostrils. The tendons in his neck were raised and corded to jaw muscles that rippled over clenched teeth. But it was his eyes that I would never forget. Flaming holes cut into a furnace of rage and cast-iron will. Maybe this was the face that made my mother cry. I froze.

"Joseph, go! Now!" My grandfather's voice again. "Stay there 'till I call you."

I stumbled backward, then turned and ran toward an old sycamore. I could hear Nico gagging.

"Chi, Nico?" *Who?* My grandfather demanded. "Baressi?"

Nico choked loudly. I peeked from behind the tree trunk. My grandfather hunched lower, putting more of his weight on the cross.

Nico moaned low in his throat and his hands flailed at my Pop Pop's forearms. But these were the forearms of an old longshoreman, thick and hard.

"Baressi, si?" My grandfather asked again.

Then in a soft and calm voice, my grandfather said, "Nico, metti le mani giu." *Put your hands down.*

Nico let his arms slide to the road beside him. My grandfather whispered something in Italian, or maybe Latin, and in one powerful motion rose up on his toes and leaned forward onto the arms of the cross. Nico's legs and arms shot up wildly and shook like a puppet. I could see my grandfather pushing down hard, rocking the tire iron back and forth until Nico stopped moving.

My grandfather stood up and threw the tire iron into the trunk of his car. He lifted Mario's legs and swung him in, too. Then he grabbed Nico under the arms and grunted as he wrestled the dead weight up and over the edge of the trunk. He glanced around before lifting a can of gasoline from the trunk, which he used splash away Nico's blood.

My grandfather looked down at his soiled and bloodied camel cashmere overcoat.

"Bastardi," he cursed between thin, tight lips.

He took off the coat, wiped his hands on it, and tossed it into the trunk before closing the lid. I continued to peek as he went to the driver's seat and used the rear-view mirror to adjust his shirt collar and comb his hair. When he had resettled his fedora, he called for me.

He swung his legs out the door to face me. "Joseph, do you understand that I have to protect myself? That sometimes men must die for others to live? Nico would have killed your Pop Pop tonight. He shot Mario, his old friend from Napoli. He may have hurt you, too."

"But Nico was your friend," I said.

"Nico was my second cousin's son. But no, Nico was not my friend. You remember this, Joseph. People aren't always what they seem to be. Sometimes it's hard to know who is your friend."

His eyes slipped from mine. He drifted back to me with a weak, sad smile

"It seems the longer you live the fewer friends you have," he said.

"You have me, Pop Pop."

"Yes, I know, Joseph. And now we have this secret."

My grandfather touched the first two fingers of his right hand to his lips and then moved them slowly to mine and rested them there.

"We must never tell another man what happened here tonight. No one, not even your father must know. Never."

I nodded unconditionally. He studied my face for a long moment and then slowly withdrew his fingers. I followed his mutilated forefinger as it fell away, remembering a year earlier when it had been nearly torn off by the metal blade of a table fan.

"Pop Pop?"

"Yes."

"Will Mario and Nico go to Heaven?"

"Mario will. Nico called you Joey, though. That is not a name men say with respect. Joseph was my father's name. Never let anyone call you Joey. For that, and other things, Nico will go to Hell."

"Will you go to Heaven, Pop Pop?"

"If you pray for me, Joseph."

I watched him drive away and round the bend in the road, the red lights on the tail fins of the Chrysler flickering between the trunks of the elms and sycamores before they disappeared. I smelled the gasoline and looked down at the spot where Nico had died. I kicked leaves from gutter and spread them over the wet area with my sneakers. Something hard and heavy banged against my toes. It was Nico's gun. I picked it up and was surprised by its weight. I tucked it in my belt under my jacket.

Before I went to sleep that Sunday, I wrapped the gun in my Davy Crocket frontier shirt and hid it with my 'coonskin cap in a box of toy soldiers and matchbox cars in the back of my closet. In my bed, I closed my eyes and smelled the meat sauce and prayed for my grandfather.

# Today

I've never told anyone that story, not even my wife. There are unquestionably a lot of reasons I haven't. I'd like to think that at least one of them has to do with me keeping my promise to my grandfather. Maybe, though, it's about living my father's life and not my grandfather's, and wanting to be defined by *my* deeds and not by the salacious nature of my grandfather's chosen work. But most likely, I never told anyone because I was afraid they might believe me.

So, why do I tell it now? Well it's not because I struggle with any deep psychological requirements to ventilate and heal from what I witnessed that night at such a tender age. I seem to have skirted any major consequences, moral or otherwise, from having kept this secret. Frankly, some recent events have more soundly trampled my psyche. It is true, though, that unlike the rest of my childhood, time and distance have failed miserably to dim even that most insignificant detail of that Sunday. Looking back, even as I stood at the curb making my promise, I knew that the weight of that moment would never leave me and, now later, nor will its occasional night rides through my darkest dreams.

And no, breaking my promise to my grandfather has nothing to do with me suddenly finding myself much closer to his age or him being long gone, that Sunday in 1963 being the last time I ever saw him. I've learned a lot about Don Carmine Napolo over the years, the side of him I never knew, him being someone I might be afraid to know today. Say what you will about him, it's all probably true and not much of it good. But he was a wonderful grandfather to me, my Pop Pop Carmine, and because of that there was never a question about me keeping our secret. Not until recently.

I told that old story because you need to hear it now, in view of this new story. They go together, hand in hand, like my grandfather and I walked to his car that chilly March night. And, I believe, knowing what I know now and what I had to do not too long ago, releases me from my promise. I think he'd understand because this involved my family and people I care about, and each of them was made fearful and diminished by it.

So now that you know the back-story and what it costs me to tell you, we can move forward to a week in May some years ago to the events that brought us here. But know first, that while great literature has been built around defining events in men's lives, don't be mistaken, this isn't one of those stories and it's certainly not great literature. The defining moments in my life have been those that most men pass through without much notice or even that expectation. No, this story has nothing to do with greatness; weakness perhaps, and from some perspective, comeuppance. I am no longer afraid who might believe it, or not. I do wonder, though, if enough time has passed to make the telling safe.

One thing is certain, none of this would have happened if my grandfather had been a cobbler. And for that, he and I are now inexorably coupled and likely to meet again someday in Hell.

So, we can continue now. I'll tell you exactly how it happened, all that I know and what I have come to learn in the years since, clearly understanding that this telling will not serve to further me from the sins - his or mine.

*Joseph Carmine Napolo*

# CHAPTER 1

## Monday, The First of May, 2001
## Edison, New Jersey

Domanski Trucking Company sits on fourteen blacktopped acres just off Exit 10 of the New Jersey Turnpike. We're in an industrial park near the crossroads of every major highway that transects the state. I stood in the yard just inside the main gate. The sun was just below the horizon, chasing the false dawn westward. Early birds were chirping in a narrow stand of pines and maples at the edge our property. The night rain had left the yard smelling of damp loam and petroleum.

Michael Cogan was behind me, bent over, head down with his hands on his knees, panting.

He said, "Are you trying to kill me?"

I looked over my shoulder and said, "A little too much drinking this weekend or just getting old?"

"For chrissake, I'm forty-six, not sixteen."

"And I'm not . . . Nancy?"

"Fuck you."

We're best friends and partners. We held each other to the promise of an early morning run, a couple miles several days a week. It wasn't a race but we secretly compete. Still, I take no real pleasure in beating him, or him me especially since there is never a wager on the outcome. I would never bet with Michael, just as I would refuse a drink with a recovering alcoholic.

Michael joined me now and we stood there in silence, both of us still too winded for more conversation. We had met as freshman roommates at Penn in Philadelphia. Sophomore year, Michael took a course in Greek

1

Mythology. He'd get sloppy drunk and hug me and announce to anyone who would listen that we were like Damon and Pythias, making sure everyone knew he was Damon because Pythias sounded like someone with a lisp. He'd jump up on the pool table at Kelly's and tell the story of these two friends who lived in Syracuse in the 4th century BC, always feeling the need to explain that he was not talking about Syracuse, New York. He'd invariably begin at the end of the story, when Pythias was sentenced to death. Damon took his best friend's place in prison so Pythias could be free to put his affairs in order. Pythias returned just before Damon was to be executed, and the king was so impressed with their loyalty to one another that he pardoned Pythias.

"I'd die for that guy," he'd slur pointing at me.

Then he'd jump down and try to kiss me on the lips.

We lived together until we graduated and remained faithful to the legacy of Damon and Pythias ever since. We shared apartments, cars, women, and eventually both went to work for different Fortune 100 companies; huge multinational, brand-rich consumer products and healthcare manufacturers. But Corporate America in the seventies and early eighties was a dinosaur world, lumbering along through swamps of waste and mediocrity, where factories were called plants as if it softened the truth of the bricks and mortar and steel. A place you had to work hard at getting fired from. Overstaffed and stifling, thick and bloated with self-important middle managers insulated from all realities of business except those exposed in corporate mission statements, company policies and standard operating procedures, each guarded and preserved as if they balanced the order of the universe.

Over the years, in spite of our corporate successes and earning our ways into the bigger boxes higher on the page of our divisions' organizational charts, we grew to hate it there. Along with the boredom and complacency, we struggled with an absence of meaningfulness and found ourselves once too often drinking a Friday night away, paraphrasing Jackson Browne in one last toast: 'when the morning light comes shinin' in, we just get up and do it all over again'. Ultimately though, it was what we had been forced to witness; the horror of too many capable men with good intentions and hardy ambitions slowly suffocating inside these massive cocoons, losing themselves in the company goo.

This was no place for the dynamic duo. After all, we had helped change the world. We stood shoulder to shoulder with other longhaired students in protest of the Vietnam War. More than once, the National Guard and State Police had hosed us off the steps of the ROTC building and chased us through the teargas across the campus, batons and bayonets at our backs. We had survived sex, drugs and rock'n'roll together and, when the opportunity presented itself, we knew we could make Domanski Trucking into a company we'd be proud to own. No excuses. No compromises. Just good men in good machines providing good service for loyal customers. Silly as that all sounds, it's the good ground we walk that's become the path to our success.

Now, in the first light of day, we stood shoulder to shoulder again. Our fleet of eighty-four Freightliners was backed up against both sides of the yard. Forty-two shining blood-red behemoths frowning at their mirror images across the pavement. The two of us stood there struggling to regain our breath, but even at rest, the power and stamina of these machines could still leave us speechless.

Finally Michael spoke.

"When we were playing hippies, whadja think you'd do when you grew up?"

I shrugged. "I never thought I'd grow up."

"Have we?"

I looked at him. He was a thicker around the middle and a bit worn around the eyes, but they were still strong eyes, still sparkling with Irish mischief.

"Hell no," I said. "Older, yeah, but I still don't know what I want to do when I grow up."

"I think we're doin' it."

"Maybe."

\*      \*      \*

By the time we had showered it was close to six o'clock. As I dressed, I could feel the terminal building begin to stir as drivers and dispatchers, dockmen and mechanics, clerks and supervisors began to circulate through the facility. I heard the time clock thump and thump. Doors breathed open and closed. Rooms pulsed with footsteps and voices, soft and loud. Computer screens blinked awake and the smell of fresh-brewed coffee, the real fuel of trucking companies, filled the halls. The good people of Domanski Trucking Company had come to bestow it life for another day.

At exactly six, Michael and I stepped up on a four-foot high riser fashioned from wood pallets stacked at one end of the loading docks; a long and narrow structure that juts out from the center of the office area. The docks were nearly empty of cargo. Friday night the second shift crew had loaded today's deliveries onto trailers. Nonetheless, there was little room on the platform. Standing before us were all but five of Domanski Trucking Company's one hundred and forty-two employees.

Michael cleared his throat and began. "Good morning and thank you all for getting up so early to come to this important meeting. It's a very special

3

day for all of us and we felt it was important that we should all start it together, just as we will move forward together."

Michael stepped aside for me.

I said, "Good morning, everyone. On Friday, you were all valued employees of Domanski Trucking Company. Michael and I were the proud owners of that great little company. But today, May First, we are all owners. As of twelve-oh-one this morning, each of you now owns a piece of our new company, DTC Transportation, LLC. Collectively you own thirty-three and a third percent of the company and the value of your shares will grow with time and good service. Congratulations!"

The new owners of DTC Transportation broke into unrestrained cheering and applauding. Michael and I joined the noisemaking. Soon the clapping was accompanied by stomping feet, in unison quicker and quicker, until we could no longer hold the rhythm together. I raised my hands and the thunder rolled and faded like a down-shifted diesel breaking into a steep curve.

"But, like all good things, this has come with a price," I continued. "The days ahead will be challenging for us all. Michael and I will continue to finalize this situation as it is not only what you wanted us to do, but also what is best for our company.

"Now, you all know Bobby Moretti, your shop steward, or as of today, former shop steward. He's worked hard over the last few years to represent those of you who belonged to Local 714. He's always been fair and honest, and a strong advocate for all you Teamsters, or should I say, former Teamsters. Michael and I are particularly grateful to Bobby for his representation and hard work on this decertification effort. Come on up here Bobby and give us an update."

Bobby Moretti was a truck driver in his early fifties. His thick hair was dark brown and his large frame moved with the strength and agility of a man half his age. Like a lot of Viet Nam vets, he still sported a bushy, late-sixties style handlebar mustache which accented his ready smile. As he approached the makeshift stage, his associates chanted, "Bob-by, Bob-by, Bob-by."

He leaped up between Michael and I, grinning and embarrassed but proud.

"Awright! Enough. I ain't the freakin' Pope." Everyone laughed and someone in the back yelled, "Bob-by" one more time.

"Hey, this is a great day but we got some problems. And it's these guys' fault." He pointed at Michael and me. "If they hadn't wanted to give us all a bonus last Christmas and give us part of their company, there'd be no problems." The crowd laughed.

"Seriously, now, that's when it all started. That's when Local 714 told us that our contract would not allow us to take the bonus or any ownership in the company. Hey, call me stupid, but I always thought a union's s'posed to improve conditions, and pay, and benies for its members. So when they drive up in their new Town Cars and try to tell us not to trust the company because they want to put some cash in our pockets and share the profits we all help earn, hey, guess what, I can't understand that. Then when we hear about how the Federal Government's investigating the looting of our union's pension fund, the misuse of our funds for Teamster elections, and how the Feds had to take over Locals all over the state because they say these guys are all mobbed up, well somethin's wrong. And then, after we all voted to decertify and to work for Joseph and Michael without the union, the National Labor Relations Board tells us we can't do that. They tell us that we're working illegally. Well this is still America and last I heard it was outlaws who founded it. So if that's the way they see it, screw the freakin' NLRB and screw the union!"

The outlaw employees broke into another round of cheering and stomping. Bobby let them go for a while and then held up his hands until the crowd was quiet.

Turning his head toward us he began again. "Joseph. Michael. Today we are teamsters with a small 't' but we got big heart. You've helped many of us individually through hard times over the years. We know your kids' names and you know ours. Hell, some of our kids work here now. You guys have turned this company around, and it's this company that puts food on our tables, not the union. Without the company, the union wouldn't even know our names. What's done is done. Now it's time to stand together and get through this. We got freight to deliver and bills to pay, so let's get it on!" More cheering.

I squeezed Bobby's shoulder as I stepped forward on the platform. "Thank you, Bobby. Ladies and gentleman, we asked you to get here very early today because Local 714 has promised us a picket line."

"Who's gonna be on that picket line? We're all here," someone yelled from the back.

Bobby Moretti shouted, "Donchya worry 'bout that. Laskowski and Catella can produce a picket line from thin air. There'll be pickets, and plenty of 'em. Look out the window, there's a few dozen of 'em out there already."

The gathering shifted to one side of the building to get a look through the windows on the loading dock doors. Michael broke through the murmur.

"Okay. Okay. Let's get back to the meeting."

When we had their attention, I began again, "Truth is, we're not all here. Five of our drivers have chosen not to join us. They will most likely be joining the pickets today. That's their right. We will *not* hold it against them. Please, under no circumstances, engage them or any other pickets in any conversation. At this juncture, nothing good will come of it. We are all owners and, therefore, principal representatives of this company. We must demand of each other that we act professionally and within the law, no matter how we are treated.

"Our attorneys have briefed us on the rules of picketing. Picketing is legal under these circumstances. But, pickets must keep moving, walking, and be spaced three feet apart. They can not picket on company property. They can not prevent or intimidate persons or vehicles from entering or exiting company property, although they will try. They can carry signs but the language must be specific and accurate. We have alerted the Edison Police and the State Police, and we will enforce the rules of picketing. We will protect company and personal property. And, of course, we will protect all of our people.

"Now, this morning and every morning until this is over, all trucks will leave the grounds together. Drivers will hook up to their trailers and line up, circling the building. Michael and I will be at the front gates. We'll roll on my signal. Office personnel will meet after this in the customer service area. Janie Steple will instruct you all on how we will cross the picket line and how to handle inquiries from customers and the media. Any questions?" I paused and scanned the crowd. "Good. Let's be smart and safe today."

Michael and I returned to the office we shared. Through the windows we could see that there were now at least a hundred men gathered outside the gates. Ron Laskowski and Albert Catella, the President and Vice President of Teamster Local 714, were holding their own meeting. These were men of the streets and the blacktop was their stage. Their twin Lincoln Town Cars served as the backdrop. Albert "Alley Cat" Catella was the most animated. Black pants and shoes, and a black leather jacket over a crisp white shirt accented his sharp features and middleweight's build. He always dressed in black and white, but today he looked pumped and ready for a prizefight.

"Jesus Christ. Who *are* all those fucking guys?" Michael thought aloud.

"Unemployed and retired Teamsters, no doubt," I guessed.

"Whadaya thinking?" Michael said without taking his eyes from the window.

"I think we better get our trucks movin'."

Michael headed to the dispatch area and I went out into the yard. I watched our drivers pull themselves up into the cabs of their trucks. One by one, the eighty-four starters whined loudly and the huge Cummins engines exploded to life. The air shook and filled with a sweet mix of diesel and morning dew. The pickets turned toward the noise and began to hoot and boo and shout obscenities.

6

I turned my back to the pickets and raised a fist in salute to the drivers. Then, in keeping with a tradition that had never been taught nor practiced, the last truck on the right lurched forward and rolled down the middle of the yard toward me, passing between the rows of rumbling red monsters huffing at each other across the asphalt. The last truck on the left quickly followed the first and, as if perfected for a truckers' rodeo, each of the remaining drivers pulled his vehicle out, alternating left and right with nearly precise pacing. It was a beautiful thing. The first time, about a year ago, it just seemed to happen, and I had to wait in the yard for my eyes to dry. Ever since I made it known that sometimes in the morning the exhaust irritated my eyes. Michael nor any of our employees ever let me know that they knew better. But this was the only lie I ever told them. Not all of them could say the same.

Michael joined me in the yard and we turned toward the gates and the pickets.

"All set inside," Michael said.

"Well then, let's go say good morning to our friends."

Laskowski and Catella had adjourned their street meeting, having successfully orientated their men on the picket line, ensuring the synchrony of their hearts and minds. As Michael and I approached the gate the pickets bunched together in anticipation.

Michael felt something come through his shoe into his foot. "What the . . . Joseph there's nails all over the place."

As Michael bent to remove the black-painted roofing nail from his shoe, the pickets burst into laughter and jeers. *Hey, get the point you fucks? What's the matter? Maybe you should sweep up once in awhile.* The pavement was littered with hundreds of the black-painted, two-inch roofing nails, the most economical, portable, and stealthy tire puncturing instrument made by man.

I looked over the pickets. I had never seen any of these men before. They were young and old. Big and small. White, brown, and black. I took in the group and walked slowly at them. As I got closer, I let my eyes move over them one by one. Still no one I knew, but I recognized them; near strangers joined and emboldened by a common belief, empowered by a simple notion that they are here to right a wrong, fortified by their numbers and sanctioned to act out their anger. They were where I once had been. A different time – a different reason, but I knew the power that one man could draw from the crowd. Even a coward, anonymous in the womb of a mob, could have his day in the sun. I knew this was a potentially very dangerous situation, one that had to be confronted directly and without hesitation.

"Good morning, gentlemen." I said loudly as I rolled aside the twelve-foot high chain link gate at the entrance of DTC Transportation.

The Teamsters had their own greetings.

*Fuck you, asshole.*

*Why ya openin' the gate? Nothin's comin' through it today.*

*Hey, scumbag, go tell your drivers they better not try to come through us.*

Michael joined me at the gate.

*How's your foot feel, asshole?*

"We need to speak to Laskowski and Catella," I announced.

*Who gives a fuck what you want?*

I started to walk through the pickets. No one would move. Michael pushed in close beside me and we used our shoulders and elbows to separate the crowd and wind a path through the thicket of angry bodies. Occasionally, a Teamster would shove one of their brothers from behind and he would slam into one of us, but we kept pushing through until we reached the back side where the leadership of Local 714 was watching with amusement.

"Beautiful day for this sort of thing, donchya think?" Alley Cat Catella said when he saw us.

Ignoring him, I turned to Ron Laskowski, a slim, former truck driver in his late fifties. He had climbed to the top of his Local with a reputation as a tough but tempered professional. "Ron, let's talk about some ground rules to keep this thing sane."

"Whadaya mean, Joseph?" Laskowski shrugged. "Because of your *insane* and *illegal* attempt to break with this Local, we're well within our rights to be here."

"We understand that, Ron. But this will be settled in arbitration or in the courts, not here. And you're not within your rights to block our gate or to throw nails around our property."

Catella threw up his hands. "Whoa, wait a minute. You accusin' us of throwin' nails? I didn't see any of our guys throw any nails, and if we did we'd put a stop to it. They must have been there."

"Oh, cut the shit, Albert," Michael said.

The Alley Cat Catella stepped forward with his right foot, rose up on his toes and pointed a finger in Michael's face. "Hey pal, maybe you two should get back onto your property. Ya never know what could happen out here. These guys are really pissed. So why don't you and your friend Joey here just go on back inside before you get hurt."

The tightening started in my chest and spread like a wild fire to every cell in my body. My face burned hot as I glared at Catella and said, "Get your finger out of my partner's face."

Catella smiled and settled back on his heels. "Heeeey, just a friendly warning. I wouldn't wanna see anyone gettin' hurt here."

"That's enough, Al," Laskowski interrupted. "What do you want, Joseph? We shouldn't be talking now."

I took a breath and turned to Laskowski. "Ron, we've worked together for over ten years. You know us and you know what we want. Our employees have made their own decision to break with the union. They're better off for it. I want you to do the right thing and walk away from this."

Laskowski shook his head. "Can't do that, Joseph."

"All right, then let's get clear on a few things. We'll be going about our business as usual. We'll respect your right to picket but we won't tolerate any abuses. Our trucks are going to roll through this gate in a few minutes. Please instruct your men accordingly. I don't want anyone doing anything stupid. Okay?"

"Whatever," Laskowski shrugged and started to walk toward his car.

Catella cupped his hands around his mouth and shouted mockingly to the pickets, "Hey, listen up. These guys want to get their trucks out and they won't *tolerate* any abuses." Then he walked toward his car.

Michael and I turned to the crowd to head back inside the gates and found ourselves surrounded by Teamsters.

Michael pointed toward the gate. "We're going back in now. Please step aside."

The men in our path just smirked or shook their heads. No one moved.

I looked at Michael. He shrugged and nodded in a way that I had come to know over the years. He was with me. I walked up to the biggest picket, paused briefly and stepped around and past him with Michael close behind. Shoulders and elbows were jostling us when suddenly an older man pushed through and spit in my face. The pickets laughed, of course. Then, as we pushed further into the horde, every man within range was spitting on us.

I looked over my shoulder at Michael. It only took a second for our eyes to speak a conversation, silent words that only many years of friendship could understand.

In a moment, Michael was at my side I leaned forward, raised my arms and began shoving men aside. Michael used his hands to push and pull at men in his way. The crowd finally gave us room but the rain of spit continued. When we broke free on the other side of the mob, spittle was dripping from our faces and hair.

*Looks like you guys need a shower.* Laughter.

*Hey, just come a little closer and we'll give you a shower.* More laughter.

*Pussies.*

*Chickenshits.*

By now, our eighty-four trucks were hooked up to trailers and lined up nose-to-tail at the gate, winding back around the terminal building. When the drivers of the first few trucks saw us emerge from the crowd they climbed down from their cabs and hurried to us. Bobby Moretti was in the lead truck and reached us first.

"Fuckin' animals," he cursed and gave us each a handful of paper towels. "Whadaya wan' us ta do, boss?" He asked me.

"First, we'll get these nails swept up. Then Bobby, get back in your truck. Get on the radio and tell the other guys to follow you as closely as they can. Take a lap around the building to get your speed up. I want you to go through the gate at twenty-five or thirty miles an hour with your air horns wide open. I don't want any of those assholes jumping up on our trucks."

"What if they don't move?" Moretti asked.

I wiped spittle from my ear. "They'll move."

# CHAPTER 2

## The Lower East Side
## New York City

Vincent "Vinny Diamonds" Venezio liked to meet with his crew, his whole crew, first thing every Monday. So between noon and one, but never later than one o'clock, Vinny Diamonds' boys would straggle into Taverna Reggia, an almost unnoticeable establishment just off East Houston Street. From the sidewalk, steep concrete steps descended to a wrought iron gate that guarded a black metal door. The windows had been bricked up years ago. The inside was dark and stained with the redolence of garlic and tobacco. Only a faded sign trimmed with grapevines, barely visible above the door, identified this as a public place. Although, the general public hadn't been inside for many years.

"Where's Dominick Patacca?" Vinny Diamonds was irritated. He had finished his pasta fagioli and not everyone was there.

"He's got sumethin' goin' in Jersey, boss," said one of the eight men at the table between spoonfuls.

"What the fuck's he doin' in Jersey? No one talked to me about anything in Jersey."

Turning to his right, Vinny bent toward Jimmy Merchanti and said, "You know about this?"

Merchanti nodded. He had mouthful of bread. "Yeah, this is the Tommy Ton thing."

"What Tommy Ton thing?" Vinny Diamonds frowned and leaned over the table to put his bulbous face squarely in front of Merchanti's. "Someone better fuckin' enlighten me."

The younger Merchanti flashed the palms of his hands. "Boss, calm down. Some mick in Jersey was a hundred large into Tommy Ton, some hockey and final four action. And ya see Tommy laid some big numbers off onto Rocco DaMeo and then the fuckin' mick stiffs him. So Rocco's lookin' for his money and Tommy Ton don't have it or he wouldn't have laid it off in the first place. And the mick, well he ain't even makin' the weekly vig. So . . ."

Merchanti swallowed the rest of the bread in his mouth.

Vinny screwed up his face. He looked like a gargoyle. "So whathefuck's this gotta do with Dominick Patacca bein' in fuckin' Jersey when he's s'posed ta be here?"

"Well, Johnny Anelli . . ." Merchanti began hesitantly.

Vinny Diamonds slapped his fat hands on the table rattling the dishes and silverware. "Don't you fuckin' tell me Johnny Onions is in this thing! You're not gonna fuckin' tell me that, are ya?" Vinny eyes were bulging out of his reddening face.

The other men at the table put their forks and glasses down, and they all looked at Merchanti. Everyone knew that Vinny hated Johnny Anelli. Given the opportunity and, of course, the proper blessings, Vinny would gladly shoot Johnny Onions several times in the head and then spread his body parts all over the tri-state area. Only Jimmy Boy Merchanti could get away discussing Johnny Onions Anelli with Vinny Diamonds Venezio. And even Jimmy Boy had to be careful.

"Look boss, a lot of the guys still like Johnny," Merchanti continued cautiously. "All he wants is ta make things right wit' you. So, uh, Johnny, he, ah, knows this union guy, a Teamster in Jersey. The union guy tells Johnny about this mick's operation. He owns a trucking company. So Johnny sits down with the mick and tells him Tommy Ton wants his money or else. Now Johnny, he knows there's no fuckin' way this mick can put his hands on a hundred grand, so he tells the guy he has to give up a truckload of somethin' to make things right."

Vinny shook his head quickly, like he was having a fit. The meaty wattle under his double chin flapped and shook even after his head stopped moving. "Whathefuck's wrong wit' you? You still haven't tol' me why Dominick Patacca's in Jersey. What is it you don't understand? I don't even wanna hear that cocksucker Anelli's name and you're sittin' there tellin' me his fuckin' life story. Get to the *fuckin'* point! *Why is Dominick Patacca in Jersey?*"

Merchanti drew a breath. "Boss, Dominick used to drive a big rig, so Johnny brought him in on the job. He thinks the load's gonna pay big. Big enough to pay off Tommy Ton and Rocco and then some, and by bringing in Dominick he's hopin' he can get straight with you, Vinny."

"Yeah, sure. Fuckin' typical. That scumbag figures he'll be kissin' three asses for the price of one. So, what's on the truck?"

"Shoes. Over twelve thousand pairs of Bennini shoes." Merchanti emphasized *Bennini*.

Vinny Diamonds sat back in his chair and looked up at the ceiling. Taverna Reggia was quiet as a graveyard and nobody at the table was breathing much either.

Finally, Vinny spoke. "Those shoes are two, two an' a half a pair retail. Shit, that's ah, an easy quarter million on the street, minimum."

Vinny Diamonds banged the table again, lighter this time. "Okay, so now I know what Dominick Patacca's doin' in Jersey. Tell me, Jimmy Boy, was that so fuckin' hard?"

# CHAPTER 3
## The Vince Lombardi Rest Area
## On The New Jersey Turnpike

Bobby Moretti was taking his time on his way back to the terminal, heading south on the Turnpike from Connecticut when his radio began squawking *Bob-by, Bob-by*. A glance in his right-side mirror revealed a DTC rig coming up fast on his left in the center lane. Right on schedule, Bobby thought and smiled to himself. Before he could reach his microphone, the other truck was along side. Kenny Diaz was behind the wheel, grinning widely and flipping Bobby the bird. Bobby signaled back in kind and motioned to the rest stop sign. A few minutes later they were having coffee inside at the Roy Rogers.

"Man, I couldn't believe those guys this morning," Kenny began, shaking his head. "Spittin' and shit. Man, I don't know if I could've taken that no matter how bad they beat my ass."

"Well, Joseph knows better than to start a fight you can't win. He's gonna take the time to think it through - do it right," Moretti began. "Now Michael, he's another story. He's a crazy fuckin' Irishman. If Joseph wasn't there today, Michael would've probably got his ass beat good, but luckily he usually follows Joseph's lead." Bobby looked Kenny in the eye. "Believe me, Joseph did the right thing today. And don't you worry, Joseph won't take their shit for long. You know how he is . . . don't fuck with him, he won't fuck with you. But if you fuck with him . . . He'll never let it go. I know, it's an Italian thing."

"Yeah, well it was great blowin' through the gate this morning. I was doin' at least thirty-five, forty." Kenny was grinning again.

"Fuckin' A. I was the first one through. Those boys didn't know whether to shit or go blind." They both laughed and slapped a low, slow five.

"Bobby?" Kenny is no longer grinning.

"Yeah?"

"How you gonna handle gettin' back into the yard?"

"Tell you the truth, I hadn't really thought about it. But now that you bring it up, I'll tell ya a little story. When I was in the Nam, and we were on the way back to our fire base after some shit-scary, senseless all-night walk through the fuckin' jungle, and for the first time all night I'm startin' to feel like I might live 'till sunup, a battalion of fuckin' gooks couldn't've stopped me. And back then all I had was my little M-16. Today I got a big fuckin' truck. But, who knows? Depends on what they do. You can follow me in if you want."

"Do you think they'll try anything?"

Bobby pushed himself away from the table. "One way to find out."

As they headed toward the truckpark, passing the fuming lines of commuters queued up at the gas pumps, they could see the tail ends of two dozen tractor-trailers parked side-by-side. Moretti stopped suddenly and put his hand on Kenny's arm.

"Hey, Kenny. Didn't we park next to each other?"

"Yeah. Why?" Kenny replied, looking up. "Uh oh. Where's your truck, Bobby?"

"That *is* my truck. Where's *yours*"

"No way, Bobby. That's trailer 5335. I had 5335 today."

"Shit. You're right, man. I had trailer 5353. Someone fuckin' took my truck!"

"*Damn*," Kenny said. "Good thing. I got a deadpiled load of those Bennini shoes. Cubed out the whole box. That's *big* bucks. What'd you have?"

"One piece. A long green metal crate, like a coffin but real fuckin' heavy. Picked it up at FirsTech, upstate. It's government stuff going to Virginia, I think. Exclusive-use, hi-tech security setup. You know, tons of paper work, special bills, government security seals. The whole nine, man."

"Holy shit! We better go make a phone call."

# CHAPTER 4
## DTC Transportation
## The Terminal Building

Michael and I shared a large corner office with windows overlooking the main gate. The company founder, Freddy Domanski, had shared the office with his son, Freddy II, and him with his son, Freddy III. We kept the original furnishings purchased by Freddy the First when his son came into the business after his three years with the 101st chasing the Nazis back to Berlin. There were two barge-size oak desks, four worn side chairs, and a wall of oak bookcases filled with industry periodicals, miniature truck models, and family photographs. The beige walls were crowded with dozens of dime-store framed pictures of the trucks that had carried the Domanski Trucking Company logo for over eighty years. The earliest was a faded black and white of Fred Domanski's first 1919 Ford. The pictures chronicled generation after generation of heavy trucks and trailers, right up to the last bright red 2001 Freightliners we had just leased. Many a visitor to this office was taken in by the display. More importantly, the photographs served as powerful testimony to the longevity of the company, which for a small regional trucker was an achievement all its own.

I remembered the first time I had seen the pictures. The still lifes of the progressively stronger and more efficient machines left me feeling oddly cold and empty. The idle trucks seemed ghost-like until I realized what was missing. They all stood alone without the men to drive them and they were, under those conditions, worthless. At that moment, I thought the essence of the trucking business, if not all things, had become forever clear to me. Only people can make things useful and good. And, of course the opposite would also be true. But, knowing well that principled and good-hearted people can be lead by circumstance or desperation to unforgivable conduct and that even the most wicked souls are capable of acts of kindness and decency, this moment of clarity quickly blurred. So, it wasn't surprising to me that that the poetry in that moment had nothing to do with trucking or business or people. It was clearly that nothing worth anything is ever that simple. Even so, I made sure that all the pictures taken since Michael and I bought the company had a driver in them, a good man standing ready.

Michael came through the door and scattered my thoughts.

"The cops are leaving. Their regular shift starts in half an hour and it'll be about an hour or so until the next shift gets here."

"How many trucks are still out?"

"Everyone that's coming home tonight is back in except for Bobby and Kenny. What's the latest?"

"They're on their way in. I spoke with the State Police. They took a report from those guys and they told me they'd put the information out on a network that alerts the state and local police east of the Mississippi. And we may be hearing from the FBI."

"The FBI?" Michael was surprised. "Don't they have better things to do, catch some drug dealers or something?"

"I'm sure they do, but it was an interstate shipment and apparently the FirsTech freight was an exclusive-use DOD shipment and . . . "

"FirsTech!" Michael interrupted. "Kenny had a Bennini load."

"Yeah, you're right. But Bobby's truck was stolen, not Kenny's"

"Oh, shit. How'd that happen?"

Now I was confused. "Whadaya mean? I told you they took tractor F24 and trailer number 5353."

"5353? What trailer did Kenny have today?"

"What difference does that make?"

"Humor me, will ya?"

I flipped through the daily dispatch printout. "Kenny had F55 and 5335."

Michael flopped down into his desk chair and grunted, "Oh, for Christ's sake."

"What's with you?"

"I don't know why I thought it was Kenny's Bennini load. I guess I just heard wrong and now that I know it's the FirsTech, well . . ."

I'm a fairly good judge of people. It's something I've grown comfortable with over the years. But Michael is not just people. I may know him better than his wife does. He's a bad liar and carries generations of Irish guilt and

17

emotion around like a sack of dirty laundry. One look and I knew something was up.

"Well, what?" I demanded.

"Well, you know," Michael paused and lightened up. He's not stupid. "It's all the government crap we're gonna have to deal with. Jesus, remember the shit we had to go through to get approved to handle the FirsTech freight? It was a near act of God to get the Department of Defense clearance. Can you imagine the bullshit paperwork this is gonna generate?"

I looked long at him. "Like you're the guy who's gonna do it anyway."

"Well, no, but you know what I'm talkin' about."

"No, not really?"

Michael cocked his head and looked confused. I watch his face slide into that Irish-hurt-feelings thing he did and thought I might be all wrong – sometimes Michael's just Michael.

"Look," I said. "FirsTech supported our application and recommended our approval. Their security check and clearance process was more demanding than the Pentagon's. And let's not forget all the other USG and DOD work we've been awarded because of FirsTech. Besides, I've already talked to Wilson Dennis at FirsTech. He's handling all the notifications to the USG."

"What'd he say about it? What was on the truck?"

I opened the manila folder on my desk. "The Bill of Lading description is electronic equipment. Wilson Dennis described it as proprietary government hardware. When I pressed him for more information on it and its value, he shut me down, said it was classified. Some military stuff, I assume."

"Where was it going?" Michael asked.

I pulled the bills closer. "The consignee is . . . It was going to FirsTech, care of The Potomac Consulting Group in McLean, Virginia."

"Oh Great. FirsTech ships it to itself and then this Potomac Consulting Group diverts it to God-knows-where. I wonder what's on that truck."

"Oh, here we go . . . I'm gonna hear this shit again?"

"It's not shit." Michael was serious. "Stuff like this pisses me off. The Pentagon, the CIA, NSA . . . God knows what they're up to that the people in this country will never know about."

"Jesus, Michael, maybe you should call Oliver Stone or Geraldo. There's gotta be a conspiracy or at least a good story here. You guys could smoke a few joints, drop some microdot, stay up all night, and try to figure it out, just like the good old days. . ." I lowered my voice to a whisper. "Hey, maybe we shouldn't be talkin' about this– ya never know who might be listening."

"Fuck you. You know I'm right. At least you used to, before you got old and conservative."

"Michael, I just want our truck and the freight back. And I don't want to lose the FirsTech business because of this. The rates are great and they pay in 15 days. If that makes me conservative, well, I'm busted."

Michael shook his head and said, "You were always good at making nothing out of something, but when you put it like that, I guess we did bill FirsTech over three hundred grand last month."

"Yeah, well over three million last year and we're on track to do a lot more this year." I was the numbers guy of the partnership. "Add that to all the other government work we do, it's over eleven million last year, about sixty percent of our revenue. All as a direct result of FirsTech's referrals and recommendations."

"I guess you're right. Do you think this is gonna cause any fallout? Did Wilson Dennis say anything . . . how'd he sound?"

"He was fine. In fact, he seemed . . . I dunno, sympathetic . . . understanding. Said he was confident that everything would be recovered quickly."

"Really? What'd he say?"

"He didn't elaborate. Just said something like, don't worry, we'll find it before it gets too far. Something to that effect, but real calm and assured. You know how he is."

"Yeah, well, if I had a name like *Wilson Dennis* I'd be calm and assured too."

"Why's that?"

Michael shrugged. "Two last names. Very blueblood white bread stuff."

"Or two first names. Always reminded me of Mr. Wilson and Dennis the Menace."

"Or Dennis Wilson, the Beach Boy."

I glanced out the window and saw Kenny Diaz's truck approaching the gate. The pickets, no longer restrained by the police presence, were tightly grouped in front of the gate, surrounding the truck as it slowed to a stop.

"Yeah, Help Me Rhonda," I said.

# CHAPTER 5

## New Jersey Turnpike Exit 15W
## Kearny, NJ

Johnny Anelli had spent the last few weeks working on this job. It had been a great few weeks. A little information here, a little more there, know a guy who knows a guy, sets up a meet with another guy, and before he knew it . . . *badda bing*, one by one, the details had fallen neatly in place. And then, to be able to grab the truck when it was parked in the rest stop - no rough stuff, no witnesses - things were never this good for Johnny Onions. Not that he didn't deserved it. After thirty-five years of doing whatever, whenever, wherever he was told, it was finally his turn. And who else could have pulled this off? Not some young, smooth-faced wiseguy with more balls than brains. Only a seasoned guy with a lot of history and some good grease could make this thing happen. Only a guy like him. Maybe *only* him.

But what Johnny found sweetest about this job only he could appreciate. He owed Tommy Ton a favor, he needed to set things right with Vinny Diamonds, Rocco DaMeo would be grateful - at least a couple points worth, and he was dead broke. Yes sir, this job had lots of mileage and a strong payday.

Johnny looked around the interior of his '93 El Dorado and was thinking he'd replace it soon with something right off the showroom floor. He was feeling pretty damn good. That is, until he spotted the silver Ford Taurus again in right the lane at the tollbooth.

Johnny had been following Dominick Patacca in the stolen DTC truck. He stayed well behind, varying his distance and changing lanes. Almost immediately after leaving the Vince Lombardi rest area, he had noticed the silver Taurus. The two antennas on the trunk and the two stiffs inside caught his attention. About halfway to Exit 15W he had spotted them again, the two antennas and Delaware plates. He looked over at them now and watched them as their cars crept along side by side in line at the toll plaza. The men looked to be in their thirties, sharp-jawed and clean cut, in crisp white shirts and dark ties. The driver was looking intently ahead to the lane on his right, in the direction of the DTC truck as it inched toward the tollbooth. The passenger was talking on a cell phone wedged between his ear and his shoulder, his hands working something on his lap.

Johnny's heart was racing and he felt his stomach curl. He lit a cigarette to calm down. He had to think. *Shit, this was probably nothing*, he thought as he blew a lungful of smoke against the windshield. First, how could anyone have known anything within minutes after taking the truck? After all, he had first seen the Taurus when they just pulled out of the rest area. That was too soon for anyone to be looking for the truck. Lots of regular people have antennas on their cars. And, the Ford Taurus was one of the most popular American cars. Companies had fleets of them. These guys are probably just a couple of copier salesmen, making business calls and playing with their laptop. Either way, Johnny Onions' time had come and he wasn't going to let anything or anyone fuck it up.

Johnny wiped the beads of sweat off his upper lip and took a long drag off his cigarette before he tossed it out the window. He reached down and flipped open the padded storage compartment between the bucket seats. He cleared away papers, matches, and cassettes so he could grab the bent up corner at the bottom of the compartment. He pulled open the bottom panel to reveal the hideout for his pistol, a Beretta Model 92F. Johnny had bought it from a guy in Brooklyn after he saw Mel Gibson using one in *Lethal Weapon*. He liked the look and feel of the gun, but its ability to spit out fifteen nine-millimeter rounds, as fast as he could pull the trigger, was what he loved about it. Johnny always kept it loaded but he checked the clip before pulling back the slide to chamber the first round. He wedged the gun under his thigh and turned his attention back to the silver Taurus.

Dominick Patacca had just paid his toll and the DTC Freightliner was accelerating toward the ramp under the sign for Harrison Avenue and Kearny. Johnny had arranged for a warehouse about a quarter mile down to be available and unmanned. Dominick had the key to the large drive-in door so he could pull the truck inside the building. Johnny watched as the Taurus took the same ramp for Harrison Avenue.

The warehouse was on the right, just before a twenty-five-foot high berm, which was crowned with railroad tracks that crossed over Harrison Avenue on a concrete bridge. Johnny stayed several cars behind and watched Patacca pull up to the drive-in door. The Taurus slowed at the driveway to the warehouse and then suddenly turned left into the lot of an abandoned scrap metal company across the street. Johnny watched in horror as the driver of the Taurus carefully backed the car in between two rusted truck bodies. The two men in the Taurus now had an unobstructed view of the warehouse and the stolen truck.

With all remaining doubt erased, Johnny Onions felt his fear and anxiety wash away, replaced with sheer determination. He had managed five and half years in New Jersey's Rahway State Prison, a maximum security hellhole, doing time for loansharking and attempted murder, by converting his fear into anger and the anger into the purest and most basic instinct to survive. The cellblocks soon whispered stories of the vicious and deadly consequences of failing to pay respect to Johnny Anelli, a connected guy, a made-man - a true Mafioso with serious affiliations. And although most of the nasty rumors were initiated by Johnny himself, jailhouse thugs, tattooed men half his age and twice his size, gave him wide berth to avoid his intense stare and the prospect of the terrifying wrath of Johnny Onions. Sometimes he missed the way evil and dangerous convicts would seek him out simply to brag that they had spoken with the legend he had created. But on the outside it was different. You were only as good as your last job. And these two guys in the Taurus, no matter who they were, weren't going to ruin his day.

Johnny drove past the warehouse and under the railroad bridge. On the other side, he turned right into the parking lot of a diner. He smelled the exhaust from the charcoal grill and realized he hadn't eaten since breakfast. A burger would hit the spot. A nice greasy cheeseburger deluxe, with lettuce, tomato, mayonnaise, and fries. Maybe later.

He looked down at his pants and shoes, wishing he had dressed more appropriately for climbing. But who would've figured. Besides he really wasn't the outdoorsy type and didn't own anything appropriate for nature walks or hill climbing. He pulled the 9mm from under his leg and slid it down the front of his pants, but his belly made it too uncomfortable. So he tucked it between his belt and the love handle at the right side of his back and zipped up his Members Only jacket. Johnny locked the El Dorado and started to climb the berm.

The hill's landscape was a patchwork of dry dirt and loose rocks, overgrown with string vines and creepers, milkweed and wild briars. His leather-soled loafers slipped out from under him several times on the way up and he had to grab at the brush to pull himself along. Johnny was winded and dirty when he reached the top. He brushed off his knees, caught his breath, and then walked along the tracks on the bridge to the other side of Harrison Avenue. There, he looked down at the roof of the silver Taurus nestled between two junk truck bodies and decided to walk further down the tracks. After about forty yards, he stopped and hiked up the waist of his pants, tighter around the Beretta.

This side of the hill appeared steeper so he held on to a small bush as he began to inch down. But Johnny quickly lost his footing and his hand slid down off the branches, leaving him only a hand full of leaves as he tumbled down the hill in a cloud of dust.

He was a mess when he finally came to a hard stop against a chain link fence at the bottom of the hill. Johnny leaned up on his left elbow and felt a sharp pain in his shoulder. "Fuck!" he cursed quietly as he looked down at himself. His pants were torn at the knees and the skin was broken and red. The palms of his hands were stinging and some of his knuckles were raw. Blood ran from a small cut above his right temple and his shoes were probably ruined. The 9mm had bruised his back but at least he hadn't lost it. But when he reached for his cigarettes they were gone as was his Zippo and all the change in his pocket. He grunted in pain as he reached for the fence to pull himself up.

Johnny crouched low and brushed himself off again while he surveyed the yard behind the Taurus to plan his approach. He drew the Beretta and held it in his right hand close to his knee as he crept along the fence. When he reached the end of the fence, he weaved through several piles of junked cars and trucks until he was behind a rusted panel truck next to the Taurus.

Johnny was perspiring heavily and his mouth felt like he had just licked out the ashtray in his El Dorado. His breathing was quick and he could feel his heart jackhammering against his breastplate. The sounds of an approaching train snapped his head up and he quickly knew that he had only seconds to act. He pulled back the slide on the 9mm to confirm the round in the chamber, drew a deep breath, and cocked the hammer as he straightened up. As the train rumbled closer, louder, he stepped in between the truck and the Taurus and walked deliberately toward the driver's door with the Beretta tight to his thigh. The instant he was at the door, the startled driver jerked up straight and away from the window. Johnny jammed the muzzle of the nine-millimeter against the glass, shielded his face with his left hand, and began squeezing off rounds as the 5:05 out of Newark thundered along the tracks above them.

The first shot exploded the window and the driver's head. The passenger was able to grasp the horror for half a second as nuggets of window glass mixed with the driver's blood and brain matter splashed his face. The next two bullets struck the passenger's neck and chest. Johnny continued to shoot as he swept the pistol across the blown-open window, but the rest of the fifteen rounds were redundant, ripping through flesh and bone that no longer lived.

Johnny bent to the window. He waved away the blue gun smoke that was curling slowly around the inside of the car. And although his ears were ringing from the fusillade, he could hear air gurgling from a hole ripped through the passenger's throat. Two final beeps sounded from a small keyboard device that rested between the legs of the passenger, its LCD screen shattered by one of the rounds. Johnny pulled back and grimaced when the driver's left eye twitched and rolled, as if he was trying to clear his vision for a final glimpse of his executioner to take with him into eternity.

After a few moments, when the driver's eye had settled into a half-closed stare, Johnny opened the door and knelt on his bruised knees in the dirt. He began to remove a leather case that was protruding from the driver's rear pants pocket. As Johnny slid the case free, the cell phone on the seat between the bodies began ringing - one of those annoying, high-pitched cell phone tones: *Brring-bingling-brring-bingling.* Johnny started, dropping the case. It flipped open on the ground and several plastic-coated photo I.D. cards fell out. As Johnny picked them up and began to read the cards, his stomach churned. His name had been William P. McNeely. The driver's picture on the first card was partially distorted by an embossed government seal. The words across the top read 'United States Secret Service'. *Brring-bingling-brring-bingling.* The next card was equally authentic looking but this one identified the driver as Special Agent William P. McNeely of the Federal Bureau of Investigation. *Brring-bingling-brring-bingling.* A third card, also in the driver's name, bore the official seal of the Department of Defense. *Brring-bingling-brring-bingling.* The last card announced Lt. W. P. McNeely, FirsTech Security Corps. And then the phone stopped ringing.

Johnny Onions sat back on his heels, held his head in his left hand and let his fingers massage his temples. Skipping lunch always gave him a headache.

## The Catskill Mountains
## Upstate New York

In a windowless room, seated behind a console crammed with keyboards and monitors, the technician pressed a speed dial button on the telephone.

"Mr. Lincoln," he said into the phone. "We just lost the GPS triangulation on Tailgate One and they're not answering their cell. I think we have a problem."

"Do we still have a fix on Cargo One?"

"Yes, sir."

"Give me the location."

"Harrison Avenue, Kearny, New Jersey, just off the Jersey Turnpike, sir."

"Why wasn't I notified when they left the Turnpike?" Lincoln was angry. "There was no reason for that vehicle to leave the Turnpike until Exit 10."

"Sir . . . I, ah . . . "

"Fuck! Dispatch Tailgate Two to that location."

"Yes, sir!"

"And then call Dennis. Tell him *nothing* of this but tell him to send in someone to finish your shift."

"Sir?"

"You fucked up, you're out. Tell him you're sick. Leave the building and just disappear. You'll be paid in full as agreed. But if I ever hear of you, you'll never spend it."

"Yes, sir."

# CHAPTER 6
## The Front Gate
## DTC Transportation

Michael and I watched from our office window as Kenny Diaz slowed his truck to a stop outside the front gate. The Teamster pickets were moving toward the truck, spreading out to surround the cab. I switched on the CB radio and tuned to channel 11, the frequency used by dispatch. Bobby Moretti's voice was loud and alarmed.

"Where the fuck are the cops," he was saying.

I grabbed the microphone. "Bobby, it's Joseph. Cops are gone. Shift change. Can you back outta there?"

"Negative. Not without runnin' a few of these guys over. They're all around us. Shit! They're up on our doors and fenders."

"Stay inside the cab. We're coming out."

Inside the cab Bobby turned to Kenny. "You keep anything in here?"

"Yeah, under the seat . . ."

Bobby reached down and pulled out a two-foot long steel rod. He held it up so the men on his side of the truck could see it. His smug smile convinced some of the pickets that he would use it if he had to.

Suddenly, the driver's side window shattered. Two men on the running board began pushing in the safety glass. Kenny reached through the opening and shoved one of them backwards. But as the man fell he grabbed Kenny's wrist with both hands, pulling him hard against the inside of the door. The second man reached in and flipped up the door handle. Before Bobby could react, the door flew open and Kenny was gone.

Michael and I ran toward the gate, followed closely by a few of our men. When we reached the gate, I looked over my shoulder and saw seventy or eighty more good souls - drivers, dispatchers, and mechanics - pouring out of the terminal, streaming through doors and leaping off loading docks.

"No!" I shouted when I saw Kenny pulled from the truck and disappear into the crowd.

Then Bobby appeared in the open doorway with the steel rod raised high in his right fist, I cupped my hands to my mouth and yelled again, "Bobby! No!"

Bobby looked in my direction and our eyes locked in a brief moment of understanding. But when Bobby looked down to where Kenny was, on the ground being beaten and kicked by the Teamsters, he glanced back at me and tilted his head, faintly acknowledging what he had to do. As he raised his fist higher, he too was pulled from the doorway, swinging the steel rod wildly until he was absorbed into the melee.

Several of our men began to roll open the gate. The pickets had their backs to the gate, cheering their brothers on to *get the scabs* and *teach 'em a lesson* and *give 'em some more, from seven-one-four.* But when the metal wheels on the gate screeched, the pickets turned to see an army of DTC men and women charging across the yard, some with tools and pallet boards raised overhead. The chanting began to subside.

I spun around to our people and raised both hands, and yelled, "STOP!"

Our employees slowed and stopped at the gateway, forming thick and angry behind Michael and me as we turned again to face the pickets. In the back of the union mob, a group of men next to the truck were still shoving and beating one other. We couldn't see Bobby or Kenny but a couple dozen men were viciously engaged.

*What are we waiting for?* A call from behind me.

*We gotta help those guys!*

*Come on, let's get 'em!*

*Let's show these fuckers!*

I felt my body heat rising. But, as much as I wanted to, I couldn't allow our people to be lowered into an all-out brawl with these Teamsters.

Michael grabbed my arm, leaned into my face and pleaded, "Joseph?"

"We can't let this happen, Michael," I said as I pulled free from his grip.

I took several steps toward the pickets and shouted, "STOP! STOP THIS!"

I instantly felt like a schoolboy dancing around while his best friend was getting his face beat in by the class bully, too afraid to do anything but jump up and down and yell, "STOP!"

The Teamsters sneered at me defiantly, as if to say, *or what?* They had sensed my hesitancy and smelled my fear and took it for the weakness it was.

I looked over my shoulder again at our people. I panned their faces, their names and personalities flashing through his mind. They would follow my lead, even into this fight. I could draw on that strength but there was tremendous risk. I could lose control. If I bluffed and was called, people would get hurt. But two of our men *were* being hurt. I needed the advantage quickly.

I looked one more time over my shoulder before turning to the Teamsters and doing what our people's eyes pleaded.

"On my signal, we're getting our men," I told the front line of Teamsters. "It will be best if you stay out of our way."

I began a countdown that all could hear. "ONE."

"TWO." Both sides of the gate were tensed and still except for a scuffle moving up from the rear through the pickets.

"THREE." I kept my tone flat. The next jump-off point was the count of five.

"FOUR." I knew I wouldn't be able to count past five and retain the advantage. There was no turning back.

I started walking at the Teamsters, leading a slow-motion charge, hoping that a path would miraculously open for us. I hated what was happening. But, I could not stand by while Moretti and Diaz suffered the punishment of this faceless anger. And, frankly, I was goddam mad that anyone or any group thought they had the right to force their will on others in this manner. Besides, the Teamsters had drawn first blood and history always seemed to forgive the victims of aggression, even when their victories resulted from horrific and devastating acts of violence. There was no longer any mystery in this night for me.

"FIVE!"

I was a few steps from a very large Teamster. I coiled my arms and balanced my quickening stride. Michael fell in step next to me with the rest of DTC Transportation at our heels. The Teamsters braced for the clash.

*Come on! Come and get 'em.*
*We'll give you some, too!*
*You're goin' down first, Napolo.*
*Let's teach these faggots a lesson!*

Suddenly, the big teamster in front lurched forward and stumbled, almost loosing his footing. Then several other Teamsters were also pushed from behind and a small group of men burst through the crowd, several of them supporting, nearly carrying Moretti and Diaz. I recognized their five rescuers. They had fought their way out.

"We got 'em, boss," said Pete Jurewicz, Katie Jurewicz's granddaddy, one of our drivers who had joined the pickets.

"We never wanted this," added Teddy "Bear" Johnston, through swollen and broken lips.

Ernie Roman, a world-class diesel engine mechanic, stepped forward in his ripped shirt and spoke for the five disenfranchised DTC men. "If you still want us, we'd like our jobs back. We don't want anything to do with these fuckin' guys, boss."

I nodded. "Put 'em down here, boys."

"Someone call 911," Michael shouted.

Moretti and Diaz were badly beaten. Michael and I knelt over them. Kenny was dazed and barely conscious. Several DTC employees were volunteer EMTs and they pushed us away from Kenny. Moretti was on his back holding the bridge of his nose to stop the bleeding. His face was cut and bruising quickly. He looked up at me and said, "Sorry, boss. I did the best I could."

"We know," I said.

A familiar voice came from the front line of the Teamsters. "My men tell me your guys tried to run them down. We had to pull them outta the truck before they killed somebody."

I straightened up to see a grinning Albert Catella.

"Lucky no one got hurt," Catella continued.

"These men *are* hurt," I shot back.

"Actin' crazy like that, no wonder they're a little banged up. You'd think they'd know better," Catella cracked, still smiling. "Know what I mean, Joey."

I started slowly toward Catella, letting the surging anger pumping from my core swell and spread throughout me like molten steel. I didn't stop until our faces were inches apart. I lowered my chin, so close that our breath mingled in the small space under our noses. We stood that way, neither of us speaking or moving, the seconds ticking as if time had somehow become viscous and mired. A rolling silence overcame both sides of the gate.

I felt the violent and ugly heat continue to seethe through me, fusing my cells into one exposed nerve. All I could hear was my own breath rushing in and out of my nostrils. My vision tunneled to a rifle barrel pointed between Catella's eyes. I was ready to take The Alley Cat's head off.

Then Catella's cheek twitched and his head lowered as he swallowed hard and turned to his Teamsters.

"Let's go home, boys," he said. "Tomorrow's another day."

I waited for Catella to fade into the crowd before I turned away. I inhaled deeply and closed my eyes. Exhaling, I lowered my head and mumbled something profane that was lost forever in the wail of distant but approaching sirens.

# CHAPTER 7
## The Jersey Shore

I had learned long ago that I required a daily commute of at least thirty minutes. This is my time in the morning to prepare for the day ahead. And in the evening, I used the solitude to reflect and decompress; down-shifting my psyche to create the separation between what I do for a living and the life I do it for. Behind the wheel I make the transition from husband and father to businessman, and back again, each day of my working life. After most days, the thirty-five or forty minutes I drive south on the Garden State Parkway works like an elixir. Often, I find myself magically pulling into my driveway not remembering any details of the ride home as if I'd just awakened from a trance, feeling lightheaded and relaxed.

This evening's commute carried me along suspended in thought, the day's events racing in and out of focus as I tried to make sense of things. The miles passed but I couldn't put any distance between my emotions and the facts. I had needed the parkway to cast its spell, to spirit me along above and beyond the anger and contempt I felt swirling around me.

I found myself suddenly sitting at a familiar traffic light. The evening breeze was briny and reeked of seaweed and marsh mud at low tide. I looked over at the royal blue sign with gilded letters. *Welcome to Monmouth Beach.* I was home.

The light changed and I looked into the rearview mirror to check what my family would see when I walked through the door in a few minutes. I saw that I looked as I felt, tired and saddened. And, I saw a large pickup truck too close to my rear bumper.

I hit the turn signal to warn the pickup but the driver gave me no more room and followed me into the turn. I paid the tailgating pickup no further attention as I traveled the last few blocks to Seaside Avenue. However, when the driver of the pickup stayed tight on my bumper as I turned down Seaside, my street, I decided to take a longer look.

The hood of the pickup was almost as tall as the roof of my Jeep. Its steel grill filled the back window. I sped up slightly to increase my scope of vision in the rearview mirror. It was a late-model two and half ton GMC with a long bed supported by dual rear wheels on each side. The pickup accelerated to close the gap, coming dangerously close to my rear bumper.

I threw up both hands in an irate wave-off and then quickly began to feel foolish. The three men in the front seat were most likely hard-working tradesmen anxious to get home after a long day. Was I so in need of a diversion for my anger that I was hunting for an outlet? I would quickly have to negotiate a new attitude for myself before I walked through my front door. I felt the greatest disappointment with myself when I failed to shield my family from my personal or professional frustrations. They were rarely the cause. And it was nothing short of shameful to make a loved one feel blame simply because you could. It was a weakness in men I despised.

After one particular episode many years ago, my cruel words and vicious demeanor sent my very pregnant wife, Cathy, running out the front door into the cold night. Blinded by her tears and wobbly from the forward-pitched center of gravity her condition imposed, she slipped on steps of the stoop and fell, nearly loosing the baby. In the hospital, waiting for the prognosis, I swore never again to direct my anger at innocent parties, especially my family. I had kept this pact. But I worked hard to be aware and in control. My family's unconditional love and a mesmerizing commute help a lot. And on the rare occasion when all else fails, I slip into the garage and take a few pulls off an old soapstone pipe I keep hidden with a small stash of pot. The effects are instantaneous and familiar. The relief is total and without compromise. Retired skypilots love to fly and a lot of us still do, now and then.

I smiled to myself as I swung the Jeep into my driveway. I was a few steps away from sanctuary. In moments I would walk through my front door and my anxieties and tensions would begin to melt away with the sounds of my arrival. *Daddy's home! Hi, daddy! I'm in the kitchen, honey. How was your day?* Hugs and kisses and home; my island of peace and comfort, safe harbor from the storms of life that rage outside my door, beyond my control.

My cell phone rang.

"Hey, it's me." It was Michael. "Where are you?"

"I'm sitting in my driveway. Why?"

"I think I was followed home."

"Really? Are they in cars or black helicopters?"

"Cut the shit, Joseph. I'm fuckin' serious. I noticed this blue Ford Econoline van about half way home. By the time I got off the Parkway I was pretty sure they were following me, so I detoured around awhile. Right now I'm sitting outside Shoprite on 36 in West Long Branch and the van's parked a few rows over. They're just sitting there."

While Michael was talking I remembered the GMC pickup. "Has anyone gotten out of the van?"

"No. Not yet."

"How long have you been parked there?"

"Five or six minutes. Long enough."

I looked into the rear view mirror and then spun around to confirm what I saw.

"Michael, I think we have a problem. I've got a pickup parked across the street. I think they followed me, too. Christ, I've led them right to my front door."

"This is *bullshit*!" Michael spat into the phone. "It's blatant intimidation. I'm not leading these assholes to *my* house. I'll sit here all night if I have to."

"Fuck that! Listen, wait ten minutes. Then call my house and tell Cathy you're having car trouble and you need me to pick you up. Don't say anything to her about this. Stay off the phone. I'll call you back."

"Whadaya gonna to do?"

"I'm not real sure, but first I'm gonna get rid of these guys across the street. I'll talk to you in a few minutes."

I walked into the house without glancing at the pickup. A few minutes later, my son, Mickey, and I came out through the garage door with baseball gloves and a bat. Mickey was my youngest. Eight years old, he was named after two of my favorite people, my father and my partner, and with a wink at my childhood hero, Mickey Mantle.

The pickup was still there, parked across the street, directly in front of my house. The three men were still inside. I tossed the ball toward the street and it came to rest in the grass before the curb.

"Go get it, Mickey. Hustle out there and throw it back hard. Hurry, there's a man rounding third. You can throw him out at home."

Mickey's little legs carried him quickly to the ball. He scooped it up and threw it with everything he had. I ran up to catch it and feigned a tag at the plate. "He's *out!* " And then in an announcer's voice, "Mickey Napolo saves the day. Three outs. The Yanks win!" Crowd cheers.

Mickey threw a tiny fist in the air and yelled, "YES!"

"Okay, Mickey, let's practice our fielding. Get ready, I'm gonna hit a few out to you."

I picked up the bat and began tapping gentle grounders to my son. After a few, I called to Mickey. "Okay, now its time for batting practice. Come over here."

When Mickey was safely behind me, I said, "Watch how daddy swings the bat."

I tossed the hard ball straight up with my left hand. My eyes followed it up and I watched as it slowed to a stop in mid-air and then reverse direction, falling into my strike zone. I wound up big with the Louisville Slugger, lifted my left foot, and put the whole day into it, pulling hard and fast through the swing, knowing I had hit the ball well from the crisp crack and firm shudder of the ash bat. The ball exploded straight away like a rocket. It was a bone-crushing line drive, screaming toward its target like a guided missile. It hit the side of the GMC pickup just in front of the driver's door with a loud thud.

"Uh oh," Mickey said looking up at me.

"Whoops," I said. "Daddy better go apologize to that man. You go in the house, Mickey. I'll be right in."

I watched him until he had closed the front door before I started across the lawn. The driver of the pickup was outside his truck, bent over inspecting the dimple the ball had left. As I reached the street, the driver stood to face me. I still had the bat in my hand.

"Hey, sorry about that, pal," I said as I crossed the street. "Guess I was showin' off a little for my kid. Have you seen my ball?"

"Fuck your ball. Look what you did to my truck. You're gonna pay for that."

"Oh, I don't think so," I said. "In fact, I think you're gonna get back in your truck and drive away from here. And I think you should never, *ever* come near my family's home again."

The two other men were sliding out the passenger door. The driver looked over at them and laughed. "This asshole thinks he can tell us where we can park. Guess he thinks he owns the fuckin' street."

They all laughed but not too loud. I'm six-foot-two, in relatively good shape and had a bat resting on my shoulder.

"Well, okay. So you're right, I don't own the street," I said as I bounced the bat lightly on my shoulder. "But be careful. This might seem like a quiet neighborhood but we've had our share of vandalism. And I'll bet that if you went to the Monmouth Beach Police they'd have a very hard time believing that someone they've known in the community for years, someone active with the Board of Education, the PTA, soccer coach, and, oh yes, baseball coach, . . . someone like *me* for instance, would ever take a baseball bat to your pickup. In fact, I'll bet that if I took this bat right now and, well . . . but that's just silly because no one would believe it anyway."

"I have witnesses. Go ahead," the driver taunted.

"It's a nice truck. But if you insist."

I walked around to the front of the truck. "I think I'll start with the headlights and grill. Okay with you?"

"Fuck you!"

I shrugged. "Okay, then. Batter up."

I stepped back and cocked the bat.

"He's serious Lou," one of the passengers said.

"Awright. Awright!" the driver shouted, holding his hands up in surrender. "I don't need this shit!" Then turning to the other two. "Let's go. Fuck this guy."

I let the bat rest on my shoulder again. "You sure? I always wanted to do this; ever since I was a kid. It always looked like fun."

The driver and his two buddies got back in the truck. As the driver reached down to turn the keys in the ignition, I stuck the bat through the open window and put the business end under his chin. I forced the bat hard into the soft flesh under his jaw and lifted up. When his head was pressed back against the seatback, chin to the sky, I said, "I saw the decals. Tell Laskowski and Catella that if I ever see anyone that even *might* be associated with Local 714 around my home or family, or Michael Cogan's home or family, or the home or family of *anyone I know*, I'm gonna start havin' batting practice. Remember to tell them I think it'll be a lot of fun, something I've always wanted to do. Can you remember that?" The driver didn't respond.

I repeated myself, "*Can you remember that?*"

"Fuck you," the driver spat.

"Fuck me. No fuck you. Here's a little reminder."

I swung the bat away from his chin and knocked the rearview mirror off the windshield.

I stepped back from the truck. "Now get off my street."

The pickup roared away with the driver's and one of the passengers' arms sticking through the windows giving me the finger.

I was about halfway back to the house when Cathy appeared at the front door. "Mickey says you broke a man's truck with the baseball."

"Just hit the ball a little too hard. No damage. Everything's fine. Even found our ball."

"Well that's good. You know, Joseph, I knew that someday I'd have to worry about the kids breaking the neighbors' windows or something. But then I've always said I've got four kids; three under twelve and one over forty."

"Ha, Ha. But it's just because your man can't contain his own super strength."

Cathy rolled her eyes. "By the way, Batman, Robin just called. He's got car trouble. He's stuck in the Shoprite parking lot. Ilene must've had him stop for something on the way home. He wanted to know if you could pick him up. I told him no."

"What?"

"Only kidding. I told him you'd be right there. But come right home, dinner's almost ready."

I threw the bat in the front seat of the Cherokee and dialed Michael's cell as I backed out of the driveway.

"Hey," Michael answered.

"I'm leaving now."

"Is the pickup still at your place?"

"No, they're gone. But they were Teamsters. There were stickers on the windows."

"Great. This is really bullshit, isn't it?"

"What's up on your end? The van still there?"

"Still here. There's two guys, just sittin' there."

"How're they parked?"

"They're backed into a space, facing me, one row over."

"Is there anyone parked behind them?"

"It looks like there's a car behind them."

"Are there cars on both sides of them?"

"Yeah. Why?"

"This is gonna be simple. I'm gonna pull across the front of the van and stop. They'll be blocked in, right?"

"Right."

"Then you drive home. I'll keep them there long enough so they can't follow you. They already know where I live. No sense in giving them the satisfaction of getting to your house, too."

"What if they start something? I should stay with you, Joseph."

"Don't worry, I've got Mickey's Louisville Slugger with me and I've been practicing my swing."

"Joseph, don't do anything stupid. Just drive away if anything happens. It's not worth it. If they really want to they can find out where I live pretty easily."

"Michael, it's the Shoprite parking lot . . . What's gonna happen? Go home I'll talk to you later."

A few minutes later, I pulled slowly down the row of cars and vans and SUV's parked at the Shoprite. When I reached the blue Econoline I stopped and put the Jeep in park. I looked over at the two men in the van. When I was sure I had their attention, I lifted the bat and tapped the palm of my left hand with it. The van's driver leaned on his horn and the man in the passenger seat gave me the finger with both hands.

I turned the radio up and watched Michael drive out of the lot. A few seconds later, my cell phone rang.

"You okay? What's goin' on?" Michael asked.

"Well, you can hear their horn."

"Did they get out of the van?"

"No. But they're both giving me the finger," I said.

"Wow, that's a little harsh. Don't you think?"

"So, who do you think invented 'the finger'?" I asked.

"Must've been the cave men."

"Cave men?"

"Yeah, sure. Before there was language they had to have some way of telling each other to fuck off. Why, who do you think invented it?"

"I dunno," I said. "But after today, I was thinking it may have been the Teamsters."

"After today, cave men - Teamsters, same thing."

# CHAPTER 8
## After Dark
## Kearny, New Jersey

Conditions permitting, Lincoln always took the chopper. It was one of the many perks that came with his position, and it was a position of his own making. He had risen through the ranks of the military and civilian intelligence communities as a shadow. Far removed from the politics of foreign affairs, he was spawned from deep within the murky netherworld of covert operations; treacherous games that had played out in steamy jungles, on arid deserts, and in unfriendly cities around the world. He never had a home or a family. He thought he had fallen in love once or twice along the way, but true love required compromises and devotions, which he could not allow. But he had always been devoted. First, as a young man, it was to his missions. Dark and dangerous assignments orchestrating murder and mayhem disguised as patriotic sacrifices. They forced him to bury his humanity at an early age. Later, having seen too many revolutionaries become genocidal despots and too many enemies become allies of convenience, his devotion turned inward to his own survival and fortune.

It was the late-eighties, toward the end of the Iran-Iraq war, when he simply disappeared from Baghdad. Nothing made sense anymore. Once again, hundreds of thousands dead and there was never going to be any profit in it. His conflicted emotions roiled, and then in the midst of the turmoil it suddenly became blatantly obvious to him. For he had seen powerful and murderous men, begging for mercy, stopped short after looking in his eyes. Even these men with the blackest of hearts, seeing their own evil staring back at them, fell silent and died frozen in fear.

38

The years had also taught him that the men who wielded power and fortunes did so by controlling other men. However, control of men through the fear of loosing their own lesser power and smaller fortunes often proved dangerous. Most ambitious men are never satisfied with their lot in life and they become restless and resentful. Driven to achieve a higher station, they will risk it all in favor of greater rewards. The value of their benefactors and mentors is minimized through rationalizations supported by other ambitious co-conspirators. And soon the cycle is completed, only to begin again.

But history has recorded the deeds of men whose power remained unchallenged. These are the most ruthless men, unwilling to be compromised at any cost. Men whose enemies, and suspected enemies, are swiftly and decisively eliminated. Men with friends and allies that remain so only because the fear of death, the loss of all we know and love, dwarfs all other fears. It was natural then, that he should amass his own fortune by providing his deep-pocketed clients with the knowledge that they held that ultimate power. He would become an agent of change, or stability, or whatever else they wanted. He would perform his services unconditionally and would demand to be compensated accordingly. And, with his personal enrichment as the primary objective, his most important client would be himself. It was all very basic stuff.

For now, his name was Lincoln, Aaron Lincoln. His identity had been erased and reinvented more often than most men buy new socks. Any record of his true identity had long ago been expunged. He was a ghost. Seen when he wanted to be seen. Accountable to no one, not even those who financed him.

Inside his refitted Bell Long Ranger, hovering 1000 feet above the scrap yard on Harrison Avenue in Kearny, he squinted his light gray eyes at the night vision image on his laptop screen. His team was at work below. The three men had secured a tarp over the silver Taurus with the bodies of his other operatives still inside. A tow truck was backed up to the front of the Taurus and the steel bed was tilted back, ready to receive the car. The Taurus, together with the bodies inside, would be made to disappear.

Lincoln swung the microphone attached to his headset in front of his mouth and said, "Tailgate Two, come in."

"This is Tailgate Two Team Leader, sir."

Over the street noise, the team couldn't hear the helicopter above them but they recognized Lincoln's voice in their earpieces.

"Switch to scramble two four," Lincoln instructed.

After giving them enough time to adjust the setting on their digital radios to the encrypted channel, Lincoln spoke again. "Let me hear what you've got."

"Sir, the tractor trailer is across the street in a warehouse . . . "

"I know that. Tell me something I don't know," Lincoln interrupted.

"The GPS locator transmitter was still attached to the inside trailer wall. Over."

"The trailer wall! Why the fuck is it on the trailer wall? "

"Uh, sir, I can't answer that. Over."

Lincoln exhaled loudly. "Of course you can't," he said, more calmly. *But I know the person who can*. He thought. His instructions couldn't have been clearer. What good was his planning if the execution was left to incompetents?

"What else?" Lincoln asked.

"Sir, the shooter came from behind. We found a fresh trail in the weeds along the fence that runs west leading to the rear of our vehicle. There were blood smudges on the back of the truck parked north of our vehicle. Neither of our men drew or fired their weapons so the shooter must have been cut before he approached the car. We have fifteen nine-millimeter casings found in and around the vehicle. Shooting occurred at very close range. And McNeely's I.D. case is missing. Over."

"Awright. Get that car up on the truck and outta there. I'm dropping down for an IR and thermal scan."

Lincoln instructed the pilot to switch to whisper mode and descend to 200 feet. Then he switched on the infrared camera and thermal imaging equipment, which was mounted in the nose pod of the chopper with the other expensive looking and listening devices. As the helicopter settled into its new hover, Lincoln spoke into the intercom while watching the fuzzy thermal images on the computer screen. "Drift slowly northwest," he said to the pilot.

He could see his men, three bright red Gumby-like figures moving around the truck and the Taurus. The hood and certain other parts of the tow truck and Tailgate Two's car glowed red and orange from engine and friction heat. "Hold!" He shouted to the pilot.

The image on the screen stabilized and Lincoln moved the joystick controller to direct the camera behind and north of the vehicles. He tapped at the keyboard to broaden the computer-enhanced infrared and thermal imaging spectrum analysis. In seconds the screen jumped alive with more varying shades of color. Lincoln was now able to draw relative conclusions from the scanned images on the screen. In the chilly evening air, the chain link fence had cooled faster than the ground. The scrubs and grass were a little cooler than the bare ground but not as cool as the fence. And the scrap metal inside the fence was as cold or colder than the fence, depending on the size of the object. Lincoln concentrated on a path directly along the north side of the fence but found nothing. Then he worked the keyboard to zoom closer and up the hill that lead to the rail tracks outside and north of the fence. After a few minutes, he saw several small items that appeared to be inorganic, as they did not match the IR spectrum of any of the surrounding area's vegetation.

"Tailgate Two. Come back," Lincoln said through the scrambled channel.

"This is Team Leader, sir." The men looked up but they were barely able to see the dark gray belly of the helicopter against the night sky.

"I want you to check something for me. One of you walk back along the chain link fence about thirty paces. I'll tell you when to stop. Take a flashlight but don't turn it on until I tell you."

Lincoln watched the red Gumby walking along the fence. When the man had reached a position parallel to the items on his screen, he said, "Stop! Turn 90 degrees right and walk slowly about 25 paces."

"Up the hill, sir?"

"Yes, up the goddam hill!"

Lincoln watched and said, "Two more steps. Stop! Now turn on your light and see if you can find anything. It should be directly in front of you."

Lincoln sat up and turned away from the screen. He drank from a bottle of water and listened to the familiar sounds of cracking bones as he rotated his head to break the stiffness in his neck. He had survived his helicopter being shot out from under him over Laos in the early seventies, but his neck was forever stiff from that day.

"Sir, I've got a pack of cigarettes that appear to be fresh and a gold lighter. They couldn't have been here long. No weather exposure. I'll bag them and keep looking. Over."

Lincoln smiled. He loved technology. He had all the latest toys. Another perk of his position. He took another mouthful of water and waited.

"Sir!" The voice was noticeably exited. "I think you're gonna like *this*. I've got a wallet."

Lincoln leaned forward as if to hear better but nothing else came. He said, "Well?"

"Well? Sir?"

"Well open the god damn wallet and see who it belongs to!" *Fucking moron*, Lincoln thought.

"I didn't want to contaminate evidence, sir. What if it's the shooter's wallet?"

Lincoln exploded. "Just open the fuckin' wallet! Whadaya think we're gonna do, turn this guy in? Take him to court?"

"Sorry, sir. Uh, let's see. I, uh, I've got a New Jersey driver's license with a photo. The wallet belongs to a John A. Anelli. 392A Garden Road, Hackensack, New Jersey. DOB 30 June 1940. Five nine, 190 pounds. Brown hair and eyes. No credit cards. Nothing else except his Social Security Card."

Lincoln was writing furiously. "Spell that last name for me and give me the SSN."

When the man on the ground had finished, he nervously added, "Maybe we got lucky here, sir."

Lincoln had already instructed the pilot to head to Teterboro Airport, which was just south of Hackensack. He replied, "Don't be a fool. There's no such thing as luck."

## 37 Indian Creek Road
## Oceanport, New Jersey

Michael and had his wife, Ilene, were clearing the dinner dishes from the kitchen table. Their two children had gone into the family room to watch TV before bed.

"You haven't said a word. How bad was it today?" Ilene asked.

"I didn't want to say anything in front of the kids. It got pretty ugly. There were about a hundred pickets. Joseph and I got spit on. Bobby Moretti and Kenny Diaz got beat up. And we had a truck stolen from a rest stop on the turnpike. Other than that, things went pretty well."

Ilene stopped loading the dishwasher and spun around, "Are you kidding? Are Bobby and Kenny okay?"

"Bobby was treated and released. Kenny will be out tomorrow if the test results are good. They're concerned about a concussion. But they'll both be fine."

Ilene closed the dishwasher door. "I thought your employees voted to go non-union."

Michael turned off the faucet and reached for a hand towel. "They did, but Friday the NLRB ruled in favor of the Teamsters and declared the vote an unfair labor practice. Big bad Domanski Trucking running roughshod over the rights of the working man. Same old story. The company's guilty until proven innocent in the eyes of the NLRB. I told you this, didn't I?"

Ilene shrugged, "You did, but I thought that if your employees didn't care, the union would have no support."

Michael shook his head. "The Teamsters, all organized labor for that matter, have lost a lot of ground since the mid-eighties. Their organizational efforts have been weak and mostly unsuccessful. The last thing they want is to lose more membership, even a little company like ours."

"But if the employees don't want the union, can they be forced to join?"

"In theory, yes. If we end up in court and lose, we'll be forced to deal with them *in good faith*, as they say."

"*In good faith?* That sounds ridiculous after today," Ilene said. "What are you guys gonna do?"

"Ride it out. See how much stamina they have. We'll sweep up their nails and . . ."

"*Nails?*"

"Yeah nails. Classic stuff. It's like an old black and white movie. All we need is a little fog and some guys . . ."

The phone on the kitchen wall rang, interrupting Michael. Ilene answered, "Hello, Cogan's."

Michael winced. He always thought it sounded like she was answering a phone in a pub.

Ilene turned to him. "It's for you." She shrugged, indicating that she had no idea who it was.

"Hello? This is Michael."

"Are you a fuckin' smart ass or just plain stupid?" Michael recognized the voice. "Do you really think you can fuck with us?"

Michael smiled for Ilene's benefit and said into the phone in a reassuring voice, "Oh, hi. I'm glad you called. Can you hold a moment while I get to my files?"

Michael handed the phone to Ilene and said, "Honey, its business. I've got to get my briefcase. Please hang this up when I get upstairs in the office."

Ilene took the phone but gave him a look. Michael did get occasional calls from the second shift dispatchers or operations guys at the terminal, but she knew their voices. Strange and abrupt evening callers usually meant one thing: Michael was gambling again.

She covered the mouthpiece and said, "Michael, this better not be what I'm thinking it is. The last time was the last time. We're not going through that again are we? You promised." Her eyes were teary but angry.

Michael held up his right palm. "I promise. Nothing like that. Just business. You know with this union thing and all."

He caught her glaring at him as he left the room. He knew that his last loosing streak had nearly cost him his marriage. After he had paid off the bookies with the combination of a home equity loan and a loan from the company, he swore to Ilene that he had quit gambling forever.

43

Michael locked the door to the spare bedroom that served as their home office and picked up the phone. "I've got it." He said and waited to hear the click signaling Ilene had hung.

"Hello," Michael said.

"Oh, donchya worry, I'm still here. Now you wanna answer my question?"

"How'd you get this number?" Michael asked.

"Let's get one thing straight, pal. I'm the one asking the questions. You give the answers. And they better be good ones. Got it?" The voice was dead serious and threatening.

"Okay, go ahead," Michael said.

"You were s'posed to give us sumthin' today and you gave us sumthin' else. This has caused a problem. We don't like being fucked with. You know what happens to people who fuck with us." It wasn't a question.

"Hey, I did my part. You guys took the wrong, ah, unit. It wasn't my fault. Look, Johnny . . . "

The caller cut him short. "No one here named Johnny."

"Well, isn't this . . .?"

"Just shut the fuck up! No names. You are a stupid fuck, aren't you?"

Michael now knew it was Johnny Anelli. There was no mistaking the rasp in his voice and the crude language.

"Now, how we gonna make this right?" Johnny asked.

"Well, I don't know . . ."

"You don't know *what*?" Johnny said, cutting him off. "I'll tell you *what*. You're gonna give us the *what* we wanted. And for thinkin' you can fuck with us you're gonna give it again and again, whenever we tell you to."

"I can't do that."

"You can and you will."

Michael heard a recorded voice requesting more money and coins being dropped into the pay phone. He took the opportunity to regroup.

"Now wait a minute," Michael said. "I tried to get square with you guys. It was against my better judgment, but I did it. You guys blew it. Now we got big problems. This thing you got is serious . . . government stuff. I don't think you understand what you've gotten into here."

Johnny laughed. "You don't think *I* understand? No, no, I don't think *you* understand. We don't give a fuck. Your ass is ours now. If you had done the right thing, this could've all been over. But, no. You gotta get cute, right."

"Listen to me," Michael pleaded. "You guys made a mistake. This isn't my fault and I'm not doin' anything like this again. I'll call Tommy Ton in the morning and make arrangements to pay him. I've always made good before. I'll do it again."

"Hey, pal, what don't you understand?" Johnny was getting frustrated. "You got no fuckin' choice. There's too much involved here now and I ain't gonna get hurt on this 'cause of you."

"Sorry, I've been dealing with Tommy Ton a long time. I prefer to settle this with him directly now. Please don't call here again."

As Michael removed the phone from his ear he could hear Johnny cursing. Michael depressed the button on the phone, hanging up on him. He waited a few seconds, lifted his finger and heard the dial tone. Then he placed the handset on the desk to ensure he wouldn't have to talk to Johnny again that evening.

Michael ran his fingers through his hair and gripped the back of his neck. He paced the room and cursed himself under his breath. He knew he had to ask me for another loan from the company credit line. But he didn't know how to tell me that he had broken his tearful promise to our wives, that he had failed miserably to control himself and had fallen off the wagon, and fallen hard. He had no choice; he was in serious trouble now. He'd have to ask for my help, one last time, and Tommy Ton would get his money and Johnny Anelli would go away.

\*      \*      \*

When the line went dead, Johnny Onions Anelli slammed the handset onto the cradle. He reached into his pocket for more quarters to shove into the coin slot. He read Michael's phone number from a slip of paper and pounded the numbers furiously. After the third attempt and the third busy signal, he banged the phone several times against the metal tray and yelled, "Cocksucker!" Then he threw the handset, which quickly whipped around on the end of its metal cord and struck him in the chin. Further enraged, he kicked savagely at the clear plastic at the bottom of the phone booth until it broke, leaving his foot protruding through the jagged opening. When he tried to pull his foot back, his pant leg snagged. Johnny tugged viciously until his cuff ripped and he fell backwards out of the booth.

His left elbow hit hard on the sidewalk. The pain shot through him like a bolt of lightening, taking his breath away. After a few seconds he managed to whimper softly, to no one in particular, "Motherfucker."

## Taverna Reggia
## Lower East Side, New York City

Dominick Patacca sat across the corner table from Vinny Diamonds Venezio looking down at his hands, twisting a cocktail straw into nervous knots. It had been a very unpleasant twenty minutes explaining the day's events to his boss and now Vinny had fallen into a silent, frozen stare looking very much like a bug-eyed gargoyle. Finally, Vinny belched and turned to Jimmy Merchanti who was seated to his right, as usual.

"Howdoya like this guy, Jimmy Boy?" Vinny said, pointing a plump, sausage finger at Dominick. "First, he sneaks off ta Jersey with that fuck Johnny Onions. Then he crawls back here ta tell me this whole lotta bullshit story about how this mick fucked Johnny. And all they got ta show for it - so he says - is a metal crate that they can't even open. On top of it all, he leaves the goddam crate with that scumbag."

Vinny put both elbows on the table and hunched over his crossed fingers to lean close to Dominick. After a couple seconds, he said, "Do I look stupid to you?"

"No, boss," Dominick replied, shaking his head.

"Then why can't any-a-youse guys believe me when I tell you that Johnny Onions is a fuckin' *piece a shit*? That motherfucker would steal his own mother's eyes and then leave her in the middle of Flatbush Avenue at rush hour. Didja ever think that maybe Johnny's jerkin' you off? That maybe there was never any goddam shoes? And that maybe Johnny knows *exactly* what's in that crate and he wants it all for himself?"

Dominick blinked and shrugged. "I never thought of that, boss, but I . . ."

"Ah, shit," Vinny sighed, wiping the sweat off his puffy face with a napkin. "You guys know goddam well we've had our problems with our friends in Jersey. Last time it cost me big. Albie got whacked, Sal did some time, and I got told ta back off. That fuckin' Anelli never had ta answer for any of it. Well, that ain't happenin' this time."

Vinny pushed himself away from the table and leaned back in the chair. "Dominick, I want you and Paulie S to go over ta Jersey tonight."

"Which Paulie S?" Dominick asked.

"Whadaya mean which Paulie S?" Vinny said, his eyes beginning to bulge again.

"Ah, Paulie Soldano or Paulie Sig, boss?"

Vinny let his head fall, spreading his fleshy double chin against his chest. "Jimmy, help me here. Is this guy trying to make me fuckin' nuts? Will you ask him if he's trying to make me fuckin' nuts?"

Jimmy patted Vinny's beefy forearm gently several times and said in a soothing voice, "Dominick, if the boss was talkin' about Paulie Sig he would've said Paulie Sig. But he's talkin' about Paulie S so he said Paulie S. Got it?"

Dominick nodded sheepishly.

Jimmy patted Vinny's arm again. "It's okay Vinny, go ahead."

Vinny looked up and continued with deliberately slow pacing, enunciating each word carefully. "Go to Jersey with Paulie S. Go to Johnny's house. If he's not there, wait until he comes home. Then bring him to me."

"Whadif he doesn't wanna come?"

Vinny sneered. "Then start breakin' every fuckin' bone in his body until he tells you what's in that crate and where it is."

"Then what, boss?"

"Then put him in the fuckin' trunk. Drive to where he says the crate is. If it's not there, start cuttin' pieces off him until he tells you. Then, when you get the crate, call Jimmy here so we can pick it up."

"Then what do we do with Johnny?"

"Then you cut that motherfucker up into little tiny pieces and flush him down the nearest toilet."

## Hackensack, New Jersey

One of Lincoln's men from the Tailgate Two team had met him at Teterboro Airport to give him John Anelli's wallet. Lincoln rented a dark blue Pontiac Grand Am with an American Express card and driver's license in the name of Peter Ansbach from Columbia, Missouri. Before leaving the rental lot, he had used a GPS navigation system in his laptop to route him to Garden Road in Hackensack. Less than twenty minutes later, he was parking the Grand Am on a dark section of Beechwood Street, one block south of Garden Road.

Lincoln stood at the rear of the car and surveyed the street. It was an older but tidy neighborhood with mature, neatly trimmed landscaping. It was after eleven o'clock and most of the houses were already shuttered for the night. The neighborhood's tall oaks and maples were near full leaf and provided a canopy that let faint, stippled light from the half moon dance across the lawns in the night breeze. Lincoln liked the cover of the darkened street and the shifting shadows.

He popped the trunk and, with a small flashlight clenched in his teeth, reached in to dial the combination lock on the oversized black aluminum briefcase he had brought. He opened the case, which appeared to be filled with business papers and files belonging to Peter Ansbach, Vice President of

Sales for the Mid-American Agchem Products Company, Columbia, Missouri. Letting his fingers feel along the inside wall of the case, he located two small, flat buttons. When he pressed them forward and down the bottom of the case lifted slightly. He opened it further to reveal the foam cut-outs which neatly cradled the equipment he kept with him at all times.

Lincoln turned off the flashlight and looked up and down the deserted street. He unbuttoned his shirt, loosened his belt, and unzipped his pants. With a quick tearing sound, he ripped a Kevlar vest from its Velcro fasteners underneath the lid of the false bottom in the case. It was actually a customized breastplate similar to a baseball catcher's equipment, complete with a codpiece. Velcro straps around the back of the neck and midsection held it in place. The codpiece assuaged a personal phobia. A little over thirty years ago, a high explosive round from a shoulder-fired RPG had slammed his helicopter into the Laotian jungle. After he had crawled a safe distance away from the burning wreck, he looked down to see his lower torso and groin area covered with blood. He felt no pain, which was not unusual immediately following severe trauma, but he was sickened by the thought he had suffered a fate worse than death. Both hands flew to his crotch. He was instantly relieved to feel his personal package still attached, safe and snug in his grip. Although he had been seriously wounded, most of the mess on his clothes turned out to be the blood and guts of his squad leader who had absorbed most of the blast. Ever since, even when his neck stiffened and ached unbearably, he never complained. He tucked the codpiece into his pants, zipped his fly, and buttoned his shirt.

Lincoln reconfirmed he was alone in the street before he switched on the flashlight again. He took stock of the equipment nestled tightly in the bottom of the case and focused on the job at hand, Mr. John A. Anelli. From his helicopter, Lincoln had used the satellite link in his powerful laptop to access databases at the FBI and the Justice Department. By routing his inquiries over the Internet, through a series of sites designed to alter the origin and name of the user, and then through the Bridgeport, Connecticut police department's computer, he was afforded valuable and confidential information on demand. He had paid a brilliant but sociopathic computer wizard twenty thousand dollars for this feature. After nearly fifty thousand dollars in illegal upgrades, Lincoln decided to do himself and society a favor by terminating the hacker. This had also obviated the need to pay the hacker for the last upgrade.

The FBI files had been the most comprehensive. Anelli was a convicted felon and a "made" member of the Napolo Crime Family, one of the original New York crime families and arguably still the most powerful crime organizations in the country today. He was a suspect in several murders and known to be involved in typical organized crime activities such as extortion, gambling, loan sharking, robbery, and hijacking; essentially, street-level crimes indicative of lower ranking soldiers. However, the physical evidence from today's murders in Kearny was also compelling and telltale. To Lincoln, it spoke of a man that was not patient or remarkably intelligent. The murder of his two men had been impulsive and sloppy. The fifteen shell casings found at the scene indicated Anelli had emptied his weapon with furious abandon, giving little or no thought to the aftermath. Anelli, he thought, should be considered a confused and explosive individual. A potentially dangerous combination to approach, not unlike a scared wounded animal, which will strike out viciously and unpredictably.

With this in mind, Lincoln began selecting equipment from his case. First he took out the loaded nine-millimeter semiautomatic pistol, a Glock 17, and two extra clips. He checked the safety, chambered the first round, and slid the handgun into the waistband of his pants at the small of his back, putting the other clips in his left back pocket. Next he drew a small, .22 caliber 9-shot revolver. He preferred a revolver to an automatic for specific circumstances. A revolver did not eject the spent bullet casings, which could be valuable to the crime scene's forensic investigators. The small .22 caliber bullet was also used frequently and effectively by mob executioners, which in this case, may prove useful. Lincoln's pistol was loaded with Eley sub-sonic .22 caliber hollow-point bullets. Like most world-class assassins, he preferred the Eley product for their quiet and deadly performance. The hollow-point bullets mushroom and fragment on impact, disbursing tiny pieces of hot lead that tear through human tissue in jagged paths of destruction. The end result renders the bullet incapable of secondary penetration and distorted beyond recognition by forensic science. He screwed a noise suppressor onto the barrel. While you could never truly silence a revolver, it would dampen the muzzle pop from the little bullet. Moreover, the silencer nearly double the length of the gun and added the extra weight Lincoln preferred for better balance.

He put the silenced pistol in his jacket pocket. Then he selected two knives in Velcro-trimmed ballistic nylon sheaths. They had been forged of hardened steel and balanced for throwing. Both seven-inch blades were double edged and sharp enough to slice tissue paper yet strong enough to penetrate bone. He strapped one to his right calf concealing the blade end in his sock and pressed the other one onto a Velcro strip that he had glued into the left cuff of his jacket. A small kit of lock picking tools, a roll of duct tape, plastic wrist restraints, a miniature night vision scope, and a pair of latex gloves completed his outfitting.

Finally, he removed a black leather ID case from his rear pocket. He slid out several sets of identification, each in the name of Clifford Dwyer, all bearing his photograph. He flipped through the ID's, all perfect replications, indistinguishable from the actual credentials issued to the agents of the Secret Service, Department of Defense, CIA and the FBI. Tonight, Special Agent Clifford Dwyer of the Federal Bureau of Investigation was calling on John Anelli, so he placed that ID in front before sliding the pack behind the clear plastic holder in the leather case.

Lincoln snapped the false bottom back in place and locked the case, moving only one digit on the combination so he could quickly access the compartment in the event of a hurried departure. He closed the trunk and started down the street to the corner of Garden Road.

The apartment complex was comprised of six two-story brick structures, two of which faced the street, with the other four ringing a common courtyard. Each building had six apartments, three up and three down. Lincoln leaned against a tree across the street to steady the night vision scope. He focused the green-tinted image to be able to read the numbers on each front door. He saw that the ground floor apartments were the "A" addresses and the second floor were the "B's". He reached into his pocket and found John A. Anelli's photo ID in the wallet. Lincoln was relieved to confirm the address 392A. A ground floor apartment would make things much easier. He studied Anelli's photograph one final time before slipping the I.D. back into his pocket.

Lincoln scanned the front doors until he found 392A. Once again he was pleased. The apartment was located in the back of the courtyard on the end of a building and there were no lights on. The apartment next door was also dark. There were cars parked behind all the buildings, which led him to believe there were back doors to access this area. Smiling at his luck, he began to move.

He crossed the street at the end of the complex and walked through the parking lot behind the building, staying to the back side to avoid the better lit area closer to the buildings. When he reached Anelli's building, he stopped behind a trash dumpster to use his night vision scope to peer into the back windows of the apartment. The kitchen and bedroom were dark and empty. The lack of window dressings, sparse furnishings and bare walls suggested a bachelor's home. The unmade bed and several weeks of clothing draped over the closet doors and dresser top was further proof that no female had even visited recently. Lincoln frowned in disgust at Anelli's untidiness as he trained the scope on the back door to plan his entry.

There were four glass panes in the door that would make it easy but noisy. He looked closely at the door handle. He needed to determine the lock type in order to evaluate the degree of difficulty and time required to quietly pick the lock. However, something was wrong. The door was cracked and splintered near the handle and the frame appeared to be broken around the lockset. Had

Anelli forgotten his key one night and simply broke into his own home? Or, was this the sign of a recent break-in?

Lincoln had a time honored motto that he attributed to saving his life on a number of occasions: Always get caught with your pants up. Tonight would be no exception. Something was not right with that door and there was no way to exact the cause. Therefore, he had to avoid the affect. He would go in through the front door.

Sticking to the shadows, he walked around to the front of the building. When he reached the front door, he unscrewed the light bulb in the fixture above the mailbox. As soon as the light went out, he thought he saw movement through the living room window. He pressed an ear against the front door but quickly snapped back and to the side of the door after he heard at least one whispering but urgent voice.

Lincoln was not feeling like his pants were up real tight. Whoever was inside had been spooked when he turned off the porch light. He had lost the element of surprise. He needed to get the high ground again to be back in control of the situation. And he needed to do it quickly, before whoever was inside had time to think through their own plan.

He took a deep breath, pulled the Glock from behind his back, and slammed the front door twice very hard with the side of his fist.

"FBI. Open this door NOW!" Lincoln screamed.

Then he jumped from the porch and ran as fast as he could around the side of the building to the rear, not slowing even a little as he leaned his shoulder into the back door. The door latch had been ripped from the frame, so when he hit it at a full run the door slammed open imbedding the handle into the sheetrock wall behind it, causing the glass panes to shatter loudly. Lincoln continued running through the tiny kitchen into the living room where two startled men were spinning around in his direction.

Lincoln raised his gun with both hands configured for combat shooting. "Freeze! FBI!" he yelled, and came to a stop about five feet from the men.

Both men had handguns at ready. Lincoln saw that one held his gun low next to his right leg, too low to react effectively. The other, taller and younger, had his right arm outstretched to the side with a large automatic in his hand about waist high. This was the one that posed the threat; the one Lincoln needed to address first.

Lincoln pointed his Glock directly in the face of the taller man. "Drop your weapons," he said, not moving a muscle.

"Who the fuck are you?" The smaller, heavier man asked.

"FBI. I'm here for John Anelli. Is Anelli here?" Lincoln asked without taking his eyes off of the taller man. The taller man hadn't even blinked.

"FBI don't come into someone's house like that. Show us some ID," the smaller one said.

"Okay," Lincoln said. "But stay cool. No one needs to get hurt here. I'm just looking for Anelli." Lincoln was trying his best to look and act like a Fed - calm, reassuring, and professional. He tried again. "Just put your weapons down so we don't have any accidents."

"ID first." The taller man finally spoke.

"Alright," Lincoln sighed. He shifted the Glock to his left hand. It didn't matter. He was a trained and expert marksman with either hand.

As he reached into his jacket, he said, "I'm Special Agent Clifford Dwyer. I'm here to ask John Anelli a few questions about a hijacking we're investigating."

Lincoln flipped open the leather case and held it out for the two men to see. The smaller man leaned closer and began looking from the case to Lincoln's face and back again. He stepped back and said, "Looks real enough, Paulie."

Lincoln folded the case and put it in his right jacket pocket, leaving his hand in the pocket, wrapping his fingers around the .22 revolver.

The taller man began to shake his head. "Somethin's not right with this." Then to Lincoln, "Where's your partner? Fed's don't travel alone."

"He's close by, outside," Lincoln said. "Look, is Anelli here or not? If he's not we'll just come back at another time. No need to have a problem here." He was making an effort to sound conciliatory.

The taller man, Paulie Soldano, looked over at Dominick Patacca. "I think this guy's here alone and I'm not so sure he's a Fed." With that his arm snapped up and he pointed his gun in Lincoln's face. Dominick quickly did the same. Lincoln let his eyes widen in fear.

Paulie said, "Now, Special Agent Dwyer, or whoever you are, whachya gonna do, shoot us both? I don't think so. Now drop that gun or I'll blow your face off."

Lincoln allowed his hand to tremble and forced a hard swallow. "I told you I don't want anyone to get hurt."

"I'll bet you don't," Dominick said.

"Just be cool and I'll set my gun down," Lincoln assured them.

Dominick and Paulie looked at each other, shaking their heads and smirking as Lincoln bent to lay his Glock on the cheap carpet. Lincoln looked up at the two men through frightened eyes, cowering pathetically below them.

"Look guys, let me explain. I've got a wife and three kids. I'm just doing my job . . ."

"Oh, shut the fuck up." Paulie tapped Lincoln on the top of the head with his gun causing Lincoln to hunch lower and creating the distraction that allowed Lincoln to slide the knife from his left sleeve.

"Guys?" Lincoln began weakly, his voice lilting and trembling. "Remember when I said I didn't want anyone to get hurt? Well . . . "

"Well, wha . . . "

An eruption from below cut Paulie short. Lincoln moved quickly and efficiently. In a blur, his legs sprang outward from under him, to create a strong and balanced crouch, while in the same motion his arms shot up fast and powerfully. The knife in his left hand sank deeply into the soft flesh of Paulie's right armpit causing him to drop his gun and fall backward over the sofa. Simultaneously, Lincoln placed the muzzle of the .22 revolver against Dominick's left kneecap and fired two quick rounds which left Dominick curled up on his side, grabbing his knee with both hands.

Lincoln straightened up and kicked the men's guns out of reach. Paulie and Dominick were both moaning loudly. Lincoln slipped on his latex gloves and used two pieces of duct tape to cover their mouths. Then he walked over to Paulie and put his foot on his right triceps, pinning his arm down, exposing the knife protruding from the armpit. Paulie's left arm rose instinctively to push Lincoln away. Lincoln blocked the attempt with his right forearm and then shot him once, through the inside crook of his elbow to deter any further interference.

"Gimme my knife back," Lincoln said as he pulled hard on the handle. Paulie moaned and thrashed in pain. The knife wouldn't come out.

Paulie's eyes were clouded with tears but he could still see Lincoln leaning forward with the silenced .22 pistol. Lincoln coolly shot once on either side of the blade. Paulie screamed behind the duct tape. This time the knife came out easily.

Lincoln bent over Paulie, waving the bloody blade in his face and said, "Sometimes they get stuck, in the bone or something. That's a little trick I learned. Frees 'em up almost every time."

Lincoln rolled both men over on their stomachs and bound their hands behind their backs with the plastic wrist restraints. He searched both men for other weapons and wallets. Then he rolled them over again onto their backs causing both men to groan in pain.

After rummaging through their wallets Lincoln held their driver's licenses in his hands. "Let's see. Paul Soldano and Dominick Patacca," he said, mispronouncing Patacca by giving the second "a" a hard rendering. "Two New York greaseballs waiting here, in the dark, for our mutual friend John Anelli. This is *most* interesting. I think I want to know more. Who wants to be first?"

Paulie grunted in pain. Lincoln cocked his head in his direction and said, "Well, thank you for volunteering."

Paulie let out a low groan. His wounded right armpit and left elbow were twisted behind his back, bearing his weight. The pain was unbearable. The slightest movement was excruciating. The armpit wound was bleeding profusely, swamping the carpet.

Lincoln sat Paulie up, squatted behind him, and put the muzzle of the .22 against Paulie's temple, angled forward toward his eye. He ripped the duct tape off Paulie's mouth and put his lips close to his ear. "Paul, if you don't answer my questions in a forthright yet polite manner, I'm going to shoot your eye out from behind."

"Oh, God no," Paulie trembled.

"Come on, Paul. It doesn't have to go that way. Just do your best to answer my questions."

Lincoln began again. "Now, why have you come here tonight to see Mr. Anelli?"

"We came to bring Johnny to Vinny," Paulie gasped.

"Very good, Paul. Now tell me who is this Vinny and why does he wants to see Mr. Anelli."

"I dunno. I . . ."

Lincoln pulled the trigger and tiny bullet fragments blew out Paulie's right eye. Paulie's head drooped forward and shook violently until he passed out. Lincoln laid him back gently on the carpet.

Dominick was breathing hard and fast through his nose, staring at them in disbelief. However, he stopped breathing when Lincoln rose and said with a broad grin on his face, "Paul and I just couldn't seem to see things eye-to-eye. Maybe you and I, Dominick, will get along better."

And for the next five minutes they did. Lincoln sat comfortably in an armchair while Dominick told him all about the Bennini shoes that turned out to be a metal crate belonging to the government. He told him all about Vinny Diamonds and Johnny Onions and that it was an inside job; that Johnny knew some guy at the trucking company. But he couldn't tell him where the metal crate was now.

"Honest, I just don't know," Dominick said.

Lincoln studied him for a moment and then replied assuredly, "You know what, I believe you."

"But Vinny will find it. You'll see." Dominick was beginning to feel more comfortable. "He's a tough guy. He always gets what he wants. When Vinny finds it, I can let you know. But you'll have to let me go so I can do that for you, right?"

"Sure, Dom. Can I call you Dom?"

"Yeah, sure, everybody calls me Dom or Dominick. Except my mother, she calls me Dommy, 'cept when she's mad at me, it's Dominick then."

"Is that so?" Lincoln uncrossed his legs and leaned forward in the chair. "Dom, just one more question."

Dominick nodded and shrugged, "Okay."

"It's an important one. So think carefully before you answer."

"Okay." Still nodding.

"How do you spell chrysanthemum?"

"What?"

"Chrysanthemum. I need you to spell chrysanthemum. Correctly, of course."

Dominick probed Lincoln's face seeking assurance that he was joking. But Lincoln's face told him nothing, not until Dominick saw his dilated pupils, eyes that transformed into black pools of incalculable depth without the bottom reaches that men of conscience and humanity possess lest they become comfortable with iniquity. Dominick began to cry.

"C - H - R - I . . ." Dominick sobbed.

Lincoln shook his head and pursed his lips. "I'm sorry, Dom. That's incorrect."

The .22 revolver thumped twice and two small red holes appeared in Dominick's forehead. Dominick fell slowly backward and didn't move. Lincoln got up and bent down to put one more bullet in his heart. Then he walked over to Paulie and put two rounds through the side of his head.

Lincoln picked up his Glock and left through the open kitchen door, pulling it closed behind him. He would abandon the Grand Am outside the airport and walk through a field to his helicopter waiting on the tarmac. It was a short flight back to New Windsor, New York. He could still get a full night's rest.

*     *     *

A short while later, Johnny Anelli parked his car in the usual space behind his apartment. He retrieved his Beretta from its hideout in the console. He knew he would have to disassemble it, wipe it clean, and scatter the parts throughout Bergen County. He hated giving up the Beretta but he had no choice. Besides, there were plenty more where that came from. Maybe, he thought, this time he would look for something a little smaller. One guy he knew had this compact Colt nine that fit nicely into a back pocket.

Johnny reached for the car door handle but a sharp pain in his left elbow made him pull up short. The concrete sidewalk had done some damage. He reached across and opened the door with his right hand. He sighed as he swung his legs out of the car and groaned in pain as he straightened up. He looked down at his tattered pants and raw hands. One knee had swelled and stiffened. His back was sore and he still had a headache. He couldn't wait to down a handful of Tylenol and get into a nice hot bath.

Johnny limped toward his kitchen door, stopping short when he was close enough to see it was ajar. After a couple more cautious steps, he could see the shattered doorframe and broken windows. He pulled the Beretta from his jacket pocket, wishing it were loaded. Crouching as low as his aching back would allow, he made his way slowly to the stoop where he lowered himself gently to the bricks and slowly pushed opened the door. When he was sure the dark kitchen was empty, he began crawling on his belly across the threshold into the kitchen. After a few painful feet, his belt buckle snagged on the metal weather strip across the bottom of the doorframe. He tried to move forward but the buckle wouldn't dislodge. Then he pushed himself backwards hoping to slide it loose, but no such luck. He tugged this way and that, smoothly at first, then rough and jerky. Nothing.

Johnny began to panic. The broken door was a very bad sign. If some guys had been sent for him and were waiting inside there were only two reasons; to give him a good beating or, God forbid, to whack him. Either way, flat on his stomach, hooked to the floor with an unloaded gun in his hand would not work in his favor. So he slid his good knee forward and brought his good arm back to push himself up. The buckle held firmly as he arched his back and pushed up, straining hard against the leather belt strap. He gritted his teeth and pushed up harder and harder still, grunting, until suddenly it jerked free, sending him wildly off balance, slamming his bruised elbow and swollen knee hard on the floor. He yelped in pain and fell sideways against the open door, which banged loudly into the wall behind it. The floor there was littered with broken window glass, some of which, of course, cut into his hands and forearms.

"Shit!" Johnny cursed under his breath as he fumbled with his empty gun to get it pointed toward the living room.

Wincing in pain, he waited for them to come. As he tried to control his breathing and blink away the sweat that had dripped into his eyes, he imagined them hidden in the shadows of his living room, ready to pounce on him or simply put a couple rounds in the back of his head. Any second, they would come to investigate the noise in the kitchen. Johnny knew he could barely stand so running for his life was out of the question. He closed his eyes briefly and thought, *I'm fucked.*

But no one came and Johnny couldn't understand why. So he reached for the handle on the refrigerator and pulled himself up. He peeked into the dark living room. No movement. No strange silhouettes sitting on his furniture.

Feeling more comfortable, he stepped into the room and stood perfectly still, listening and waiting for his eyes to adjust to the darkness. Slowly the gray shapes lightened as his night vision improved. He began to see the disarray. His couch was toppled over. The throw rug and side tables were pushed aside. The table lamp was smashed, lying on the floor next to a pair of shoes. And the shoes had feet in them! *Whathefuck* . . .

Then it all flashed through Johnny's brain like some kind of surreal music video. Dominick Patacca and Paulie Soldano dead, bound and bloody, in his living room. In *his* living room! *Wham!* Two guys from Venezio's crew. Vinny Diamonds had made his move. *Bam!* Now Everyone, Vinny, the cops, the Feds, everyone would be coming after him. Friends and strangers, good guys and bad, everybody would be hunting him down! *Thank you, ma'am!*

He stumbled through the small apartment stuffing clothes into an old suitcase and a couple plastic grocery bags. He frantically dumped two dresser drawers on the bed until he found the box of nine-millimeter shells. Staggering around, circling and twisting his head, he tried to remember where the things were that he shouldn't leave behind. Where was the stuff he should take because he could never ever come here again? Where were the important papers, the mementoes, the photographs, the few little things in life that meant something and were irreplaceable? Where were they? *What* were they?

He stopped spinning and limped toward the door, realizing that he had none of those things.

## Monmouth Beach, NJ

At 11:20 p.m., I closed my book and switched off the lamp on the nightstand. Next to me, Cathy's face was lit by a shaft of soft silver-blue moonlight. Asleep she looked remarkably young and beautiful, as if midlife was somehow years away. Studying her features and listening to her breathing was as peaceful as prayer. I smelled vanilla in her hair, closed my eyes, and fell asleep without wondering.

# Prologue - Continued

**Monday Night, March 1963**
**Greenwich Village, New York City**

"Per favore lasciaci." *Please leave us,* my grandfather - the great Don Carmine Napolo, said to a group of men standing near the door. When the door closed behind them, he gestured to the four men remaining in his study.

"Vieni e siediti." *Come sit,* he said as he swept his arm across the room.

As the men arranged themselves on the imported leather chairs and sofas, Don Carmine reached for a book of matches on his desk. When the four men had settled, quiet now in their chairs, he raised up the matchbook in his left hand and opened the cover.

"This matchbook is like this thing of ours. Each match a soldier, a friend ready to do what we need done. If we are careful with these matches, if we obey the rules that we learned as young men, they will serve us well. We can use them to light candles to our saints and to fire the gas that cooks our fine meals, and then after, they allow us to enjoy the cigars our Cuban friends send to us." The men chuckled.

He bent one match from the book, and without separating the stalk, rubbed the head across the striker. He waited for the flame to fully blossom. "But, if we are not careful, the flame from just one of these matches can ignite the whole matchbook and destroy this thing of ours. And right now we are exposed, about to be uncovered and burned. It is time for us to close the cover on our matchbook, to protect what is ours, and to extinguish this flame that burns too close to us."

Without taking his eyes of the seated men, he squeezed out the flame between his thumb and forefinger.

"I tell you this because our friends in Washington have advised me that one of our own will break his vow of Omerta. Our ungrateful President and his brother have their Judas. They will put him in front of television cameras and he will tell the world what they have, until now, only suspected. These two sons-a-bitches believe they can cleanse their hands, and their father's hands, by showing the world they are better than us . . . by trying to destroy us. This is not the way to treat those who have been your friends.

"When these bastards needed our support, we brought them the money and the unions to guarantee the election. In return, it was understood that we would require certain favors and cooperation on some matters from time-to-time. This is the way things work, in our world and in the world of politics.

"First, it was Cuba. It was in our *mutual* interest to eliminate Fidel Castro. They knew we sought to return to Cuba, to our casinos and resorts and all that we had built there. And, this new young President of the free world needed to break the communist stronghold so close to our shores. We sent our soldiers to Cuba to try assassinate Castro. True, they failed but we sent them willingly and without regret. In '61, we worked hand-in-hand with the CIA to finance and train a liberation army. We joined forces with them in this very private and secret war. The President and his brother were kept well informed of every aspect of this operation, and it had their blessing. *But*, when it came time for this President to do the *only* thing that was required of him, he looked the other way. He *refused* to send the air support he had promised, and many good men died. The Bay of Pigs? No, the Bay of *Betrayal*!"

Don Carmine paused to let his anger settle into the room.

"Next," he continued. "In their arrogance, they go after Hoffa - Jimmy Hoffa, a man of honor and a great American. He's done more for the working people in this country than any other man since FDR. This is also the man who helped us deliver them the votes of not only the Teamsters but of all organized labor. Millions of votes. And in thanks, they try to destroy him and his union because they know he's a friend of ours. Again, *betrayal*!" The Don paused and looked around at the men in the room. "*Si, un altra volta, che tradimento! Bastardi!*

"And then, there's Hoover, who only a few years ago, publicly denied the existence of something called the Mafia. Now these two snot-nosed punks use their offices, and perhaps other means, to force Hoover to publicly lick their asses. It's not enough that Hoover must use his FBI on the side of the coloreds to support this civil rights thing of theirs. No, that's not enough for these two fuckin' Abraham Lincolns, now they make Hoover turn his FBI on us.

59

we still have strong and powerful friends in Washington, and at the
the CIA, and elsewhere who will remain loyal to us. Some because
Others because they, too, have grown to hate these brothers from
Boston. They, too, understand these spoiled rich boys will stop at nothing to
have their way. We will capitalize on these alliances to go forward and forge
our future. *We have worked too hard and too long to let these Irish bootleggers
destroy this thing of ours!*"

Don Carmine unclenched his fist and stared at the crushed matchbook
in the palm of his hand. He shook his head as he turned his hand to let the
matchbook fall into the waste basket.

"You have all heard about last night, the attempt on my life." The men
nodded solemnly. "Have you heard that this attempt was made at *my son's
home?* Have you heard that *my grandson* was a witness to these events? Mio
nipote carino!" *My sweet grandson!*

Carmine paused to scan the room, to look each one in the eyes, and
to regain his executive composure. Then he began to speak again, more
calmly.

"I am told by our Washington friends there will be other attempts on
my life. I know that Baressi is behind this." The men in the room began to
shuffle and murmur.

One of the men sprang to his feet. "Don Carmine, we gotta take care of
this now! Baressi's been trouble before. Now we got the right."

"Siediti!" *Sit down!* Carmine glowered at the man until he took his
seat. "No one will move on Baressi until I give the word. Now sit quiet and
listen to me.

"I am the head of this family. I am also the head of the Commission,
Capo di tutti Capi, The Boss of Bosses. What I say here will not be challenged.
Capisci?"

Without waiting for a response, he continued. "The Judas in Washington
was my driver and bodyguard. What he knows and what he will tell the world
will be much about me and this family. Beyond that, he knows very little
that can harm us, or our friends. However, he knows enough to create the
excitement and public attention these two Irish scumbags thrive on. I will
certainly be called to testify, and though there will be no hard evidence for
me to fear, the television cameras and reporters will all be there to indict me.
Even our most loyal friends will become nervous and guarded. In the end, it
will cause us irreversible damage and fucking Camelot will grow stronger. *I
can not, will not, allow this to happen!*"

The Don breathed in deeply and let his gaze roam the rosewood paneled
walls and the priceless art work that he so loved. He looked up at the ornate
plaster castings that decorated the ceiling of his study and remembered the

chapel ceiling in Livorno he had replicated. Slowly, he let his eyes drift down and resettle on the men in the room.

"On the battlefield," he continued. "Sometimes one man is put into a position where he knows that his actions can save the lives of his comrades, even though it may result in his own death. These brave men are forever honored for their courage and sacrifice. Their families go on, strengthened by their memory." Don Carmine paused. "We will let Baressi come for me."

Some of the men shouted out. "*What?*" "*No!*" "*Never!*"

Don Carmine scowled at them and they quieted.

He continued, "With me gone, our Judas will be telling tales of a dead man. The press will declare Baressi the new Boss. They think we are so simple that a bullet can change everything. Fabrizio Benedetto, my friend, you are young but you will become the new Boss of this family, Giovanni the Underboss and Frank will remain Consiglieri."

Benedetto rose slowly and approached him. "Don Carmine, we cannot accept this. There is always another way. We will survive this thing in Washington as we have other things before. We . . ."

Carmine raised his hand. "No, I have made my decision."

"But, Don Carmine, with all respect, this decision of yours is flawed. Baressi will get what he wants. The Commission may even consider his move justified if he uses your own example of the publicity these hearings will generate. Our Judas, as you call him, will live on in custody of the Feds. And, worst of all, the President and the Attorney General will still have what they wanted, plenty of publicity and you gone. They will twist the facts to suit themselves. Above all, with you gone our family is weakened, we'll become targets."

Placing his hands on Benedetto's shoulders, Carmine said, "Fabrizio, I am gone no matter what. The doctors tell me I have a cancer. It's inoperable. I have only months to live."

Several of the men gasped. Benedetto lowered his head, shaking it slowly. Then he grabbed Carmine's hand and lowered his lips to the knuckles.

Looking up, Fabrizio said, "Don Carmine, we will follow your instructions. But please, let us hear that you have thought this thing through."

"Let's sit, Fabrizio." Carmine gestured toward the empty chairs. "I will not leave you weakened. Everyone will receive what's due them. Our good friends in Washington will see that the spotlight is brightly focused on Baressi. The press and the prosecutors will have a new Mafioso Boss to drag out for public scrutiny. That publicity and my death will distract attention from this family. The Commission will have no choice but to shun Baressi and his entire organization . . . they'll be too public. After a while, you will seek and receive the Commission's approval to hit Baressi and Tagnalli, his

Underboss. When it's done, his Capos will come to you one by one to beg your forgiveness and to pledge their loyalty. This family, the Napolo Family, will grow stronger and richer.

"A few months from now, after the circus in Washington has folded its tents, you will be contacted by someone called McBride. He will give you a time and a place where our Judas will be made available to you. Too late for us now, but better than never."

"What about the Irish brothers?" Benedetto asked. "They go on like nothing has happened?"

"Did I not say that *everyone* will get what's due them?"

"Yes, but what should we do? Should we . . .?"

"*You* do nothing. Just know that *everyone* will get what's due them."

Benedetto looked into my grandfather's eyes and knew that somehow this would be done.

Looking around the room, my grandfather said, "I need to speak with Fabrizio alone now."

One by one the men in the room hugged and kissed their Don good-bye. It would be the last time they would see him. When they left, Don Carmine looked over to Benedetto who had tears in his eyes.

"Fabrizio, please. I couldn't stand to let the cancer chew me up. It's better this way. Now I need your help with a couple things."

"Certamente." *Of course.*

"You will see that my dear wife's grave is properly kept. I made sure that Angelo the florist has what he needs to continue to deliver her fresh red roses every week of every year, for the rest of his and his son's life. He knows the grave blankets I like for the Holy Days. Make sure my death does not cause Angelo to become lazy or forgetful. Perhaps an occasional reminder . . ."

"Ci penso io, la faceio riposare come una santa." *I will see that she rests like a saint.* "And your son?"

"My son, the dentist, has never accepted anything from me, except for the occasional loan from a father to his son, but nothing more. I never insisted because I never wanted this life for him or his children. My heart is broken that my grandson had to witness that horror last night. He's tough though, tougher than his father in some ways, but this was not something a young boy should see. For this, for my grandson, you will personally make certain that Baressi's death is long and terrible. He must know that I am there with you."

"Consider this done."

"Grazie, mio vecchio amico." *Thank you, my old friend.*

"Che altro posso fare?" *What else can I do?*

"I have made arrangements which have guaranteed the future of this family and secured its position of power. From time to time, this man called McBride will contact you. Trust his information and follow his instructions as if they were mine."

"You leave me in the care of another Irishman? Who is this McBride?"

"McBride is just a name. Consider him your guardian angel, Fabrizio. The men using that name may change. But listen to them as if it was me speaking to you. Promise me you will trust them as you trust me."

"Basta." *Enough said.*

"There is more, Fabrizio."

"Of course, tell me."

"Mario's and Nico's bodies are in the trunk of my car, down in the garage. Mario deserves a proper burial. His family in Napoli should know of his death."

"And the son-of-a-bitch, Nico?" Fabrizio asked. "He should be thrown in harbor with the rest of the trash."

"Leave him. I'll take care of him myself."

"You? Why?"

"He was blood to me."

"Don Carmine, he was to be your assassin!"

"Yes, and that's why I'll take care of this."

"I don't understand, but okay."

"Do you know where Nico lived?" The Don asked.

"Sure, he had a small place over in Brooklyn."

"His son, Nicolino, is now an orphan. His mother died giving birth to him. He's a handsome, bright young boy, six or seven years old, about the same age as my eldest grandson, Joseph. He's been alone now for at least a day, waiting for his father to return. Go get him. Be sure no one tells him of his father's death. He's of my blood and my responsibility now. I will tell him his father died bravely."

"Then what will we do with him?"

"My mistress, the widow Antonelli, has always been fond of him. She'll raise him as her own. I have made arrangements to move them away from here and seen that they have everything they will ever need."

"Should I check in on them, and on your son and his family? From a distance, of course."

"No. No contact. Never. When I am gone I want the notoriety of the Napolo name to go with me. What I have done dies with me. Soon this will be your family, the Benedetto Family. Please see to this, Fabrizio."

"Don Carmine, avete la mia parola." *You have my word.*

"Good. Now go. Deliver this boy, Nicolino, to the widow. And tonight when you return, old friend, you and I will have a great meal with the finest wines. A last supper together."

"You know something else, don't you, Don Carmine."

"Yes, in the next few days, Baressi will put a bomb in my car." The Don smiled thinly. "Prego che sia grande." *I pray it's a big one.*

# CHAPTER 9

## Tuesday Morning, May 2, 2001
## Monmouth Beach, New Jersey

I woke purposefully, immediately alert, my mind churning through yesterday's events. In the dark just before the false dawn, my thinking is most clear and true. Alone with my coffee, just ahead of the rush of the things that would become today, I am best able to separate fact from emotion. But this morning the simple truth was not elusive. People got hurt yesterday, and if the situation wasn't defused others could get hurt today. This was unacceptable.

But Laskowski and Catella would not walk away, even though no DTC people would be on their picket line. They would quietly encourage disruptive behavior, feigning ignorance and shock at unlawful or violent acts against DTC or our employees. Sooner or later, something neither side could anticipate would happen. Something nobody would wish upon the other. An accident maybe, caused by mounting frustration or fear, would result in serious injury or worse. Whatever it was would be unnecessary and it would forever change things.

I finished my coffee and headed to the shower. I stood for a long time under the hot water, letting the warmth relax me. The radio in the bathroom was tuned to the sole fledgling country music station in the greater New York area. Lately, I'd been listening to less rock for the simple reason there was less rock to listen to. I missed the memorable melodies, the lyrics and stories of rock 'n' roll's better days. Country music sometimes filled that void for me. I listened with my eyes closed.

*Like a runaway freight train,*
*On an old short line,*
*This things' got me feelin' like*
*I'm ridin' off the rails tonight.*

Something unnecessary that would change things forever, I thought again. Maybe it *was* necessary for things to change. Of course, it was. Things had to change for DTC to get back to business. The NLRB would do nothing to challenge the union. The lawyers and the courts would drag it on and on, every wasted day a new opportunity for disaster. Best case, the longer this went on, the more client goodwill it would cost DTC. Even loyal customers would eventually tire of the contingent operating procedures required to ensure the safety of our drivers. No late pickups. No early deliveries. No emergency shipment accommodations. Change was not only necessary, it was a matter of survival. And successful change was proactively engineered to stay on track, not reactively adopted as the wheels rode off the rails. I wanted to be the one driving that train.

The song continued as I stepped out of the shower.

*There's this turbine inside me girl,*
*It's got me pumpin' away,*
*Got to get you eye to eye*
*To see what you gotta say.*

I dressed quickly, kissed my sleeping wife good-bye and, after peeking in on our three children, left quietly. I felt renewed. I would use the commute, the hypnotic miles, to further my thinking. With luck, a good plan would come into focus.

Standing outside my Cherokee, I dialed Michael's home.

"I'm glad I caught you," I said.

"Good morning. What's up?"

"Well, I'm standing in my driveway, ready to go, but I've got three flat tires."

"Are you kiddin'?"

"Wish I was. All three punctured in the sidewalls. Can ya pick me up?"

"Sure. See ya in ten."

After I buckled himself into Michael's front seat, Michael handed me a large 7-Eleven coffee and said, "Hey, look on the bright side. They only cut *three* of your tires?"

"Yeah, I wonder why?"

"You know you've always been the lucky one." The smile slipped from Michael's face. "So whadawe gonna do?"

"I've already called Danny down at the Mobil. He's gonna take care of the tires for me this morning."

"Not that! What are we gonna do about the union? We can't let this stuff continue. For chrissake, it's only been one day, what's next?"

"I'm not sure. But I was thinking about it this morning in the shower. Our problem is that we've been on the defensive. They're setting the pace. All we're doing is reacting to them."

"Well sure, they've done this before. They've had practice."

"Yeah, but we've gotta get control of this thing. We need to play some offense and soon." I pointed at the windshield. "Let's go, it's getting late."

We rode in silence for a while sipping coffee, both deep in thought. After we entered the northbound lanes of the Garden State Parkway, Michael said, "Joseph, there's something I need to talk to you about."

"So talk."

Michael exhaled loudly. "I've got a big problem. I'm sorry, but I fucked up again."

I turned to look at him. Michael kept his eyes on the road. I gave him time to look at me but he didn't. He couldn't.

"Whadaya mean 'fucked up again'?" I said.

"Gambling."

"Oh shit, Michael, are you serious? How bad?"

Michael finally turned looked at me. "Bad. Almost a hundred grand."

"Jesus! A hundred grand! What the fuck is wrong with you?"

"Hey, I know this is bad timing but . . ."

"Screw the timing, Michael. What about the promises you made. The last time almost cost you your family. What about that?"

"I know. Ilene can't know about this. I can't do that to her."

"You should've thought about that before you started betting again. It's a little late now."

"Look, I'm sorry but I don't need a lecture right now . . ."

"No. You need professional help. You're a fuckin' junkie."

Michael stomped on the accelerator and swung us into the left lane past a woman talking on her cell phone. She gave us a look that rivaled the disgust that I was feeling.

"Joseph, I swear I'll do whatever it takes this time to quit, but right now I need your help. I need to raise the hundred grand, quickly. And there's more. It gets worse."

"Worse?" I sighed. "Lemme hear it,"

"I owe this bookie Tommy Ton. He's not a bad guy but I know he's connected. Anyway, this guy named Johnny calls me one day and tells me Tommy Ton wants me to meet with him. So I meet this guy Johnny at a diner on Route 1 . . . "

"Skip to the chase, will ya,"

"Okay. The weekly vig is almost ten grand. Obviously, I can't make those payments. So, they gave me an ultimatum. They wanted a truckload of merchandise, something they could sell quickly. They promised me no one would get hurt and that would be the end of it."

"And what did you tell them?"

"I had no choice, Joseph. They were threatening me."

"What do you mean, you 'had no choice'? What the fuck did you do?"

"Joseph, I'm sorry. But I thought that so long as no one would get hurt, insurance would cover it, and ya know . . ."

"And ya *know*? Know *what*?" I was loud. "For chrissake, Michael, did you think just for a moment that maybe it was a crime, probably several felonies? Did you think that it could ruin your life, your family, our company? What about me and my family?"

I simmered for a moment. "Tell me what you did."

"I set them up to take the Bennini load yesterday. They were supposed to take the truck when Kenny on his way back from the Bennini warehouse. He's a creature of habit. He always stops for coffee at Vince Lombardi. I trusted Kenny to follow our procedures, to never resist a hijacking, to just give them what they want. But I don't know what happened. Well, maybe I do. They got the trailer numbers mixed up. They took the wrong load."

"Great. So now they have some classified government hardware."

"Yeah, and they're not happy."

"Whadaya mean *they're not happy*?"

"This Johnny character called me at home last night. He threatened me again. He thinks I fucked with him. Now he wants more freight."

"What did you tell him?"

"I hung up on him. But I'm sure that's not the end it. This guy's pretty scary."

"So whadaya want me to say, Michael? *Oh, it's okay, good buddy, I understand.* Well I fucking don't understand! We don't need this shit right now!"

"Look, I think I can talk to Tommy Ton. I think that if I can get him the money, right away, then he'll be happy and this thing will blow over."

"So I simply agree to let you take a hundred grand and give it to this wiseguy because you *think* that will end it. What if it doesn't? You can't trust these fuckin' guys. They've got something on you now. You conspired with them. You're as guilty as they are of a Federal crime. Don't you think that gives them some leverage over you?"

"I don't know. It's the only thing I think of right now."

I sipped my coffee and stared out the window, watching the trees and shrubbery that bordered the parkway zip past. I struggled to control an anger of incredible intensity that was beginning to well up inside me. It was an incomprehensible scenario. I understood the strength of men's weaknesses; the allure of the rush that men sought in their drink or their drugs, or their women . . . or their gambling. But what drove otherwise responsible and intelligent men to forsake even the most invaluable elements of their lives was a mystery to me. At what point in the process does a man say to himself, *'this is all that matters in my life'*? What is it that allows these men to rationalize their behavior and move beyond for what most men is *enough*? And should I care?

No, I concluded. My first concern should be my family, and my parents, and brother and sister and their families. Should something like this become public, it would be devastating for them. As it was, when someone heard I was in the trucking business, they most often replied, *'Oh.'* No follow up questions. No further information sought, just a silence that screamed, *Of course, Napolo . . . Mafia . . . trucking . . . Mobbed-up - well that confirms it!* Michael knew this. In fact, on more than one occasion, times when the Napolo name would have been ill-perceived, we had decided that Michael would represent the company to a prospective new customer. Michael would only refer to 'my partner' until the company's integrity had been established on an undeniable record of outstanding service. I couldn't believe that Michael had put us in this situation. But that was short thought. Michael was an addict and when it came to supporting his habit, nothing was improbable.

When I felt our speed dropping as we approached the Raritan toll plaza, I refocused and turned to Michael.

"This is what I'll agree to," I said. "We'll take the money from our credit line. You'll sign a note with the company to be backed by an insurance policy, which you will pay for. Your collateral will be your home and you'll have to allow the company a lien to secure it."

"I can't have Ilene find out about this," Michael pleaded.

"Your wife won't have to be made aware of a lien as she would a second mortgage. This is for her, not for you. I also want a contract from you that stipulates you'll seek professional help for your problem and, should you ever gamble again, you'll voluntarily resign from the company and forfeit your stock into a trust for your children. You'll have five years to pay back the company, principle and interest."

"Five years?"

I scowled at him. "Take it or leave it."

"I guess I'm in no position to argue."

"No, you're not. Now when we get in, call this Tommy Ton and tell him you'll have the money tomorrow morning. Set up a meeting for us this afternoon."

"Us?"

"Yes, *us*. Before I hand over a hundred grand to these guys, I want to make goddam sure that this thing is settled for good. I don't want this shit coming back to haunt us. We've worked too hard and too long to let something like this drag us down. Besides, with a name like mine, I want to be sure none of this mess will ever stick to us. Michael, you know better than anyone that if someone named Cogan gets involved in gambling or *hijacking* it's just another crime story on page five. But, if Joseph Napolo gets arrested for jaywalking, it'd be front page news, a whole goddamned feature edition about the Napolo Crime Family, and Eyewitness News will be broadcasting from the infamous curb where Don Carmine's grandson stepped *brazenly* into the street."

Michael nodded solemnly. "I'm really sorry about this, Joseph. I'll do whatever you want."

"I've just told you what I want. After this is done and the papers are signed we won't ever discuss it again. Unless, of course, you fail to perform your side of the agreement. In which case, Michael, we won't ever talk again period, except through our attorneys."

When we arrived at the gates of DTC Transportation, Michael put the truck in park and turned to me with his right hand extended. "You have my word that I'll never compromise you again like this. I'm truly sorry and truly grateful that you're my friend."

I looked at Michael's hand and then into his eyes. They held steady and began to puddle with what might have been true remorse. I felt the heave of our many years wrenching the anger from my gut as I reached for his hand and said, "You're a real asshole."

"Yeah, I know."

# The Hudson Valley
# Upstate New York

Stewart International Airport, in New Windsor, NY, serves the Hudson Valley area west of the Hudson River near Newburgh, just over fifty miles north of New York City. The former US Army base, now owned and operated by the New York State Department of Transportation, is not a bustling airfield. It is, however, utilized by a wide variety of aircraft. The Army and

Air Force Reserves, as well as the Air National Guard maintain training facilities and operations centers at Stewart. Several commercial airlines fly in and out daily. A couple air freight carriers maintain local operations there and the New York State Department of Corrections in conjunction with the US Marshals uses Stewart as an air transfer terminal for prisoner relocations. In final complement to the diversity, there is also an ever-changing assortment of private and corporate aircraft. All this is accommodated in a sprawling mix of older military buildings and a few newer facilities, which border the tarmac and dot the surrounding complex.

Aaron Lincoln, as the proprietor of Air Services Corporation, had taken a lease on an old red brick building, which formerly housed military airport emergency crews and vehicles at the end of runway North 1A. He had selected the site due to its distance from any of the other buildings, assuming correctly that no one would visit him without specific purpose and not without using the only road that ran parallel to the runway, giving him plenty of warning. His landlord, the New York State DOT, was a bureaucratic dinosaur headquartered in Albany that took eight months to sign his lease and, so long as the rent was paid on time, had no interest in the business of their tenant in Building EM North.

Amidst the comings and goings of the other airport tenants, Air Services' aircraft, a Bell 206L-4 Long Ranger helicopter was rarely noticed. And, as it was wheeled into the garage on an erratic yet keenly orchestrated schedule, the occasional observer could never be sure if the helicopter was flying or at rest behind the huge wood sliding doors of Building EM North. It would be safe to say that the same observer probably didn't care either way.

Lincoln was satisfied with the arrangement but it was not his nature to be comfortable. It was seven o'clock in the morning and he had just finished his daily electronic sweep of the entire building. No internal eavesdropping devices were detected. All incoming communications and electrical lines were free of significant impedance fluctuations. And the sensors located on all four sides and the roof of the building verified that neither lasers, thermal imaging equipment, nor infrared scanners were painting his headquarters.

Lincoln had just settled behind his desk when his pilot and crew chief walked into his office wiping their hands on shop rags. Randell, the pilot, was the first to speak.

"The bird's fueled and we repaired a small hydraulic leak we found during the pre-flight. We can be ready to fly in ten minutes."

"We still need to PM those rotor bearings," the crew chief added. "Nothing critical yet, but we shouldn't push her more than another 10 or 15 hours."

"I'll see that you get the downtime soon," Lincoln said. "But I need you both and the chopper on standby until further notice. I've got a developing situation and . . ."

The satellite telephone on Lincoln's desk was ringing.

"Excuse me," he said as he motioned to the two men with his forefinger to leave the room.

"You know where we'll be," the pilot said as they headed for the door.

When the door closed behind them, Lincoln answered the phone. "Have you reached the correct number?"

Lincoln heard three familiar tones, his signal to switch on the encryption device connected to the satellite telephone. While he waited the required 8 seconds for the encrypting software to cycle, he glanced at his watch.

"It's exactly seven hundred hours, New York time," Lincoln said, after ten seconds had passed. "Your timeliness assures me of your serious intent."

"We are in a serious business, my friend." The caller's English was heavily accented - Middle Eastern with a touch of French, Lincoln thought.

"Serious yet profitable," Lincoln replied.

"Aaah, is that to say our profits are secured?"

"I take it your buyer is interested in the item."

"Yes. Are you positioned to offer delivery on schedule?"

"Unfortunately, there may be an unavoidable delay. But the item is as promised."

"Unavoidable delays concern me. For me, this speaks of complications. I am now feeling uncomfortable. Please, put me at ease." The caller spoke in the deliberate rhythms of a well-educated person conversing in a second or third language.

"Our agreement doesn't require me to make you feel good. But, as a gesture of goodwill, I will confirm that within the last twenty-four hours the item has been diverted from its intended delivery path and I shall soon have possession."

"I am overwhelmed by your generosity, but I'm afraid our benefactor will seek a more exact representation than 'soon'."

"Soon will have to do, for now. If that's not good enough tell him I've got other buyers ready to step up to the plate."

"The thought of sharing a meal with you is a most unpleasant one."

"What?"

"Never mind. I will relay your message and contact you again according to our schedule. Hopefully, you will have more definitive information for me at that time."

"Since you haven't made me suffer through the usual haggling over my fee, shall I assume you have finally grasped the meaning of non-negotiable?"

The caller sighed. "You may assume all eight figures are agreed to and that your terms are acceptable. The down payment, as you call it, will be deposited today in Luxembourg according to your instructions. But, my friend, it will do you well to know that we have a *very* clear understanding of the term 'non-negotiable'. Know, too, that we have a strong distaste for compromise and a complete lack of tolerance for failure. We will act with extreme prejudice in that event."

Lincoln clenched his teeth but spoke calmly. "You should know better than to threaten me, so I'll pretend you forgot who you were talking to just now. Forget again and I'll find you, maybe asleep in your bed, and wake you up with your heart in my hands."

The caller laughed deeply. "You are most colorful, my American friend, and very funny. But it is you who have forgotten. *I have no heart!* Remember that!. Now enough of this nonsense. I will contact you again as planned. Please make every effort not to disappoint me."

The phone went silent and Lincoln hung up smiling. He loved the game but hated the players, which for him made the rules clear and simple to follow. Trust no one. Fear no one. And never let them think you can't deliver, on a promise or a threat. When this deal was done, he thought, after delivery was made and payment received, he was going to find this sand-monkey son of a bitch, visit him in the middle of the night and wake him by stuffing a pig's heart in his mouth. A little prank, but these things get around quickly. It would be good for business.

He leaned forward to speak into the intercom. "Randell."

"Yes, sir."

"Roll out the bird. I wanna be airborne in ten minutes."

"Where to, sir?"

"FirsTech."

Lincoln double-locked the office door as he headed toward the private bathroom he had built off his office. Inside the bathroom, he pushed the lock on the door handle and slid the deadbolt locks at the top and bottom of the door into place. He then pulled exactly ten sheets off a roll of paper towels, the fluffy quilted brand, and laid five on the floor in front of the toilet. The remaining five he folded and placed mindfully on top of the toilet seat. Removing the wood hangers from the back of the door, he began disrobing, neatly hanging his clothes until he was completely undressed except for his shoes and socks. Carefully, he slid off one shoe and sock and then the other, letting his bare feet step only on the paper towels in front of the toilet. Then, after he had fitted disposable latex gloves on both hands, he seated himself gently on the paper towels and began his daily bowel movement - naked and bent over, gripping his ankles with his head between his knees.

# The Catskill Mountains
# Upstate New York

The gleaming black Mercedes limousine stopped at a gatehouse manned by two heavily armed private security guards. The guards waved to the driver who had lowered his window and the steel gates swung out for the limousine to exit the compound. The long, low vehicle slid quietly through the gate to begin its daily journey down the private mountain road that wound through the compound's surrounding forest. Seated behind darkened windows, deep within the luxurious interior, the sole passenger was filling his mug from the coffee pitcher secured in a heated receptacle when the red light on the overhead phone console began to blink. He reached up to push the speakerphone button.

"Good morning," the passenger said.

"It is mid-afternoon here in the land of Allah." The caller's accented English was familiar to him.

The passenger quickly reached up for the handset that disconnected the speakerphone. "Well, here in God's country it's a beautiful spring morning."

"I am glad for you. I spoke with our mutual friend just minutes ago. A most untoward experience, I might add."

"Yes, I'm sure, but he's usually quite effective and, for our purposes, without equal."

"Perhaps, but he has yet to possess the item. There appears to be a problem. Are you aware of this?"

"Yes. There was an unforeseen incident, which our friend could not control. But, I am sure he has the resources to fully recover. If needed, we are developing a backup scenario to assist him. Covertly, of course."

"I will leave it in your able hands, then. For now, we must arrange for the account in Luxembourg to reflect a deposit transacted before the end of business today in the amount of seven and a half million US dollars."

"I will see that everything appears as it should."

"I trust that you will. Enjoy your spring day in God's country, my friend."

"Thank you."

The passenger smiled as the Mercedes continued quietly down the mountain road. On either side, tucked between white pines and cedars, the hemlocks and beeches, ash and tamaracks were filling with young leaves. It had been a particularly wet April and the mountains had drunk freely. The undergrowth was bursting with new growth, thick and lush. The Catskills were indeed God's country, he thought as he looked out through the tinted glass at a mother deer hovering protectively over her new fawn. They stared back at him, still as statues at the edge of the rich forest. Perhaps, he reasoned, he was in some way responsible for this doe's good fortune. His security patrols strictly enforced the no trespassing signs posted on his property's perimeter, especially during the hunting season. Still smiling, he reached up and touched the phone console.

"Call Virginia four one five." He spoke distinctly into the air.

The voice-activated phone silently dialed the pre-programmed number. He sipped his coffee while he waited.

A pleasing female voice answered. "Fifty-five hundred."

"I would like to speak with someone in customer service, please."

"May I have your order number, sir?"

"Yes, it's 17-12-29."

"Thank you. That would be Mr. McBride. Just a moment, please . . . have a nice day, sir."

## DTC Transportation
## Edison, New Jersey

Michael and I returned to our office feeling gratified and renewed. We had just watched our drivers steer the fleet of bright red Freightliners through the morning ritual. One by one, hauling long red and white trailers, they fell in line, nose to tail like giant circus elephants. As planned, they began circling the yard, gaining speed and momentum to propel themselves past the pickets. Michael and I had thrown open the gates and stood ready to roll them closed behind the last truck. But after the first lap around the building, when the lead truck failed to break and head out the gate, the conspiracy was revealed. The air horns sang a loud and defiant protest as the drivers continued to circle the yard. They accelerated, lap after lap, to speeds unsafe for big rigs in tight turns, until suddenly the circle broke and eighty-four thirty-ton bleating, thundering monsters were unleashed - out the gates and into a narrow corridor cut through the scattering pickets. Road dust and diesel fumes kept the Teamsters at bay until the gates were closed. The last truck carried a large banner across the back doors of its trailer. It read, *For Bobby & Kenny, Fuck you!* But as the truck noise was carried away down the road, it was replaced by the curses of the Teamsters and the sound of roofing nails, already swept up once this day, raining onto the pavement.

Michael and I had just settled behind our desks when the intercom on Michael's desk chimed.

"Michael?" The voice came from the speakerphone on his desk.

"Yeah. Who's this?"

"It's Ripton. I got the night crew's report. You're not gonna believe it. They pulled over two hundred nails outta the tires last night and we had to replace twenty-seven of 'em. The guys were saying they peppered the road for about a quarter mile outside the gate."

Michael said, "Make sure everyone knows to check their personal vehicle tires."

"Tell you what," I added, "Let's agree to a daily procedure for the shop to check all personal vehicles. I'll have Janie put up a notice that the company will repair or replace all personal tires that are damaged by nails."

"Okay, Joseph," Ripton replied. "We may need some overtime for this, though."

"No problem, Rip. Whatever it takes."

Michael hit the button disconnecting the intercom and turned to me. "What time do you want to go see Tommy Ton? We've got the State Police scheduled to call to complete the report this morning, we gotta get a hold of Laskowski and Catella, and we should be back here this afternoon when the trucks start coming in."

"Where is this Tommy Ton?"

"He's got a small restaurant in Secaucus, just off a Route 3."

"Well, let's go for lunch. Maybe he'll buy."

"Maybe, but don't count on it," Michael said. "Oh, and by the way, Janie reminded me this morning that tomorrow night's FirsTech's Annual Partners in Excellence, Supplier Quality Awards Dinner."

"Jesus, that's embarrassing." I said. "Yesterday we lose a high-security load and tomorrow night they're giving us the Carrier of the Year Award."

"Yeah, for continuous improvement and commitment to quality, or something like that," Michael added.

I sighed. "I guess we'll have to go."

"You guess? Shit, we better go. We need the points."

"Where is it?"

"I don't know." Michael rummaged through the stacks of papers on his desk. "Here it is. It's at a place called The Smoke and Gun Club in Livingston Manor, upstate New York in the Catskills."

"Great, that's at least a two hour drive."

The speaker on my phone interrupted. "Joseph, Bobby Moretti on line three for you."

I snapped forward to hit the button. "Hey, Bobby, how are you? How's the nose?"

"Nothin's broken, just bruised and swollen. Don't think I can drive for a couple days. The doctor says a week but I'll be back sooner than that."

"Don't rush it, Bobby. But if you want to get out of the house, you can come in and dispatch or something. It's up to you."

"Yeah, maybe. I'm gonna get on my old lady's nerves before too long. Have ya heard anything about Kenny?"

"He's going home this morning. They kept him overnight at the hospital. We talked to his wife last night. He has a mild concussion and a few stitches in his scalp from hitting the pavement. He's pretty banged up, though. Lot's of cuts and bruises. He'll be out for a while."

Bobby said, "That's too bad. He's a good kid. So, ah, how's it goin' there today?"

"Well, our boys put on a little show this morning in tribute to Kenny and you. But nothing's really changed. They're still out there in force, roofing nails and all," I said.

"They sliced Joseph's tires last night," Michael added.

"No shit! Where?"

"At his house," Michael replied. "They followed us home."

"They followed you home? What are you gonna do about that, Joseph? That's not right, coming to your house and all."

"We'll straighten it out with Laskowski," I said.

"It's not Laskowski. It's Catella." Bobby sounded serious. "Watch him, they don't call him The Alley Cat for nothin'. And he ain't no truck driver. Never was. I think he's just got the right friends, or the wrong friends . . . ya know what I mean, doncha, Joseph?"

"Yeah, low friends in low places . . . I get it." I looked up at Michael to make sure his words found their mark.

"Oh, ah, that reminds me. Have you guys seen the news today?" Bobby asked.

"No. Not yet," I said.

"A couple of guys from the Napolo Family got whacked in Hackensack last night, so I was real glad to hear your voice today, Joseph."

I frowned. "Not funny, Bobby."

"Just kiddin', boss. Sorry. I know . . ."

"Forget it," I said. "What did they say about it?"

"Hold on, I got the paper right here. Says that they found two soldiers from the Napolo Family tied up and executed gangland style in the apartment of another known member of the family. Says they're lookin' for this guy. His name's John Anelli, a.k.a. Johnny Onions. Sounds like Family problems."

"Did they say anything else about this guy, Johnny Onions?" Michael asked.

I looked over at Michael. His face was ashen.

"No, just that he's a suspect. I guess that's not much of a leap, right?"

"Well, okay Bobby," I interrupted. "You take care of yourself. Let us know if you need anything and, if you're up to it, stop by."

"I just might. I'm gonna go nuts sittin' around the house."

"We'd be happy to have you. Either way, keep in touch."

"Oh, I'll be in regular touch. I want to hear what my old friends at 714 are up to. You guys just be careful. They have more experience at this kinda stuff than you do."

"Thanks, Bobby. We'll be fine. Take care."

I disconnected the call and leaned back in my chair. I stared across my desk at Michael.

"What?" Michael finally said, his arms outstretched.

"Michael, tell me this Johnny Onions is not the same Johnny who you met with. Let me hear that you didn't make a deal with the Napolo Family. Tell me, please."

"What makes you think I would do that?"

"What the fuck, Michael. You looked like you were gonna throw up when you heard his name. Come on, pal, I need to know that you didn't make a deal with my grandfather's old friends."

"Joseph, I don't know," Michael shrugged and looked into this lap. "I'm not sure."

I stared at him until Michael looked up and locked eyes with me. "No, I'm sure. It's him."

I remember finding it almost funny, the way you feel when someone witnesses you painfully stubbing your toe on the same thing for the third time.

I think I groaned before I said, "Man, you're a real asshole."

Michael put his head in his hands. "Yeah, I know."

## The Starlight Motor Lodge
## South Amboy, New Jersey

The Starlight Motor Lodge was a noisy place, day or night. Nestled between the intersections of Routes 35 and 9, adjacent to the Garden State Parkway, the traffic sounds were never-ending. But the single-story circular complex was perfect for Johnny Anelli's purposes. All the rooms opened to an interior courtyard and you parked your car right outside your door where it couldn't be seen from the road. Even though he had switched license plates with a Dodge Caravan last night, he liked the additional privacy. And, at thirty-one dollars and fifty cents a night, or one-forty-five per week, the price was right. However, you get only what you pay for, especially in Jersey.

It was nine o'clock in the morning and Johnny had been awake, on and off, all night. Car doors opening and closing, loud drunken voices in the parking lot, and downshifting trucks on Route 9 Bridge kept waking him until the sun sliced through the gap between the dirty draperies. Johnny squinted and tried to brush the golden slash of light away from his eyes but only managed to incite the floating dust particles to dance more defiantly.

He sat up and looked around the room. *What a fucking nightmare this place is*, he thought. Through the thin walls, people arguing on one side of him and a couple making wild love on the other, had drowned out his television, which received only three channels of distorted greenish-red faces. The pillows were stained and lifeless. The mattress was like a wafer filled with whipped cream and had compressed to the boxspring under his weight. He had nearly stuck himself with a used hypodermic needle lying in the drawer between the bible and the yellow pages when he ordered pizza. And when the deliver boy arrived, Johnny, fresh from the shower, dropped the pizza because the only bath towel was so small he had to hold it in front of his loins with one hand and try to balance the pizza and collect his change with the other. Of course, the pizza slid out of the flimsy box and fell top down onto the dirty green shag carpeting. Johnny tried to carefully pick the dust and dirt and carpet fiber off the cheese. But after one crunchy bite, he threw the whole pie at the wall where it splattered and slid down behind the cheap dresser. This morning he could still smell it. But that was okay. It was a better smell than the disinfectant the chambermaids had used.

Johnny cursed as he rolled off the bed. He felt wobbly from lack of sleep and an assortment of sore bones and muscles. He removed the chair that he had lodged under the broken door handle and sat with a loud grunt. After inspecting his bruised knees and elbows and the cuts on his hands and forearms, he picked up his Beretta from the nightstand and made sure he could manage a good grip. He took the gun into the bathroom and placed it on the counter next to the sink. Leaning on the sink, looking from the mirror to the Beretta and back again, he wondered when, if ever, he would be able to live without having a gun within reach. No time soon, that was for sure. There were two dead wiseguys in the apartment of a third, who was a paroled felon. He didn't need to read the papers to know that the entire law enforcement community was looking for him. If they found him, he would be immediately returned to prison. Possession of firearms definitely was, and cavorting with even the cadavers of known criminals probably was, a violation of his parole.

But, comparatively, this was only of minor concern. Vinny Diamonds was his real problem. Whoever killed Soldano and Patacca had written his death warrant. Even supposing they hadn't been sent to whack him in the first place, Johnny knew that Vinny now had clear and undeniable cause to seek revenge. No one would or could intervene on Johnny's behalf. He had, as far as they all knew, broken the rules. He was a dead man. In prison he wouldn't last a week. At least on the streets he had a chance to get away, far away.

Johnny splashed cold water on his face and held his hands and arms under the faucet to rinse the cuts. Staring at his hands, he wondered, *Who the hell killed those guys last night?* Who could've done it and, more importantly, why? It didn't make any sense. But it really didn't matter, because he knew for everyone else the only sensible answer was, *Johnny Onions killed those guys!*

He only had two choices. Leave and disappear, like he was in the witness protection program, into the weave of some Midwestern town that had little to offer and, therefore, no attraction for the Mob. Some place where there were no people like him. But what would he do? Get a job? What job? He had never worked a day in his life. Could he even do some menial work with a paycheck on Friday that barely paid his rent? What, maybe Wal-Mart or Home Depot waiting on pasty white gavones in plaid shirts and cowboy boots? No fuckin' way! Leaving was out of the question. He had to stay and somehow work this thing out.

He had heard of guys who were able to buy their way out of trouble. They made cash payments in tribute and restitution. All things were forgiven and they were allowed to live, not as they had before, but live nonetheless. But, in this case, it would have to be a very large tribute. Vinny would not come cheap. On top of it all, Johnny didn't trust Vinny. What would keep him from taking the money and then one day putting a bullet behind his ear anyway? Johnny needed a foolproof plan and right now he didn't have one.

What he did have, though, was that goddam metal crate. Although he had no idea what it was or even how to open it, only he knew where it was and it would be at least a couple days before anyone would find it. It had to be worth something to somebody. He also had an Irish guy named Michael Cogan who owned a trucking company and was at least partially responsible for this mess. And Cogan had cargo; cargo that could be easily turned into cash – as much cash as he needed. Johnny suddenly felt like he wasn't so alone anymore. Whatever happened was going to involve Michael Cogan, that was for sure; Cogan and his cargo, probably the damn metal crate for starters.

Feeling a little better, Johnny turned on the shower and waited for the water to heat up. He slipped off his boxers, pushed back the mildewed shower curtain, and lifted his right leg over the edge of the tub into the shower. As he shifted his weight to lift his other leg, his right foot slipped on the soap scum on the bottom of the tub. He lost his balance as his leg abruptly went out from under him. On the way down, he grabbed for the shower curtain, pulling the metal rod onto his head. His crotch hit first, crashing onto the edge of the tub. As he continued backwards, the big toe on his right foot jammed into the tub's faucet, ripping his toenail. And, just before the lights went out for Johnny Onions, as his upper body flopped out of the tub, whipping the back of his head toward the rim of the toilet bowl, he wailed, "Motherfucker!"

## Queens, New York

It was summertime. He was a young boy, nine or ten years old, sitting on the rear bumper of a very big truck. His buddies from the neighborhood were sitting on either side of him, dangling their skinny, puppet-legs over the edge of the large square bumper. He couldn't see their faces but he knew their names: Wally, Jimmy, Allen, Pete, Tony, Joey, and his little brother, Sal. They were watching a huge steamroller work slowly back and forth behind the truck. Suddenly, the truck's backup bell started ringing and the truck lurched. The shiny black diamond plate bumper they were perched on was slippery, so they held on tight. Jimmy, the daredevil of the group, began saying, *Whoa, I'm gonna fall off. Help me! Help! Whoa!* Even though they knew he was kidding, when he wiggled to the edge to pretend he was slipping off the bumper, they started to say, *Quit it, Jimmy!* and *Cut it out, man!* The backup bell rang again, the truck stopped, jerked violently, and began moving forward. Jimmy lost his grip and fell off the bumper, which now seemed a lot higher off the ground. The steamroller had changed direction and was now coming straight toward the rear of the truck. Jimmy was smiling and waving up at them, ignoring their screams, as the massive steel drum rolled over him without the slightest effort.

Somehow he could now see behind the steamroller. Jimmy had been squashed into a perfectly round red spot on the pavement. The back-up bell tolled again and the bumper underneath them jumped. Tony fell off this time and he went under the roller drum and became a perfectly round yellow spot. Now he felt himself slipping further and further off the bumper. When the backup bell sounded a third time, his little brother Sal fell off and, as he went under the roller, he looked up with sad eyes and called out to his older brother for help. But he couldn't help and Sal became a little green spot. He started crying which only served to weaken his grip. He was sliding down, slipping off. He was sure to be next.

The bell woke him this time. He reached for the phone on his night table.

"Yeah," he said breathlessly.

"Vinny?"

"Yeah." Still breathing shallowly.

"You okay?"

81

"Yeah." Mouth making dried-out noises.

"You sure?"

"Yeah." Trying hard to swallow.

"It's Jimmy."

"Jimmy!"

"Yeah, Jimmy."

"Jimmy who?"

"Boss it's me, Jimmy Boy, Jimmy M."

"Oh, it's you, Jimmy Boy. Sorry, I was sleepin'. What time is it?"

"It's almost nine-thirty."

"Oh. Why you callin' and wakin' me up so early?" Vinny wiped the nightmare sweat off his neck with the bed sheets.

"Dominick and Paulie. Somethin's happened. How soon can you get out to a payphone?"

"Half an hour," Vinny grunted, as he swung his legs out of bed and ran his fingers through his wet hair.

"Call me at the number in Brooklyn. We got a serious problem."

Vinny Diamonds hung up the phone and lumbered into the bathroom. As he stood naked over the toilet, urinating and passing morning gas, he looked into the mirror at his obese profile. What a nightmare, he thought.

# CHAPTER 10

## Offices of Teamsters Union Local 714
## Keasby, New Jersey

"Mr. Napolo and Mr. Cogan are here to see you and Mr. Laskowski." The receptionist's eyes darted back and forth from Michael to me as she listened to the person on the other end of the phone. She blushed as she hung up the phone.

"Mr. Catella said, um, he asked if, ah . . ."

"We know Mr. Catella," I interrupted. "Feel free to tell us exactly what he said."

"Oh, I don't, ah, think you, ah . . ." She stopped, shaking her head in tight, rapid arcs.

Michael noticed there were no rings on the important fingers so leaned forward and touched her hand. "What's your name?"

"Tina." She smiled coyly.

Michael cocked his head to let the Irish charm ooze more freely. "Tina, that's a nice name for a nice lady, a pretty lady." His flirtations made her blush. "Now, Tina, don't be upset. That Albert Catella can be a little rough sometimes, can't he? But he's just a big pussycat. We get a kick out of him. Why doncha tell us what he said . . . please?"

"Okaaay." She took a deep breath. "Mr. Catella was wondering if you guys understood English."

"That's it?" Michael said softly.

"He, ah, also wanted me to ask you what you didn't understand about what he told you on the phone earlier today."

"Oh? Jeez, I guess we could have misunderstood him. Was there anything else he wanted you to ask us?" Michael said.

"No. But he wanted me to give you a, ah, message."

"And what was that, Tina."

She looked at Michael, then me and back to Michael again before she continued. "Well okay, but these are his words, not mine. He told me to tell you fuckin' guys to crawl back to where you came from or he was gonna throw you both the fuck outta here." She had lowered her voice to say the 'f'' word.

Michael shook his head and patted her hand. "I'm awfully sorry you have to hear that kind of language."

"That's okay, Mr. Cogan. I'm used to it around here."

"Excuse me a minute, Tina, I have to talk to my partner."

We stepped through the glass door and stood in the foyer with our backs to the reception area.

"There's no goddam way we can leave now," I said as soon as the door closed behind us.

"What are we gonna do? Just barge in there?"

I tilted my head. "Remember in Godfather II when Pacino gave the 'In My Home' speech?"

"Not really."

"Remember when they tried to assassinate Pacino at his house, in his bedroom with his wife and kids there?"

"Yeah."

"Just follow my lead."

"Where're we goin'?" Michael raised his eyebrows.

"We're goin' on the offensive and we're goin' in pissed."

"Well okay, why didn't you just say that?"

We walked up to the reception desk smiling warmly. Tina looked up but before she could speak I said, "Tina, where are Mr. Laskowski and Mr. Catella?"

Tina saw that I was no longer smiling. She looked over to Michael for help but he just shrugged.

I pressed on. "Tina, we are not leaving here until we speak with them. Now, tell me which of these rooms they're in."

"But they're in with the Pension Trustees. It's the quarterly meeting. They can't be disturbed."

I leaned forward with my hands on her desk. "Tina, which room?"

She must have seen in my face that no matter what she said we were not going to leave. She sighed and pointed to a door on the right wall. "They're in the conference room."

I straightened up and Michael stepped forward. "Tina, why don't you go outside and smoke a cigarette."

"I don't smoke," she sneered between her teeth. "And I don't like being bullied. I'm takin' my break."

"Thanks for your help, Tina," Michael called after her as she stomped toward the ladies' room in the hall.

Michael turned back to me and, with a wave of his arm, said, "Lead on, Mr. Pacino."

I put my hand around the door handle, looked at Michael, and took a deep breath. I turned the handle and threw open the door. Ron Laskowski was seated on the far side of the room at the head of the oblong conference table. Albert Catella was at his right and four other men were seated loosely around the rest of the large polished tabletop. They all jolted in surprise at the two of us in the doorway.

"Excuse us, gentlemen." I said. "We need to speak with Laskowski and Catella . . . in private."

The Alley Cat sprang to his feet. "Are you guys fuckin' nuts? Get the fuck outta here!"

I ignored Catella and spoke to the other men at the table. "Gentlemen, we'll just be a few minutes. Please wait in the reception area."

The men at the table looked to Laskowski and Catella for guidance. Laskowski began to say something but was cut off by Catella.

"You guys stay put," Catella said to the men at the table.

"Joseph, what's this about?" Laskowski said, still seated.

I said to Laskowski, "I was trying to keep this between us but . . ."

"Fuck this, Ron!" Catella shouted. "You can't let these assholes bust in here like this."

I slammed an empty chair against the table and started moving toward Catella with Michael close behind. The other men at the table froze. Catella was standing with his arms folded across his chest. "Look at this bullshit. Two tough guys, eh," he said.

Laskowski was on his feet now. "Albert's right," he said, "You guys can't come in here like this. Who the fuck do you think you are?"

As I continued toward them, I leaned down and swept my forearm across the table where they had been sitting, scattering papers and file folders to the floor, backing Laskowski and Catella up against the wall. The other men at the table began to rise up out of their chairs. Michael spun around and snapped a pointed finger in their direction. "Sit Down! You guys had your chance to leave."

One of them, a thin, dark-suited man stood and said, "Hey, ah, we're with Rorer Securities. We've got nothing to do with union business. We're just managing the pension fund."

"Sit!" Michael barked. The Rorer-man sat quickly.

Laskowski and Catella were up against the wall. I stopped in front of them and said, "Now that I have your attention, I'll tell you who the fuck I think I am, Ron." I moved even closer to Catella. "I'm the guy you wished you never fucked with. Last night, three of your men followed me home. TO MY HOME! WHERE MY WIFE AND *CHILDREN* LIVE! WHERE MY CHILDREN PLAY! And you have the balls to ask me who the fuck I think *I* am! Who the fuck do you think you are to bring our business to my home?"

"Hey, I don't know nothing about this," Laskowski said.

"That's bullshit!" Michael said.

"Hey!" Catella shouted. "The man said he knows nothing about it."

I turned to Catella but spoke to Laskowski. "Our drivers have been assaulted. Our trucks have been damaged. Our employees have been spit on and verbally abused. And, you have terrorized my family. You're in charge here, Ron, and I hold you responsible and accountable."

"Imagine that, Ron," Catella said, looking at me. "And this thing is what, only two days old. Imagine how these two pussies are gonna feel five or six weeks from now."

I felt my lips curling over my teeth and my fists tightening. I've never been comfortable with physical violence but I wanted to pound the shit out of Catella. I knew, though, that no matter how good it would feel, it would be over in seconds and the result would be months or years of legal bills. Moreover, it would be just what Catella wanted. But, Pacino would not have let this pass unanswered.

"Here's something for you two to imagine," I began quietly. "Imagine that my people aren't allowed to hold a vote and decide this issue for themselves. Imagine that we're videotaping every move your pickets make. The physical attacks. The spitting. The roofing nails. It'd look like a newsreel from 1955. Then imagine that I contact my old friend who's a top producer at ABC News and show him the tape and tell him that not one of our employees is on that picket line. Imagine how the Teamsters and the NLRB will be portrayed. Begin imagining how you'll defend your support of these thugs. And then imagine that I tell ABC what I know about the leadership of this local. That a certain individual here has never driven a truck. That this individual may have close associates who should never be spoken of in the same breath with Teamsters. Can you imagine what a story they could make out of that? National news, I'm sure."

"And they'd believe you?" Laskowski smirked. "To me it just sounds like a union buster's sour grapes."

I smiled. "Remember my last name, Ron. I think they'll be very interested."

Laskowski looked at me long and sat down with a huff. Catella uncrossed his arms and stuffed his hands in his pockets as he spun away to pace along the wall.

Finally, Laskowski spoke. "Okay, Joseph. We don't need to blow this outta proportion. This should stay be between us. It's nobody else's business. Let Albert and me finish up this meeting and then we'll discuss this with the NLRB. Maybe there's a solution that hasn't been considered yet. Give us until tomorrow afternoon."

"Until then the videotape will be rolling," I said.

"Whatever," Laskowski shrugged.

Catella turned to me and said, "Now why don't you two get the fuck outta here."

"Our pleasure," Michael said.

I stopped in the doorway and looked at each of the men at the table, bringing my eyes to rest on Laskowski and Catella.

"One more thing," I began. "Since you know where my family lives, I thought it only fair to find out where your families live." I pulled a piece of note paper from my pocket. "Does 129 Eastbrook in Carteret sound familiar, Ron? How about 17 Maryland Avenue in Woodbridge, Alley? Now, if anyone I don't know even drives by my home or Michael's home, we're gonna consider it personal, not business. If that happens we're gonna pay you both a personal visit, at home. Then we'll resolve our differences on a personal basis, man-to-man. These other gentlemen here can serve as your witnesses to this promise." I paused for reactions. There were none. "We'll look forward to hearing from you tomorrow. Have a nice day, gentlemen."

As soon as they were inside Michael's truck, Michael turned to me and said, "We were pretty good in there, weren't we?"

"Good? I don't know about good. I guess we did what had to be done," I said coolly.

Michael put the keys in the ignition but let his hand fall away without turning them. "That's right, we did. But, by your condescending tone, I'm hearing something else."

"Is actin' like a couple of thugs *good*?"

"Oh, cut the shit, Joseph," Michael shot back. "What was the alternative? Wait around four or five days for Laskowski and Catella to decide that they can't keep postponing a meeting without violating the good-faith bargaining rule. In the meantime, we take whatever shit they can get away with. You said it yourself; it was our plan to get on the offensive. We did what we had to do in there and we got their attention."

"The end doesn't always justify the means, Michael."

"Oh come on, so we acted like tough guys. Big fuckin' deal. No other approach would've been more effective, or more efficient. But, if you need to rationalize this, I think acting is the key word here. Look, when we go meet customers, we act the way we think they want us to be. We recite the lines and the buzzwords we know they want to hear, so they can feel good about giving us their business. When we meet with the bankers, we act exactly like we think they need us to be to get their approvals. We negotiate with our suppliers like their products or services are instantly replaceable at a better price. At the terminal, no matter how good or bad things are, we act confident and knowledgeable in front of our employees so they'll feel secure and comfortable. And then we go home and for our kid's sake we act like the world's a wonderful place because that's our job."

I considered Michael's comments for few moments. "Today, I acted a lot more like my grandfather than my kid's father."

"I thought you were acting like Michael Corleone."

"I was, until I used my last name. That kinda switched things from Hollywood to real-life, didn't it?"

"Yeah, but your grandfather's been dead a long time. If they let it mean something, shame on them."

"Sure, he's been dead for forty years, but they still call it the Napolo Crime Family."

Nothing more needed to be said. We both knew that it had indeed meant something, and just as intended, it had carried the necessary weight to at least temporarily silence the opposition.

Michael started to drive out of the parking lot and while he waited for the traffic to clear, he thought aloud. "Videotaping?"

"So I lied."

"And wasn't Arnie Weichtner an *accountant* at *N*BC?"

"NBC, ABC what's the difference?"

"He went to work for Price Waterhouse in the mid-80's, didn't he?"

"Yeah, he's a partner now."

"You still wanna be involved in this Tommy Ton thing?" Michael asked, as he accelerated out of the lot.

"Definitely. Let's go get some lunch in Secaucus. It's important and we're on a roll."

"Is that r-o-l-e or r-o-l-l?"

"Both."

"Whatever you say, Mr. Pacino."

# CHAPTER 11

## Tonzollo's Ristorante & Pizzeria
## Secaucus, New Jersey

One August two generations ago, Luco Tonzollo packed up his cobbler's tools and left Palermo, Sicily for America with his young wife and baby boy. After two steamy weeks in New York's Little Italy, the ambitious and affable Luco accepted an offer to move across the river to New Jersey. A small ristorante in Secaucus needed a hardworking and loyal manager. The former proprietor had repeatedly resisted the weekly protection payments to the Black Hand. Failing to heed their warning and without their protection, he fell prey to the murderous criminals stalking the streets of America, just as the Black Hand had warned. Luco and his family were allowed to move into the small apartment above the establishment and run the business as their own. As promised by their benefactors, they enjoyed a guarantee of loyal patronage and protection from the criminal element, so long as the weekly payments were made. Under this arrangement and with a well-deserved reputation for delicious Sicilian dishes prepared by Luco's wife, the business thrived.

One day, after three successful years had passed, Luco was cleaning the store room in the back of the kitchen. Coming upon the canvas satchel that held his cobbler's tools, he paused and sat on a produce crate. He began to unhook the straps of the satchel but stopped suddenly and looked around the clean, well-stocked kitchen. No, he nor his son would ever have to repair another man's shoes to earn a living. Some day he would own this restaurant and, in time, he would pass it on to his boy, and his boy to his son. Then, nodding his head, Luco Tonzollo stood tall and straight and tossed his cobbler's tools into the trash bin.

Eighty years later, Tonzollo's Ristorante & Pizzeria stands wedged between The Thai Barbecue and a Latino bodega that sells more than its share of lottery tickets. As Luco had dreamed it, his grandson Tommy was now the proprietor. Grandma Tonzollo's famous gravies and homemade ravioli's were still prepared from her original recipes but today a Puerto Rican kid named Andreas was the head cook. Reggie Hooks, a black guy that went to high school with Tommy, made the pizzas and tended bar. Mrs. Lu Tran filled in for both of them when she wasn't waiting tables.

Tommy Tonzollo, however, didn't inherit his grandfather's or father's love of the restaurant business. He had watched them work the long hours, in good times and bad, to keep the business vital. His grandfather had never taken a vacation. His father had taken time for a brief honeymoon in Atlantic City and once took his mother to a musical on Broadway. Both men had worked in the restaurant right up to the day they died.

As a boy, Tommy was bored to tears whenever he was forced to spend time in the restaurant. He did his homework in the kitchen in between the menial chores his father would assign him. When he was a teenager, he waited tables after school until closing time. One table, however, only his father would serve. Every afternoon, at about half past two, their special patron would arrive. He always sat against the rear wall at a large table near the phone booth. His father would frantically insist that the table was set and the phone booth cleaned well in advance of his arrival. It wasn't long before Tommy understood his father's behavior - the nervous preparation, the way he snapped at the other employees until every detail was perfect; how he hovered nearby but out of earshot throughout the meal; and the way he made Tommy sit in the telephone booth to answer the phone. Some days Tommy would be in the phone booth for hours, stepping out only to let Mr. Baluccio or one of his associates take a call. He and his father always received a generous tip for their services.

After high school, Tommy worked full-time at the restaurant. He still spent the late afternoons in the phone booth but soon, against his father's silent protestations, he began taking Mr. Baluccio's calls. His tips quickly grew much larger than his father's. And, as he had a natural talent for names and numbers, it wasn't long before he became Mr. Baluccio's right hand man, Tommy Ton.

In the fall of 1961, his father died. Then one day, a month or so later, Mr. Baluccio just stopped coming in and Tommy Ton inherited his second business, all before his twentieth birthday. Since then, the restaurant struggled to pay for itself and the bookmaking paid for everything else.

We found the restaurant without any trouble. Michael had obviously been there before. On the way, Janie Steple had called us. The State Police had found Bobby Moretti's truck but it wouldn't be released until after the crime scene investigators had completed their work. The cargo was gone but the truck was in good condition. She told them the pickets were generally behaving, except for scaring away the coffee truck that had come for the terminal's mid-morning brake. FBI Special Agent Dwyer had called and would try back later. I called Wilson Dennis at FirsTech to give him an update on the hijacking. I hung up feeling that Wilson had politely listened to information that was old news to him.

Michael slid the Explorer into a parking space directly across the street from Tonzollo's Ristorante & Pizzeria.

"This is it? Tonzollo's?" I asked, pointing toward the tired facade.

"Yep, we're here."

"I get it now. Tommy Ton's not the name of a *fat* wop bookie. Or is it?"

"No, he's a wop bookie of average height and weight. But let's remember this is a serious guy. Let me do the talking, okay? I wanna keep you out of this."

"I'll appreciate that. Just so you don't forget what we're here for. Remember, unless I'm convinced that this payment will make everything disappear, this guy Johnny, everything - forever, than I'm gonna have a problem givin' this guy that kinda money."

"I'll do my best and I know how to talk to this guy, so lemme handle it. All he wants is his money. I'm sure once he knows we're serious about paying him tomorrow, he'll agree to whatever I want."

"Alright, just introduce me as your friend, not your partner. I'll nod once in a while and look bored. But don't take any prisoners, Michael. We gotta walk outta there with exactly what we came for."

"Leave it to me, we will."

I captured Michael's gaze and held it for a few seconds. "No prisoners, Michael," I said, finally. "This ends here, today."

The inside of Tonzollo's was dark, like a cave. No pizza-parlor-plate-glass windows. No bright florescent tubes suspended in the white drop-ceiling tiles. No gaily painted murals of Venice. I paused inside the vestibule to let my eyes adjust. There were no customers, and everything was ninety years old and dusty. The floor, the tables and chairs, the booths, and the wainscoted walls were worn to bare wood in all the right places. A hammered tin ceiling soared 14 or 15 feet overhead and dripped down four ancient belt-driven ceiling fans that slowly stirred the air. A magnificent mahogany bar covered the entire right wall. It appeared to be one massive structure that rose majestically from the floor, cascaded up the wall to the ceiling where it splashed out over the heads of any patrons lucky enough to be seated on of her stools. The rich, dark wood was tired and dry, thirsting for a long, slow drink of wood oil and all the mirrors were cloudy, but the brilliance of the cabinetmaker's craftsmanship could not be dimmed. I liked the place. I didn't think I was going to like the man who wouldn't even keep it clean.

Mrs. Lu Tran greeted us with a soft bow. "Two for lunch?"

"No, but please tell Tommy that Mikey C's here to see him," Michael replied.

Mrs. Lu Tran bowed again and scurried toward the kitchen. When she was far enough away, I said, "Mikey C?"

Michael shrugged. "What can I say, that's my name here."

A few seconds later, Tommy Ton came through the kitchen doors, moving sprightly with a telephone in his hand, dragging the cord behind him. He was in his late fifties, about five eight or nine, thin but with a middle-age paunch. He wore a black and gray synthetic ensemble that used to be called a jogging suit. His thick black hair was matted on one side, a sure sign he had not yet showered this day. A day-old beard made him look even more Sicilian.

"Come over here, Mikey. Let's sit down." He motioned to the corner booth closest to the kitchen. It was a large wood booth with high bench-backs. Michael introduced me as his friend and we both slid into one side of the booth.

"You guys wanna eat somethin'? I was just gonna have some sausage and peppers."

"No, that's okay," Michael replied, quickly.

"Come on, eat. Your friend here looks hungry." Tommy turned toward the kitchen and shouted, "Mrs. Tran." She floated in to the end of the booth. "Bring us a nice antipasto and then some sausage and peppers." Then to Michael and me, he said, "Glass of wine?"

"No, thanks." We answered together.

"I gotta a new house red. It's real nice, you gotta try it. Mrs. Tran, bring out a bottle with three glasses, and three bottles of Pellegrino."

For almost an hour, the three of us sipped the wine, which was good, and ate the lunch, which was excellent. Michael and Tommy talked sports, and more sports. After that, they talked about sports again. Tommy Ton was a natural host, accommodating and gregarious. Throughout the meal, he politely excused himself to take frequent phone calls. Each call was brief and nearly identical: "Hey, howya doon? Yeah. Yeah. Sure, you got it." He wrote nothing down. He was a real character and I found myself having a hard time disliking him.

After Mrs. Tran had set three double expressos on the table, Tommy said to Michael, "Let's talk some business. First, who's this guy?" Pointing at me.

"He's a friend of mine."

"I got business with you, not your friend. He has to take a walk." Tommy was talking to Michael as if I was invisible.

"He's part of this today. He needs to be here."

Tommy's face hardened. "He's part of this if I say he's part of this. What's this about, Mikey?"

"Without him, I can't pay you. So, he stays."

Tommy looked at me for what seemed like a long time. "I don't know if I like this." Then to me he said, "You a cop?"

"No. But, as Michael said, without me there's not gonna be any money."

Tommy eyed us for a few seconds. "Okay, both of you stand up. I'm gonna pat you down. I don't want anyone else but the three of us hearing this."

"You think we're wired, Tommy?" Michael asked, incredulously.

"You better fuckin' not be. Stand up, both of you, over here." Tommy motioned to the end of the table outside the booth.

Michael and I slid out and stood at the end of Tommy's bench. Tommy expertly patted our chests, backs, waists, buttocks, groins, and legs. He had done this before, or had it done to him.

"Okay, so your Michael's angel," Tommy said to me after we were reseated.

"Something like that."

"So, you guys are gonna have my money tomorrow? All of it? Ya know there's another week's vig due. I need a hundred and seven."

Michael said, "We got the money, Tommy, but we need to get a few things straight."

"Like what?"

"Well, like this thing with this guy Johnny."

"Whoa there pal, whatever you got goin' with Johnny Onions is no concern of mine. I'm not involved with that and right now ain't a good time for anyone to be associated with that asshole. Haven't you heard the news? The whole fuckin' world's lookin' for that guy right about now. I don't even want to hear his name again. Got it?" Tommy Ton pointed a finger at Michael. I clenched my teeth. There were a lot of fingers being pointed lately.

"The only reason I got involved with him was to settle up with you," Michael said. "The deal I had with him was all about my debt to you."

Tommy smiled and shook his head. "Wrong. The deal you had with him, was the deal you had with him, period. Word on the street is that somebody fucked up - you, the other guy, don't matter. All that matters now is that I still don't have my money."

"Look Tommy, I got a wife and two young kids. I fucked up. I know this is all my fault, but I gotta use the only leverage I have. The money comes with the condition that this other guy is told to back off and never to contact me again, for any reason. And once I pay you, I'm done - with you, him, everybody and everything else goes away forever. I can't have any of this left over to come back and bite me."

"I got a couple problems with this," Tommy began. "First, you're right, *you* fucked up. Making a deal with that guy was a big mistake. Why doya think they call him Onions? 'Cause he stinks, that's why. Everything he touches turns to shit. That scumbag managed to weasel his way into this by goin' around me. You got tempted. You saw an easy way out. Your problem, not mine. Second, all this other stuff . . . I don't give a fuck about your wife, your kids, you, nothin'. The only thing I care about is the money you owe me and when you're gonna pay."

Tommy Ton was losing his patience. I was no longer concerned about liking him.

There was a long silence. Michael was looking down at his hands. Tommy Ton was staring at Michael. His face had become snarled and red.

Finally, Michael said, "I don't know, Tommy."

"You don't know?" Tommy Ton started to shake. "Fuck you, you don't know! You call me up. You tell me you got my money. You come here, to my place. You and your fuckin' friend, you sit down with me, drink my wine, and now you don't know! Well, I know. You have my fuckin' money here tomorrow ten o'clock or it's your ass. You got it?" Tommy Ton's finger was up and aimed again, an inch from Michael's nose.

I folded my hands in front of me on the table. I leaned forward toward Tommy Ton and said quietly, "Why don't you take your finger out of my friend's face." It wasn't a question.

Both Michael and Tommy Ton turned their heads slowly toward me. Tommy Ton turned back to Michael and said, "This guy doesn't say two words for the last hour. Now he's gonna tell me what to do?"

"Joseph, it's cool," Michael said.

"Cool?" Tommy Ton said. "I got news for you two boy scouts. It ain't cool. Tomorrow at ten or else." Tommy Ton started to push himself out of the booth.

"Or else, what?" I said, softly.

"What's with this fuckin' guy?" Tommy Ton said to Michael. I was invisible again. "Oh, that's right, he's your angel. Tell him that all he needs to know is that if I don't get my fuckin' money tomorrow he just might be the friend of a real angel. You got it?"

Michael sat back and let his head fall against the bench back. He rolled his eyes toward me. I shook my head and took a deep breath. This was not heading in the right direction. The noise of my exhale turned Tommy Ton's head.

"Tommy Ton," I said. "That's what they call you? Right?"

Tommy Ton scowled at me.

"My name's Joseph Napolo. And Michael's a friend of mine. We came here today like gentlemen to reach an agreement with you but you chose to insult us and show us no respect."

"What's your name?"

"Napolo. Joseph Napolo."

"Oh." Tommy Ton sat back a little.

I paused for affect. "What was the original amount that Michael owed you, before any vig?"

"I don't know, about eighty grand."

"Here's what we'll do for you." I was speaking almost in a whisper but Tommy Ton was listening. "Tomorrow, we'll be prepared to deliver you eighty thousand dollars, at our convenience. But first, here's what you're gonna do for me. When we leave here today, you'll go to the nearest library. You'll look up my last name, do all the research you want, find out who my grandfather was. Then leave the library, go to the nearest Catholic Church. Light a candle and say a prayer that my friend, Michael here, doesn't even stub his toe or nick himself shaving. Say another prayer that we never hear from this Johnny Onions again. *You* got it?"

Tommy Ton silently studied every inch of my face. My lips were drawn tight across my teeth but I wasn't smiling. Michael was also looking at me, with his jaw dropped in disbelief.

Finally, Tommy Ton said, "I gotta make a call."

"Go ahead," I said. "But make it quick."

Tommy Ton slid out of the booth taking his telephone with him. He stepped just inside the kitchen door and dialed. He peeked through the small glass window in the door every few seconds, keeping an eye on us.

Michael folded his hands in front of his mouth and whispered to me, "Are you fuckin' nuts. This guy could come outta there with a gun. God knows who he's talkin' to."

"Relax," I said between my teeth.

Just then, Tommy Ton stuck his head through the door. "What was your grandfather's favorite wine?"

"Brunelleschi Chianti. He imported it for himself."

Tommy Ton went back to the phone. "What did he drink after dinner?"

"Strega. And only one espresso. He had high blood pressure."

To the phone again. "What was his favorite beer?"

"He hated beer."

Tommy Ton nodded a few times, hung up the phone and then came back to the table, dragging the phone cord.

"There's one more question."

"Okay, one more."

"What was wrong with his hand?"

"Nothing was wrong with his hand. But his right index finger was crooked at the last joint. He caught it in the metal blades of an electric fan. He was trying to pull out a piece of paper that had been sucked into the back of it. The blades were whipping the paper and the noise was annoying him. He yelled, 'Figlio di puttana,' when it happened."

Tommy Ton's face softened and he smiled. "Joseph, my God, why didn't you say somethin' earlier? I didn't mean no disrespect, it's just that in my business . . ."

"Forget it, Tommy. Do we have a deal?"

"Sure, sure, but this is over my head now. There's someone you gotta go see – in the city. He's the one that can fix this. I know he, ah, well, we all got a lot of respect for the old man, ya know?"

"The old man?"

"Your grandfather, the great Don Carmine."

I took the address, telling Tommy I would check my schedule and get back to him by five o'clock. Tommy Ton continued to apologize to me, until I told him to stop. Then he started apologizing to Michael. I ended it by getting up from the table. Tommy Ton walked with us to the door.

In the doorway, I put my arm around Tommy Ton's shoulders and spun him around to face the inside of the restaurant. I squeezed him close and said, "Tommy, I need a favor."

"Sure, Joseph. What can I do?"

"Clean this place up. It's a shame the way you've let it go. Call in a service. Spare no expense. It's your family name on the sign out front, for chrissake. Have a little respect, will ya?"

Tommy Ton bobbed his head agreeably. "No problem. I can do that . . . whatever you say."

We walked to Michael's truck in silence, squinting in the bright daylight. It was a beautiful Spring day and the warm sun felt good to me. In fact, I thought, I felt too good. One minute, we were in way over our heads, powerless, being threatened, about to walk out with our tails between our legs. Then, with the only thing my grandfather left me, his name, and a few carefully phrased suggestions . . . I could begin to imagine the power my grandfather had wielded 40 or 45 years ago. It's no wonder that mobsters, or entertainers and politicians for that matter, find it difficult - if not impossible - to walk away, to give it all up, to look themselves in the eye and say, 'it's over, I've had enough'. It was too seductive, if not addictive. I was beginning to understand it. I would have to remember not to start enjoying it.

"I don't know what to say," Michael said, as soon as they started to pull away from the curb. "I feel like I'm dragging you into something that . . ."

"You know, it sounds like you're about to apologize to me again. I'm getting tired of people apologizing to me. Frankly, it's too goddam late for that. I'm already in much further than I wanted. So let's stop the namby-pamby bullshit and start figuring out what just happened and what the hell we're gonna do about it. Jesus Christ, Michael, that fuckin' guy was threatening your life in there and I don't have any doubt that he was serious. What the fuck - you owe him a hundred grand. And what was I supposed to do? Sit there like some fuckin' douche bag and let him threaten you? Fuck him and fuck you!"

Michael knew better than to say anything. I needed a few minutes. Luckily, his cell phone rang. It was the office so he pressed the speaker phone button.

"Michael Cogan here."

"Michael, I'm glad I finally got you. It's Janie. Some guy named Johnny's called here three times looking for you. He gave Samantha a real hard time the first two calls, so I told her to pass him to me if he called again. What's this guy's problem? Do you know him?"

"Why? What did he say?"

"He said to tell you that you can't hide from him forever and that you'd better be here the next time he calls. Are you coming back? I really don't want to talk to him again. He sounds like a real low-life. Is he some kinda bill collector or something?"

"Yeah, um okay, Janie, we're on the way back from Secaucus. If he calls again tell him I'll be back in an hour."

"Good. Is Joseph there?"

"Yeah, hi Janie," I said.

"Your wife called. She wanted to know if you were gonna make your son Joseph's sports dinner tonight."

I looked at Michael and shook my head. "No, I don't think so. Michael and I have an important meeting in New York City tonight."

# CHAPTER 12
## FirsTech World Headquarters
## Liberty, New York

Officially, Wilson Dennis was Execute Vice President of Risk Management for FirsTech, a little-known multi-billion dollar defense contractor. He had corporate responsibility for insurance and product liability, but the primary focus of his position was security. This was his second career, but his compensation package at FirsTech was worth almost forty times as much as his last and highest annual salary in his first career. This wasn't unusual though. The pay scales of the United States Government have never been competitive with those in private industry. However, his first career had been essential. Only in the employment of the most powerful intelligence agencies in the modern world could someone acquire the skills and experience that were prerequisite for his position at FirsTech. In fact, as FirsTech's customers were the defense departments and the intelligence agencies of the United States and its allies, top secret clearance had been a base qualification for the job. Wilson Dennis had all of these qualifications and more, which was why FirsTech's founder had handpicked him for the job.

Wilson's hair was still wet when he walked into Nicolas Pucci's office. Nicolas was on the phone but he smiled warmly and motioned him over, signaling he'd just be a minute. Wilson settled into a large wing-backed chair covered in stripped silk fabric.

It was a palatial corner office on the top floor of the FirsTech complex, befitting the Chairman and CEO of this very successful, privately held company. The office, and the entire executive floor, were expensively furnished and appointed in a classical American Federal motif, reminiscent of the executive offices in the White House, which Wilson had visited on more than several occasions. Stars, stripes, bald eagles and various recombinations of the same were tastefully recurrent throughout the decor. The lobby and the other office areas of the complex's top three floors were similarly decorated. This was, of course, psychologically comfortable for visiting representatives from the Pentagon or from one of the many U.S. and foreign intelligence agencies with who FirsTech enjoyed long-term contracts. The bottom five floors of the complex were underground, housing state-of-the-art research and development and manufacturing facilities.

Nicolas hung up and smiled again at Wilson. "I'm glad to see someone's putting our gym to good use," he said, cordially.

"My wet hair gave me away?"

"That, and your red face."

"Well, that about sums it up," Wilson chuckled. "I've grown afraid of hair dryers. It feels like they're gonna blow off the precious few strands I have left up there. And, I think that someday I'm gonna kill myself tryin' to stay in some kind of reasonable shape so I can live longer. But, I guess I don't have to worry until you tell me my face is blue."

"Guys like you don't die in the gym."

"Guys like me usually don't get this old." They laughed, even though it was probably true.

Nicolas leaned back in his chair and interlocked his fingers behind his neck, letting his elbows fly out to either side of his head, framing his handsome Mediterranean features. "So, let me hear the latest. I saw Lincoln's helicopter come and go this morning. Where is he on this thing?"

"Well, after I let him rant and rave about my peoples' incompetence for failing to secure the locator transmitter and a backup device to the cargo, he went on and on, laying the groundwork to exonerate himself from any culpability. I countered quid pro quo by lashing into him for allowing his so-called well-trained units to be ambushed and eliminated. What I really loved though, was being able to take a few well-placed pot shots at that hi-tech chopper he loves so much. He reacted like I was talking about his wife or his mistress. So I asked him if he was actually fucking that helicopter or just wishing he could. You should've seen him. I'm sure that maniac wanted to kill me. Probably would've under different circumstances."

Nicolas laughed again and said, "Sounds like the generation gap between you two spooks has widened even more."

"Maybe. Hey, you and Lincoln, you're about the same age, same generation anyway, still in your forties – he's early fifties maybe. Things are different now. And I know we've had this discussion before, but in my day there were rules, an unwritten code. If you broke them, you paid – one way or another. Not many dared cross the line. It was a very small world. Your uncle and I mourned those days on many occasions. In fact, the first time we met to discuss this company and this job, back in the sixties, we spent most of the afternoon talking about how the world, our worlds, were changing. I was a young, but old, cold warrior, in my early thirties. He was a lot older and wiser, and certainly not Government Issue, but we hit it off immediately. Deep down, we were a pair of nostalgic fools for two lives lived, each our own, and gone forever. But, hey, our worlds changed - so fuck 'em all - we did too. And look at us now." Wilson held up outstretched arms. "This was his vision we built and he was so proud of what we accomplished. I loved that old man. I miss him every day."

Nicolas had heard this speech many times before. And sure, he was the Chairman, CEO and majority stock holder of a multi-billion dollar hi-tech government contractor, with little time in his day for repeated trips down memory lane, but Wilson Dennis was more than a valued executive, more than his trusted counsel and confidant, he was family. So, out of respect, he listened intently each time. He replied, simply, "Me, too. He raised me like a son."

"Anyway, back to business," Wilson said. "Let me give you the details of my meeting with Lincoln. I think you'll agree that some of them are problematic. First, it's important to know that our FBI sources are telling me that the two guys they found shot down in Hackensack, New Jersey last night were, in fact, Napolo Family soldiers, and that they were found in the apartment of a third Napolo guy, another soldier, just as the media reported. Obviously, they like the third guy for the hits. Publicly, they're goin' with Family problems on this one - an internal dispute. Privately, they're leaving open the possibility of a wider problem, maybe something between Families, but with what we know, it's not likely.

"Here's where it gets interesting. Lincoln told me that he has absolute confirmation that it was the Napolo Family that took out his men and that they have our cargo. He's looking for the same guy the Feds want, the third Napolo guy. In an uncharacteristic slip, Lincoln even mentioned his name; it's John Anelli, 'Johnny Onions' on the street."

Wilson paused and looked at Nicolas as if to say, *Ring any bells?* When Nicolas realized what he was doing, he shrugged and gave him a look that replied, *Are you kidding?*

"Anyway, this is where the problems begin," Wilson began, again. "Lincoln's looking for Anelli because he says that Anelli and his accomplices conspired to hijack a truckload of shoes. He believes that they got our merchandise by mistake. This is quite disturbing on two fronts." Wilson leaned forward with his elbows on his thighs and continued. "First, the Feds are in no way connecting the Hackensack hits with the hijacking, which means that Lincoln has developed this information on his own."

"Lincoln doesn't have access to that kind of information, does he?" Nicolas asked.

"No, not normally. But my bureau contacts gave me something that the media didn't get; the two guys in Hackensack were tortured before they were executed. In view of the emphasis that Lincoln is putting on that fact that his information is *absolutely* confirmed, and because he would *never* use such definitive language without cause, I'm betting that Lincoln was in Hackensack last night - that he's responsible for the torture and murders. But, how he connected Anelli to the hijacking in the first place, I don't have a clue."

Nicholas raised his right palm. "So, you're saying that somehow Lincoln puts Anelli in the hijacking, gets his address, finds two guys there, tortures them until he hears what he needs to hear, and then kills them? I don't know, Wilson. For chrissake, the truck didn't go missing until almost five o'clock. That's a lot for one evening."

"Never underestimate Lincoln. He's a very resourceful guy. A little crazy and very dangerous, but highly focused and, as I said, resourceful."

"Not to mention a cold-blooded son of a bitch," Nicolas added. "But I'm still not convinced. What am I missing?"

"Look at it this way, Nicolas. For our purposes, it really doesn't matter how he managed to connect Anelli to the hijacking. What's important is that the only way he could've put all this together was by getting it from someone on the inside. Someone on the inside of the Napolo Family. And, as you said, he doesn't have those contacts. Until, perhaps, last night in Anelli's apartment."

"Okay, let's say I buy it, for now. Lincoln's responsible for Hackensack," Nicolas conceded. "So, now the law enforcement community is chasing Anelli for the murders and, at the same time, Lincoln's chasing him for our merchandise."

"Exactly. The poor bastard would probably turn himself in to the Feds if he knew Lincoln."

"In a heartbeat," Nicolas agreed. "And, based on what I'm hearing, I'll bet that the Napolo Family would also like to know where Mr. Anelli is. You know he won't fair much better if they get a hold of him first."

"Correct, which is why we need to now consider getting more directly involved. Anelli may be the only one who knows where our merchandise is. That's certainly Lincoln's assessment. If the Feds or the Napolo Family get to him first, there's a good chance that Lincoln won't have the opportunity to recover the merchandise."

"*That* would be a serious problem."

"There's something else." Wilson leaned in closer to deliver the worst of it. "Lincoln says he's also confirmed, without any doubt, that it was an inside job, that the owner of the trucking company conspired with Anelli on the shoe hijacking."

Nicolas grunted and looked down at his desk, shaking his head. "*This* is not good."

Wilson sat back, giving Nicolas time to think.

Tired of waiting, Wilson said, "And, true or not, if Lincoln thinks it's so, he'll be calling on Domanski Trucking. He'll do whatever he deems necessary to recover that equipment. There's too much money at stake."

Nicolas looked up at Wilson. "Lincoln'll eat those guys for breakfast."

"Yes, he will. But we hired him and we're still pulling his strings."

Nicholas shook his head. "That's not good enough, Wilson. Lincoln can slip off those strings any time he wants. Jesus, this whole fuckin' mission is built around him doin' just that - we're counting on him to go south. We've provided him with the opportunity *and* the motivation."

Both men sat silently. Neither of them had a quick fix to offer. They both knew that reeling in Lincoln would jeopardize, if not abort, the mission. That was not a viable option. There had been too much planning, with too many different agencies. Too many wheels were in motion. Nicolas got up and walked over to the wall of windows behind his desk and looked out over the mountains and forests he loved so much. He had spent the best part of his youth in the Catskills - fishing, skiing, hiking - and he felt calmed by the view. He wanted to open the windows to smell the sweet pines and musty undergrowth that floored the forest, but he couldn't. The fixed mirror-coated windows were triple-paned and bulletproof. The spaces between the panes were filled with a temperature-controlled gas that prevented infrared, thermal imaging, and laser eavesdropping. All to make him safe and secure. He felt trapped.

Finally, he turned around and said, "Get to our inside man. Warn him. Stay close to Lincoln. Keep his strings short. Use any excuse you can think of to keep in touch with him. And make sure Napolo and Cogan attend the Awards Dinner tomorrow night, and that they're seated at my table."

# DTC Transportation

Michael and I arrived back at the terminal just before three o'clock. The two moonlighting Edison cops providing security cleared a path through the mob of Teamsters for Michael's Explorer. As we drove past the pickets, we heard the usual greetings; *Assholes! Dickheads! Dirty scumbags! Roll down your windows. We'll give you another shower, motherfuckers!* And then spittle of varying sizes and colors began splattering against the windshield and side windows of the truck. We ignored the taunts and spitting, as did the two cops. After all, the PBA was a union, too.

A few minutes later, we were both settled behind our desks, returning phone calls. After several calls, I felt Michael looking at me. I caught Michael's eye and said, "I just lied to Cathy. I told her we had a negotiating session with the union tonight and that I didn't know what time it'd wrap up - that we might be late."

"I'll tell Ilene the same thing," he responded, without hesitation.

When he hung up, I said. "It doesn't bother you, does it?"

"What?"

"Lying to your wife."

Michael threw up his hands. "What do you want from me? So, it doesn't bother me as much as you. I guess I've had more practice - with the gambling stuff and all. But, it's not like we're goin' out on dates or something. It's business."

"I guess. But, as my father used to say, if you can't talk to your wife and kids about your business, it's time to find a new job."

Michael didn't respond. I could tell he was frustrated by my emotional wanderings. Some of it was just me thinking out loud. It was a luxury we were both accustomed to after so many years together. Michael knew well enough to just leave it alone. Best thing was to change the subject.

"By the way," Michael said, to create the shift. "Bobby Moretti's here, helpin' out in dispatch. Came in a few minutes ago. Said he didn't want to miss any of the action."

"Oh yeah, how's he look?"

"Like he went a couple rounds with Mike Tyson."

I felt like I owed us one. I said, "He's got bite marks?" We smiled at each other.

The intercom on my phone beeped. "Joseph? Michael?"

It was Samantha Burke, our receptionist. "Yes, Sam?"

"Special Agent Dwyer, from the FBI, is here to see you and Michael."

Michael walked over and hit the mute button on my telephone. "There're a couple messages from him. He was probably trying to tell us he was coming by today."

Michael pushed the mute button, again, allowing me to reply. "Okay, Sam, please bring him back."

Michael and I began straightening our desktops, as if the FBI was in someway concerned with tidiness, knowing that what while we indeed had something to hide, none of it was on our desks. When we heard Sam's chatty voice in the hallway, we stopped suddenly and sat back in our chairs, folding our hands in front of us on our desks, like two schoolboys hearing the teacher in the hallway.

"Here they are," Sam said, as she showed the Special Agent into the office.

The agent had an unusual presence that was as immediate as it was unfathomable. He was above average height, lean and fit, in his late forties or early fifties. His face was long and angular, led by a blade-sharp nose. His eyes were small and his sharply hair cut bristled on the top of his head, both furthering his avian appearance. He wore a dark blue suit that was expensive and well tailored, but the floral pattern on his tie was out of style. But you always came back to his eyes - aluminum gray, cold and soulless, like the water in a long-abandoned granite quarry, deep and dangerous. If you lingered there, you stood at the ledge of a bottomless chasm that seemd to emit an immutable force greater than gravity, making it impossible to feel safe being so close.

As Samantha closed the office door she made a face behind the agent's back. Her expression told us that there was something about this guy that she didn't like either. Aaron Lincoln had always had a problem with first impressions.

Lincoln leaned toward Michael with his hand extended, "Mr. Napolo, I'm Special Agent Clifford Dwyer. With a last name like yours, I'm surprised to see you're having union problems. Teamsters, no less."

Michael shot a glance at me and extended his hand. "Nice to meet you. But I'm Michael Cogan." Nodding toward me, he said, "This is Joseph Napolo."

"Oh, I'm sorry. I uh . . ."

I came around from behind my desk, took Lincoln's hand, and said cordially, "It happens all the time. Everyone thinks the darker one must be the Italian. But my mother's from northern Italy. She's a blond."

"Lucky for you," Lincoln responded, giving my hand a final squeeze that was a little too hard. Neither Michael nor I knew exactly what he had meant.

"It's okay, I'm happy to be mistaken for Italian," Michael said, to break the uncomfortable silence. "Guess it's the black Irish in me."

"Well, that's better than being just plain black," Lincoln chuckled loudly.

Michael and I looked at each other. We knew what the other was thinking; *What's with this guy?* There was another deafening silence.

I broke the ice this time. "That never happens, does it Michael?"

"No."

Lincoln snickered and said, "Well, I guess you're damn glad for that."

I saw that Michael's mouth was wide open, feigning shock. It was time to have some fun, I thought.

"Special Agent Dwyer," I said. "I think you should know that Michael is married to a beautiful African-American woman and that they have five beautiful children."

Lincoln turned toward me and looked at me intently. "Is that right?" Then he looked at Michael and asked again, "Is that right?"

"Would he lie to the FBI?" Michael responded.

Lincoln looked back at me. Tilting his head back and to the side, his eyes narrowed, he said, "Why not? He's the grandson of Carmine Napolo."

I straightened and locked eyes with Lincoln. Neither of us flinched. Apparently, the fun was over. I said, "Now that we clearly understand your prejudices, Special Agent Dwyer, can we get on with discussing the theft of our tractor trailer? I assume that's why you're here."

"Certainly, can I sit down?"

"Be our guest."

Lincoln began arranging his chair so he could comfortably see both of us. He was trained to keep his adversaries well within his field of vision. Then he snapped open the locks on the black attaché case he had placed on his lap. He flipped the top of the case up and away from him, so it shielded the contents from our view. Inside the case, a green light on a small electronic device was flashing, indicating that no eavesdropping equipment was operating in the room. Lincoln removed a pad of paper from the case and closed it, leaving it to rest on his thighs. I sat down behind my desk after Lincoln had finished.

"First, I want you guys to understand something," Lincoln began. "Don't ever think you can jerk me off. I, the bureau, know all about you two." He glanced briefly down at his pad and then looked at Michael. "Your wife's name is Ilene. She's *white*, forty-four years old, and you have two children, a boy and a girl." Lincoln checked his notes again. "You, Mr. Napolo, are also married with three children, your wife's name is Cathy, with a 'C'. I know all your children's names and ages. I also know that you two boys were roommates for four years at the University of Pennsylvania and you've been friends ever since. You participated in campus anti-war activities and associated with the anti-war, anti-establishment group called Students for a Democratic Society, although neither of you were committed enough to actually join the SDS. I'm guessing you probably thought it'd be easier to get laid by the hippie chicks if you hung around with the left wing, counter-culture types. Neither of you were in the armed forces; too privileged or, more likely, too afraid to join even though the Vietnam War was winding down by the time you two were of age. Mr. Cogan was arrested in '73 for possession of less than 28 grams of marijuana, a misdemeanor. The charges were dropped, though, because the Philadelphia Police Department lost the two joints they had in evidence. You both worked for several large companies before you bought this company in 1990 with second mortgages on your homes and a sweetheart deal from the former owner. You've paid off your notes and the former owner, as of last December."

Lincoln paused for our reaction. There was none. Michael and I were products of the Nixon-Hoover era, when this kind of detailed information was routinely assembled and catalogued. We knew that our anti-war activities virtually ensured that we had dossiers on file. When Lincoln saw he wasn't getting to us, he pressed on.

"Since college, on paper you've been upstanding citizens. Good credit. Paid your taxes. Active in your communities. Good employers. Respected company. Outwardly, a pair of fucking choirboys."

"Special Agent Dwyer," I broke in. FBI or not, I had had enough. "We're very impressed with the quality and the quantity of your information, but what does any of this have to do with the hijacking of our truck? Quite frankly, I'm offended by your tone and the content of this conversation. I think it's uncalled-for, if not unprofessional."

"You're offended? Oh, that's too bad. Frankly, I was hoping to insult you as much as you insult me and the bureau."

Michael pushed his chair back. "What the hell are talking about? I'm about ready to ask you to leave and call in a formal complaint."

"Go ahead." Lincoln was smiling. "While you're at it why don't you tell them all about you and your partner here." He spoke to me now. "Napolo, who do you think you're kidding? Sure, you've done a real good job hiding behind your respectable life, putting it out there for everyone to think that you're a hardworking stiff. We know better, though, don't we? That guinea mobster blood of yours runs thick, doesn't it?"

I gripped the arms of my chair. I took a deep breath and locked eyes with Lincoln. Something was not right, with this guy. FBI agents were supposed to be skilled professionals. All the movies and TV shows couldn't be that wrong. This wasn't the way it should be, I decided.

"Agent Dwyer, can we see your I.D.?"

"Sure." Lincoln removed a leather holder from his inside jacket pocket and held it up for us to see. I leaned across my desk to examine it more carefully. After a moment, I realized that he had no way of knowing if the credentials were genuine. Like most people, I had never been in the same room with an FBI agent before. I looked at Michael and shrugged.

"Go on," I said calmly to Lincoln.

"Oh, I've got your attention now, huh?" Lincoln smirked.

I smirked back at him. "Let's say, I'm interested to hear where you think you're going with this."

"Well then, let's get right to it," Lincoln replied, still looking directly at me. "The bureau's sources have confirmed that the hijacking of your truck was planned and carried out by members of an organized crime family. We've learned that they intended to steal a truckload of shoes, but something went wrong and they ended up with the FirsTech shipment. Now here's the interesting part, Mr. Napolo. The crime family that's involved here is the *Napolo* Family. And, even more interesting, our source has told us that this was an inside job - that the owner of the trucking company was involved."

Lincoln paused, raising his eyebrows, waiting for me to respond.

Michael must have felt compelled to speak. "Agent Dwyer, with everything else you know, how is it that you don't know that Joseph, or his father for that matter, have never had anything to do with the Napolo Crime Family? That was Joseph's grandfather. But he died years ago, when we were kids."

"He got blown up in his car, as I recall." Lincoln shook his head in mock sympathy. "But, I'm not here to debate whether or not one or both of you are involved in this, or why. I have confirmed that you are and I really don't care why. The way I see it, Mr. Napolo here, or maybe both of you, saw a way to make a little extra cash. So, you contacted some of his grandfather's goombahs and made a deal. The only question now is, how will we proceed?"

"Proceed?" I said.

"Yes. I need to decide how this thing is going to be put down. Let's see . . ." Lincoln rubbed is chin and looked up at the ceiling. "Is this a simple theft gone wrong? Oh, no. I think this is a much bigger than that. And what could be bigger than treason?"

"Treason!" Michael said.

"Yes, treason. This shipment was highly classified equipment. Vital to national security. And it's missing. It could be on its way to one of our enemies right now."

The blood instantly drained from Michael's face. I felt like I'd been punched in the stomach. The agent was making assumptions and drawing conclusions based in fact. The FBI's informant apparently knew enough to be dangerous, but not the whole story. All in all, there were enough circular references for this to become a major problem.

"I think we should terminate this conversation until we're able to retain legal counsel," I said.

"I agree," added Michael, quickly.

"Not a wise decision," Lincoln said. "Not until you have the opportunity to hear my offer."

"Your offer?" I repeated.

"Yes. A most unusual offer. Normally, the bureau would not be approaching suspects like yourselves until we have developed additional evidence to support the informant's claims. We'd spend the hours and days necessary to find the corroborating evidence a federal prosecutor would require for a bulletproof indictment. At that time, maybe we'd send in a pair of agents to test the suspects' reaction to a limited amount of that evidence. More likely, we'd simply make the arrest. But this case is different. We don't have the luxury of the time it may take to find additional evidence. Besides we know, without a doubt, that our information is solid. The informant was in no position to tell us anything but the truth.

"Now you've noticed that I came here alone today," Lincoln continued. "I'm here in an official capacity to make you an unofficial offer. In the interests of nation security, our primary concern is the repossession and safekeeping of the missing equipment. To that end, we're prepared to make an exchange for the equipment."

"An exchange?" Michael said.

"Yes, a trade, an exchange. You know, you give us something, we give you something. But if you *take* something, we take something." Lincoln eyes twinkled when he spoke.

"What does *that* mean?" I said, as if the words were spoken in a foreign language.

"Before I tell you, you should know that this offer is the kind your grandfather no doubt made on some occasions. You know, the kind you can't refuse. Simply put, we get the equipment or we get you."

"I'm asking you again, *what does that mean?*" I said, slowly speaking the last part of the sentence.

"It's pretty simple. We're offering a special reward of one million dollars for the safe return of the equipment. However, it is a limited offer which expires in forty-eight hours."

"A million dollars?" Michael blurted.

Lincoln nodded. "Yes, sirree. Cash. Tax free."

"You guys can do that?" Michael asked.

"We'd never admit to it, but yes we can."

I looked at the two of them in disbelief, and said, "Assuming that we had no involvement in this situation and, therefore, no knowledge of the equipment's whereabouts, what happens if we don't - can't - return the equipment?"

"Oh, I'm not exactly sure. Shall we toss it around, though?" Lincoln said, looking up at the ceiling again, his eyes squinted again, feigning a thoughtful moment. "Okay, let's try this. First, we'll leak the treason and the Mafia thing to the media, setting the stage for when we arrest you in front of the television cameras. It'll be a very public event, guaranteed to be a real media spectacle. Your trials are front-page news and the lead story on every network's primetime news show. The government's prosecution will destroy your company and bankrupt you personally. In the meantime, people you never met will be getting rich from movie and TV deals. There'll be an endless string of best selling books that will argue juicy mob conspiracy theories for years to come. Even your closest friends will claim their fifteen minutes of fame when they defend and/or vilify you in the tabloids and on Cable news shows. Every moment of your lives will be picked apart and made unsavory and distasteful, to even your own children. Your wives will divorce you. You'll spend the rest of your bitter lives in a federal penitentiary, proclaiming your innocence to a world full of deaf ears. Your infamy, Mr. Napolo, may even eclipse that of your grandfather."

I glanced at Michael. He was pale and taut, resembling a statue helplessly watching a flock of pigeons descend upon him. I sensed Michael was having trouble finding his next breath, overcome with the repulsiveness of Lincoln's threat.

"This is crazy!" I said. "I can't believe the FBI goes around making deals and threatening people like this?"

"Oh, I'm sorry, I forgot to tell you," Lincoln replied. "The FBI never does that. In fact, the FBI will deny any knowledge of this visit, or this conversation."

Michael came back to life. "That'll be pretty hard, considering that by now Samantha has probably told the whole company that you're here."

"Forget that," I said to Michael. "I'm not comfortable making any kind of deal with this guy, with or without legal representation. This is crazy!" Then to Lincoln. "No one here has admitted to anything. You come in here with some weak information about the Napolo Crime Family and draw the ridiculous conclusion that we had something to do with this. Suppose my name was Smith? Would you still be threatening us? I doubt it. I want you to go now. Get some real evidence, and then come back and talk to our lawyer." I needed to buy some time. Too much was going on for me to think clearly.

"Look boys," Lincoln said, leaning forward for emphasis. "I really don't give a shit who knows I'm here and I don't give a shit about lawyers or anybody else. You don't seem to understand . . . I've given you two choices here. These are your *only* options. *I* am now in total control of your destinies. Don't make the mistake of not believing that. If I want to make a deal with you guys, then there'll be a deal. If I want you arrested, you'll be arrested. And if you think you can fuck with me, you better believe that if I want you dead, you'll be dead."

I couldn't believe that I had heard Lincoln correctly. But one glance at Michael confirmed I had.

"Are you serious?" I stood and pointed to the door. "Get the fuck outta this office. I'm not gonna listen to this shit anymore. I want you to leave our property. Now!"

Lincoln nodded as he snapped the locks on his attaché case and flipped open the top. He placed his pad inside and let his wrist linger over the edge of the case. Lincoln looked up slowly. His gray eyes had dilated and turned black. He stretched his neck to one side, then the other, and rolled his head around, so we could hear his vertebrate bones making tiny cracking sounds. His hand shifted inside the attaché case.

Suddenly the door opened. Bobby Moretti was in the doorway, looking down over Lincoln's shoulder.

"Everything okay in here? I heard some yelling." Moretti didn't look up from the opened attaché case.

Lincoln brought the top of the case down quickly, leaving his hand inside, and looked up over his shoulder at Moretti. "This is FBI business, please leave the room."

"I dunno . . ." Moretti's eyes were locked on the attaché case as he spoke, "Joseph, what's goin' on in here?"

"Our meeting's over Bobby. Everything's fine. He was just leaving."

"I'll walk him out then." Moretti didn't look up until Lincoln slid his hand out of the case and snapped the locks closed. Lincoln stood and addressed Michael and me.

"On behalf of the bureau, I would like to inform you that there will be no further investigation of this incident. We are convinced that we have identified the perpetrators. They have been made an offer that they can't afford to decline. I expect the missing cargo to be secured within 48 hours. I will be in touch with you to arrange its return. Of course, if the 48-hour deadline passes uneventfully, the perpetrators will come to understand the true meaning of *dead*line." Lincoln over-emphasized 'dead'.

I looked at Moretti. "We're through here," I said in disgust.

"Here's my card," Lincoln said, as he flipped it onto Michael's desk. "You can page me if anything jogs your memory. Either way, I'll be in touch, boys." Lincoln smiled and turned to follow Moretti down the hall.

Bobby Moretti escorted Lincoln into the parking lot, walking a few paces behind him. Lincoln pulled keys from his pocket and as he bent to unlock the door of a car with a rental company decal on the windshield, Moretti asked, "When did the FBI start driving rented Chevys?"

"None of your business," Lincoln replied.

"When did the FBI start carrying silenced .22 revolvers in their briefcases?"

Lincoln straightened up and, without looking at Moretti, said, "Again, none of your business."

"I thought you guys were carrying the big Sig Saurs now."

Lincoln turned and scowled at Moretti. "What's your fuckin' problem?"

"You look familiar," Moretti said, ignoring his last question. "How do I know you?"

"You don't."

"No, I do."

"You know, you're a goddam pain in the ass. Is that why your face is bashed in? Someone get sick of your fuckin' questions?"

"I don't like you either," Moretti said, unfazed by Lincoln's growing impatience. "But I never forget a face. It'll come to me. I know you."

"Whatever." Lincoln huffed and got into the Chevy. Moretti stepped back and folded his arms across his chest. The window of the Chevy slid down and Lincoln stuck his face through the opening.

"Tell your bosses they'd better play ball. Tell them there'll be no further warning. They'll know what I mean."

"I think I'll just tell them that I know you," Moretti said, coolly.

"You'll tell them what I said, if you know what's good for them."

Moretti shrugged and walked to the gate where the pickets were grouping to confront him. As he rolled back the gate, he said to them, "Get outta the way, boys. The company's attorney's comin' through. Better move, he's a real prick lawyer. Said he's gonna get you guys good . . . that you're all fucked. Shit, you shoulda heard what this guy was saying. He said you're a buncha fuckin' asshole losers . . . that all Teamsters are pieces of shit. And, man, there's no talkin' to this guy. We tried to tell him that you're just working stiffs like us, but he wouldn't listen. He really pissed me off when he said you guys were a bunch of dumb fucks, and that if you could doing anything else but drive a truck, you wouldn't be here. Guy just fuckin' hates Teamsters; thinks you're real scumbags. Come on. Outta the way. Here he comes now."

Moretti watched as Lincoln began inching the Chevy through the seething mob. Invectives and spit rained freely. After a few seconds, Lincoln began gunning the engine and pumping the brakes, letting the car lurch and jump into the pickets. The cops finally came out of their cruiser but it was too late. The pickets were all over the car. They were crawling over the trunk, roof, and hood, beating at the windows with their fists and boot heels. Moretti could no longer see the Chevy. It had been swarmed and completely covered with Teamsters, like maggots on a piece of rancid meat. The police stood back helplessly and watched as the car was absorbed by the mob.

Moretti closed the gate, locking out the madness. As he walked back to the terminal building, he heard glass breaking and Teamsters cheering. The cuts and bruises on his face began to sting from a widening grin that stretched his cheeks. It felt very good.

# CHAPTER 13

## FirsTech World Headquarters
## Liberty, New York

"I know you're running late for your meeting with Van Houten and Franks at the club this evening, but I wanted to give you an update on the situation with Lincoln before you left." Wilson Dennis said, as he lowered himself into an armchair in front of Nicolas Pucci's desk.

Nicolas huffed and said, "Those NSA assholes pray for me to be late. They love the club. The later I am, the more wine, caviar, and oysters they can stuff themselves with. It's like it tastes better when they think they're getting away with something."

"You know, it's incredible to me that the largest, most sophisticated intelligence agency in the world wouldn't presume that we'd be watching their every move, especially under our own roof," Wilson said, smiling and shaking his head. Slapping his thigh. "How funny was that video of those two last year? Franks standing in the door of the cigar room playing lookout, while Van Houten's stuffing handfuls of Cohibas and Partagas into his briefcase."

"That was priceless," Nicolas agreed.

"No, the priceless part was later, when you started admiring Van Houten's case. I thought he was gonna shit his pants."

"That was great, wasn't it?"

"A classic moment. Your uncle would've loved it. He was great at playing with guys like that."

"Except that my uncle wouldn't've let him off as easy as I did. He'd a made sure Van Houten left with a load in his pants."

"No doubt," Wilson said.

"So, lemme hear about Lincoln's afternoon," Nicolas said, as he began to organize the files and papers on his desktop.

"Well, he left here and flew to Teterboro, where he rented a car under one of his aliases and drove to Domanski Trucking or DTC Transportation, as they're now called. There, he impersonated an FBI agent and spent fifteen or twenty minutes with Napolo and Cogan."

"Do we know what went on in the meeting?"

"No, not exactly, but Napolo and Cogan stayed behind closed doors for about an hour and a half after Lincoln left. They were overheard arguing loudly at several points during that time."

"That's it? That's all we got?" Nicolas had stopped working, shifting all his attention to Wilson.

Wilson heard the dissatisfaction in Nicolas' voice and responded quickly, "No, there's more. We heard something about a 48-hour deadline, with some kind of threat associated with it."

"That's not much more."

"No, but tonight we're bugging their office. We'll be listening and we'll be close by if anything happens."

"Okay, Wilson, just stay *real* close to this from now on," Nicolas said, with less bite. "We can't have Lincoln running this thing his way. It's too dangerous."

"Understood," Wilson nodded. Then smiling again, he said, "Hey, want to hear something that'll make you laugh? It's about Lincoln."

Nicolas stuffed several file folders and his laptop into a soft-sided leather attaché. When he had closed the zipper, he said, "Somehow laughing and Lincoln don't seem to fit together, but why not."

"Okay. As you know, the Teamster Local is picketing Domanski Trucking. It's been an unfriendly situation. Well, as Lincoln was leaving there today, trying to drive through the picket line, something set off the pickets and they trashed Lincoln's car, with him inside. They broke all the windows and stomped in the roof and the trunk and the hood. They were trying to drag Lincoln out of the car when the local cops finally got it under control."

"Are you kidding?" Nicolas said, as he locked his desk.

"Nope. And listen to this. The car's damaged so badly that Lincoln can't drive it, so what does he do . . . he shows the local cops his bogus FBI credentials and has them set up a relay with the state police to get him back to Teterboro Airport."

"What balls!" Wilson had Nicolas' full attention again.

"And this is not the end of the story. About an hour later, a gray and black helicopter appears and settles into a low hover over the pickets at DTC. It's just floating there about 300 feet over their heads. Suddenly, the chopper drops down to about 50 feet, both side doors open, and they start dumping out bags of white powdered lime. Of course, the rotor wash whips it down hard onto the pickets. I was told they were scrambling around, frantic, looking like a bunch white mice on an electrified grate."

Nicolas' mouth had dropped open as he slowly shook his head in disbelief. Even in the midst of all that was happening, of all that was at stake, Lincoln's base reaction and immediate priority had become revenge, or what guys like Lincoln called 'pay back'. Raw vengeance, swiftly and decisively served up, even at the risk of compromising the mission at hand. He would have to remember this, he thought.

"The Teamsters would have no idea who did this, would they?" Nicolas finally said.

"Now that you mention it, no."

"Do we know which Local is it?"

"Seven-fourteen, out of Keasby." Wilson thought for a moment. "You know, they'll probably blame it on Napolo and Cogan."

"Probably." Nicolas nodded.

Then after a moment he added, "I think I'd better make a call on my way to the club."

## Northbound on The New Jersey Turnpike

"Ron, I'll tell you one last time, we had *nothing* to do with that. For chrissake, your men trashed an FBI agent's car. They might have seriously injured him if the police didn't break it up. Why don't you call the FBI? Maybe it was their helicopter." I winced and moved the cell phone a few inches from my ear. After a few seconds I said, "Ron, I'm on a cell phone and when you scream like that I can't understand a word you're saying."

I listened for a few seconds before hanging up. Michael let his eyes drift from the Turnpike traffic and said, "So, what'd Laskowski say?"

"He asked me if I could understand two simple words, 'fuck you', and then he hung up."

"Wonderful. So I guess we can expect to hear from the NLRB bright and early tomorrow."

"That'll be the least of it. He's contacting their attorney to see if they can file any criminal charges."

Neither of us wanted any more conversation. We had left the terminal after a long and heated discussion. On our way out the door together, not one of our employees would look up. Obviously, we had been arguing too loudly and word had gotten around. Only Bobby Moretti had dared to address us. He had purposely stepped into our path, smiling, and said, 'Hey guys, it can't be that bad. And remember, no matter what, we're all behind you. It'll work out, you'll see.' But, Moretti was no Pollyanna and his optimism did little to ease the tension between Michael and me. We had driven fifteen minutes north on the Turnpike in total silence until Laskowski called.

After a couple more miles, I said, "You're taking the Holland Tunnel, right?"

Michael, affecting a perfectly effeminate lisp, replied, "Oh, does thith mean we're talking again?"

"It means you better get into the right lane or you're gonna miss the exit."

"Thank you, dear." Michael was still talking like a sissy. "I juth don't know *how* I would be able to find my way around without you. Thank heaventh you're coming into the big thity with me tonight."

"Cut the shit, will ya."

Michael shrugged and turned the Explorer onto the exit ramp, passing under the sign for the Holland Tunnel. When he had finally negotiated through several lanes of high-speed merging traffic, he turned to me and said in his own voice, "Alright, so maybe trying to collect the FBI's million dollars is a bad idea. But maybe, just maybe, if we worked together - like we always have - we could figure a way to use their offer to come outta this thing whole."

"You don't give up, do you? You're already in way over your head and you still wanna roll the dice one more time . . . with the FBI no less."

"And what's our alternative? Wait until Friday and see what happens? I'm still waiting to hear a better idea."

I knew my old friend well. Michael by nature was impatient, driven by a need to be meticulous. Everything had to be put in its place, and quickly. Unfinished business was loose ends with tentacles that tickled his gut. Michael would squirm until a resolution was adopted. Unfortunately though, it was the tickling he sought to quiet, not the tentacles that caused the tickling. And, the more Michael squirmed the easier the solutions came, too often impetuously. It was, I had decided, the way of an addict. The solution, in this instance, is the drug or the bet, and once it's rationalized everything is good again. But Michael was my friend and you take your friends how they are.

"Michael, you're right," I said, in as normal a voice as I could find within me. "I don't have all the answers for you right now. You'll have to give me some time on this thing. But one thing I *do* know is that thinking we can middle a deal with the FBI on one side, and these other characters on the other, is just fucking crazy. You're *way* outta your league, and the quicker you realize that the better off we'll both be."

Michael recognized the finality in my statement. So, knowing that further conversation on this matter would be an exercise in frustration, but in pursuit of the last word, he said, "I guesth I'll have to sthop dreaming about all the nice thingth I could've bought with my share of the million dollarth."

I shook my head. "You're a real asshole."

"Yeth, I know."

## Lower East Side, New York City

We circled a two or three block area around East Houston Street in Little Italy for about fifteen minutes until we finally found a parking space on Elizabeth Street near the corner of East Houston. When we finally found Taverna Reggia, we realized we had driven by the place several times. In fact, we had even walked past it once, before Michael spotted the dimly lit wrought iron gate with the grape vine sign above it.

"This is it?" Michael asked.

"Yeah, Taverna Reggia. This is the place."

"It's in the cellar?"

"Jesus, Michael, they're not *cellars* here. They're below street level."

"So's my cellar."

Pretending to ignore Michael's last comment, I went down the steps and waited for Michael to join me in front of the iron gate. The latch on the gate wasn't locked but its age required me to tug at it forcefully before it would open. We closed the gate behind us as quietly as possible and stood in the dark for a moment in front of the black metal door. I reached up and knocked hard, three times. We waited, both wondering if the place was as vacant as it looked. Then, after the noises of two locks and a deadbolt, the door swung outward a few inches and stopped, opening oddly toward the street instead of into the building.

"Yeah, who is it?" A raspy voice from behind the door.

"Joseph Napolo and Michael Cogan," I said, as I moved around to look into the opening of the door. "Is Mr. Venezio . . . " The door closed abruptly, cutting me off in mid-sentence.

Seconds later the door swung out again, this time more quickly, forcing us to back up against the iron gate. A tall, very large man in his late fifties leaned out, holding onto the door handle.

"Cumon in. Vinny's expectin' ya."

I forced a smile and thanked him as Michael and I squeezed past his stomach. The interior was well lit but not bright. The room wasn't as small as it felt. The ceiling seemed lowered by the haze of tobacco and kitchen smoke. There were four men casually grouped at the far corner of a small bar on the

117

right wall. Three more were seated at a round table in the left corner of the room. They were all stone-still, heads turned and eyes locked on us, looking as if a cameraman had just said, 'Okay now, hold it and remember, no smiles.'

We took several short steps, stopping on the far side of a worn throw rug covering the granite floor in the foyer area. We heard the door slam and locking sounds behind us. When the noises stopped another fatter man slid his chair back from the table and smiled as he pushed himself up. The other men began looking back and forth between the smiling fatter man and us. The fatter man lumbered around the table and waddled toward us with outstretched arms.

"Welcome, Joseph. Welcome. I'm Vinny Venezio," he said, as he threw his arms around Michael, giving him a bear hug and a kiss on the check.

Michael patted Vinny's back politely and looked sideways at me for help.

"Vinny, I'm Joseph. That's Michael Cogan, my partner."

Vinny's arms flew away from Michael and stopped in mid-air as he stepped back, his face bulldogging as he screwed up his nose. After glancing back and forth at us a few times he shrugged and said, "Of course, of course." And then he hugged and kissed me.

When Vinny released me and stepped back a bit, I said, "Sorry we're a little late, Vinny. We're having some problems that we had to deal with before we could leave."

"What problems?"

"Nothing, really. Just a little problem with our union."

"Problems with your *union*? What union?" Vinny asked.

"Teamsters."

"Teamsters? Ya tellin' me Joseph Napolo's havin' problems with the *Teamsters*?" Vinny was acting shocked.

"It's a contract issue. We'll resolve it," I said, wishing I hadn't mentioned anything.

Vinny turned to his men and with his hand on my upper arm announced, "This is why I asked all you guys ta be here tonight. I wanchya ta meet Joseph Napolo, the old man's grandson. He was jus' tellin' me he's havin' a problem with the Teamsters in Jersey. A *contract* issue. Maybe we oughta go over ta Jersey and tell those Teamsters they'd better reread their fuckin' contract. Tell 'em they must've skipped over the grandfather clause." Vinny belly-laughed. His crew joined him, slowly at first and then more confidently as Vinny continued to roar. After catching his breath, he continued, "Yeah, maybe we should . . . And, this here is Joseph's, ah, partner Michael, ah . . ."

"Cogan," Michael finished for Vinny, with a smile and quick wave.

"Yeah, and they're here tonight as my guests. But . . ." Vinny continued slowly for emphasis, waving a pudgy forefinger, "We did *not* have any guests tonight, capisci?"

Vinny looked around the room. "Good. Let's eat somethin' and then we'll talk."

Vinny steered me over to his table, ignoring Michael who followed behind with the big man from the doorway. I guessed it was a pre-war building and that the restaurant was part of the original plans. At one time it was probably a fine little ristorante in a well-to-do, desirable neighborhood. The thousands of dinners and glasses of wine served here were reflected in shiny traffic patterns around the tables and through the kitchen door where the mottled terrazzo floor had been worn smooth. Dark bentwood chairs encircled a dozen empty tables draped with overlapping squares of white cloth. In the center of each table there was a small dusty brass lantern with an unlit candle inside.

At the corner table, Vinny's table, Vinny motioned to a fit, well-dressed younger man and said, "Jimmy, move over. I want Joseph to sit next to me. And, Jimmy, remind me tomorrow about those Teamsters."

Jimmy Merchanti shrugged and said, "Sure, boss. Do you want we put a few a tables together so we can all sit together?"

"Good idea, Jimmy. This is a special occasion."

I put my hands up in protest. "Really, Vinny, you don't have to make a fuss here. We . . ."

"Joseph, Don Carmine, was always very kind to me and my family. Out of respect for him, I *must* fuss. Jimmy, tell him what we spent on the wine."

"A lot."

"That's right. And Tony's been cookin' all afternoon. And we don't talk no business until after we eat, so . . ."

Vinny looked at us with expectant eyes, as if we actually had any choice.

"So," I said. "Where's the wine?"

The dinner was impressive. The table was set with baskets of warm semolina loaves and imported Italian breadsticks, small bowls of roasted garlic in olive oil, and mountainous cold antipasto platters that were ladened with shrimp, lobster tails, calamari, and scungilli salad. The antipasto plates were replaced by steaming bowls of escarole and bean soup. Then manicotti in marinara sauce, followed by three-inch thick veal chops topped with portabello mushrooms in thin dark brown gravy. Enormous trays of broccoli rabe and sautéed zucchini and onions, rounded out the main course. A chilled garden salad dressed with a light balsamic vinegarette finished the meal. When the dinner plates had been cleared, espresso pots and demitasse cups were laid out with bottles of sambuco, anisette, Strega, and two large carafes of grapa.

Vinny leaned back and rubbed his stomach. "So, Joseph, Michael, some cookies or cheesecake? We got tortoni, spumoni, maybe some lemon ice?"

"Vinny, no thanks. It was delicious but I'm stuffed," I said leaning back in my chair.

"Me, too. What a meal, though. Thank you," Michael added.

"So, just lemon ice then, to clean the palate," Vinny insisted.

After dessert, Vinny told everyone to fill their glasses. When the bottles had all been resettled, he wiped the perspiration from his face and the back of his neck with his napkin, pushed himself up from his chair with a grunt and waited for the men at the table to give him their undivided attention.

"I wanna say a toast to our guests, and to a great man, Don Carmine Napolo, may God rest on his soul." He bowed his head and made the Sign of the Cross, kissing the tips of his thumb and forefinger when he finished. The hard-looking men at the table follow suit. Then raising his glass, he continued, "To men of honor and respect, living and dead, who have been our friends . . ." Then nodding to Michael and me, ". . . and to our new friends, salute."

The men at the table raised their glasses and responded in unison, "Salute."

"Now," Vinny said as he sat down. "I want to tell Joseph a story that I want you all to hear."

Several men at the far end of the table were speaking quietly to each other. Suddenly laughter erupted. Vinny smacked the table and swung his big head in their direction. The men, at once silent, looked up to see his bulging eyes and sneering mouth. One of them said, "Sorry, boss."

Vinny very slowly turned away, letting his anger linger with them until they had each looked away or down at their expressos.

"Okay," Vinny turned to me. "Back in the early '50's, when I was fifteen or sixteen years old, my mother got sick with cancer. She was suffering terribly. At night, in my bed I could hear her moaning and crying. And there was this fuckin' doctor sayin' there was nothing he could do for her. *Nothing.* You see, we were very poor. My father worked for old Mr. Abetamarco, the neighborhood grocer. He was a hard worker. He would start at four or five o'clock in the morning, seven days a week, to bake the bread and the pastries. Then he would meet Mr. Abetamarco at the market to help him carry the fresh produce, and the meats and fishes back to the grocery. At night, he would come home long after dark, so tired . . ." Vinny stopped and pursed his lips for a few seconds.

He cleared his throat and began again. "You see, my father loved my mother very much. She was his whole life. He begged and pleaded with this doctor to help her, but he refused because my father couldn't pay his bill. He said there was nothin' more he could do. So he just sent her home to die. My father couldn't stand to see her like that . . . in so much pain. He became bitter and angry, blaming himself because he couldn't pay for her proper care. He began to drink and not come home every night.

"Then one day, in the middle of the afternoon, he came running into the house so happy he was crying, tears on his cheeks. He ran to my mother's bed and held her hand and told her everything was going to be all right. Then he called me and my brother in and he just keep saying that everything was going to be alright and we all cried, tears on our cheeks.

"The next day, a private ambulance came to our apartment and took my mother to St. Vincent's Hospital. They put her in a private room and fresh flowers were delivered every morning. A team of the best doctors in New York operated on her, only after consulting with a specialist, a doctor from Bologna, Italy who flew over to see her. The whole time, a nurse sat at her bedside twenty-four hours a day, to give her medications and to see to her comfort. The cancer finally killed her. But her last weeks were made comfortable and dignified.

"At her funeral, which was a beautiful funeral, more than I knew my father could afford, I finally asked my father how he had been able to do what he had done for my mother. My father told me about a regular customer at the grocery who he had come to know, and then he took me over to a handsomely dressed gentleman sitting in the back row with two younger men at his side. My father told me that I should thank this man for all he had done for my mother. Which, of course, I did.

"When my father and this man walked away to talk, I asked the younger men with him who he was. They laughed at me and said, 'You don't know who Don Carmine is?' The next day, I made it my business to find out.

"Soon after the funeral, my father quit the grocery and we moved to a nicer apartment. We got a car and a television. Except for missing our mother, things were going great. One day, a year or so later, my father came home and told me that the fuckin' doctor who had refused to help my mother had been killed in an accident - a garment delivery truck had run him over in the street, like a fuckin' dog. God's way, he told me. A few years later, I think I was 17 or 18 years old, I also started working for Don Carmine. And now you know why I will be forever loyal to his memory and defend his name with my life."

I looked up from my espresso and caught Michael trying to look as serious as possible. No one spoke. There was nothing to say.

"What do you think of that, Joseph?" Vinny asked.

At that moment, I happened to be thinking that God had probably very little to do with the doctor getting run down by the garment delivery truck. Just before that, I had been wondering what my grandfather had required Vinny's father to do in return for his mother's medical treatment. A small favor or two? Or just one big favor?

"I'm glad your mother received the treatment she needed and that her suffering was minimized," I replied, almost clinically.

"And all because of your grandfather. You should be very proud."

"Oh, you don't know." I wanted to move on.

I realized Vinny was waiting on my next words, which didn't come. Then nodding sympathetically, he said, "I'm sure it's a difficult thing to say . . . in words. Ya know, with all us here, an' all."

"That's right, Vinny," I said solemnly, hoping to end the exchange.

Vinny closed his eyes and patted my forearm in a tender, almost fatherly way. I saw the corners of Michael's lips curl into a tiny, private smile. Then Vinny slapped his palms together and said loudly, "Alright boys, Joseph and I have some business. First, I gotta take a shit. Put these tables back where they belong so when I'm done we can talk in private." He turned to me. "Joseph, I'd like Jimmy to sit with us. Awright?"

"Sure," I shrugged. "Michael, too. Okay?"

Vinny waved a no-problem-wave as he hurried off to the men's room. Michael and I sat at the table with Jimmy. We didn't talk, but I know that the way men conduct themselves during uncomfortable silences speaks loudly about their character, and I was sure Jimmy was studying me. So I went to school, too.

Jimmy looked to be in his late thirties. He had thick, wavy dark brown hair neatly combed straight back. His face was a familiar type; smooth olive skin, soft brown eyes with lazy lids, centered by a classic Roman nose. He was trim and fit, though not bulky. One of those guys that looked neat and pressed no matter what they wore. I thought he would probably be considered good-looking, although except for extraordinarily handsome or really ugly guys, I was never any good at judging other men's looks. I sensed Jimmy was smart - smart enough to make sure that he was being perceived as a genuinely warm and friendly guy. So when he smiled cordially, I decided to watch him carefully. He was obviously Vinny's trusted aid. There were reasons for that, and good looks and charm were not the only important ones.

"You guys getting to know each other?" Vinny said, as he sat down.

Jimmy winked at me and said, "I think we are, Vinny."

"Good. Now let's hear more about this problem Tommy Ton was tellin' me about. A little problem with the outcome of a few sporting events?"

"It's my problem," Michael said.

"Oh, I know it is," Vinny said. "Joseph probably knows better than to bet on things you have no control over. Don't you, Joseph."

"I never enjoyed gambling."

"How much you into Tommy Ton for?" Vinny asked Michael.

"Something over a hundred grand, with the vig."

"Aw, fuggedaboudit," Vinny said, holding up the fleshy palms of his hands.

"We've offered to pay the original amount without the vig, about eighty grand," I said.

"You heard me, Joseph. I said, fuggedaboudit."

"Eighty grand's still a lot of money," Michael said.

"Whathefuck?" Vinny huffed, turning to Merchanti. "Jimmy, don't they speak fuckin' English in Jersey anymore? I haven't been there in a while. Maybe Jersey ain't even part of America anymore. Help me here. Tell these guys I said *fuggedaboudit!*"

Jimmy touched his thumb to his first and second fingers and shook them. "Guys, Vinny said fuggedaboudit. You don't owe nobody nothin'. Understand?"

I had to chuckle. "Oh, sorry, Vinny. I think we've been watching too many movies. That's very generous, much more than we expected. Thank you. You can do that?"

"It's already done."

Michael said, "Really Vinny, that's ah, incredible. Thank you. Thank you very much."

"You should thank Joseph for being your friend. This is for him, not for you. You and me ain't done talkin' yet."

Vinny hunched over the table to get his face closer to Michael. "Listen to me, Michael. Why do you think we're in the bookmaking business? Because we lose money? Fuck no. We make money, big money, on stupid fucks like you. You can't beat the odds, Michael. If that was the case, we'd be outta business. Right?"

"I guess so."

"You *guess* so?"

Vinny shook his head and sat back. "Jimmy. Joseph," he panted. "What are we gonna do with this fuckin' guy? *I guess so*, he says. It don't sound like he's learned his lesson. First, he loses big, bigger than he can pay. Then, he goes and *guesses* he can play around with a scumbag like Johnny Onions and come out a winner." Turning to Michael. "Well, you lost, again! And you're still saying, *I guess so?*"

Although I found myself enjoying Vinny's tirade, I thought it was time to rescue Michael and get down to business. "Vinny, Michael has already agreed to give up gambling under stiff contractual terms that will cost him dearly, if he defaults."

"Who's this *contract* with, Joseph?"

"Me."

Vinny thought a moment. "Well, okay. But, now you're gonna hear the terms of *my* contract, Michael. Since your bad luck has caused my good friend Joseph trouble, Jimmy's gonna put the word out – no one's gonna take any of your action. And, if they do, they'll answer to me. And, if you try to bet on anything, anywhere – even a fuckin' high school football game, and I find out, fuggedaboudit. First, I'll tell Joseph, and then you and me are gonna have another talk, a *serious* talk." Vinny turned his head to me so Michael couldn't see him wink his right eye. "Okay with you Joseph?"

"Fine by me."

Vinny turned back to Michael. "Anything about this you don't understand?"

"No. I understand," Michael said, sheepishly.

"Alright, then, let's talk about Johnny Onions. Jimmy, tell 'em what we know about this cocksucker."

"Well, first you guys should know that there's some history here, some bad blood between Vinny and Johnny. A few years ago, Vinny's brother, Sal – you know, he ate we us tonight, well he and Johnny were runnin' a thing in Jersey with . . ."

Vinny let his demitasse cup fall loudly onto the saucer. "Jimmy, cum'on for chrissake, we don't need all the fuckin' details here."

Jimmy looked at me and raised his eyebrows as he began again. "Well, anyway, Johnny made a side deal that went bad and it came back on Sal. Vinny took some serious shit from our friends in Jersey. They forced Vinny to make retributions. Sal had to stand up for it and he did eighteen months upstate. And one of Sal's guys had to disappear from the earth."

"Now tell them what happened to Johnny Onions," Vinny said.

"Nothin'. As usual, Johnny was playing both sides and he got protected. Even so, since then Johnny don't come across the river from Jersey too often, right Vinny."

"Fuckin' right he don't," Vinny added.

"Now, this is what we know about this thing yesterday," Jimmy continued. "First, Johnny slides in between Tommy Ton and Michael here; tries to make out on something he's got nothing to do with. He drags in one of our guys, they go back awhile and he needs him to drive your rig that they're gonna take – tells him they're set up for a truckload of shoes. As you guys know, there was no fuckin' shoes. Just some kinda metal crate, something for the military. The two of 'em try to get it open but, after a few minutes, Johnny tells our guy Dominick that they can't stay in the warehouse too long, like he's nervous about somethin'. So Dominick, dumb fuck that he was, he leaves Johnny with the crate, like you can believe anything Johnny says.

"Then last night, Vinny sends Dominick and another guy over to see Johnny, at his place in Hackensack. And, unless you've been asleep all day, you know what happened there."

"This motherfucker," Vinny added, lips curling over his teeth. "In the afternoon, he's your partner. A few hours later, he's tyin' ya up like a fuckin' bracioli and shootin' ya in the head."

"What can you guys tell us?" Jimmy asked.

I swept my hand toward Michael. "Go ahead, tell them what you know," I said.

"Everything you said was true except that there really *was* a truckload of shoes. The trailer numbers for the two loads were similar. Both trucks were in the rest stop and Johnny took the wrong one. He *was* expecting shoes to be in that trailer. He has no idea what's in that crate. Neither do we, for that matter, other than it's highly classified government hardware. We do a lot of DOD high security hauling."

"What's DOD?" Vinny asked.

"Department of Defense," I replied. "We're an approved DOD carrier, which means we get a lot of work from defense contractors and various branches of the military and other government agencies. This crate, though, is apparently very sensitive. The FBI's involved, as a matter of national security. It's very serious, Vinny. We need to get this thing, this crate, back to them."

"National security? The Feds? Jesus Christ, that asshole really fucked up this time," Vinny hissed.

"Johnny called me last night, all pissed off," Michael continued. "He thinks I fucked him over – like I did this on purpose."

"He called you *last night?*" Jimmy jumped in. "What time?"

"About nine or so. I told him that it was *his* mistake and that I was done dealing with him, that I would square with Tommy Ton directly. He didn't like that and told me that I'd be done dealing with him when *he* said I was done."

"Then what," Vinny probed.

"I hung up on him. He tried to reach me several times at the office today but we were out when he called."

Vinny rubbed his forehead and then looked over at Jimmy. A silent sidebar ensued, with both men making slight facial contortions as they thought.

Vinny finally said, "As far as I'm concerned, Johnny Anelli's a dead man. After last night, no one's gonna get in my way. He's outlived his protection. Eventually we'll find this motherfucker. The word's out. Someone'll call us. And that'll solve both our problems." Then, after a breathy, garlic belch, he said, "But I think Michael can help us here, don't you Jimmy?"

"What can *I* do?" Michael asked.

"He's not gonna let go of you just 'cause you said so," Jimmy snickered. "Johnny's gonna be reachin' out for you. Believe me. We know how this goes – he's gonna try to work you. You heard him last night. And he needs you right now 'cause he ain't got no one else. He'll be in touch with you again. Probably, soon."

"Listen to Jimmy. He's right," Vinny said. "Johnny don't have two nickels. You're one guy he'll be thinkin' he can squeeze a little, maybe a lot. But, when he contacts you again, you put him off – make an excuse, have him call you back, and then call Jimmy. That'll give us time to set up."

"Then what?" I asked.

"Whadaya think?" Jimmy said.

I swung my head in Jimmy's direction. "*I* think there's another issue here. We need to get the government back its hardware and Johnny's the only one who knows where it is."

"Fuck the government!" Vinny shouted. "That's their fuckin' problem. We're gonna take care of *our* problem and then we all go on with our lives, without ever havin' to think about that fuck Johnny Onions again."

I was having a couple problems with the way things were going. First, we were about to become key players in a mob execution. Second, without the crate we were was still exposed to the FBI's threats. Neither situation was acceptable.

I said, "Vinny, my grandfather did your family a favor once. Now I need a favor from you, for my family. I need to get that crate back."

Vinny sat back and looked at Jimmy, who shrugged. Then, in a warm voice, he said, "Joseph, I can promise a lotta things. I'm a guy that can make a lotta things happen. But, some things, ya know – all I can tell ya is, well . . . lemme think a minute."

It was Michael's and my turn to have a speechless conference. After a few seconds, Michael raised his eyebrows and cocked his head, the Irish devil sparkling in his eyes. I squinted at him. There was something congealing in Michael's mind, and I wasn't sure, but I was afraid that . . .

I felt my eyes widen as I remembered the million dollars. I began to mouth the word, *NO*. But it was too late. Michael was smiling and looking at Vinny and Jimmy.

"Ya know," Michael began, calmly. "The FBI's offering a million dollar reward for the return of that crate,"

I closed his eyes and let a low moan escape. I couldn't believe it. Throwing a million dollars on this table was like offering sight to a blind man. Nothing else would matter now.

"What?" Vinny asked, even though he had heard it clearly.

"Wait a minute!" I blurted. "This is a mistake. The agent who told us this was, in my opinion, not to be trusted. There was something wrong with that guy and his deal. I'm absolutely certain about that, and Michael knows it, too." I leaned in to him. "Don't you, Michael?"

"Hey, you already know what I think," Michael responded, avoiding my glare. "The FBI's the FBI. If you can't trust them, then who?"

"Vinny, I gotta agree with Joseph," Jimmy interjected. "We need to know a lot more about this thing before we can get involved with the Feds. We don't need any a their shit right now."

"Jimmy, who said anything about *us* gettin' involved with the Feds?" Vinny said. "I think even Michael knows that *that* wouldn't be a good idea. But what's stoppin' Michael from gettin' our friend Johnny Onions involved. He's a greedy fuck. He won't be able to pass it up. Whadaya think, Joseph? This could work out just fine. The government gets its crate back like you want, we whack up the million bucks, and Johnny, leave him to us - we'll take care a him."

I couldn't stop staring at Michael. Not even long enough to respond to Vinny.

Michael took a deep breath and said, "Joseph, I know you're uncomfortable with this, so maybe you should just stay out of it. Let me work with Vinny and Jimmy. It's all my fault anyway. If anything happens, you know nothing about it."

Vinny leaned forward. "Hey, sure, that's not a problem, Joseph. You don't wanna be involved, okay, we understand. We'll work with Michael and let you know when it's done. Awright?"

I looked around the table. The three of them, collectively pretending to be waiting for my response, my approval, was a laughable sight. They knew as well as I did that there were no words, nothing I could say, that would change their minds.

"Okay, I'm out of it," I acquiesced. "But, for the record, I don't think you guys should go anywhere near this FBI thing. And, Michael, as you said, I don't wanna know anything about it. Not a word after we leave here tonight. I do hope you get the crate back. I'll be grateful for that. But, that's all I'd ever want from this. You guys can split the million dollars, if you collect it."

"Then no hard feelings, eh?" Vinny asked me.

"No hard feelings."

"No matter what happens, right?" Vinny probed, just to be sure there would be no offense, no disrespect, and no misunderstanding.

I waved a hand. "Whatever. Just leave me out of it." Then turning to Michael, I said, "You're on your own here, pal."

"I know," Michael nodded, avoiding having to look me straight in the eye.

I waited until Michael had stopped bobbing his head. "And, by the way, you're a real asshole."

Michael looked me in the eye and, for the first time in over twenty-five years, did not respond. I heard him loud and clear.

## Stewart International Airport
## New Windsor, New York

Lincoln had locked himself in the old brick building at the end of runway North 1A and armed his array of doubled-backed security devices that virtually sealed him inside an electronic cocoon, but he was feeling unsettled - pacing, waiting for a phone call. At exactly eleven p.m. the satellite phone rang. He walked quickly behind the large table that served as his desk but hesitated to pick up the phone. He hated to dance and, without the hard answers he needed, when he answered the phone he was going to have to do a good jig.

After the third ring he snatched up the handset. "Have you reached the correct number?" he said, listening for the electronic encryption tones. Ten seconds later he said, "Good evening."

"Good morning, you mean, it's seven a.m. here. It's a new day. Do you have news for me that will ensure it is a happy one?"

Lincoln wasn't sure which he hated more; the caller's accent or his self-assured tone. Both were equally grating, he decided.

He said, "I will be able to make you extremely happy no later than Friday of this week."

"Two days from now?" The caller was obviously displeased. "This is unacceptable and in default of our agreement. What is the reason for this?"

"The reason is none of your business. You only have to be concerned with your end of this deal. How do I know you have the money?"

"I wish you would not use such childish tactics to evade my questions. If you checked, which I'm sure you have, your Luxembourg banker should have told you that I have met my commitment. Now please respond to my question, like an adult."

"Who the fuck do you think you are?" Lincoln seized the opportunity to continue his evasion.

"In the most forthright verbiage I can think of, I am the person who has you by the balls, Mr. *Aaron Lincoln*."

Lincoln jerked the handset away from his face and stared at it for several seconds before returning it slowly to his ear. "How do you know my name?" He asked slowly, to mask his trepidation.

"Please understand, Mr. Lincoln, that my benefactor is very careful about who he does business with. As his representative, I am responsible to know certain things, everything - in fact, about the associations I bring to him. Therefore, I would be negligent if I did not know all I need to know about you. This is just good business, Mr. Lincoln. Wouldn't you agree, Mr. Lincoln?" The caller was purposely repeating his name, taunting him.

Slowly lowering himself into his chair, Lincoln sensed his breath quickening and fought to control the rising panic that caused it. He covered the mouthpiece with the palm of his hand and drew a deep breath. Then, unable to formulate a response that was both logical and retaliatory, he blurted, "The deal's off! I'm withdrawing the item. You have *me* by the balls? Think, again. Your money didn't even get warm in Luxembourg. It's four banks and two continents away by now, waiting for the only person in the world who knows where it is, me. You and your benefactor and the camels you rode in on can go fuck yourselves."

"Really, Mr. Lincoln. Are the Turks and Caicos Islands actually *two* continents away from Europe? I think not, Mr. Lincoln. Now let's stop with these foolish outbursts and get on with our business."

Lincoln felt a blast of heat, rushing to the top of his head. Perspiration formed on his upper lip and brow. Who was he dealing with? His bank routings had never been compromised before. They had been cleverly, and very expensively, designed to be invisible transactions, lost amidst the thousands of US Dollar wire transfers that crisscrossed the globe twenty-four hours a day.

"Mr. Lincoln, are you still there?"

Lincoln focused to recompose himself. He was trained to strategically withdraw, to retreat if necessary, and live to fight another day. "Okay, you son of a bitch. Let's talk turkey."

"Turkey? Why do you suggest Turkey? It is not a friendly state for my benefactor to do business in. Turkey is unacceptable! I will not entertain any further deviations from our original plan!"

"Forget it. Relax, I made a mistake," Lincoln surrendered. He just wanted to end the conversation. "But Friday's the best I can do. Take it or leave it."

"Well, then . . . okay, Friday it will be. However, Mr. Lincoln, there will be no more extensions. If I do not receive confirmation of delivery from my Lufthansa agent at Newark Airport by seventeen hundred hours Friday, your time, our contract is terminated. Is that clear."

"English is *my* first language."

"Good for you, Mr. Lincoln. Then you will also understand when I tell you that my benefactor accepts news of unfinished business with an ill temper. He will react poorly to your failure to deliver. His instructions to me will be of the most final consequences for you."

"That's the second time you've threatened me," Lincoln spat between clenched teeth.

"Just to be sure we understand each other. No offense is intended, Mr. Lincoln."

Lincoln struggled to control himself, not wanting to further dilute his position with an uncontrolled explosion of murderous invectives that were teetering on the tip of his tongue. Summoning a tone of indifference, he said, "Do we need to speak again before Friday?"

"No, so if you have anything else for me to know, let me hear it now. But please be brief, Mr. Lincoln, my breakfast is ready."

"Choke on it."

Lincoln heard the caller laughing as he slammed down the phone but his attentions had already moved on to a more critical matter. Slowly, like fingers over Braille, his eyes groped the walls and ceiling of his fortified quarters. Was someone there with him, silently observing him, exposing him, mocking, and snickering at him? Was there new technology that he had failed to guard against? Had some revolutionary combination of photoelectrons and powerful computing been used to penetrate his digital world? Or, was it something that predated all technology – a human source. Was that possible after all these years? Not one person, still living, knew more than one partition in the labyrinth of deception he had diligently constructed. Yet, this camel jockey . . .

The cell phone on his desk rang, collapsing his thoughts. "Yeah?"

"Sir, this is Tailgate Two. Our video surveillance of the New York location has recorded something interesting. Can we upload it to you?"

"Hold on." Lincoln tapped his keyboard and his laptop jumped to life. After a few more keystrokes he picked up the phone and said, "Send it."

Lincoln waited while the file downloaded, anxious to see what the remote camera had recorded. When the video camera icon popped onto the screen, he clicked on it and a black and white infrared image appeared. It was the sidewalk and entranceway in front of Taverna Reggia. The date and time stamped across the bottom of the screen told him the recording was made at nine forty-eight this evening. He clicked on the play button. The image flickered but remained the unchanged for about ten seconds. Then the door to Taverna Reggia opened and a large man came out through the gate and walked up the stairs to the sidewalk. After checking the street in both directions, he went back down to the open door where two men now stood with their backs to the camera, obviously talking and then shaking hands with men inside the doorway. The two men turned and started up the steps. The large man closed the gate behind them and then disappeared inside, closing the door behind him. Lincoln squinted at the screen, trying to see what his men had found so interesting. Then, when the two men had reached the sidewalk, the headlights of a passing car illuminated their faces. Quickly, Lincoln clicked on the pause button and pushed the pointer to the toolbar on top of the screen. He selected a drop-down box and enlarged the image to five hundred percent. The monitor blinked and the faces came into focus.

"Napolo and Cogan," Lincoln said to himself.

He sat back in his chair and smiled.

## Monmouth Beach, New Jersey

I walked around the front of Michael's Explorer and stepped up on the curb in front of my house. I heard the window motoring down behind me. When Michael called my name I hesitated before turning back to the truck.

I said, "It looks like my tires are fixed."

"Yeah, looks like."

"So I'll tell everyone you're taking some time," I said, continuing the awkward small talk.

On the way home, we had agreed that Michael would not come back to work until the business with Vinny and Johnny and the FBI was finished. One way or the other, it would be over in a few days. Either way, I had made it clear that I wanted no further involvement for myself or the company.

"They're gonna think it's a strange time for me to take off, with the union stuff and all. Should we tell them something else?"

"Like what?"

"Like, ah . . . oh, I don't know."

"At this point, I think the less said the better."

Michael nodded and looked down at his lap. I felt myself turning away again, but I pulled around and extended my hand through the open window. When Michael grabbed hold and we locked eyes. I squeezed hard and said, "Good luck, man."

In the dashboard light, a moist film on Michael's eyes sparkled. When he blinked, tiny tears clung to the ledges of his lower eyelids.

He cleared his throat and said, "Thanks, man."

I spun away quickly and walked into my house. When I had closed the door and was twisting the deadbolt closed, I looked out through the windowpanes on the side of the door. The street was dark and empty, and lonely. Michael was gone.

*        *        *

"How'd it go?" Cathy was heading down the stairs in her bathrobe. "Were you guys able to settle anything?"

I had nearly forgotten that I had told her we were going to a meeting with the union. Now I needed to avoid giving her any details, which would be furthering the lie.

"No. Just a lot of the usual posturing that leads to nothing except another meeting."

Cathy was at the bottom of the stairs now and she hugged me. "I'm sorry, honey. I know this thing is really upsetting you. You look exhausted."

"I'm fine. It's been a long day, that's all."

I pulled her close and ran my hands down her back and over her buttocks. She was naked under the robe and freshly powdered after her shower. Her damp hair smelled like lilacs. I filled my lungs with a long, slow breath, letting the clean smell of her wash me. I kissed the top of her head and when she looked up my lips wandered down her face until I found her mouth. We kissed softly at first and then harder and deeper. Maybe it was our being in the foyer, or knowing that one of the kids could unexpectedly wake and appear at the top of the stairs, or the familiarity of the kiss and the knowledge that this was a prelude we no longer needed to doubt or rush lest it go unfulfilled. Maybe we stopped because of all of those reasons.

"I love you," I whispered in her ear as she nuzzled my neck with her face.

"Mmmm, me too," she cooed.

I pulled back a little, not wanting to let go, and said, "Hey, tell me about little Joseph's awards dinner. How'd he do?"

Her eyes twinkled. "Oh, you would've been so proud of him. He won the Cappy Barnes Award."

"The what?"

"The Cappy Barnes Award. His coaches and teammates voted him the most sportsmanlike player. That's the Cappy Barnes Award. It's a very big deal. He got a big trophy. He tried to wait up for you, so you guys could decide where it should go on his shelves. Let's go upstairs and see if you can wake him up for a minute."

I let her go up the stairs ahead of me, as I shut the lights and double-checked that I had locked the door. Cathy turned and waited for me at the top of the stairs. She hadn't bothered to tighten her robe after our embrace and now it hung loosely, exposing the deep cleavage of her breasts and a creamy left thigh. When I reached the top step, she put her hands on my shoulders and whispered, "Go kiss your kids and meet me in the bedroom. I might even turn on some of that damn country music." Sliding her bare leg between mine, she smiled seductively and added, "Lock the door when you come in."

I kissed her. "You got a date, but gimme a minute. I've gotta go back down and make a quick call. I should check on things at the terminal."

Downstairs in the kitchen, I took a glass from the cabinet and let the tap water run on my finger until it was cold, as cold as I knew it would get. My thoughts drifted toward Michael, but I quickly let him go. It was too late to let all the impressions and emotions of this day come rushing forward. Their stamp would be indelible, forever changing things, as every day changes the next. But I knew, as it is with all difficult things, that ruminations of all pending issues and unpredictable consequences were best left to the light of a new day.

However, some things can't wait for tomorrow. Some things are better done in the dark. I filled the glass and held it up to look through the crystal clear water. Between mouthfuls, I pulled a slip of paper from my pocket and dialed Ron Laskowski's home number.

Three rings later, a groggy voice answered. "Hullo?"

"Ron, this is Joseph Napolo. Earlier today, I told you what would happen if you continued to harass my family, didn't I?"

"What?" Laskowski was waking up. "What are you talking about?"

"I just had a couple of your men in my driveway honking their horn and shouting obscenities. They woke my family. Scared my kids."

"I don't know what you're talking about. We've got nothing to do with this."

"That's bullshit, Ron."

"Oh yeah, well maybe some of my guys were pissed off about that helicopter stunt you pulled today. Ever think of that?"

"Ron, here's what I think. Grown men scaring women and children in the middle of the night is depraved and cowardly. One more time and the gloves are comin' off. You hear me?"

"Joseph, let's talk in the morning. Lemme find out what's goin' on. I honesty don't know nothin' about this."

"You better straighten this out, Ron. Fucking with my business is one thing. Fucking with my *family* is a whole different story. Remember what I told you two today."

"Awright! Awright! Anything else?"

"Yeah, I'm waiting, Ron."

"You're waitin'? Waitin' for what?"

"For an apology, Ron. Something like, I'm sorry. Sorry that I can't control my men. Sorry that members of *my* Local disturbed *your* evening. Very, *very* sorry that your wife and kids were afraid of the mean men in the driveway. Something like *that*, Ron."

Laskowski sighed, "Sorry, Joseph."

Hoping Laskowski wouldn't hear the smile on my face, I said, "Good night, Ron."

I went up the stairs two at a time, each step making me lighter, taking me further from Laskowski and Catella, away from Tommy Ton and Vinny Diamonds, far from Special Agent Clifford Dwyer. They would all be there in the morning, waiting for me, but for now I had more important things to attend to.

Little Joseph wouldn't wake to my light taps on his shoulder and my daddy-is-very-proud-of-you whispers in his ear. So I sat on his bed for a few minutes holding the trophy, using my sleeve to wipe the smudges off the brass plate that read "Joseph Napolo III" and then to blot the proud-father tears that had welled in my eyes. I looked in on the two younger ones, kissed their cheeks and covered them to their chins, tucking them tight as if the night could creep under their blankets and darken their hearts. Little Mickey smiled at me in his sleep.

As I walked down the hallway, Michael came into my head again, and with him a parade of doubt. Should I have protested more loudly and insisted that Michael not pursue the FBI's bounty? Maybe I should have used my new-found influence with Vinny and demanded that Michael not get involved. Had my easy acquiescence to their wishes been a matter of convenience – an easy way out for me? Did I simply throw Michael to the wolves hoping he would come home unscathed, knowing the odds were against it? Was I the friend I professed to be?

I found myself standing outside our bedroom door. Inside, Cathy had the radio on. A whining pedal steel guitar and a lonely fiddle wept a sad cowboy melody. The singer's rich, deep voice resonated with pain and sorrow. I stood in the hallway and listened.

*Remember the old stage*
*From Dodge to Santa Fe?*

*We robbed it one day*
*Twenty years ago May,*
*And a boy made his play,*
*Pulled his gun, took a stand,*
*I left him cold dead in the sand.*

*And why's it always too late when you learn,*
*That you're only gonna get what you deserve,*
*And there's never any changin'*
*Those mistakes of your agin',*
*Why's it always too late when you learn.*

Some music had a way of taking me back to my teenage years and first loves lost, and the long days after a break up when every song on the radio spoke to your pain. Was I so starved for an intellectual resolution to this day's events that I was seeking emotional shelter in country music lyrics? Jesus, I was too old for that. But, the song sang a truth, because what's past does indeed become forever unchangeable.

I stepped back from the door and leaned against the wall. I pushed both hands into my hair and let my fingertips roughly knead my scalp. There was no way I could abandon Michael – no matter what he's done. I was closer to Michael than my own brother. There's a lot of history there. I met Cathy through Michael. It was junior year. Michael and Cathy had been dating for a month or so, maybe even sleeping together. I suspected so, but never asked because I was smitten and never wanted to know. Still don't. Michael did the right thing and stepped aside. Then Cathy introduced Michael to Ilene and the rest is history. Three years after graduation, we married seven months apart. Since then we've spent holidays and family vacations together. Godparents to each other's children. Adoptive parents in each others' wills. Michael might have his problems, but he would never let me down when it came to the kids. And maybe Michael was just trying to do what he thought was the right thing; clean up his own mess, save face, protect his marriage, salvage our friendship - Damon and Pythias.

I looked down the hall at the doors of my children's bedrooms. What would I tell them if they asked? What would they learn from me about loyalty and love and truth of heart? Who was I kidding? There was no way I could so simply extricate myself from what had happened and just sit back, above it all, hoping for a conclusion that suited me. Life didn't work that way, and neither did true friendship.

I exhaled loudly and a low groan escaped. I had no choice. The right thing to do now was to find a plan, anticipate the obvious and prepare for the worst. I needed to be ready to help Michael and do what needed to be done. Whatever that was.

But no quick comfort arrived.

Not until Cathy called, "Joseph, come to bed."

## Starlight Motor Lodge
## South Amboy, New Jersey

Johnny Onions felt the ache in his head before he woke up, wincing in the half-sleep where we share our real life pain and suffering with our dreams. He was unable to prevent the slow return to consciousness and with it the full impact of his headache. The effect of the handful of Tylenol he had swallowed earlier had worn off and, if anything, the pain was worse. While he slept, night had fallen but the bathroom light dimly lit the room. He glanced at his wristwatch on the nightstand. It was almost midnight. He had been asleep for almost five hours.

Swinging his legs off the bed, he started to get up, but as he rose the room spun wildly. Johnny closed his eyes to steady himself, pinching his eyelids tightly against the motion and the shooting pains that were piercing his brain. The spinning didn't stop, though, and his stomach began contracting in nauseous spasms. Gulping air through his mouth to combat the bile rising into his esophagus, he stumbled into the bathroom. There, the light from the naked fluorescent bulb punctured his squinted eyes like hatpins boring through to the back of his skull. He reeled back and a powerful fountain of vomit arched through the air hitting the mirror above the sink, sending pale chunky matter ricocheting onto every surface in the dingy bathroom. Johnny heaved again, this time on the floor between his feet.

He made it back to the bed and rinsed his mouth out with flat Diet Pepsi from the can on his nightstand. Then he ripped open two packets of the Tylenol he had bought from the vending machine in the lobby and chased them down with another mouthful. The vomiting had stopped the spinning, but the stench from the bathroom was threatening to make him sick again. He opened the door to his room for ventilation and began stuffing his things into his suitcase. When he finished, he slipped the Beretta into the pocket of his Members Only jacket, leaving his hand firmly around the grip while he leaned out his door and checked the parking lot. Nothing appeared strange about the strangers in the lot so he limped to his El Dorado and left the Starlight Motor Lodge.

Luckily, he didn't have far to go. The Highway Motor Lodge was directly across Route 35. It was almost identical to the Starlight. Same circular single-story design. Same-looking Indian guy behind the bulletproof glass in the lobby. Same vending machine, selling mostly condoms and few toiletries. And, no doubt, the same shitty rooms with the same shitty beds. However, Johnny was pleasantly surprised to find it was cheaper than the Starlight. Only twenty-nine dollars a night.

"How come the Starlight's two bucks more a night than this place? You got TV's here?" Johnny asked suspiciously.

"Of course. Color." The Indian guy looked insulted.

"You got the dirty movies like the Starlight?"

"Closed circuit. All night, just like them." The Indian guy smiled.

Johnny leaned closer to slot at the bottom of the glass. "So how come you're two bucks less?"

"Price war."

"What?"

"Price war."

"Oh yeah, like the gas stations." Johnny passed thirty dollars through the slot. "So who's winning?"

The Indian guy shrugged. "I don't know. I only work here two days a week."

"Maybe you should start servin' free coffee in the morning. That'd bring 'em in."

The Indian guy rolled his eyes. "Yeah, sure. I'll tell the boss."

Johnny took his room key from the slot and headed toward the door. Then he turned back to the clerk. "Does the soda machine take bills?"

"Sometimes. You come back here if it doesn't take your dollar."

Johnny nodded. "So where doya work the rest of the week?"

The Indian guy motioned across the street. "The Starlight. Same guy owns both places."

"I thought you looked familiar."

After Johnny had thrown his suitcase on the bed in his room, he walked back to the lobby and got five dollars in quarters from the Indian guy. Johnny hated feeding singles into vending machines; never seemed to work for him. He bought five packets of Tylenol and a Diet Pepsi. On the way back to his room, he stopped at the bank of payphones mounted to the wall outside the lobby. He found Michael's number crumbled up in his back pocket.

The phone rang three times before Michael answered sleepily.

"Hullo?"

"You know who this is?" Johnny asked.

Michael recognized the raspy voice. "Yeah. I'm - ah, glad you called. Hold on."

Johnny heard the muffled sounds of Michael telling Ilene that it was the terminal calling and that he was going to take the call downstairs. He waited.

"I've got it, honey." Then, when the phone clicked, signaling that the bedroom extension had been hung up, Michael said, "I was hoping you'd call."

"Oh yeah, why's that?"

"There have been some developments that I need to discuss with you."

"So discuss."

"I can't. Not here. Not now. Can you meet me tomorrow morning?"

Johnny had planned on having to force Michael to meet, threatening him, if necessary. He was unprepared for this invitation.

"What's this about? Why do *you* want to see *me* all of a sudden? Maybe things didn't work out with Tommy Ton the way you thought they would, huh?"

"I told you. There are some new developments."

"Whathefuck does that mean? You gotta gimme somethin' now. I don't have no time to fuck around with you."

Michael thought for a moment. "Okay, let's just say that with what I think *you have* and what *I know,* we can make a lot of money, quick."

"What's a lot?"

"We spilt seven figures."

Johnny's interest had been piqued, but he didn't like the eagerness in Michael's voice. "I dunno. Where?"

"Anywhere you want. But it's gotta be tomorrow. Time is of the essence."

Johnny massaged the back of his head. The pain was thunderous. It sounded too good, too convenient to him. This could be a setup. He needed a place that he was familiar with, where he could spot a trap.

"Okay, met me at the old Amboy Iron Works factory on State Street in Perth Amboy. You know where that is, off 440, the State Street exit? It's the last exit before the Outerbridge Crossing"

"I'll find it. What time?"

"After lunch. Say one o'clock, in the back lot. Just park around back and wait for me."

"I'll be there."

Again, Johnny heard Michael's enthusiasm. He didn't like it. It was making his headache worse. "You better be. And, you better be alone."

"Don't worry about it," Michael said, assuredly. "Relax, it's cool."

*Relax? It's cool?* This guy thinks I'm scared, Johnny thought. "Hey, you read the papers today?"

"Yeah, I did." Michael's tone indicated he knew that Johnny was referring to the hit in his apartment.

"Well, then you know I'm the wrong person to fuck with. I see anyone else there, cops, anyone, they'll be reading about *you* in the papers. You understand?"

"Yeah, I understand."

"One more thing. I'm gonna need a little, ah, call it an advance on our business deal. Say five large."

"Five hundred dollars?"

"Five thousand."

"Five thousand dollars!" Michael stammered. "I can't . . . "

"Fuck that *you can't* shit!" Johnny exploded. "You bring the fuckin' money or we got nothin' to discuss, except maybe what *I* wanna talk about. And remember this - the way I see it, we're partners in this shit, and I'm the *senior* partner. And when partners disagree, it can get real nasty for the junior guy. So you better come alone and bring the fuckin' money!"

"Okay," Michael sighed. "I'll, ah . . ."

"Good. See ya t'morrow, *partner.*"

Johnny returned to his room and locked himself in, placing a chair under the door handle, knowing it would give him another second or two to react to an intruder, time enough to roll off the bed and take aim with his Beretta. In the bathroom, he turned on the shower, stripped off his clothes, and angled the bathroom door so the full-length mirror on the door reflected a view of the door to his room. Stepping carefully into the tub, he rechecked the mirror. The angle was wrong, so he stepped out and closed the door slightly. This time it was perfect. He could stand under the hot water and see the door to his room in the mirror.

While he let the shower massage the back of his head and neck, Johnny inspected his body. The cuts on his hands and knees were minor, more like scratches with a few deep scrapes. His elbow had been sore all day, but he was surprised by how swollen it was and how the bruising had spread halfway down his forearm. Gently cupping his scrotum, he winced when he thought of how hard he had slammed onto the edge of the tub. To the touch, they were still tender and the left one felt enlarged. Then, his big toe started to sting from the shower water so he peeled off the bandage he had applied in the Thrift Drug parking lot. He grimaced when he saw what was left of his toenail. A small jagged piece protruded from the base of the nail. The rest of the area was raw and pulpy. He put his weight on his heel to keep the toe out of the water and closed his eyes to let the hot water work its magic as his aching body.

After a few minutes the water started to get cold, forcing Johnny out of the shower. The bath towels were just as thin and scratchy as the ones at the Starlight but at least they were a little bigger. He found that if he wrapped the towel around his hips, under his belly, he could actually tuck the ends together. Lifting his injured big toe so it wouldn't touch the matted shag carpet, he hopped over to the bed and opened his suitcase. He rummaged around inside looking for the Thrift Drug bag containing the gauze and surgical tape he had bought. He quickly became impatient and dumped the contents of his suitcase onto the bed. Still no Thrift Drug bag. Then he remembered that he had left it in the car.

Johnny grabbed his car keys, cinched the towel tighter around his hips, and pulled the chair from under the doorknob. Walking on the side of his foot to keep his toe elevated, he hobbled over to his car, which was parked directly outside his door. As he fumbled with his car keys, he heard a door slam. Instinctively, he ducked, crouching behind his car. The bending action stretched his girth and pulled the ends of the towel apart. He felt it slip loose and fall to the ground, but he was too busy looking around the parking lot, trying to make sure his ass was covered, to worry about covering his ass.

Unable to see any immediate threat, he cursed himself for leaving his room without the Beretta. He picked up the towel and held it over his crotch as he ran to his room. Looking furtively over his shoulder, he twisted the doorknob but the handle didn't turn. Then, realizing that it was *this* door, the door to his room that had slammed close, and that he was now locked out, Johnny crashed his fist into the door and screamed, "Son of a bitch motherfucker!"

# Chapter 14

## Wednesday Morning
## DTC Transportation
## Edison, NJ

After receiving the call at 3:18 a.m., it had taken me less than forty-five minutes to reach the terminal. The fire was out by the time I got there. As I drove into the yard I noticed the heavy gate chain had been cut, probably by the Fire Department. I parked by the office and walked through a snake pit of fire hoses, trying to avoid the puddles on the blacktop. The air was chilly and the light wind was thick with the smell of burnt rubber, chemicals, and hot steel. The wet macadam reflected the pulsing red and blue lights from the fire trucks and other emergency vehicles, rendering the scene all the more surreal and carnival. I could see three firefighting teams at the business end of their hoses pouring water onto the smoldering remains of two of our Freightliners. Spray from their hoses misted in the wind and flickered red, white, and blue as I approached a group of uniforms standing in the headlights of a police cruiser.

"Gentlemen, I'm Joseph Napolo. One of the owners."

The men opened their circle to allow me a space. One of them, a middle-aged firefighter with a bushy gray mustache, leaned forward with his hand extended.

"I'm Deputy Fire Chief Dave Sadowski, Mr. Napolo." Then, nodding toward one of the policeman, "This is Sergeant Thomas of the Edison Police."

"Thanks for getting this under control so quickly, guys." I said, shaking hands with them both. "It looks like it could've been a lot worse."

"Luckily we had a little help on this one," Sadowski confided, as he looked over to Sgt. Thomas.

ɔmas, looking ramrod straight in his starched uniform shirt stretched
ʽer his police-issue body armor, nodded toward the adjacent building.
"Your neighbor here, DDS, has a night guard that patrols the plant. As he
was making his rounds in the front office, he saw a flash – probably the initial
incendiary device – and then he saw two men running along the outside of
your fence and then up the road. He didn't see a car. He said they just ran
up the road outta sight. By the time he looked back over here, the first truck
was already burning. He called 911 right away."

"As you can see, two of your trucks were destroyed," Sadowski added.
"The third one can probably be restored. The heat did a job on the windows
and paint, and blew the tires, but I think we got here in time to prevent any
major damage. Good thing that guard called when he did, though, or you
coulda lost that whole row of trucks."

"I guess I owe my neighbor and his guard a big 'thank you' call in the
morning."

Sgt. Thomas stepped in front of me. "Mr. Napolo," he said. "I know you
have our guys here on the first two shifts, but I think you should consider
putting on a twenty-four seven security detail, at least until this union thing
is settled. Whether it's our guys or a private outfit doesn't really matter, you
just need a deterrent, some kind of visible presence."

"I think that's good advice," I agreed, angry with myself for not having
thought of it sooner. Now it would be a reactive gesture, an afterthought,
similar to putting up a traffic light at a dangerous intersection after someone
finally gets killed.

"Can you guys cover it?" I asked Sgt. Thomas. "I'd feel better having
one of your cruisers parked out front instead of some security guard's private
vehicle."

Thomas nodded. "I'll post it when I get back to the station. I'm sure
you'll get some takers."

"Thanks I'd appreciate that."

"You got a coffee machine inside the building?" Sadowski asked.

"Coffee we have," I assured him.

"Good. It's gonna be a long night," Sadowski continued. "DEP's on the
way. They'll supervise the diesel cleanup. And, the arson squads'll be here
soon – both the county and the state. We'll wait 'till they all get here to take
your statement. That'll kill three or four birds with one stone."

"My statement?" I huffed. "I'll give it to you right now." I looked over
at our burned Freightliners and said, "United Brotherhood of Teamsters,
Local 714."

\*       \*       \*

"Jesus, Joseph, why didn't you call me? For chrissake, the place is burning down and you don't even call me! What the fuck!" Michael was incredulous.

I spoke calmly into the phone. "I dunno, man. I thought about it, but I didn't want to distract you. I wanted you to be able to concentrate on this little, ah, - side venture you've undertaken. Frankly, I'm a little concerned."

"*A little concerned!* You are *unfuckingbelievable!*" Michael was shouting. I moved the phone an inch or two away from my ear. "These guys try to burn down our business and you're *a little concerned?* What the fuck is wrong with you?"

"I'm concerned about *you*, Michael," I clarified. "I can handle Laskowski and Catella, but I'm not so sure about you're situation."

Michael exhaled. "We've been through this. I'm a big boy. I know what I'm doing. I just can't believe *this* shit. Have you spoken to Laskowski yet?"

"Oh yeah, I called him at home about two hours ago."

"You called him at four thirty in the morning?" Michael was slowing down. "What did he have to say?"

"He's coming here at nine. The police want to talk to him, and then he and I are gonna talk. I'll handle this, Michael, don't worry about it. Now, what's up with you?"

There was a brief silence, inside of which I suspected Michael was cycling his thoughts, knowing that I wouldn't let Laskowski and Catella get off easy, deciding what he should tell me.

"Anelli called me last night," he finally said. "I'm meeting him at one today."

"He called you?"

"Yup, just like Vinny and Jimmy said he would. And, as they predicted, he's starting to squeeze me. He wants me to bring him five grand or he won't meet with me. Says if I don't bring the money then things go back to his terms."

"What does *that* mean?"

"I took it to mean that if I didn't bring the money then *he* was going to start running the show. Probably start demanding more freight or money – some kind of extortion – using my involvement as leverage."

"That's great, Michael. This just gets better and better, doesn't it?" I paused and waited for Michael to respond. He didn't.

"So take the five grand out of the credit line account. You've got a check, right?"

"Yeah, I've got one or two in my case."

143

"Have you contacted Jimmy or Vinny yet?"

"Joseph, it's six-thirty in the morning. I thought I'd wait a while and then beep Jimmy. Oh, I almost forgot. I need that FBI agent's number. What was that asshole's name?"

"Dwyer, I think. Hold on, I see his card on your desk . . . Yeah, it's Special Agent Clifford Dwyer. All it has is a pager number."

I gave Michael the number and we discussed the damage to our trucks and reviewed other mundane details of the business as if our friendship hadn't missed a beat. We finished by promising each other a day off as soon as this was all behind us; eighteen holes of golf followed by a big fat joint, single-malt scotch, two thick steaks, and a couple of twenty-dollar cigars. I could hear Michael smiling. I smiled back, suppressing a haunting notion that the future we were forging was still too unshaped for such agreeable plans. But for the moment, it was a distraction we both needed.

"So where're you meeting Anelli?" I asked him, easing back to it.

"I don't want to tell you. I promised I would meet him alone and if no one else knows where we're meeting, then there's not much chance of anyone else being there. Besides, we agreed that you would have no involvement in this and I think that's the way we should leave it."

"Well, I'm changing the rules a little. There's no way I can't be at least *in*directly involved. For chrissake, you're meeting with someone who most likely killed two guys the other night. Have you considered this - that this guy's dangerous, that someone should know where you are? What if something happens?"

"Of course, I've thought about, but . . ." Michael hesitated. "Hell, maybe you're right. I'm meeting him in Perth Amboy, on State Street, at the Amboy Iron Works – an old foundry."

"Jesus, Michael, I know where that is - near the refinery. There's nothin around there but tank farms and old abandoned factories. The whole area looks like a bomb hit it."

"I'm sure that's why Anelli picked it. There's no one around. He's not exactly in the position to be goin' anywhere public."

"Or maybe he doesn't want any witnesses."

"Yeah, well either way, it's too late. I'm committed now. If it makes you feel any better I'll ask Jimmy Merchanti to back me up somehow. But you've got to promise me that you won't come anywhere near that place. Do I have your word on that?"

I sighed. "Okay. Not that I feel much better with Merchanti backin' you, but I guess it's better than nothing. But I want you to call me afterwards. Just let me know you're okay. I'll give you two hours. If I don't hear from you by three then I'll . . . ah. . . I don't know what. I'll do something."

"Fair enough."

Neither of us spoke for a few seconds. We both knew the conversation was over, but neither of us knew how to end it.

Michael broke the silence. "How'd little Joseph do at the dinner last night?"

"Good. He got a trophy – some kind of sportsmanship award."

"Hey, that's great. Tell him his Uncle Michael's proud of him."

"I will."

"Okay, man, I gotta get goin'. Good luck with Laskowski, today. You gonna Pacino him?"

"Yeah, I'd like to make him a fuckin' offer he can't refuse, but I'll probably go with something a little less dramatic."

"Well, good luck."

"You too. And remember, Michael, we need that crate. Don't lose sight of that. I'll talk to ya later."

I reached behind me and flipped the toggle switch on the portable stereo on my credenza. Springsteen's CD *Lucky Town* was loaded and started to play but I wanted to hear something less engaging, something that wouldn't distract me. So I switched to FM and hit the preset for the country music station. As I flipped through my address book looking for our insurance agent, I heard a sad harmonica playing through a song's bridge. I continued to listen as the next verse began.

*And oh I love those quiet nights,*
*With my beer and you with your wine.*
*Rollin' 'round in the TV light,*
*Spill the drinks, lose track of the time.*

*But ooooh lately,*
*Seems like nothin's ever funny that I do.*
*And ooooh baby,*
*To keep you here you never know what I might do,*
*All for you.*

I stared across the room, trying to remember when life was so simple and straightforward as heartbreak, and wondering if it ever would be again.

# Bella Collina
# Livingston Manor, New York

As his driver held open the rear door of the Mercedes limousine, Nicolas Pucci stopped and turned to look back at his home. His uncle had told him that the mansion had been built to resemble Thomas Jefferson's Monticello. It was true that the red brick was trimmed with white wood and black shutters, and a protruding rounded portico supported by alabaster columns braced an enormous white dome that centered the structure, but that's where the similarities ended. Unlike Monticello, his uncle's mansion was one of huge proportions. The massive columns soared over sixty feet to the roofline. Wings jutted back off either end of the building, forming a rear enclave that terraced down to fountained pools and lush gardens containing species of plants and trees found no where else in North America. Seven full-time gardeners tended to the grounds and two large greenhouses. Several out buildings housed the staff, equipment, and workshops that were required to maintain the estate. One of those buildings, protected by enormous decorative concrete planters, served as the private security force's operations center. The latest technology, some of which was developed in FirsTech's R&D labs, monitored every square foot of the estate's three hundred mountaintop acres.

Nicolas lived alone in the West Wing, in twenty thousand square feet spread over three floors, serviced by two of the five elevators in the mansion. The East Wing contained living quarters for the household staff, the gymnasium, a theater, an indoor pool and spa, and medical facilities that would do a rural hospital proud. The grand, domed center section of the mansion was home to The Smoke and Gun Club - a very exclusive club, with one surviving member, Nicolas Pucci. Joseph Antonelli, his uncle, had been the founder and only other member.

Nicolas turned and looked out over the roof of the limousine, over the round fountain pool in the center of the circular drive, down the long cobblestone approach from the gatehouse. The air was damp and lightly perfumed with the scents of humus and wild honeysuckle. Towering weeping willows that bordered the wide drive were budding. Soon they would form a beautiful canopy of wispy tendrils that, on the slightest breeze, waved a gentle hello and then goodbye to the invited few. He let his eyes sweep over the sloping lawns leading down to the thick forest and the misty valley below. Beyond, more of the Catskill Mountains were lit in hues of dark green and purple by the morning sun. The name his uncle had placed in the wrought iron scrollwork over the main gate was apt. *Bella Collina*. It is a beautiful hill, he thought.

Nicolas sipped his coffee as the limo eased through the estate's outer acreage. When the red light on the overhead phone console began to blink he glanced at his watch. It was exactly 7:00 a.m., which made him smile.

"Good morning, my friend," Nicolas said.

"We are always on opposite ends of the day. One day we must meet and share the same hours of the same day. But until then we are stuck with this business of ours." The middle-eastern caller was pleasant but Nicolas sensed tension in his tone.

"Many men are stuck in much less rewarding businesses. Wouldn't you agree?"

"Oh, please do not misunderstand me. Our commerce is both noble and profitable. We are truly blessed in that way. It is, I suppose, the nature of what we do that often makes it, how shall I say, inconvenient. As it is with our friend at the moment."

"Inconvenient?" Nicolas recognized the caller's misuse of the word, but he stayed on common ground to further the conversation.

"Yes, we spoke this morning – last night, your time. He was unable to firmly commit to a delivery. Therefore, it was necessary for me to assume a more dominant position. I have given him a deadline of Friday, 1700 hours, New York time."

"How did he react to that?"

"I believe he is sufficiently motivated. I gave him enough information to get his attention."

"What kind of information."

"He now knows that his identity is no longer secure. I also applied a strict penalty for failure."

Nicolas didn't appreciate the caller's initiative. It was a dangerous strategy. Lincoln was not one to be trifled with. He was smart and he had a career's worth of contacts all over the world that he could trade on. If he was pushed too hard, to avoid risking a compromising result, he might flare off and seek another buyer. Moreover, Nicolas' knew that Lincoln was a volatile sociopath, someone who should not be overly stimulated by conditions threatening failure or exposure. And, he certainly didn't need Lincoln running amuck, obsessively pursuing a deadline at all costs. It could be disastrous. Control of this project was essential to its success.

"I am sure that you used your best judgement, but . . ." Nicolas searched for the right words, not wanting to insult the caller. "In the future, please check with me before you push any buttons. We can't afford to lose control of either end of this deal."

"Oh, I understand that but I don't think I have caused any problems. I simply wanted to apply some pressure, to our mutual advantage."

147

Nicolas frowned. "Well, we'll just have to watch it closely from our end. When will you contact him next?"

"I hope never. We agreed that there was no reason to talk again before the deadline, unless of course you think I should. Perhaps, a call to confirm he's on schedule?"

"No. Leave it as it is, for now. Let's see what develops. I'll contact you if I need you again on this project. If you don't hear from me, assume all is well."

"Only my bank balance will confirm that."

Nicolas looked up at the speaker in the overhead console. "It will. But, not until you have made final delivery."

"That, my friend, will be no problem. Our buyer is anxious. The madman is crazy with the thought that he will be able to shoot down American jets and cruise missiles."

"Then our little present should drive him insane."

## Queens, New York

Vinny Diamonds was awake, sitting on the edge of his bed when the phone rang. He had had the dream again. The same dream as yesterday. He and his friends, just boys, sitting on the bumper of the big truck, only to fall one by one under the giant steamroller. And, although it was cartoonish the way the boys appeared in death – squashed into brightly colored circles on the road, it scared the shit out of him again today. He squeezed his eyes tight trying to blot it out, but there was one image he couldn't shake. The look on his younger brother Sal's face as he went to his death under the roller filled his head. It was a face filled with the terror and hopelessness of the moment, distorted in horror, the eyes begging and pleading with Vinny for help despite the knowledge that his big brother, his protector was as helpless as he was. Vinny reached mechanically for the phone feeling extremely sad.

"Yeah?"

"Vinny, it's Jimmy. You up?"

"Yeah, I'm up. Why?"

"It's early. I'd thought you'd still be sleepin'"

"Well, I'm up." Vinny glanced at the red digital numbers on the clock radio. It was eight forty-seven. "What's so important that you're callin' me at this hour, Jimmy?"

"Our friend from Jersey has a meeting today with our other friend from Jersey."

"For chrissake, Jimmy, it's too fuckin' early for this shit! Whathefuck's the matter with you? I just woke up. Talk straight, will ya? Who the fuck from Jersey is meeting who?"

Jimmy hesitated but decided that Vinny's bad mood overrode any security issues. "Johnny called Michael last night. They set up a meet today. Michael s'posed to go alone but he wants me there to back 'im."

"Where's the meet?"

"In Jersey, just over the Outerbridge, at some old factory. Whadaya want me ta do?"

Vinny stood and paced to the end of his bed and back. "You go with him, like he wants. But I want you ta go heavy. Stop and get something clean and quiet from Two Toes. This way Johnny tries anything . . . *anything,* you hear?"

"I hear."

"And don't you let nothin' happen to this Michael. Joseph would never forgive me."

"Don't worry about it, Vinny. Only thing that's gonna happen is to the other guy."

"You make sure of that, Jimmy."

## FirsTech World Headquarters
## Liberty, New York

"Wilson," Nicolas said into the speakerphone on his desk. "I got your message. What's up?"

"Good morning to you, too, Nicolas. Have we become too busy for simple courtesies? They make for a more enjoyable life. Don't you agree?"

"Gimme a break, Wilson," Nicolas pleaded, trying not to be disrespectful.

"No."

"Okay. Good morning, Wilson." Nicolas said with as much patience as he could muster. "Better?"

"Yes, better."

"Good. Your message said something about Domanski Trucking. What's going on?"

"Well, our bug caught a conversation between Napolo and Cogan this morning. Napolo was in the office and Cogan was at home. It was early, about six-thirty. A few of their trucks were torched overnight. They think the union did it."

"Sure, they're probably pissed off about Lincoln's helicopter stunt."

"No doubt," Wilson said. "But I think they might be wrong."

"Why, what do you know?"

"I'll get to that, but first things first. Take me off the speaker." Wilson waited to hear the background sounds go quiet. "It appears that Lincoln may be on the right track, that Napolo and Cogan are somehow involved in the hijacking."

Nicolas exhaled noisily. "Lemme hear it."

"I listened to this morning's tape several times. Cogan's somehow involved with this John Anelli – the one from Hackensack, you remember?"

"I remember. Go on."

"I think that Cogan got caught up with this guy somehow. Anelli's got something on him. And, it sounds like Anelli does in fact have the crate. Cogan's meeting him today to work out some kind of deal. We have the location."

"Does Lincoln know any of this?"

"The meeting? No, I don't think so. But this certainly confirms his understanding of the situation – of Napolo and Cogan's involvement. In fact, when Lincoln called me this morning, he pushed me for help getting the union out of the way – to call them off of Domanski Trucking. He's quite insistent that Napolo and Cogan are key to the recovery of the item, and after yesterday he can't get at them while the Teamster pickets are there. Then - listen to this - he said that he had, quote, 'turned the heat up a little' between the union and the company'. When I told him we had heard about the lime he dumped on the pickets, he just laughed and said that was not what he was talking about. But, he continued to tell me that he had, and I'm quoting again, 'put a few burning issues on their bargaining table', and that if we had any influence, now would be a good time to use it."

Nicolas thought for a moment. "So Lincoln burned the trucks? Is that what you're saying? He burned the trucks, because in his warped mind that's going to bring an end to the picketing?"

"You tell me what it sounds like. Hell, if I can stretch here and put his spin on it, escalating the situation just *might* bring things to a head."

Nicolas knew that Wilson and Lincoln were originally cut from the same cloth. Facilitating change through covert operations that relied on dirty tricks and surreptitious mayhem was a time-tested mainstay of their craft. Nicolas understood that, he just didn't think on those levels. Wilson had to lead him to the fact of the matter.

"Okay, let's see what we can do to help," Nicholas conceded. "In the meantime, make sure Lincoln doesn't find out about this meeting today. I don't want him anywhere near it. What's *your* plan for this meeting?"

"We'll have a dozen or so units on the ground with the some expensive equipment and, if the timing's right, we'll have satellite coverage. But I'm still waiting to hear back on that."

"What's your gut here, Wilson?"

"Well, we'll see and try to hear everything that goes on, and we should be able to track everyone coming and going, but we'll be too far away to be effective if the meeting goes bad. If Cogan or Anelli have any ideas other than talking to each other, we may not able to stop it."

"Well, I hate to say it, but Anelli's the one we need. If push comes to shove, make damn sure he's the one that walks away."

# CHAPTER 15
## DTC Transportation
## Edison, NJ

In between sessions with the police, fire, and arson squads, I spent the best part of the morning conducting impromptu meetings with groups of our employees, answering their questions and allaying their concerns. I had to listen to the arson investigators postulate on the type of device that had been used to incinerate our trucks. I explained to them that as far as I was concerned, it only mattered who had done it, not what. Then, I had to listen to the quick denials from Laskowski and Catella as they passed in the hallway on their way to the conference room to meet with the law enforcement officials. Finally, I listened in frustration to Sgt. Thomas telling me that as Laskowski and Catella both had alibis and, assuming they would be verified, there was nothing that could be done except for continuing the investigation. All in all, the morning had proceeded exactly how I guessed it would. Until, I came upon Laskowski and Catella waiting patiently outside my office door.

"Joseph, can we talk to ya?" Laskowski spoke softly. "Privately?"

I crossed my arms and looked them over slowly, making sure I didn't answer to quickly.

"Please Joseph, we gotta talk, it's important." Alley Cat Catella was whispering.

I waited again, looking long at the two of them before I led them into my office. As I motioned for them to sit, Catella brought his forefinger to his pursed lips, signaling for silence. Then he walked over to the radio and switched it on, turning up the volume until it was uncomfortably loud.

Laskowski took me gently by the elbow and guided me over to Catella, so the three of us were huddled around the blaring radio.

"Where's Cogan?" Laskowski asked.

"He's not here. What's *this* all about?" I asked, pointing to the radio.

"We shouldn't talk in here; too many ears in the hallways," Catella said tensely. "Can we go for a walk?" Then seeing my eyebrows rise, he added, "Just outside here, in the yard."

I thought for a moment and began to see the value in getting them some place where we wouldn't be overheard. I nodded and Catella put his finger back to his lips as he turned off the radio.

The three of us walked out of the building past the teams of investigators that were combing through the wreckage of the two trucks. Yellow crime scene tape had been strung to cordon off the area. A young Edison cop lifted it so they we could pass. When we had rounded the far side of the building, I stopped and turned to face the union men.

I planted myself and said, "Alright, this is far enough."

Catella looked over both shoulders and then gave Laskowski a slight nod. Laskowski cleared his throat and said, "Joseph, first we want you to know that Local 714 had nothing to do with this fire and we have no idea who was at your house last night."

"Why do I have such a hard time believing that, Ron? The arson squad has already confirmed that some kind of device was used to start the fire. A witness saw two men leaving the scene seconds before the device went off. *Somebody* did this. It didn't start by itself. Local 714 looks like a good suspect to me."

"I think we're being set up," Laskowski said.

I waited long enough to be sure that Laskowski was serious. "Oh, okay," I chuckled. "I think I've heard enough. I'm going back to work."

I started to walk away and Catella grabbed my arm. "Wait."

I looked down at his hand on my forearm and leaned into Catella's face. "Get your hand off me."

Catella loosened his grip and put his hands up in surrender. "Sorry," he said. "But we need to talk to you. It can't wait,. Please."

I studied Catella's face. There was a new facet there. What exactly it was eluded me for the moment but I had the immediate sense that it was harmless, something akin to a sharp and dangerous knife that had suddenly lost its edge. Then I recognized it. Catella was concerned, perhaps genuinely troubled with something. But a knife is still a knife.

"Alright," I said. "But the first piece of bullshit I hear, I'm walkin' away."

Catella's lips turned up at the corners. "Good. Thanks." Turning to Laskowski. "Go ahead, Ron."

"When I said *we* were being set up I meant *us* – all of us, you guys and us. Something's going on here. We don't know exactly what but we know that it involves you and Cogan."

"I'm still listening," I said.

Laskowski continued. "Yesterday, in our offices, you mentioned your last name. Everybody's heard the name Napolo, but . . . well, we did some checking. We never connected you with the ah . . . you know, Napolo *Family.*"

"Joseph," Catella interrupted. "We didn't know who you were - that he was your grandfather. Why didn't you say something?"

"Because that was a long time ago. It doesn't matter now."

Catella smiled. "It does matter, Joseph. Have you noticed the picket line today?"

When Bobby Moretti had told me the pickets were quiet today, I hadn't thought twice about it. With all the police activity this morning, I assumed they were just behaving themselves. I looked over Catella's shoulder at the front gate. There were only about a dozen pickets pacing slowly back and forth off to one side of the gate. A few of them had signs draped over their chests but it was an orderly procession. It was a picket line straight out of an NLRB training video.

I looked back at Catella. "And, of course, this has nothing to do with last night?"

"No," Laskowski replied firmly. "It has to do with what we're trying to tell you."

"So tell me."

"Look," Catella said. "If we had known who you were, there would never have been no picket line. Things woulda been worked out right from the git-go. No problem. Hell, if this thing didn't happen last night . . .well, you understand why we couldn't pull them off today, right? It'd look too suspicious. As it is, everyone thinks we're responsible for the fire."

"I still do," I said.

"Whydoncha let 'im finish," Laskowski snapped. "Then tell us what you think, okay?"

I looked hard at Laskowski for a moment and then nodded. I was becoming interested to hear where this was all going. I turned back to Catella. "Okay, but let's get to the point here, Albert."

Catella looked to Laskowski who gave him a small nod. "So yesterday morning we find out who you are, right? It really bothered us. After all, your grandfather was, ya know, a, ah, good friend of organized labor and the

Teamsters. We shoulda been more respectful, but we didn't know, so who could blame us, right?"

I saw that Catella was waiting for a confirmation, probably hoping for absolution. But I liked Catella's new attitude too much, so I looked down my nose at him, deadpanned. "Sure, whatever, you say, Albert."

Catella shot side-glance at Laskowski before continuing. "Then, we hear that our men trashed an FBI agent's car out here. That's sumthin' the Teamsters don't fuckin' need right now, ya know. So me and Ron contact the FBI in Newark, to apologize – to try to smooth things over, ya know. They check all their offices in Jersey and tell us that no FBI agent ever visited you yesterday. Then, we hear about this unmarked helicopter dumpin' lime on our guys. So then we figure that the Feds did it in retaliation, or sumthin', and they don't want it connected to them, so because of that they're denying the agent was even here. Know what I mean?"

I had heard every word but I didn't acknowledge it. Catella stared at me a moment before continuing.

"Meantime, one of our guys has the plate number off the agent's car. Another one of our guys has a brother who's a Woodbridge cop. He runs the plate for us and guess what – the plate comes up on the stolen list. Last I heard, FBI agents don't steal cars or license plates."

I crossed my arms and spread my feet as if the ground was about to shake.

"So what's your point, Albert? Obviously, your man didn't get the right plate number."

Catella exchanged glances with Laskowski again. Laskowski looked down at his feet and nodded imperceptibly.

"Okay, Joseph," Catella said. "Now there's something you gotta understand here. Ron and I run this local, but there are some things that I do that Ron don't have to know about. It's union business that's not really union business, if ya know what I mean."

"I can use my imagination."

"So Ron's gonna walk over there. Okay?"

"Whatever . . ."

When Laskowski was out of earshot, Catella looked me hard in the eyes. "I got a call late last night from New York. You and I have mutual friends." Catella waited for a reaction that never came. "They told me what we'd already figured out - about your grandfather. Then we had a little talk about a guy named Johnny and this crate he took. But that wasn't news to me either. Ya see, I've known all about the situation with Johnny and Michael Cogan."

Catella paused again but I kept my face vacant. Catella shifted his feet and squinted at me. "Ya see, Johnny and I go way back, to grade school in

Perth Amboy. In fact, if Johnny was in some kinda trouble, and he had nowhere else to turn, the one person in this world he'd trust – maybe even call - just might be me. I'm not saying he did. But if he did, I think he'd tell me that he had nothin' to do with those guys getting shot in his apartment the other night. You heard about that, right?"

I lowered my chin.

Catella continued. "And I'd believe him. Ya know why?"

I felt my eyebrows lift.

"Because he would know that I wouldn't give a shit either way. Shoot a couple guys or not, I could care less. Not my business. So when I tell you that Johnny had nothin' to do with that thing in Hackensack, and that Local 714 had nothin' to do with your trucks gettin' burnt up or those guys showin' up at your house last night, and that there's sumthin' wrong with this FBI agent, ya know ya gotta start thinkin' about what's goin' on here."

"No, I don't, Albert."

I turned and walked toward the terminal building, leaving Catella and Laskowski gesturing questions to each other across the black top.

## Amboy Iron Works
## Perth Amboy, New Jersey

Johnny Onions caught himself wiping his right eye again. In the car on the way over, he had thought it was a smudge on his sunglasses. But after wiping the lens several times he had given up, thinking the cheap green plastic had become scratched or somehow distorted. Now, inside the old powerhouse sitting in his El Dorado, parked beside the steam boilers that used to generate heat and electricity for the Amboy Iron Works, Johnny removed his glasses and tried to blink away the blurred vision in his eye. But the fuzziness remained. He held the palm of his hand over his right eye. His left eye was fine. Then he covered his left eye. The room was completely out of focus. He glanced down at the dashboard and found that he could read only the largest characters on the instrumentation. He switched back and forth between his left and right eyes, watching the images snap in and out of focus, until he felt queasy and his head started throbbing. Then he leaned forward and looked into his rear-view mirror and studied his face.

He looked like shit. Dark puffy bags drooped under his eyes. His skin was sallow and seemed to hang too loosely, pulling down at the corners of his eyes and mouth. The constant pain in his head was etching deep furrows into his brow between his eyebrows. But what troubled him most was the droop. Starting with his eyelid, the right side of his face sagged noticeably.

He touched his right cheek. Then his left and right again. The right side was numb. He looked into the mirror again.

"God damn it!" he cursed, as he grabbed the rear-view, twisting it hard, up and away until it snapped off the windshield. He held the mirror in his hand for a few seconds, staring at it, wondering what he should do with it. Then he threw it into the back seat and said, "Fuck it!"

He took a few deep breaths and tapped six Tylenols out of a fresh bottle he had bought on the way, rinsing them down with a gulp of coffee. Then he reached into the console between the front seats, lifted up the bottom panel and pulled out the Beretta. He depressed the button under the slide that released the clip and let it fall into his hand. By pressing on the top round he could feel that the magazine was full so he guided it back into the bottom of the handgrip and drove it home. He racked the slide, chambering a round. After he had eased the hammer down into the safe position, he stretched his right arm across the passenger seat and sighted on the handle of a tool cabinet on the far wall. When he closed his left eye, everything beyond the front sights of the pistol was a total blur. He tried sighting with his left eye, but he found he had to hold the gun in an unnatural position to line it up properly. Then he tried aiming with both eyes open but that only served to double his vision.

He let his arm fall and placed the Beretta on the passenger seat. What the hell, he thought. It's not like he had ever shot anyone that was more than three or four feet away. Most of the time, it was a matter of inches. Up close and personal. Good name for a TV gossip show. Maybe it already was. Was it? He realized he was blinking his right eye and he rubbed it again. Sure, he probably just needed glasses, maybe even bifocals. Might even be the reason for his headaches. He made a mental note to get to the eye doctor when things settled down.

Johnny lit a cigarette and settled back to look around the cavernous powerhouse. Dusty shafts of light filtered through holes in the roof and broken dirty windows that had been built high up on the walls. Overhead, dual coal conveyors punched through the wall and angled down to feeder chutes at the boiler's furnace doors, iron mouths gaping for one last mouthful before being abandoned. Above the boilers, huge twin turbines, frozen with rust and corrosion, dripped rainwater through the catwalks onto the wood block floor. And then there were the pipes. Everywhere, pipes. Water pipes. Steam pipes. Pipes stuffed with electrical wiring. Spare pipes of every size stored in racks along the walls above dozens of bins filled with pipefittings.

Just beyond the bins, in the far corner, was a workbench. His father's wood stool was still there. And, he was sure that, if he wanted to, he could still find his initials, next to his father's, carved into the seat of the stool.

Giovanni Anelli would occasionally bring his son, Johnny, to work with him, to show him the monstrous machines he kept running so the foundry could make artillery and tank parts for the US Army. Twelve-hour shifts, seven days a week for the whole war and he never complained. He was proud to do it, he would tell Johnny. Proud to be helping America blow the Nazi devils back to Hell.

Johnny remembered staring into the turbines, mesmerized by the giant spinning blades, too hot and too loud to hear his father explaining how the coal made the steam, made the turbines turn, made the electricity. He remembered his father's sweat and smell, and how he had wondered how anyone could drink hot coffee in a place like this.

Johnny looked at his watch. It was eleven o'clock. He had been there over an hour. He sipped his Dunkin' Donuts coffee. It was cold.

*     *     *

Johnny woke with a start and quickly checked his watch. He had dozed off but thankfully it was only five after twelve and he hadn't slept through his one o'clock appointment with Michael Cogan. He stuffed the Beretta and a flashlight from the glove compartment in his jacket pockets. Locking his car, he thought about having to leave in a hurry and then unlocked it. He made his way to a metal door tucked under a maze of pipes behind the boiler. Several good tugs later, the rusted hinges loosened. Inside, it was pitch-black but he knew there was a stairway. He turned on the flashlight although, even after all these years, he could've found his way down in the dark. When he was a kid, the steam tunnel was his favorite place. Cooler and quieter than the powerhouse, he would spend hours here, hunting rats with his slingshot and the ball bearings he would take from his father's workbench. His father had told him that the tunnel was over a half-mile long. Inside the tunnel, steam pipes and electrical conduits ran underneath State Street, under the basement of Amboy Iron's corporate office building, continuing all the way to the foundry building on the far side of the property. Johnny descended into the darkness and began the long, damp walk, stomping his good foot and waving the flashlight to chase the rats along the way.

When Johnny reached the end of the tunnel, he climbed the stairs that led up to the basement of the shuttered foundry and pushed open the door. He was now inside a brick shaft that housed the steam pipes and electrical conduits that had powered the facility. It was just how he had remembered it to be. Steel ladders ran up two sides of the shaft, affording access to the tunnel through small metal hatches on each of the three floors. Johnny squeezed through the hatch into the basement. He spent the next thirty minutes going over each of the floors, opening closets and offices, walking around the rusted machinery on the shop floors, and using the windows to check the parking lots and the surrounding buildings. As far as he could tell, there was no one else on the property.

*       *       *

On the roof of an abandoned Chevron Oil building adjacent to the Amboy Iron Works, two men lay prone on the flat tar roof hidden behind the decorative concrete parapet. One man peered through high-powered binoculars mounted on a tripod and wired to thermal imaging equipment. The other squinted through the scope mounted on his 50-BMG-caliber McMillan sniper rifle. They both wore headgear that held tiny video cameras, earpieces and sensitive lip mics for communicating with each other and the rest of the surveillance teams.

The man behind the binoculars spoke. "Yankee Team has visual. Dark green Ford Explorer entering back parking area. Jersey plates xray-charlie-three-four-eight-alpha. Driver only, zero passengers. Confirm target vehicle."

"Target vehicle confirmed. Home Plate has video from Yankees." The voice that emanated from a step van parked behind the Chevron building spoke to all the teams' earpieces. "Stand-off Teams report."

"Sox still have one thermal image of target number one in factory. Zero visual. Stationary, first floor rear."

"Pirates have zero visual. Zero thermal. Front clear."

"Yankees report activity." The voice in the van again. "Sox report thermal movement."

"Yankees have visual on white male, marking target number two, tan pants green shirt leaving target vehicle, approaching east rear entrance."

"Sox have thermal of number one in factory moving south, first floor."

"Yankees have visual on number two stopped five meters from rear door."

"Sox now have thermal *and* visual in rear doorway. White male, number two, dark pants dark jacket light colored shirt."

"Home Plate has five-by-five video from Yankees and Sox."

"Yankees have number two moving again. Heading to rear doorway. Will lose visual in doorway."

"Sox have visual on number one and two. Request target acquisition."

"Acquire target number two and hold," the voice instructed.

The Sox Team sniper let the crosshairs in his McMillan's scope come to rest on the back of Michael Cogan's head and whispered, "Target number two acquired. Holding."

"Sox any audio?"

"Negative. Number one and number two entering building. Will lose target acquisition in 3 . . . 2 . . ."

"Hold!" The voice shouted.

"Sox holding. Now zero visual. Number one and two inside building. Thermal on number one and number two moving lateral north first floor, ten meters. Now stationary."

"Rangers report."

"Front clear."

"Pirates move to front entrance. Orioles move to south wall. Philies move to north wall. All ground units prepare to breach. Report activity."

Sox Team's man with the thermal imaging equipment watched the red figures behind the corrugated metal and glass walls of the old factory. They paced one way then the other without leaving the general area.

"Sox have thermal on number one and number two, stationary, one-five meters north of east entrance."

"Brewers move to east entrance and hold." The man in the van sat back and scanned the twelve video monitors broadcasting from his teams' headgear. When the Brewers Team was in place outside the rear entrance, he said, "All ground units lock and load. Prepare to breach on my command. All shooters take at-will measures to protect number one."

\*　　\*　　\*

Jimmy Merchanti rose up slowly from the floor, lifted the blanket from his face and cautiously poked his head between the front seats of Michael's Explorer. Keeping the blanket over his head, he looked over the dashboard at the rear entrance of building and let his eyes adjust to the sunlight. He saw two men dressed in black SWAT uniforms squatting just outside the doorway with their suppressed Heckler & Koch MP5 submachine guns at ready positions.

"Oh, shit!" Merchanti said, as he squirreled himself back under the blanket on the floor of the back seat. Twisting onto his back, he wrestled the Browning .22 automatic from his waistband and screwed on the silencer. Holding the pistol in both hands with his arms extended between his legs, he lay in the dark under the blanket, trying to control his breathing, listening, and hoping Michael had locked the doors.

\*　　\*　　\*

The voice from the van was loud and deliberate in their earpieces. "Ground units go on my count. 3 . . . 2 . . . 1 . . . GO! GO! GO!"

Reacting instinctively to the loud banging and breaking glass echoing through the cavernous first floor, Johnny Onions and Michael Cogan both hunched down. They caught each other's eyes for just a second, but it was long enough to confirm that neither of them knew what was going on. Then, over Michael's shoulder, Johnny saw two armed men coming through the rear door. Pushing Michael aside, he spit, "Son of bitch," and yanked the Beretta from his jacket. Holding the gun sideways like Mel Gibson, he fired four quick rounds in their direction, forcing the Brewers Team to dive for cover.

Johnny turned to Michael who was wide-eyed and frozen. There were two red laser aimer dots dancing across Michael's chest. Johnny spun around and saw the broken red lines of the laser beams reflecting off dust particles in the air. He brought the Beretta up and pumped the trigger three times in the direction of the red beams. Bullets chipped the floor and sparked off the steel columns as they ricocheted in the cavernous factory. The red dots disappeared from Michael's chest. A man cried out and fell noisily to the floor, gripping his thigh. A second man came out from behind a workstation and dragged the wounded man to cover. Johnny swung around and fired two more shots towards the rear door, keeping the Brewers down, and then spun again to shoot two more times at the workstation.

Johnny started to limp to a door against the rear wall. He yelled to Michael over his shoulder. "Let's go! Follow me!" Without a thought, Michael started to run after Johnny.

Inside the door was a staircase. Johnny said, "Go up one floor and wait for me."

Michael hesitated. Johnny yelled, "GO!"

As Michael took the stairs two at a time, Johnny peeked through the door. Three pairs of SWAT types were running across the factory floor toward him. Johnny ejected the clip from the Beretta and rammed a fresh magazine into the bottom of the handgrip. He racked the slide, threw open the door and swept the opening with the Beretta, firing six lighting-quick rounds, screaming, "FUUUCK YOOOU!" The running men dove into the dust on the factory floor.

Johnny slammed the door and slid the locking bar into place. As he ran up the stairs, he could hear rounds from the submachine guns ripping through the door and ricocheting in the stairwell below him.

\*　　\*　　\*

"Jesus H. Christ!" the man in the van said to himself between clenched teeth. He had been listening and watching the jerky video images being transmitted by his teams as they ran and ducked and ran and dove and fired and ran. It made it difficult to fully assess the situation but he had seen enough to know that they had lost control. He pressed the button to activate his microphone.

"Control fire! Control fire! Ground units continue pursuit. But control fire. Number One must come out breathing. Stand-off units report activity."

"Sox have targets number one and two thermal on second floor moving north."

"Rangers ditto."

"Pirates with Brewers on second floor. No visual. Where are they?"

The man in the van broke the silence. "Sox, Rangers, report."

"Sox here. We, ah, lost thermal. Just disappeared."

"Rangers ditto, thermal gone."

"Equipment check, goddamit!"

"Sox equipment checks 5-by-5. Have Pirates and Brewers thermal, moving west and north. Nothing else."

"Rangers' equipment checks 5-by-5. See Pirates and Brewers. Targets gone."

"Gone? What the fuck is gone?" The voice from the van. "Ground units report!"

"Philie 1 with Philie 2 down, code yellow, first floor clear."

"Orioles, stairwell clear."

"Pirates, second floor clear."

"Brewers, second floor clear."

In the van, the police scanner had come to life. Dispatchers from Perth Amboy and Woodbridge were sending cruisers to check out reports of explosions and possible shots fired in the vicinity of State Street. The man in the van slammed his fist onto the console and cursed under his breath. "All units break off, code red. Repeat, code red break off. Go stealthy to pickup."

The man in the van cradled his head in his hands and let out a long sigh that noisily fluttered his lips. Then he straightened up and, after a deep exhale, reached for a phone on the console and pressed a speed dial number. He winced as he waited for an answer.

"This is Lincoln."

"Sir, this is Home Plate. The mission has been compromised and aborted. The targets have evaded our surveillance." The man in the van cringed, waiting for the response.

"Are you serious? What the fuck happened?"

"Sir, one of the targets was armed. He opened fire on our units and . . ."

"And what?" Lincoln screamed. "You knew he was armed and likely to use his weapon at the slightest provocation. How the fuck did you lose them?"

"The local police were dispatched, I had to abort or risk . . ."

"I don't want to hear anymore." Lincoln cut him off. He was already moving on to his next plan. "Now make your call to Wilson Dennis like a good little FirsTech security guard. He should be real pleased with you, too. If I were him, I'd put you and your fuckin' team in the gate house at Pucci's place. Maybe that duty's more your speed."

"Yes, sir," the man in the van replied, but Lincoln had already hung up.

*     *     *

After climbing down from the second floor of the foundry on the steel ladders inside the power shaft, Johnny Onions and Michael Cogan made their way to the powerhouse through the steam tunnel. They had stopped along the way, underneath Amboy Iron's corporate offices, to see if they were being followed. Johnny thought that they would have a better chance escaping into the office building than shooting it out in the dark tunnel. But, after several minutes of listening for footfalls and catching their breath, they continued on, stopping and listening every fifty yards or so, until they had reached the stairs up to the powerhouse. Now they were propping steel rods against heavy metal tool carts to brace the door to the stairwell closed. If they had been followed, it would now take their pursuers thirty or forty loud seconds to get the door opened.

"Follow me," Johnny said, breathlessly, rivulets of sweat running down his face.

By now Michael was behaving like an obedient toddler. Since the shooting started he had had no mind of his own. Whatever Johnny said, he did. Nothing in his life had prepared him for this. He hadn't been able to process anything except for the fear and one thought, or more accurately, one of my thoughts. *You're in way over your head, pal.*

"Where are we?" Michael asked, as he followed Johnny around the boiler.

Without turning around, Johnny replied, "What the fuck does it matter where we are? Just so those assholes aren't here with us. So just shut the fuck up and stay with me. Ya hear?"

Michael nodded as Johnny led him around to the El Dorado. Johnny opened the driver's door and reached inside. Closing the door, he placed a box of nine-millimeter bullets on the roof of the car. Michael watched him quickly reload a clip from his pocket and then the one from the Beretta. Johnny turned, racked the slide, and pointed the cocked pistol in Michael's face.

"Okay, who the fuck were those guys?"

Michael turned his face to the side and raised his hands. "Whoa, relax. I have no idea who they were. You told me to come alone and I did."

"Relax, bullshit! Last time you told me to relax I end up gettin' shot at by a SWAT team. That's not my idea of relaxation." Johnny moved closer and pressed the muzzle of the Beretta against Michael's temple. "One more time. Who'd you call? Who were those guys?"

Michael's mouth was dry. He had to force the words out. "Please, I came alone. Why would I jeopardize collecting a million dollars?"

Johnny let the words be absorbed and mingle with the other thoughts whirling around inside his aching head. He recalled the expression on Michael's face when the ambush had started. Total surprise, like a deer frozen in the headlights. Not the reaction of someone expecting that kind of company. And the red laser dots on Michael's chest. None on his. They were aiming at Michael, not him. It didn't make sense.

Johnny said, "Lemme see the five grand."

"It's in my back pocket."

"Take it out, slowly," Johnny instructed, pushing Michael's head back with the pistol.

Michael opened the envelope so Johnny could see the wad of hundred dollar bills. Johnny grabbed the envelope and let the Beretta fall from Michael's face. He took a step back as he inspected the contents, keeping the gun pointed at Michael's chest.

Michael breathed again. He examined Johnny's face. It didn't look good. Puffy, moist, and pale. The right eyelid hung heavily, and it may have closed over his eye if it had not been for the lower lid being dragged down with the cheek toward the drooping corner of his mouth.

"Are you alright?" Michael asked.

Johnny looked up from the envelope. "What?"

"You don't look good. You feel okay?"

"Don't worry about that. You got other stuff to worry about."

Michael nodded. "What do I have to do to convince you that I had nothing to do with this . . . that I came alone?"

"Forget that." Johnny dropped his arm and held the Beretta at his thigh, pointed at the floor. Michael's eyes followed it down. "I think those guys were gonna shoot you."

"You mean *us*," Michael countered.

"No, I mean *you*. Nobody was aimin' at me until I started shootin'. Before that, they were just aimin' at you. You better think real good about who knew you were comin' here today, 'cause they almost got you killed." The left side of Johnny's face smiled. "'course maybe that was their plan."

Michael shook his head. "That's impossible."

Johnny lifted his eyebrow, the one that was still working. "Impossible? Why? 'Cause you didn't tell anyone . . . or 'cause the person you told you thought you could trust?"

Michael looked away. The only people who knew the location of the meeting were Joseph and Jimmy, and probably Vinny. It made absolutely no sense for Vinny and Jimmy to be involved with any type of law enforcement. He was sure they had some final plans for Johnny but it wouldn't be at the expense of loosing their share of the million dollars. Certainly, a SWAT team was not their style. That left Joseph. Had he told anyone? Maybe out of concern for his safety, Joseph had alerted someone. No, that would involve too much explaining, too much exposure. Who then? Think. Who benefits if he's killed? Jimmy and Vinny would get a larger share of the money. But, with him dead they would lose their link to the FBI, and then, no money. No, definitely not Vinny and Jimmy. Then, Joseph? But Joseph never wanted any of the money or any part of this whole situation for that matter. But suppose he *had* been killed? What if he had died in a police shoot-out along side a known organized crime figure who was suspected of double murder? That could be used to explain a lot. The gambling debt, the hijacking, the lost FirsTech cargo, it could all be conveniently wrapped, tied, and laid to rest with him. But no way, not Joseph. Not his best friend. Couldn't be. Could it?

Michael looked back at Johnny and shrugged, "I don't know. It doesn't make any sense."

"Oh yeah, well until it does, me and you are gonna stick real close." Johnny waved the Beretta toward the El Dorado. "Get in the car. You're driving. We gotta get outta here."

Michael made no protest. At that moment, he felt just as safe with Johnny Onions as anyone else.

# CHAPTER 16
## The Lower East Side
## New York City

Aaron Lincoln smelled his fingers and reached for another pre-moistened towelette. For lunch, there was nothing quite like a Jersey submarine sandwich. It started with a perfect loaf of soft-crusted Italian bread, loaded with salami, ham, provolone, capicola, and pepperoni. He had ordered it with 'the works' - shredded lettuce, tomatoes, thinly sliced onions, and hot peppers, doused with olive oil, extra vinegar and topped with a sprinkling of salt, pepper, and oregano. And when the guy at the counter spoke with an accent and didn't ask him if he wanted mayonnaise, he knew he had found the right place. Real Italian sub shops never ask if you want mayonnaise. Even so, he had only allowed himself the luxury of about a quarter of the sandwich. By experience, any more would disturb the delicate intestinal balance he had achieved over the years. Nothing, not even a Jersey sub, was worth upsetting the precise timing and comfortable consistency of his daily constitutional. He sniffed his fingers again. Almost. One or two more towelettes and the smell of the sandwich would be gone.

The clean-cut young man driving their rented car had watched him out of the corner of his eye the whole way over from Teterboro Airport. First, Lincoln had spread layer after layer of napkins over his lap. Then he carefully unwrapped and inspected the sandwich. After gingerly flipping the sandwich and lifting off the bottom piece of bread, he rearranged the order of the meats and cheese, placing the provolone on the bottom, then the ham, the salami, the capicola and the pepperoni. He ate with his eyes closed, slowly chewing each small bite interminably until the food was nearly dissolved, leaving little work for the remaining components of his digestive system. Now, as they sat in the car, parked less than a block from Taverna Reggia, the young man stared at Lincoln's reflection in the curve of the windshield as he rubbed his hands with the towelette, scrubbing between the fingers and around the fingernails, deep in thought like a surgeon prepping for a major procedure.

And Lincoln was thinking. In a little over forty-eight hours he had to locate and deliver the hardware. The money involved was important but the primary issue for him now was the success of the mission. Failure was not an option. Aside from the Middle Easterner's threats, which he would have to take at least somewhat seriously, there would be irreparable damage to his reputation. It was a small world. And he not being a likeable person, bad news would travel fast. It would weaken his position. Prospective clients, heretofore willing to put up with his demands because of his enviable track record, would use it to negotiate lower fees and reduced up-front payments. His competition, such as it was, would be emboldened. And his enemies, those he had double-crossed or destroyed or friends of those he had murdered, beholding a chink in his armor would seize the opportunity for revenge. No, failure was definitely not an option.

He lifted his fingers to his nose again and, satisfied there was no more Jersey sub smell, he tossed the last towelette into a plastic bag, which he tied tightly closed. Without looking at the younger man, he said, "Weapons check. Lock and load."

The younger man withdrew an H&K MP5 submachine gun from a special harness in his suit jacket and screwed a eight-inch long noise suppressor onto the barrel. He opened and checked the breach, inserted a 30-round magazine, cocked the weapon, and returned it to its holster. A second later, he had two pistols, a nine-millimeter Glock 17 and a .32 caliber Walther, in his lap. After checking both guns, he put the Glock in his shoulder holster and slid the Walther into a ballistic nylon holster strapped just above his ankle.

Lincoln had watched it all, making no attempt to conceal his scrutiny of the other man's activities. Satisfied, he said nothing. The other man understood and waited as Lincoln began his own inspections. First, Lincoln checked his own Glock 17 and returned it to the waistband holster in the small of his back. Then he took the silenced .22 caliber revolver from his suit jacket pocket, swung the cylinder open, and after checking the load, snapped it closed again with a flip of his wrist. What a cowboy, the younger man thought. Finally, Lincoln pulled an Israeli-made stainless steel Desert Eagle .50 caliber autoloader from his shoulder holster. It was the highest caliber handgun made and with its ten-inch barrel, it was a very large, heavy, and deadly serious looking weapon. It was much too heavy and unwieldy for everyday carry but Lincoln loved it for its intimidation factor. The visual impact of this massive pistol was worth a thousand verbal threats. Not to mention that the horrific devastation to human tissue caused by just one round of the giant .50 caliber magnums was genuinely impressive. Used properly, Lincoln could scare the shit out of a room full of men with this pistol. And, if that didn't work, eight shots and just over two seconds later there'd be plenty of blood on the walls.

Lincoln resituated the Desert Eagle underneath his suit jacket and looked over at the younger man. "Fix your tie. You're supposed to be an FBI agent. Try looking like one."

The man straightened his tie in the rear view mirror and turned to Lincoln. "Okay?"

"Yeah, better. Got your ID ready?"

The young man patted his breast and nodded. "All set."

"Let's go get this over with then. This body armor's chafing me," Lincoln said, adjusting the codpiece inside his pants.

## DTC Transportation
## Edison, New Jersey

I had just glanced at the clock on my desk when my private extension rang. It was almost one forty-five.

"Hello." No need for business formalities. Cathy and Michael were the only ones who had the number.

"It's me." It was Michael.

"How'd it go?"

"Not too good," Michael spoke in an even voice. "We were set up. They tried to shoot us."

"Shoot you!" I straightened as I slid to the edge of my chair. "Who, Anelli?"

"No, I don't know who they were." Michael's tone was flat as a board.

"You okay?"

"Yeah, I'm okay. Look, I need you to tell Ilene I had to go away for a couple days, sudden business."

There was a distance in his voice as if someone was there with him, listening. "What's goin' on, man? Talk to me, Michael. Who set you up, Anelli?"

"No. I'm with him now. In fact, he probably saved my life."

"Who then, Venezio?"

"No. These guys were dressed like SWAT."

"SWAT? Police shot at you?"

"I'm not sure but I don't think they were cops."

"Michael, you're not making any sense. Who were they then?"

"I don't have a lot of time to talk," he said, still flat and cold. "I called because I need the pager number on that FBI agent's card. It's on my desk."

"I gave it to you this morning."

"I left it in my truck. I need it again."

"I really don't think you should go through with this, Michael. I didn't like it from the start and now, after this . . . There's something not right with this whole thing and . . ."

"Look Joseph, I already know how you feel about it. Besides it too late now. I don't have a choice. So just cut the shit and give me the goddamn number."

"Whoa, buddy, let's remember who we're talking to. I'm on your side, remember?"

"Are you?"

"What the fuck does that mean?'

I listened to the background noise for longer than was comfortable. Finally, he said, "Just give me the number, willya."

"Michael, I've been thinking about this, about last night. I'm sorry I acted like such an asshole. I think we need stick together on this. We can figure somethin' out. You and I, we've always been able to find a way. Remember that time in Philly, when we were kids in college? We thought we'd never get outta . . ."

"Joseph, forget it. Just believe me, I need the number. *Now. Please.*"

I wasn't getting anywhere and knew better than to push him anymore. I crossed to Michael's desk and read him the number scrawled on the card.

"Thanks," he said, without a trace of warmth. "By the way, did you tell anyone where I was going today?"

"Me? No. Who would I tell?"

"I dunno. You tell me."

"What are you getting at, Michael?"

"Just that if I believe that you didn't mention this to anyone, then I don't know how anyone else would have known where I was. And *if* that's true, then you better be careful, too, pal."

"Whadaya mean '*if*'?" I paused, waiting for a response. When none came I said, "Hey, *pal,* we better straighten this out *right now.* I don't like the sound of what you're saying here."

"Can't talk now."

"Then how can I reach you – your cell?"

"No, it's in my truck. I'll find you. I gotta go. Please don't forget to call Ilene. Tell her I'll try to call her tomorrow. And don't forget what I said. There's somethin' goin' on here. Watch your back."

I heard the clicking and coin-drop sounds of a pay phone. "Michael? Michael!"

I leaned back and stared across the room at Michael's empty desk. It had to be Catella. Catella and Anelli were boyhood friends. They grew up together. I understood the strength of that bond. It could survive years, even decades of separation, endure the divergence of careers and position, and transcend the power of money and the love of a woman. And Catella had told me that he had talked to Anelli. That was it. Catella was the connection, the common denominator. So, how much did Catella's old friend tell him? Did he know about the hijacking? Just how involved was he? And, most importantly, would he be a loose end to contend with?

## Taverna Reggia
## Lower East Side, New York City

"Lemme see sum ID," said the big man in the door of Taverna Reggia blocking Lincoln's view of the interior. Lincoln shifted to one side to see past his bulk, but the big man moved with him and scowled, "ID. Both of ya."

Lincoln made a thin, quick-like-a-blink smile and flipped open his leather ID case. "I'm Special Agent Clifford Dwyer and this is my partner, Agent Craig Henderson. Now get your fat ass outta my way."

The big man narrowed his eyes and turned his girth sideways in the door. Lincoln used his shoulder to try to push past him in the narrow space that remained, but the big man held his ground. Keeping his eyes forward to scan the room ahead of him, Lincoln brought his left elbow up hard and fast into the soft wattle meat under the big man's chin. He heard a grunt and felt the doorway widen as the big man stumbled back with his hands on his throat. As he took his first step inside Taverna Reggia, Lincoln pulled out the big shiny .50 caliber Desert Eagle. Henderson came in quickly behind Lincoln and poked the suppressed H&K subgun into the big man's gut, pushing him back into the room.

"FBI," Lincoln shouted, as he assumed a loose but combative pistol-shooting stance. "Hands in the air!"

Lincoln surveyed the room. In the far-left corner, five men were seated around a table playing cards. On the right, two more men were standing at the bar and Henderson was moving the big man into the middle of the room. Eight men. Two more than his surveillance team had seen enter through the front door today. Two more than Lincoln had expected, which meant there had to be a back door into the kitchen, which made sense. The men in the room were all looking at Lincoln but none of them had yet raised their hands. This is a tough crew, Lincoln thought, and they're too spread out for an effective field of fire.

Henderson had locked the front door and returned to Lincoln's side. Lincoln looked around the room and smiled, "Okay, now I want all you guinea fucks hands on your heads, move to the bar, and go face-down on it."

Lincoln saw all the men turn to look at the fat man seated at the table with his back to the wall. The fat man had straightened up in his chair and was glowering at Lincoln. Lincoln brought the front sight on the Desert Eagle across the room and settled it on between the fat man's eyes. So that's Vinny Diamonds Venezio, he reckoned.

Lincoln half-turned to Henderson and, without taking his eyes off Vinny, said, "Let these *gentlemen* know that when I ask them to do something, they should fuckin' do it."

Henderson stepped forward and brought the H&K up to his shoulder. Aiming into the big doorman's face, he said, "Move to the bar."

The big man snorted a couple times and cleared his throat. Drawing his head back and whipping forward quickly to increase the velocity, he spit a wad of phlegm in Henderson's face and sneered, "Fuck you."

Lincoln had been watching out of the corner of his eye, and as the big man had readied his spit, he reached under his jacket with his left hand and snatched the Glock from the holster in the small of his back. In an instant, he pointed the Glock at the men at the table, swung the .50 caliber toward the big man's head, and squeezed the trigger.

The noise from the magnum was deafening but the big man heard nothing. The large bullet had entered his left temple, snapping his head wildly to the side and lifting him onto his toes as it ripped ferociously into his skull. The mushrooming round tore through his brain and blasted a hole the size of a baseball out the far side of his head. Brain matter exploded out the exit wound as his body followed his head down, crushing a table on the way to the floor.

The men in the room stiffened and froze. Lincoln turned to Henderson, "Let's rock and roll! Put 'em on the floor!"

Henderson swung the muzzle of the H&K toward the Vinny's table, flipped the selector to full-auto, and squeezed the trigger. The submachine gun jumped to life, spitting rounds inches over their heads as they dove under the table. Henderson lowered his aim and cleared the glasses and ashtrays off the splintering tabletop. He continued to fire as he swept to the right across the double doors leading to the kitchen and along the back wall, shattering plates and bowls stacked in a hutch. The bullets continued to stitch a path around the corner of the room and over the top of the bar, starting bottles dancing in splashes of wine and liquor to a cacophony of rapid-fire chatter from the silenced gun, until the magazine was empty.

Lincoln began to move before the last shell casings had hit the ground. And before anyone dared look up from under the table, Lincoln was on them. With a pistol in each hand, he kicked over the table, exposing them. Grinning down the barrels of his guns at the five stunned men cowering on the floor, Lincoln said soothingly, "Hey now, don't look so worried. We're not really from the FBI."

Lincoln grinned broadly as he belly-laughed, causing his pistols to bounce gently. He was enjoying himself. But suddenly, he stopped cold. His face clouded with rage as his pupils dilated, turning his eyes into black stones. His nostrils flared as he hissed slowly, "Now, move to the bar. Everyone except you." He pointed the Desert Eagle at Vinny.

Henderson had reloaded the H&K with a fresh clip and was herding two men out from behind the bar. The card players shuffled over to the bar with hands on their heads, looking furtively over their shoulders at Lincoln, who had snapped on a pair on latex gloves and was securing Vinny to a chair with yards of duct tape. A final gray strip of tape covered Vinny's mouth.

Vinny's crew lined up along the bar. Lincoln joined Henderson tying their wrists behind their backs with plastic restraints and duct taping their mouths. Then they kicked out their feet, spreading their legs, and leaning them over so their faces rested on the bar. When they were done, Henderson stepped back. When he had the H&K shoulder-aimed at the men bent over the bar, Lincoln holstered his pistols and began to search them. He patted them down first, looking for weapons, and found none. Anyone who squirmed or resisted in the slightest way received an elbow to the kidney or a knee to the thigh muscle. Then he rifled their pockets, pulling them inside out, tossing the money, loose papers, and the occasional betting slip on the floor. The wallets were piled on the nearest table.

All the while, Vinny watched from across the room. Sweating, eyes bulging, breathing quickly and noisily through his nose, he tried not to look at Joey Freeze and his brains oozing onto the floor. But his chair had been dragged to within three feet of the big dead man. It was as if Lincoln had known they had grown up together. Vinny closed his eyes and shook his head. He would have to find a good mortician. He could never let Joey's mother see him like this. No, old Mrs. Malacci wouldn't hold up seeing her little Joey with two big holes in his head. Poor Joey Malacci. Big and tough, but he wouldn't hurt a flea, unless Vinny told him to. Joey Freeze they called him. He always liked it freezing fuckin' cold. He'd drive around with the air on in December. Hell, one time Vinny had seen him sweating sitting in the stands at a Giants game in December. Well, he wouldn't sweat no more.

Then he looked over at Lincoln and Henderson. *These motherfuckers will die for this*, he promised himself.

Lincoln sat at the table with the wallets and spread them out in the order of their owners lined up at the bar. "Let's see who are new friends are," he said.

Lincoln removed a driver's license or credit card from each wallet and began to read. "We have, Mr. Gerald Ferrini, Mr. Anthony Musto, Mr. Francis Migliaccio, Mr. Anthony Virelli, Mr. Anthony Canella, *and* Mr. Salvatore *Venezio*. Hmmm, whadaya know, six guys and three of 'em named *Anthony?*"

Lincoln looked over his shoulder at Vinny and, raising his eyebrows, said. "Vinny, this is a very *toni* place you have here."

Lincoln belly laughed again, slapping the table causing the wallets and ID's to jump. Then he abruptly stopped, glanced up at Henderson and shrugged. "I thought that was goddam funny. I guess wiseguys don't have much of a sense of humor." Then to Vinny again. "You goombahs outta lighten up. There's more to life than spaghetti and meatballs, ya know."

Vinny grunted from behind the duct tape. It was muffled, but Lincoln understood the two words: *Fuck you!*

"Vinny. Vinny." Rising to his feet. "With language like that you can see why we had to tape your mouth shut. But don't worry, your time to talk to me is almost here. In fact, we're gonna play a little game." Pacing between Vinny and the table. "I think you'll like it. It's called Ding Dong Dago. Ever hear of it?" Turning to the men at the bar. "You guys? No? That's okay, I'll teach you. It's easy and loads of fun." Pausing to glance thoughtfully up at the ceiling, he concluded, "Well, fun for me, anyway."

Lincoln walked back to the table of wallets. "First, we mix up the ID's like this. Then, I cover my eyes and . . . pick one at random." Holding up a driver's license. "And the first lucky player is . . . Mr. Anthony Virelli! Tony, come on down!" Nodding to Henderson.

Henderson was able to select Virelli by reading the body language and side glances of the men at the bar. He followed Lincoln's gesturing and moved Virelli so he was standing in front of Vinny, with Joey Freeze on the floor between them.

"Okay, Vinny," Lincoln began. "This is a game of knowledge. That's right, I'm going to ask you questions that will test your knowledge of certain events. It's an easy game because these events have not only occurred in the very recent past but they are also events that I know you have direct knowledge of. Any questions so far?"

Vinny didn't have a clue where this was going, but when he saw the fear in Virelli's eyes he thought that it was probably justified. He stared back at Lincoln with all the defiance he could muster.

Lincoln smiled. "No questions? No, of course not. You have duct tape on your mouth. So let's begin.

"Here's how this game works." Lincoln pointed to the wall clock over the front door. "That will be our game clock – our shot clock, if you will. I'm gonna ask you a question and you'll have thirty seconds to answer it correctly. Of course, your answers must be one hundred percent true and honest. If you fail to answer correctly within thirty seconds, then it's Ding Dong Dago. Simple, right?

"Okay Vinny, here's your first question. What arrangements have you made with Joseph Napolo, Michael Cogan, and John Anelli? And where is the item that you hijacked two days ago? Oh, I'm sorry that was two questions." Ripping the tape off of Vinny's mouth and leaning close to affect a stage whisper. "I'll be fair; just answer the first question." Looking up at the clock. "You have thirty seconds."

Vinny stretched his fleshy cheeks against the sting of the tape and looked up at the clock. He had twenty-five seconds left. Vinny thought, *What the fuck is Danny Gallagher doing?* Was he still in the kitchen?

Danny was a neighborhood kid, in his early twenties. He'd been hanging around for years and they had been paying him to clean up, take out the trash, and such. He knew the streets, the wiseguys and the cops, and played both ends well. Did he know that there was a sawed-off 12-gauge hidden in the steam table or did the he just run out the back door when he heard the shooting? Who would blame him? Maybe he was getting help. Vinny realized he would be real happy to see a handful of New York's Finest come busting threw the door right about now.

"Ten seconds left on the shot clock, Vinny," Lincoln taunted.

"Why don't you go fuck yourself?" Vinny retorted.

Lincoln shook his head dramatically. "Oh no, I'm sorry, Vinny. You can't answer a question with a question in this game. Perhaps I should have explained the rules more carefully. Let's see what the judges say." Lincoln turned away and pretended to be listening intently to the imaginary judges. When he turned back to Vinny, shaking his head again in mock sympathy, he had the silenced .22 revolver in his right hand. "Just as I thought, Vinny. The judges have ruled against you. And, the shot clock says it's Ding Dong Dago time."

Vinny's eyes widened at the sight of the twenty-two. Reacting to Vinny's expression, Virelli began to turn to look at Lincoln. But Lincoln was already in motion, lifting the twenty-two and squeezing off two quick shots into the back of Virelli's head. Virelli went boneless and crumbled, falling across Joey Freeze's body, his face flopping hard against the floor at Vinny's feet. Vinny bolted up against the duct tape, trying to jump back from the horror.

The men at the bar grunted and cursed from behind their duct tape gags. Some of them had been watching in the mirror over the bar. All of them had heard the *thump, thump* of the suppressed pistol and then the *crack* as Virelli's head hit the floor. Henderson moved in to quiet them, pushing their heads back onto the bar with muzzle of the submachine gun, leaving them off balance and once again neutralized.

Danny Gallagher had also been watching through the separation between the swinging doors to the kitchen. He had crawled slowly out from behind the steam table, cradling the 12-gauge shotgun and clasping the wound in his side. One of the nine-millimeter rounds from Henderson's H&K had passed through the kitchen doors, through the thin metal sides of the steam table, and into the soft flesh of Danny's left side. The bullet had exited his back without damaging any vital parts but he was bleeding like a stuck pig. Surprisingly, it didn't hurt too much.

Danny quietly opened the breach on the shotgun. It was loaded, two shells, one in each barrel. One for each guy. The machine-gun guy had his back to him and the other guy was putting tape back on Vinny's mouth. If he was quick, he could get them both. At least knock them down long enough for Vinny's guys to kick the shit out of them. He began to imagine how Vinny would repay him. They called him The Irish Kid. Maybe now they'd stop calling him *kid* and let him do more than clean up the place. Maybe . . . But he didn't have time to think about it now. He had to act fast, before the guy was done taping Vinny and before the machine-gun guy turned around.

Lincoln saw the kitchen door moving in his peripheral vision. His mind flashed. *The kitchen! Fuck! We didn't check the goddam kitchen!* He sensed himself instinctively reaching for the Desert Eagle as Danny was coming through the door.

"Gun!" Lincoln shouted, but it was too late. As Henderson began to spin around, the shotgun exploded. The center of the blast caught Henderson in the left shoulder, peppering his face, head, and neck with the pellets, and blowing him back onto a table. As he slipped down between the table and chairs on his way to the floor, Henderson tried to bring up the H&K in his right hand, but his timing was off. His finger found the trigger and locked around it before he could get the gun up to its target. The automatic subgun erupted too low and too wide. Then the recoiling weapon twisted in his weakened one-handed grip, spraying hot lead in a wild arch that zipped diagonally along the bar where Vinny's crew was bent over.

As Vinny's men were dropping, Lincoln's Desert Eagle fired; three times in less than a second. The tightly grouped fifty caliber slugs slammed through the center of Danny Gallagher's chest, knocking him back into the kitchen. He was dead before he hit the floor.

"Son-of-a-bitch!" Lincoln shouted, when he looked over at Henderson and the other men on the floor. Keeping the Desert Eagle trained on Vinny's men, he walked over to Henderson and yanked away a chair that had fallen on him.

"Shit!" Lincoln cursed. Henderson was conscious but already going into shock. The left side of his neck and face was a bloody mess, dotted with buckshot. Pieces of his ear, nose, and lower lip were missing. The top of his shoulder bone was exposed. Lincoln pried the empty H&K from Henderson's grip and slid it into the corner of the room. Then he turned his attention to the men lying along the bar. Only two of them were stirring. He quickly stepped over and rolled them on their backs. One of the men appeared to be unharmed. The other had been hit once in the thigh.

Lincoln pointed the Desert Eagle at the two men. "Stay on your backs," He ordered between clenched teeth. "If you move, I'll kill you."

Then he checked the other three. Ferrini and Musto were dead. The other one had been hit twice across the back and was moaning and coughing blood. Lincoln recognized that under these conditions a lung wound would be mortal but, more importantly, he couldn't stand the man's moaning and coughing. So he pulled out the .22 revolver and fired twice into the top of the dying man's head. Frankie Migliaccio's last breath was a long gurgling sigh.

Lincoln returned to Henderson's side. As he knelt, Henderson gagged and vomited blood. A thick bright red stream ran over his chin and down his chest. Lincoln guessed that his stomach was filling with blood from the throat wounds. Henderson's bloodied lips quivered but no sound came out. His young eyes searched Lincoln's face for answers. But Lincoln had none. So he turned away and pounded over to Vinny, throwing chairs that were in his path.

"Look what you've done here, Vinny!" Lincoln screamed, as he took Vinny's head in his hands and twisted it hard toward Henderson and the other dead and wounded. "Look! Look at this mess! You did this! Do you understand?" Then moving Vinny's face close to his. "Do you? DO YOU?"

Lincoln released Vinny's head and grabbed the back of the chair he was taped to. Grunting against Vinny's weight, he shoved hard and the chair pitched forward. Vinny shut his eyes as the chair tumbled over, squeezing them more tightly as he felt himself falling onto the bodies of Anthony Virelli and Joey Freeze.

Still strapped to the chair as it settled on its side, Vinny's cheek splashed into something warm and sticky on the floor. His eyes blinked and focused on the dead face of Joey Freeze. He was inches from the death-stare eyes, with his own face in a thick puddle of blood and brains that had leaked from the head of his loyal friend. He recoiled but the movement caused the bloody goop to slosh into his ear.

Vinny closed his eyes to the fight off a wave of nausea. He tried to let his mind's eye float away, but the images were too powerful. He drifted back to the surprised look frozen on Joey's face. It had a soft boyish quality, reminding Vinny of their childhood together, the Brooklyn street corner their gang had claimed, down the alleyway they retreated to when the cops took the corner back. Stickball. Mr. Calandriello's fruit stand. Saturday matinees. His mother's meatballs. And now *this*. It was a bad dream. A nightmare. Like *his* nightmare, sitting on the back of that truck, watching helplessly as his friends slipped off under the steamroller. Colored dots in the road. He felt himself starting to slide down off the bumper of the truck. He could hear the madman, Lincoln, dragging someone, one of his friends, across the floor. It wasn't over yet. The steamroller was coming closer.

Lincoln righted Vinny's chair by first pushing it over so that Vinny went face down on the floor, in the blood again. Then he put a foot on the back rung of the chair and stepped down as he pulled it back up. When the violent motions stopped, Vinny opened his eyes and saw Tony Canella and his brother Sal standing before him, just on the other side on the bodies of Virelli and Joey Freeze. Their duct-taped faces and quick breathing relayed their distress.

Henderson coughed and started to gag. Lincoln went to him and stood there, shaking his head. Henderson was starting to drown in his own blood. Lincoln knelt and bent to put his lips near the younger man's disfigured ear. Vinny and the surviving members of his crew watched as Lincoln whispered to Henderson. Whatever Lincoln was saying, seemed to calm Henderson and quiet his gagging. Lincoln straightened up and took the .22 revolver from his jacket pocket, holding it behind his back.

"Close your eyes, Craig, and try to relax. Trust me. You're gonna be fine," Lincoln lied.

Without immediate medical attention, Lincoln figured, Henderson would be dead within an hour. Moreover, there was no way Lincoln could take the bloodied man to the car without attracting attention. And there was no way he could leave him behind alive. So, as soon as Henderson closed his eyes, Lincoln brought the pistol around and shot him twice in the head. Then one more time in the heart.

Lincoln coolly turned to Vinny and the other two men. All traces of playfulness were gone from his demeanor as he removed the empty shell casings from the revolver and placed them in his pocket. While he reloaded the pistol, he spoke slowly and softly without looking up, "Game's over Vinny. We've made too much noise in here, so I've gotta go soon."

Lincoln closed the reloaded cylinder on the pistol, walked over to Vinny and ripped the duct tape off his mouth. Then standing to the side, he stretched out his arm to its full length so that the end of the silencer on the pistol was a couple inches from the side of Canella's head.

"Okay Vinny *Diamonds*, let's try this again. I want to know where my merchandise is." Cocking the pistol, he continued, "I want to know all about it, everyone that's involved and what their part was, starting with Anelli, Cogan, and Napolo."

Vinny looked up at Canella. His eyes pleaded with Vinny but they both knew that Vinny couldn't, wouldn't help him. Vinny was old school, a stand-up guy, and it was no secret how he felt about the growing legions of New York wiseguys who had made deals with the Feds. On many occasions, Vinny's crew had sat witness as he loosed contemptuous and vicious tirades, holding nothing in reserve in his condemnation of their cowardice and betrayal. No, not under any circumstances would Vinny tell this crazy bastard anything. Especially when it involved the grandson of the great Don Carmine Napolo; the legendary godfather that had knowingly gone to a horrible death rather than expose his Family to the Senate investigations. This was the man that had forever inspired the members of the Napolo Family to remain faithful to the old ways and, in doing so, perpetuated their unchallenged position as the most powerful crime family in the nation. In fact, out of respect, or perhaps fear, not one Napolo soldier had ever broken his vow of Omerta. To do so would be to desecrate the memory of this great man. The same man that had eased Vinny's dear mother's suffering with his kindness and generosity.

Vinny looked at his brother, Sal, and then over to Lincoln. Smiling, Vinny said to Lincoln, "I guess you don't hear so good, do ya? I already tol' ya ta go fuck yourself, didn't I?"

Canella bowed his head and groaned. Lincoln locked eyes with Vinny and without breaking his stare, fired twice into Canella's head. Canella collapsed from the inside out and dropped heavily across Virelli's legs.

Lincoln stepped over Canella's body and leveled the gun at Sal's ear. The brothers looked into each others' eyes and measured the moment. It seemed Vinny had always taken care of his little brother. Sal had been only six when their mother died. Vinny had packed his lunches for school and, on the nights his father didn't come home, gave him dinner and a bath, too. But this was the life they both had chosen, and like the steamroller that crushed little Sal in his nightmare, Vinny knew there was nothing he could do to stop what was about to happen. And even if he told this lunatic everything he knew, which wasn't much, Vinny was certain that there was no way either of them were ever going to walk out of Taverna Reggia again.

"This is your brother, isn't it Vinny?" Lincoln said. "Are you gonna make me kill your brother?"

Vinny saw that tears had puddled above the lower lids in Sal's eyes but he wasn't crying. Vinny drew a deep breath to hold back his own tears and shook his head. Then Sal shrugged as if to say *what the hell*.

"Last chance, Vinny," Lincoln snarled.

Vinny scowled at Lincoln and gazed one more time at his brother. Sal's eyes were dryer and the edges of the duct tape rose as he formed a smile. Then Sal nodded and winked. Vinny winked back at him and turned to Lincoln.

"Fuck you and your mother."

Vinny put his head down and closed his eyes. He heard the .22 spit and Sal falling to the ground, followed by a low moan and a second shot.

Silence. Vinny saw a bright blue dot on the road in the back of his eyelids.

"Vinny, you are one sick motherfucker," Lincoln chided. "He was your brother for chrissake. What's the fuck's wrong with you?"

Vinny smirked. "Nothin's wrong with *me*. I won. Donchya see? There ain't nothin' left that you can do to me now. There's no one left."

"I still got you, you dumb fuck."

"Then you got *nothin'*."

Lincoln reached down to his ankle and came up with a knife. "Oh, but I do."

He waved the knife close to Vinny's face. "I've got your ten fingers and your ears and your eyes and your nose and your dick. And I'll slice them off one by one until you're begging me to hear what I want to know."

Lincoln pounced and clamped his hand down on Vinny's wrist over the duct tape, trying to spread Vinny's fleshy hand so that his thumb was across the wooden armrest. Vinny reacted quickly, moving his thumb and fingers around and underneath the armrest and squeezing hard. Lincoln tried to twist up the thumb but Vinny resisted with an iron-grip. Tired of struggling, Lincoln pressed the tip of his knife blade against the back of Vinny's hand into the space between the wrist and hand bones. Vinny steeled himself, as the knife tip broke the skin and began to penetrate the soft tissue at the edge of his wrist bone. Vinny took a deep breath as he watched Lincoln reverse his grip on the knife, preparing to bare down on it with his weight. Lincoln paused to look up and lock eyes with Vinny. Then, after a moment, he smiled and shrugged and began to push down on the blade.

Vinny sucked in more air as he watched the blade sink into his skin. But suddenly, Lincoln stopped and pulled the knife from Vinny's wrist. Sirens wailing in the streets had caught his attention.

"Doesn't sound like you're gonna have time for all this," Vinny said between heavy breaths.

Lincoln straightened up and listened to the sirens. There was no way to know which way they were heading, but they were getting louder. And although sirens were as regular as traffic lights in New York, he couldn't take the chance that the gunfire from the .50 caliber and the shotgun hadn't attracted some attention.

Lincoln shrugged and smiled resignedly. "Maybe your right, Vinny. But I got one more question."

Lincoln flipped the knife around in his hand and held his arm outstretched. Vinny's eyes went to the shiny blade tipped with his blood. It was pointed to heaven.

"How do you spell chrysanthemum?" Lincoln asked him.

"*What?*" Vinny answered, as he looked up at Lincoln, exposing his spongy neck.

"Wrong."

Out of the corner of his eye, Vinny saw the blur of Lincoln's hand and a glint off the razor-sharp blade as it arced toward him, just before it sliced deeply across his throat. Lincoln jumped back a safe distance to avoid the spray of blood. He stood still and stone-faced, lips moving slightly, watching the pulsating red fountain squirting from Vinny's carotid artery pump slower and slower, until it was a trickle.

All the while, Vinny heard Lincoln muttering and, in the moments before he died, he realized that Lincoln was reciting letters, spelling something. As he felt himself slipping away, down off the bumper of the big truck and into the path of the steamroller, Vinny put the letters together: *chrysanthemum*.

Lincoln dropped the knife at Vinny's feet and began to work quickly. He scooped up the dead men's ID's, stuffed them back into their wallets, and scattered them on the floor around the table. To prevent the analysis of any hair or fibers that may have adhered to it, he removed all the duct tape from the corpses and stuffed the flattened wad into his jacket pocket. He removed Henderson's ID case and checked his pockets to be certain there was nothing else to identify him. Then he went to the center of the room and spun around slowly, taking in every detail, like an artist surveying his canvas, searching for flaws in the craftsmanship that would sully his art. He spied and removed a ring from Henderson's finger, which prompted him to feel the dead man's neck and wrists for any other jewelry. Finally satisfied, he pulled the Desert Eagle from his shoulder holster, wiped it clean, and dropped it on the floor as he walked toward the kitchen. The ballistic markings on the Desert Eagle's .50 caliber slugs and shell casings are too unique, too traceable. It was a throwaway gun. He had purchased a dozen Desert Eagles with that in mind. He figured he had seven or eight left.

He stopped again just in front of the kitchen doors and turned to look around the room one more time. Pushing the approaching sirens out of his mind lest they distract him from this final inspection, he studied the bloody scene with a clinical eye. He didn't allow his concentration to break until he was absolutely sure that nothing was left behind to distract the criminalists from the conclusion that this had been anything but a Family matter. Then, to be sure, he reached into his pocket and threw Johnny Anelli's wallet on the floor near the table with the other wallets.

Stepping into the alley behind Taverna Reggia, Lincoln used a spatula from the kitchen to slide the lock on the back door into the receiver as he closed it behind him. It would now appear that the door had been locked from the inside, further leading investigators to the conclusion that the victims had known their executioner. After tossing the spatula into a trash bin and folding a newspaper he had retrieved from the top of the heap, he peeled off the latex gloves and stuffed them in his pocket. Looking every bit a businessman returning from lunch with today's news tucked under his arm, he strolled casually out of the alley.

When he rounded the corner and reached his car, he fished out his keys, making sure to pause and look with great interest at the small but gathering crowd around the two police cruisers in the street. Four police officers were listening intently to an excited older woman who was motioning quite animatedly toward Taverna Reggia. When the officers started down the steps to the iron gate in front of the restaurant, Lincoln got in the car and drove slowly away.

Stopped at the red light at the end of the street, he reached for the radio knob and, smelling the submarine sandwich, he reminded himself not to forget to take the leftovers when he abandoned the rental car. Jersey subs were great left-overs.

# CHAPTER 17
## DTC Transportation
## Edison, NJ

Passing through the dispatch office on my way out to the loading docks, I tried to mask the different emotions that I was struggling to control. Bobby Moretti looked up from dispatch console and gave me a knowing nod. He had burst into my office thirty minutes ago to tell me to turn on the television. All the New York stations and the cable news channels had interrupted their scheduled programming to report on the murders at the Taverna Reggia. I sat glued to the set for almost an hour, working the channel changer on the remote. File footage of Vincent "Vinny Diamonds" Venezio, reputed Underboss of the Napolo Crime Family, and old black and white photos of my grandfather, Don Carmine Napolo, flashed across the networks. Talking head experts on organized crime likened the "Slaughter in SoHo" to Pearl Harbor, a devastating first strike in an inevitable Mob war. There were theories and ruminations ad nauseum on New York crime family rivalries that may have sparked a power struggle or demanded a vendetta. And amid frequent recaps of the "bold midday bloodbath", there were speculations on the reaction and health of the aged and reclusive Napolo Crime Family Boss, Fabrizio Benedetto, and had his weakened physical condition been perceived as an opportunity to challenge the supremacy of the Napolo Family.

CNN was calling it The May Massacre and had already selected ominous theme music suggestive of the Godfather movies to play over hastily assembled graphics depicting silhouetted fedoras and smoking Tommy guns in the segues between commercials. The reporters live at the scene were scrambling for the latest information. Varying from station to station, they were reporting unconfirmed death tolls ranging from six to ten, including Underboss Vincent "Vinny Diamonds" Venezio. A few of them announced the names of some of the other lesser-known yet infamous dead men, noting that Vinny's brother Sal was among the deceased. Several made note of the conspicuous absence of the rising Family star, Jimmy Merchanti. Most of them reminded the audience of the execution-style murders of the two Napolo soldiers in Hackensack only two days earlier. And they all drew comparisons to the Saint Valentine's Day Massacre in Chicago over seventy years ago.

I was watching two retired crime fighters on MSNBC, a former head of New York City's Organized Crime Taskforce and a former Special-Agent-In-Charge of the FBI's New York office were speculating on the motives and consequences of this apparent Mob war when the first phone call came in. It was Alley Cat Catella. He was calling to tell me that the local Fox station had learned from an inside source that John Anelli was the primary suspect in both the Taverna Reggia slayings and the Hackensack murders. Catella used this to advance his theory that 'sumthin's not right here' and that I should be careful. When I refused to probe him for more, Catella volunteered that he knew for a fact that Johnny was in New Jersey all day. And when I continued to act with indifference, Catella guilefully suggested that I could verify this with Michael Cogan.

"Don't be stupid," Catella huffed in frustration. "What do I have to gain by tellin' ya this? Nothin', that's what. I'm tryin' to do the right thing here."

"The right thing for me or your friend?" I maintained my aloof posture even though I knew Catella's concern was justified and it was likely that his intentions were pure.

"Look, Joseph," Catella sighed. "We didn't go to your house last night and we didn't torch your trucks. Believe me or not, we didn't do it. But you gotta trust me on *this* because I think you outta be real careful until everything gets figured out."

I was beginning to believe him. The State Police Arson Squad had found parts of the incendiary device used on our trucks. They told me that it was a relatively sophisticated design with military-issue fuses. Hardly the type of setup used by amateur arsonists, like a couple of Teamsters. And, of course, no one had actually come to my house last night.

"I don't know what else I can say," Catella concluded.

"I can think of something."

"What's that?"

"That you'll let my people have their decertification vote."

"That will happen. It's in the works," Catella confirmed. "Laskowski needs a couple days though, to let it play out right."

"And until then?" I pushed.

"Things'll be nice and quiet."

"They better be."

I began to hang up and then stopped. I was never comfortable playing the hard-ass. I did it well when I had to, but it was against my nature. Besides, I was beginning to believe everything Alley Cat was telling him.

I returned the phone to my ear and said, "Albert?"

"Yeah."

"Thank you. Thanks for . . . um . . . everything."

The next call came seconds after I had finished with Catella. It was a shaken Jimmy Merchanti calling from a phone booth in Greenwich Village, not far from Taverna Reggia.

"Have you heard what happened?" I heard the agitation in his voice.

"Yeah, I've been watching it on TV."

"They fuckin' shot Vinny and Sal and all . . ." Jimmy's voice wavered and he stopped himself. I stayed quiet while Jimmy breathed heavily.

"Motherfuckers!" I heard Jimmy slam his fist against something. "They think they can do sumthin' like this and fuckin' live?"

More heavy breathing.

After a few seconds, I explored the silence. "Who's 'they', Jimmy?"

"I don't know." He said it softly and slowly, like he couldn't believe it himself. "I made a lot a calls. You know we have friends *everywhere*. All over town, all over Jersey, all over. Nobody knows nothin'. And *somebody* should know *sumthin'*." Jimmy hesitated. "Joseph, there's sumthin goin' on here that ain't kosher. I'm not sure what, but I don't fuckin' like it. One thing I *do* know is that I'm gonna find the motherfuckers who did this. And when I do, I promise you, they'll wish they were never fuckin' born. But until then, I'll be watchin' my back real close. And I think you should do the same."

This was the second time in five minutes that I had heard that sentiment. Both times from guys who were entrenched in a world where things weren't always black and white. Where two plus two didn't always equal four. I found myself having trouble not believing it was true.

"Have you heard from Michael?" Jimmy said.

"Yeah. He called a little while ago. He's with that guy Johnny."

"They're okay?" Jimmy asked apprehensively.

"Yes, but there was some trouble."

I suddenly remembered my morning conversation with Michael.

I said, "Weren't you supposed to go with him today? What happened?"

"Yeah, I went with 'im. That's the reason why I wasn't there with Vinny and the guys. But I waited in the car. Michael went in to meet Johnny and then, before I knew it, the place was surrounded by cops."

"Cops? You sure?"

"Yeah, they ah . . ." Jimmy paused to think. "Well, I just assumed they were cops - SWAT guys – ya know, black outfits, helmets, boots, machine guns, shit like that."

"Yeah, but how do you know they were cops? Did they have any wording on their backs, like Police or FBI?"

"Ya mean like on TV? No. No, I don't think they did. But maybe that's just on TV, ya know?"

"Maybe. What else did you see?"

"Not much. Michael went into the building with Johnny and then the cops, or whoever they were, went in. After that I had to hide in the back of Michael's car. I heard some shooting though. You said they're okay?"

"That's what Michael told me."

"Thank, God. How they hell did they get outta there? There was a lot of those SWAT guys. How the fuck did they get away?"

"Michael didn't say. He just said he was taking care of business."

"Like the deal's still on?" Jimmy asked brightly.

I was struck silent by my disbelief. In the midst of all that had just happened, Merchanti was instantaneously electrified by the renewed prospect of a big score. His friends had just been brutally murdered, probably still lying in their own blood, the victims of a cold-blooded assassination, yet I was convinced that Merchanti had promptly calculated that with Vinny out of the picture, his share had just doubled.

"I'm afraid that's all I know," I finally replied, masking my disgust.

"Look, man, it's very important, for all concerned, that we are able to keep in touch – for a couple reasons. Ya know what I mean, Joseph?"

I considered the pros and cons of Merchanti's assertion. I had let myself become involved in a situation that had become deadly serious and I wanted nothing more than to extricate myself from it. But now, more than ever, I needed to stay involved. However, this was all new to me and I realized that I didn't possess the skill and experience factors that would enable me to react quickly and effectively, with any degree of confidence. And things were happening too fast for me to calmly sift through the rubble and intellectualize a plan. For now, every resource was important.

I reached for a cell phone that was resting in its charging cradle on my credenza. It was an extra one we kept in the office. The phone's number was written on the back.

"I can give you a cell number that I'll have with me at all times. But first I want to hear more about this afternoon, when you were with Michael."

"There's not much more. I told you what I saw."

"Yeah, but you didn't tell me how *you* got outta there, did you?"

"What the fuck's that s'posed to mean?" I could hear his hackles rising.

"Nothing. I just want you to tell me exactly what happened after you heard the shots, up to when you left."

"Why?" Jimmy's back was still up. "What're you thinking?"

"Look, just tell me what happened after the shooting stopped, or I hang up and we go our separate ways."

"Okay, okaaay." Jimmy exhaled heavily. "Lemme see . . . after the shots, I stayed under the blanket in the back seat of Michael's truck. I laid there for about five minutes and then I heard the SWAT guys talkin'. They were standin' right outside the truck."

"How'd you know they were the SWAT guys if you were under the blanket?"

"Because they were saying stuff about the shooting and how they didn't know where they – ya know, Johnny and Michael – went. They were saying that it was like they just disappeared."

"What else did they say?"

"Not much, they were talkin' about a guy named Phil. They were saying they had to wait because Philly's down. Didn't make sense to me "

"Then what?"

"They tried the doors on the truck but they were locked. One guy asked if they should break in but they didn't because I think the sirens scared them off."

"Sirens?"

"Yeah, like police sirens, coming closer. And I think this Phil guy showed up right about then and they left. After a while, I looked out and I didn't see nobody so then I left."

"Do you have Michael's truck?"

"No, it's still there. Michael took the keys."

"Then how'd you get back to New York?"

"I called a cab from a gin mill down the street."

Jimmy's lack of hesitation and forthright tone led me to believe that he was probably telling the truth. But, in this case, the truth was not too telling.

"Jimmy, think," I pushed. "Was there *anything* else? Anything you forgot? Something they did or said that you didn't tell me? Try to remember."

Jimmy exhaled again. "Man, that was it. That's the whole thing."

"Shit, I was just hoping that . . ."

"What a minute," Jimmy interrupted. "Now that you mention it, there was something that caught me funny. While they were waiting for this Phil, one of them said something about the Beach Boys."

"The Beach Boys?"

"Well, yeah, one of the Beach Boys," Jimmy said, as if he suddenly felt foolish mentioning it.

"Like in the Surfin' Safari, Help Me Rhonda Beach Boys?"

"Yeah, like, California Girls. That's my favorite."

"Jimmy, what'd he say, exactly."

"One of 'em said that Dennis Wilson was gonna be pissed. Go figure."

It took a moment, but when it hit, I felt like a penny under the steel wheels of a mile-long freight train.

"Jimmy, could they have said Wilson Dennis and not Dennis Wilson?" I waited.

"Yeah, maybe . . . now that I think about it, that was it, Wilson Dennis. That's what he said. Why, who's this Wilson Dennis? You know him?"

I let the phone drop to my shoulder as I flopped against the back of my chair. As I tried to order my thoughts, my cheeks began to tingle from burst of heat rushing to my head. My mouth was dry when I spoke again.

"I'm not sure," I lied.

I deflected Jimmy's follow-up questions. I had too many of my own. I redirected the conversation by giving Jimmy the cell phone number in exchange for Jimmy's pager number. We promised to keep each other informed, especially if either of us heard anything from Michael. But Jimmy wouldn't let it go.

"Joseph, I'm not stupid, ya know. I think you know sumthin' that you're not tellin' me and I think that's not a good thing - for me or for you, cause there's no fuckin' way that this ain't all connected somehow. So, I don't know why you're not tellin' me what you know, because we're all in the same boat here. Now me, I gotta figure out what's goin' on here before I can get back to my normal life. Until then, I'm gonna be real careful. And if I were you, I'd be thinkin' the same thing. Capice?"

I knew he was right. In some way, all this was connected. But the thought of Wilson Dennis and FirsTech being involved with Vinny Diamonds and Johnny Anelli, on any other level than the pure coincidence of the hijacking, was incongruous. But then, there was something peculiar about Wilson Dennis' demeanor when I had initially informed him of the hijacking. I distinctly remembered feeling that Dennis had already known about the hijacking, even though it had happened less than ten minutes earlier. And what was it that Dennis had said to me? *Don't worry, we have a lot of resources, we'll get it back* or something equally confident. But maybe I was reaching, creating conspiracy where none existed. Either way, for now, this had to remain with me, if only for the simple reason that I couldn't yet make sense of it, let alone explain it to Merchanti.

"Capice," I said. "I'll tell you more when I can."

"Sooner the better, Joseph."

"Stay in touch," I said as I hung up.

I leaned back in the chair and stared across the office. My mind raced but my thoughts were scattered like pieces of a jigsaw puzzle and the box top with the picture wasn't anywhere around. I would have to start from scratch and rebuild the events of the last couple days, piece by piece. I glanced at my watch. It was almost four o'clock. I reached for Special Agent Clifford Dwyer's business card and dialed Samantha at the front desk.

"Sam, please hold all my calls except for Michael and my wife. I don't want to be disturbed for awhile."

"Okay, but Mr. Dennis from FirsTech has been holding for awhile. What should I tell him?"

Occasionally, we are witness to occurrences that defy ready explanation. Some are proven tricks of the mind, like déjà vu or visual flashes of things or persons that come and go from the corners of our eyes. Others are events that seem to occur at random yet, at their center, are intrinsically connected to one another. Still others are true coincidences.

In May of 1970, a couple of friends and I told our parents that we were staying at one anothers' for the night. We hitchhiked to Washington, D.C. to join hundreds of thousands of young people gathered at the Washington Monument in protest of Nixon's Vietnam War policies. At the foot of the lawn sloping from the base of the monument, a stage had been erected. For the next 48 hours nearly every rock band of that era played for the protestors. Dylan, The Stones, The Jefferson Airplane, The Beach Boys, Taj Mahal, Black Sabbath, and many others whose names have been lost in the haze of time and the dry refreshments we took that night, played for the cause.

By the time we arrived in was dark and the lawns around the monument were blanketed with students and hippies sitting hip-to-hip in the dark, peacefully listening to the music. It was an exceptionally cool evening and the air was filled with a sweet mix of wood smoke from few dozen camp fires and marijuana from thousands of joints. As we stepped slowly over and through the seated crowd searching for a bare spot, voices from below spoke offerings of all the popular drugs. Hands reached up to steady us or to offer bottles of beer as we stretched our steps across our stoned brothers and sisters until we finally arrived at a patch of earth large enough for the three of us. As soon as we were settled we realized that we didn't have a bottle opener for the beer we had collected. My friend Doug was seated on the left. Andy was in the middle with me on the right. Doug was asking people around us if they had an opener. The guy sitting next to me leaned forward and said, "Hey, Dougie, I got one. Got an extra beer?"

It was Doug's older brother Chip. He had been in Viet Nam. He was still wearing his fatigues, a floppy duty hat, and muddy jungle boots. He hadn't been home yet. It was the first time Doug had seen him in over a year. Doug looked at him for a long moment and said, "Holy shit, Chippie! Thanks, man. Welcome home."

We used his bottle opener which dangled from a key chain along with a feathered roach clip and a peace symbol fashioned from the base of a brass 40 millimeter M-79 "Thumper" shell. We gave him a beer and settled back with the music. I know I will never experience a more powerful or more righteous coincidence in my lifetime.

Catella, Merchanti, and now Dennis? I knew immediately that I would not sully that ingenuous and hallowed moment by believing this was in any way a coincidence.

I returned the phone to my ear and said, "Put 'im through, Sam."

"Joseph, Wilson Dennis here. How are you?" Dennis was light and cheery.

"Fine Wilson, and you?" I was equally pleasant.

"Outstanding." Dennis' standard response.

"Glad to hear it. Any news on your end about the hijacking?"

"Oh, no, nothing yet. But, statistically it's the second twenty-four hours that tend to yield the most. By then, the trucks are usually found stripped and abandoned, which of course doesn't apply in this case. However, this is also the timeframe in which the cargo starts to hit the streets. The bad guys generally want to unload their swag as soon as possible. Depending on the type of merchandise, its street value, and some good old dumb luck, this is where the trail back to the culprits usually begins."

"Does your cargo *have* street value? I thought it was military hardware."

"*Everything* has a street value." Dennis' tone was suddenly somber.

Sure does, I thought, a million bucks.

"I guess you're right, Wilson."

"But, Joseph, that's not why I called." Lighter again. "This is more social than business. I was just making sure that you were coming this evening, and that you were going to be staying over tonight for tomorrow's tournaments. We didn't receive your RSVP. Maybe there was a mix up. You did receive the invitation?"

With all the events of the day, I had forgotten about the FirsTech awards dinner up at Nicolas Pucci's club. But what was this about staying over and tournaments?

"To tell you the truth, Wilson, Michael's had the invitation on his desk. I haven't even looked at it. Hold on."

I crossed to Michael's desk and found the invitation. There it was: Partners In Excellence, Quality Awards Dinner, Guests of Honor . . . Overnight Accommodations at The Smoke and Gun Club at Bella Collina, Thursday Activities . . . Tournaments: Golf, Tennis, Billiards, Nine-Ball, Skeet and Trap Shooting, Target Pistol, and Combat Pistol. Leave it to Michael to leave out the details.

"Jeez, I apologize, Wilson. Michael and I have been going in two different directions this week. We didn't RSVP?"

"No, but we assumed you would be here for the dinner to accept your company's award. I was just checking to be sure that you would be staying for the tournaments."

*The Executive Vice President checking on reservations?*

"Sure, of course I'll be there."

"That's great. And you'll be staying over?"

"I hadn't planned on it. I have a busy week."

"Oh, but Nicolas Pucci and I were hoping you would. We looked forward to spending some time with you, on a more casual basis. The opportunity to have some fun with your business associates is important to us. Frankly, we think it's good business. Now I understand it's the eleventh hour, but perhaps you could rearrange your schedule. I can promise to have you back in Jersey after lunch tomorrow."

Under normal circumstances, I would readily welcome an invitation to schmooze a senior executive and the CEO of a very valuable customer. However, this didn't feel much like an invitation, because an invitation I'd feel free to decline.

"Well, I might be able to change my plans."

"Outstanding. Do you shoot?"

"You mean *what* do I shoot? Like in golf?"

"No, I meant *do* you shoot – like in handguns? Nicolas and I have a long-running rivalry on the pistol range. Why don't you join us? We could use some new blood."

"Actually, golf's more my speed," I said.

Dennis chuckled. "I didn't think golf and speed could ever be used in the same sentence. Besides, you can golf anytime, anywhere. We have world class shooting ranges at the club, both indoor and outdoor. Even our most well placed military and government guests find our ranges impressively appointed."

"I've never really shot anything, except a shotgun and that was years ago. When I was thirteen or fourteen, my father and I went skeet shooting with a friend of his."

"Skeet's fun - a gentleman's sport, but if you've never shot a handgun, you owe yourself the opportunity, if for no other reason than to gain an appreciation of the sport and the skill that's involved. It's an awful lot of fun. There's nothing quite like running a box of ammunition through your favorite piece. Guaranteed to take your mind off what's troubling you. Hey, if nothing else, you'll walk away with a whole new perspective on Hollywood's gunfights. So whadaya say?"

It was clear that Dennis was doing his best to convince me to spend time with Pucci and him. But more importantly, I realized that Dennis had not mentioned Michael. The omission was obvious and I didn't fail to register its significance.

"Well, my golf clubs are home in my garage and I wouldn't have time to get them if I'm going to make the dinner tonight at seven. But I'm afraid I may not be much competition on the pistol range."

"Don't worry about that. We'll give you a quick lesson and you'll do fine. I guarantee you'll do a whole lot better than your first round of golf. Now, we start early and it'll probably take less time than eighteen holes, so you can plan accordingly."

"So, it's pistols at dawn?"

Dennis chuckled again. "Well, actually, it'll be after the club's famous buffet breakfast. And, there's no way a real man can turn down a big artery-clogging breakfast, followed by a morning of high-caliber gunplay."

My turn to force a chuckle. "Well, now that you've put it that way . . ."

"Good. Then pistols it is. The club has a fine selection of handguns you can choose from, if you don't have your own."

I thought for a moment.

"In fact, I do have a gun, a pistol - an old, ah, family heirloom. I keep it here at the terminal, away from the kids. But it's been in storage for a long time and I don't know what kinda shape it's in."

"What kind of gun is it?"

"I think it's a forty-five. I haven't looked at it in years. Probably hasn't been fired in, oh, thirty-five or forty years."

"If it's that old and it's a forty-five, it's probably a Colt 1911. They're durable pieces and the club's gunsmith's a true master with handguns. In fact, autoloaders are his specialty and I know he'd loved to spend some time with an old 1911. You should bring it. If nothing else, we'll get it cleaned up and see if we can run a few clips through it."

"Okay. I will."

"Outstanding. By this time tomorrow, I'm sure you'll be well on your way to becoming a die-hard shootist. We'll see you at the club later, then. Directions are with the invitation."

"Thanks for calling, Wilson. I'll look forward to seeing you."

I took a ring of keys from my desk drawer and headed out to the loading docks through the dispatch office. I nodded at Moretti and the other two dispatchers as I walked through the office, but Moretti held my glance.

"Whadaya need, boss?" Moretti asked.

"I just need something out of the storage cage," I replied without slowing down

I unlocked the gate to the chain-link cage where the company files were stored along with office supplies and, occasionally overnight, high value cargo that would be loaded in the morning for delivery. There were also two pallets ladened with some of my personal items. Four years ago, the last time Cathy and I moved the family, the terminal had served as temporary storage while the contractors finished the renovations on our new home. When we moved in, the items still in the cage were deemed unfit for the new house, but each in its own way was too valuable to discard. I found my old stereo speakers, kitchenware, lamps, and a tapestry from our first apartment, along with a few boxes of contents and importance long forgotten. Finally, I found the Philco nineteen-inch, black and white television box. A triangular banner on the top right hand corner on the box read, "Indoor Rabbit Ears Antenna Included".

I carried the box to the back corner of the cage and sat on a half-pallet of copy paper. I unfolded the flap on the box and looked down into my past at the ghosts of my youth. I dug through sections of plastic-log walls of a Fort Apache set, a Christmas gift from my parents when I was six or seven. There were cowboys and Indians and horses mixed in with World War II soldiers, all forever posed in their battle stances, ready after all these years for a little boy to meticulously set them up and then, imitating battle sounds, knock them down dead. I found a leather cowboy gun belt with silver plastic bullets across the back and a holster on each hip. A buffalo was stamped into the oval tin belt buckle and the holsters were decorated with silver grommets and real brown and white pony fur. The guns were missing from the holsters but I remembered the silver metal Peacemakers with the white plastic handgrips. I remembered shooting dozens of red rolls of gunpowder caps and how the gun smoke leaked from barrels. The smell of the gunpowder came back to me as I rubbed the pony fur on the holsters.

There was a metal fire truck, a tow truck, and a dump truck, a WWII Sherman tank and a German half-track staff car. I made a mental note to bring the box home to my boys. You can't buy stuff like this anymore.

Underneath a cigar box that held a couple dozen Matchbox cars, I found the Davy Crockett 'coonskin cap and fringed frontier shirt. I picked up the cap with its fur tail and was surprised to see that it too was genuine fur, probably rabbit. There was a chipboard patch sewn onto the front of the cap.

Fess Parker, the actor, wearing his own 'coonskin cap was pictured on the patch under the words, *Walt Disney's Official Davy Crockett*. As I unrolled the fringed shirt, I could hear the theme song playing in my head.

> *Davy, Davy Crockett,*
> *King of the wild frontier . . .*

And then the pistol, a .45 automatic with the silencer still attached to the barrel, rolled out of the fringed shirt into my hands. I read the etching on the side of the slide. Dennis was right. It was a Colt 1911.

I was sure that without a permit possession of the gun was unlawful, but due to its age and condition it was probably something I could explain if I had to. The silencer, on the other hand, was not something that someone named Napolo should be caught with. So I unscrewed the silencer and wrapped it back up in the fringed shirt, placing it at the bottom of the box underneath the toys.

As I dumped Matchbox cars out of the cigar box and placed the forty-five inside, I thought about that night a long time ago in front of my parents' house; the night I found the gun in the gutter after my grandfather's Chrysler pulled away. I remembered how heavy the gun was that night and how it had smelled like the caps I used to shoot off in my pearl-handled Peacemakers. I thought about Mario and Nico. But foremost, I was reminded that it was the last time I ever saw my grandfather and that for all these years I had kept our secret. Not even Cathy, my soul mate, knew what happened that night.

On my way back to my office with the cigar box, Bobby Moretti stopped me in the dispatch area.

"Found what you were lookin' for?" Moretti asked, nodding to the cigar box.

"I'm all set. Everything okay here?"

"Everything's fine. Danny Kelly's delayed at Camber Foods, as usual. He's not even backed in yet. So we're gonna swing Hector Vazquez by Tilton's to get the pickup."

"That's good. I don't want to get shut out there again. We missed that pickup once, last spring, and Ralph never lets us forget it. You know how it goes, Bobby . . . you're only as good as your last mistake."

"Tell me about it. Fuckin' customers. We jump through hoops everyday and you miss once, you're a piece of shit."

"Yeah, but I've thought real hard about how we'd pay the bills without having any customers . . . so far no good answers."

Moretti shrugged and chuckled. "Well don't worry. Hector's on the way. He'll be there in time."

"Good."

I started to walk away and then turned around in the doorway. "Bobby, can you do me a favor? Ask one of the guys in the shop to gas up my Jeep. I have to go up to FirsTech tonight."

"Tonight?"

"Yeah, for dinner. I'll be back after lunch tomorrow."

"Michael goin', too?"

I barely hesitated. "Yeah, Michael will be away too. Please keep an eye on things here for us, will ya? If anyone needs us, get my cell number from Sam."

"You got it, boss. Anything else?"

"Yeah, have them take my golf clubs out of the back of the Jeep and put them in my office."

# CHAPTER 18
**Bella Collina**
**Livingston Manor, NY**

Wilson Dennis shifted his weight in the chair and checked his watch. He had arrived early so when Nicolas Pucci asked him to wait in the study while he finished dressing for dinner, he did so without complaint. But it had been almost twenty minutes and what man takes more than five or ten minutes to get dressed? Sure, Nicolas was the old man's nephew and Wilson had spent many hours of his life waiting for the old man, but that was different. There was no questioning the way the world seemed to revolve around his uncle and his timetables. That was just the way it was. And, while he liked and respected Nicolas in his own right, he was not the old man and this was bordering on rude.

Just then, Nicolas stepped through the double doors into the study, dressed in a dark green double-breasted suit, over a crisp white shirt split by a rich silk tie and a cordovan belt that matched his glove-soft loafers perfectly. Wilson knew most of Nicolas' suits and accessories were custom-made for him in Milan and guessed that he was looking at several thousand dollars worth of tailoring. A few paces into the room, Nicolas stopped short, hooked his thumbs playfully under his lapels and then stared off into the corner, placing one foot forward as if he was posing for a fashion photographer.

Smiling broadly, he said, "Sorry to keep you waiting, Wilson, but you can't rush perfection."

Dennis felt a pang of guilt over his impatience. He had known Nicolas since he was a boy and he had watched him grow up on this mountain, all the while being carefully groomed by his uncle to someday take over the company.

After prep school in Connecticut, undergraduate at Columbia and a Harvard MBA, he had returned to begin the final phases of his tutelage. Since then, the serious pursuits of FirsTech's business, and everything that came with it, left little time for anything else, especially clowning around with his best friend. This was a rare, boyish moment that would have been trusted with no one else. His uncle had made sure of that.

Dennis shook his head and smirked, "It must be intimidating for you to get up every morning knowing that you have to try look as good as the day before."

"Nah, perfection knows no limits. I wake up excited to see how far I can push that envelope."

"Must be nice. At my age, you hope you just wake up."

"Jesus, Wilson. You sound like your ninety and infirm."

"Just getting myself mentally prepared for it. It's not that far off."

"You're gonna end up talking yourself into it early."

"You'll see. Getting old is no fun," Wilson said as he sat back and crossed his legs again.

Nicolas raised his eyebrows and pointed at Dennis' legs. "Are you sure you should be doing that?"

"Doing what?"

"A guy your age, crossing your legs like that. Better watch out you don't crack a hip or something."

Wilson started to look down at his legs but caught himself. "All right, fuck you."

Nicolas laughed, "That's better." Then moving to a chair across from Wilson, he continued as he sat. "So what's going on?"

"It's been an interesting day, Nicolas. Unfortunately, interesting in this usage is not good. First, we lost control of our surveillance of Michael Cogan's meeting with John Anelli. Shots were fired, one of our men was hit - nothing serious, but we had to withdraw quickly to avoid contact with the local cops."

Nicolas frowned. "Wilson, what the hell happened? I thought we were there to collect information and start a tail on those two. Not start a fire fight, for chrissake."

Wilson nodded. "We debriefed the teams and apparently our team leader gave orders to enter the building shortly after the meeting began. For the record, Anelli fired first. Four teams hot-breached the building and Anelli probably panicked."

"And our men returned fire?"

"Yes. But we don't think either Cogan or Anelli were hit."

"Why did our men enter the building? Was something going wrong?"

"No. Cogan and Anelli had only been inside a few minutes. The team leader had his own agenda." Wilson hesitated. "He was working for Lincoln."

Nicolas sat back in the chair. "What?"

"My fault," Wilson said, pointing a finger at his chest. "As you know, one of my men abruptly resigned on Monday after the hijacking. A good man but he was the guy in the control room when we lost our surveillance team in Kearny. He said he felt responsible for their deaths and in good conscience he had to resign. I personally got involved and assured him that even if he had reacted sooner, there would have been little we could have done, given the circumstances. But he insisted on leaving immediately.

"Anyway, something didn't sit right with me. His demeanor was off, more worried than remorseful. So we held him and, after a little pharmacological intervention, he told us what was really on his mind. He was on Lincoln's payroll and scared. And rightly so, I guess. He was found this morning at the bottom of the stairs at his apartment, with a broken neck. Luckily, while he was under the influence of our pharmaceuticals, he was able to give us the names of two more of our men that he knew were doubling for Lincoln. Apparently, Lincoln pays a whole lot better than we do. One of those guys was today's team leader."

Nicolas arched his eyebrow. "So you knowingly let this guy run the operation today?"

"Yes, under the 'keep your enemies close' philosophy, I made the decision to use him hoping to get a line on Cogan and Anelli that ran through Lincoln. That way, we could've traced Cogan, Anelli and Lincoln, making sure we were there to protect our interests when they eventually got to our equipment. In retrospect, it was a flawed plan. I expected that Lincoln would simply be fed information about the meeting and any subsequent movement. However, I failed to consider that Lincoln would alter the mission objectives."

"Wilson, when did you start underestimating guys like Lincoln?"

Wilson threw up his hands. "Nicolas, as I said, it's my fault."

"Okay," Nicolas said, not wanting to waste anymore time on the obvious. "So where are we, now?"

"We're nowhere good. Our teams had to move out quickly so we lost Cogan and Anelli. The good news is so did Lincoln. The bad news, the cameras we put on Vinny Venezio's restaurant after Napolo and Cogan visited last night caught Lincoln and one of his men entering the establishment this afternoon. Lincoln came out alone a little while later."

Nicolas leaned forward. "Jesus Christ, are you kidding? *Lincoln* killed those guys today?"

Wilson nodded slowly. "Apparently so. The FBI thinks Anelli did it. They found his wallet inside the restaurant. From their perspective, it makes perfect sense. My guy in the New York office told me how they see it. According to him, Venezio sends two shooters to Anelli's in Hackensack the other night. But Anelli gets the drop on 'em and before he kills them he gets them to tell him that Venezio had sent them there. Then today, Anelli goes into the big city for some payback. Neat, logical, with evidence to support it. But that's not the way it's gonna play out."

Nicolas shook his head. "I hope not. That scenario has New York Mob war written all over it, with the Napolo Family at its center. We don't need that."

Wilson nodded. "Well, I've taken care of it. When the Feds run the fingerprints of the unidentified victim inside the restaurant, Lincoln's man, the computers are gonna identify him as one Igor Steponovich, or Johnny Steps as he's know in the streets. Igor's with the Russian Mob in Brooklyn, a very bad actor. Murder's his specialty. As you know the Feds have had a very difficult time making any cases against the Russians. No one talks. Everyone's afraid and with guys like Igor running around, they should be. They kill your whole family, here *and* back in the old country. Even the Italians tread lightly around the Russians. On the surface, they stay out of each other's way, but the truth is, the Russians continue to gain ground. And even though there's a lot of pent up resentment, so far the Italians have worked hard to avoid any serious confrontations with them. But, by tomorrow this time, Benedetto and the rest of the New York Families will be feeling differently."

"How's that 'taking care of it'? The Feds can't get to the Russians so feed them to the Italians? Mob war nonetheless, Wilson. Just not the Italians killing each other off."

"It was the best I could do. I've been assured that the Feds will see this in the proper light and pursue it accordingly. They're gonna take some very public action and then stay in the shadows and let it play out. Thinning the Russians' ranks appeals to them. Especially since the *right* Russians are gonna be taken out; it'll weaken them and maybe give the Feds an inroad."

"So Benedetto's going to get what he needs to win this thing?"

"We're gonna give him more than he needs, or knows about. It's gonna be over very quickly and the Feds won't have a clue or anyone with a name ending in vowel that they can or want to arrest. In the end, they'll just be happy to have the devil they know come out on top."

"How are they going to get around finding Anelli's wallet?"

"They'll conclude that Anelli was there playing cards and managed to get away. He'll be sought as a material witness."

"And what about the real Igor Steponovich? What's he gonna say about all this?"

"As of about an hour ago, he ceased to have any opinions, about anything."

Nicolas opened his mouth to say something but nothing came. Both men sat in silence for a moment, not looking at each other.

Finally, Nicolas swung his gaze to Wilson. "Okay, back to *our* problem. Right now we have no idea where Cogan, Anelli, or Lincoln are, do we?"

"No."

"Therefore, we're no closer to finding our shipment that we were a couple days ago."

"Bottom line. No."

Nicolas exhaled loudly. "In fact, the only thing we know for sure is that Aaron Lincoln's a fucking psychopathic killer and that we already knew, didn't we? I thought you had this guy on a string, Wilson."

Wilson didn't answer.

After another prolonged silence, Nicolas asked, "Where's Napolo?"

"He should be on his way here. I talked to him earlier and convinced him to join us, as we discussed."

"Well, that's good. At least we can keep an eye on him for a while."

Wilson looked up. "I've been thinking that maybe we should do more. If I were Lincoln, and I couldn't find Cogan or Anelli, and the results of my visit with Venezio were less than I had hoped for, which I think they probably were, the next person I'd be interested in talking to would be Joseph Napolo."

Nicolas stood up and walked over to the wet bar. He pulled two crystal glasses from the cabinet and filled them with ice. Then he turned to Wilson.

"How much more?"

"As much as we have to."

Nicolas thought for a few seconds. "Okay. Let's play it by ear."

Then he nodded at the glasses. "The usual?"

## The Sheraton Hotel
## Woodbridge, New Jersey

"Mute the TV. This might be him," Michael Cogan said to Johnny Anelli as he reached for the ringing phone on the nightstand.

"Hello."

Michael listened to man on the line and then said, "No, you're right, the computer is wrong. I'm in room 512." He shook his head at Johnny. Then he said into the phone before hanging up, "No problem."

Johnny hit the mute button again so he could hear the CNN announcer. The May Massacre was being featured almost continuously. They had been watching for almost two hours and in the second hour nothing new had been reported, just regurgitations of tired information and reruns of file footage and earlier interviews. Michael had heard all of Johnny's speculations about old vendettas and more recent grievances that might have resulted in the murders of Vinny Diamonds and his crew. And he had to listen to Johnny rant about Vinny; how Vinny had fucked him over a few years ago and that Vinny was a fuckin' prick and that probably Vinny had finally fucked with the wrong guy and that someone had saved him a lot of trouble because after the other night it was gonna be him or Vinny and fuck Vinny it wasn't gonna be him 'cause Vinny tried to whack him first and that's not kosher but it was too bad that those other fuckin' guys got hit 'cause sum of them guys were okay. Mercifully for Michael, they hadn't talked much in the last half-hour or so. Probably because they were both getting nervous wondering if Special Agent Dwyer was going to return their page.

Johnny clicked off the television. "You sure about this guy? It's been almost two hours since we beeped him. This better not be bullshit."

"Look, I told you several times, he was serious. Maybe he's busy. Relax, I'm sure he'll call."

"Relax! That your favorite fucking word? Well, fuck *relax*. I got a goddam splitting headache, my toe hurts like a son of a bitch, my fucking eye's botherin' me, and I'm sitting here waitin' for sum motherfuckin' FBI agent to call. Relax? Fuck you, relax."

Johnny stood up and grabbed his Beretta off the table. Michael's eyes went to the gun.

"Oh, don't worry," Johnny said, when he saw Michael staring at the gun. "I ain't gonna shoot you, not yet. Maybe not at all, if this ain't bullshit. But if it is . . ." He pointed the Beretta at Michael's face.

Michael winced and put his hand up. "Alright, I don't need to hear it again, okay?"

Johnny shrugged and stuffed the Beretta in his waistband in the small of his back. He pulled on his Members Only jacket and said, "I'm goin' down the hall to get some ice and a Diet Pepsi. You want anything?"

"No thanks."

"By the way, I'm leavin' the door open so I can hear the phone ring or you talkin' on it, so don't get any ideas."

"Don't worry about it."

"*Don't worry*? Huh, what happen to *relax*?" Johnny said as he left the room.

At the end of the hallway, Johnny looked back toward the room before he entered the alcove with the icemaker and vending machines. The hall was empty.

He placed the ice bucket on the tray under the chute of the icemaker and pressed the button. While the icemaker turned and dropped cubes into the bucket, he looked over at the drink machine.

He said to the machine, "A dollar for a fuckin' can of soda?"

Then ice cubes began spilling out of the bucket onto the floor. He lifted his finger off the button and kicked the ice cubes away from the front of the machines. Shaking his head, he put a dollar bill in the drink machine and pressed the button for his Diet Pepsi.

Then he moved over to the snack machine. Hostess Twinkies! He fuckin' loved Twinkies. Hadn't had one in years. He fed a dollar into the slot. But the machine spit it out. Johnny reversed the dollar bill and pushed it back in. But out it came again. "Shit!" Then he pulled a fold of bills from his pocket. No more singles. He cocked his head and listened, thinking he heard the elevator, so he looked into the hallway, but it was still empty.

He went back into the alcove and ran the dollar bill back and forth against the vertical edge of the machine as he gripped each end, trying to smooth it out. This time the machine took the bill all the way in, paused, and shot it out again, this time onto the floor. Johnny took a deep breath and grunted as he bent down to retrieve it.

Back in the room, Michael had turned the television back on. He was flipping through the channels when he heard the door close quietly.

"Thanks for leaving the door open."

Michael didn't recognize the voice. He spun around and saw the man he knew as Special Agent Clifford Dwyer and two other men standing in the room.

Michael jumped up from the bed. "I was waiting for you to call."

Aaron Lincoln just stared at him as he nodded toward the bathroom. One of the other men went in. Michael heard the shower curtain being slid across the rod. The man returned and shook his head.

"How did you know where to find me?" Michael asked.

Lincoln didn't break his stare. "Caller ID. And then you told me your room number a few minutes ago. Remember?"

While Lincoln was talking, Michael noticed that one of the men had a gun in his hand.

"Where's Anelli?" Lincoln asked Michael.

Michael's eyes moved across the three of them before he answered. "He's not here."

"Oh yeah, where is he?"

"I don't know. He left."

With that, Lincoln's right arm shot forward and he grabbed Michael around the throat forcing him back onto the bed. Lincoln bent over the bed applying his weight to Michael's neck. He leaned his face close to Michael's and smiled. "Where'd he go?"

"I told you. I don't know." Michael managed to whisper. "He dropped me off here, said he'd be in touch."

Lincoln tightened his grip, digging his fingers into the sides of Michael's throat. "When?"

Michael tried to answer but he couldn't even breathe let alone speak. His eyes were beginning to tear and he felt nauseous. Where was Johnny and his goddam gun when he needed him?

Johnny was still standing in front of the snack machine, straightening out the corners of the dollar bill between his fingertips that he had wet with his spit. Then he rolled the bill tightly, unrolled it, folded it lengthwise, and smoothed it out again. As he unfolded it and flattened the crease, he rechecked the miniature replica of the dollar bill above slot and lined up his single so George Washington's head was in the right direction. Then he carefully, without much force at all, guided the bill slowly into the slot. The machine began to whir and suck in the bill. The whirring stopped and Johnny felt the tension leaving his chest. He waited, staring at the LCD readout. Nothing happened. He pressed the coin return lever several times until the machine started again. Out came his dollar. Johnny stared at it hanging from the slot, breathing deeply. Then he looked over at the Twinkies poised on the edge of the rack in the spiral dispenser. They looked a little smaller than he remembered, but he didn't care. He fucking wanted them.

Johnny removed the bill from the slot, and doing his best to control himself he feed it in again and again, until on the third time the machine stopped and the red LCD flashed $1.00.

"Damn." He realized that he hadn't breathed during the last three attempts.

He very carefully punched the letter and number combination for the Twinkies, making sure he accidentally didn't get the Trail Mix or some other crap that he couldn't stand. Finally, the metal spiral holding the Twinkies began to turn, pushing them to the edge of the shelf. But when it stopped, the Twinkies didn't fall. They were dangling from the tip of the spiral.

Johnny put both hands on the machine and gently rocked the machine. But the Twinkies hung on. This time he tipped the machine, lifting the front legs off the ground and dropping it hard. The Twinkies shook but didn't drop. He stood and watched them swing back and forth until they stopped, still hanging on.

"Cocksucker!" He cursed under his breath.

Johnny stepped back trying to control his urge to kick the shit out of the machine. He leaned against the wall and took out a cigarette and lit it. Then he checked the hallway. Still empty. Fuck it, he thought, and pulled out the Beretta. He reversed the pistol in his hand so he could use the grip as a hammer on the front glass of the machine. He shielded his face and cocked his arm. Then, as he began his backswing, the Hostess Twinkies broke free and fell into the bin.

"That's right, you son of a bitch!"

Johnny put the Beretta away and fished the Twinkies out of the machine. Sure enough, they were smaller than they used to be. He started to put the Twinkies in the pocket of his jacket but changed his mind. He didn't want to crush them, so he put the Diet Pepsi in his pocket instead. He grabbed the ice bucket off the tray and walked out of the alcove.

In the hallway, he looked up and froze. Four men were standing outside the elevator, way down at the middle of the hall. The doors had just opened and they were stepping inside. One of them looked his way and hesitated. Johnny squinted. It was Michael Cogan. They locked eyes for a split second before one of the other guys shoved Michael hard into the elevator. The elevator doors closed and Johnny sidestepped back into the alcove. But his left foot came down on one of the ice cubes that he had spilled and his leg slid out from under him. Johnny dropped the ice bucket and reached for the doorframe, but he was going down too fast.

His ass hit first. Then his sore elbow, quickly followed by the back of his head against the ice machine. He sat there a moment, listening for sounds in the hallway. It was quiet.

After few seconds, he looked down at his left hand and uncurled his fist. The Twinkies were smashed and oozing through the plastic wrapper. His chin dropped to his chest and he whimpered, "Motherfucker."

# CHAPTER 19

**Route 17 North**
**Ten Miles South of Liberty, NY**

In the early days of transforming Domanski Trucking Company, Michael and I had worked long hard hours. In those days, we had one simple rule: every day we would each call on at least one account, either an existing or a prospective customer. So after a pre-dawn trip to Philadelphia or Baltimore or New York, making deliveries and pickups in one of our rigs, and after a quick change of clothes back at the terminal, we'd make sales calls. Then, upon returning to the terminal, we often found ourselves on the docks sorting freight or driving forklifts or cutting invoices late into the night.

I don't remember exactly when, only that it had been after several months of solid black ink, that Michael and I had decided to add a private bath and lounge area adjoining our office. The long days continued for a couple more years, but a few hours sleep on a couch instead of the office floor, made the overnights more tolerable. A hot shower and clean clothes in the morning almost made it bearable. Certainly, the mid-day transformations from truck driver to businessman, from jeans and work shirts to worsted wool suits and starched white button-downs, were made more civilized by a quick shower. We still keep a couple of changes of clothes in the closet. So, like a hundred times before, I showered, put on a clean suit, packed some toiletries and a change of clothes, and headed out to see a customer. This time though, contractual performance metrics, rate negotiations, or annual tonnage commitments weren't on my mind as I drove north to FirsTech.

I had called Cathy and Ilene soon after I left the terminal. I told them both that Michael was going with me to FirsTech, joining me there, heading up separately from another meeting. Ilene was curious why Michael hadn't called himself and I had made up a story about Michael's cell being dead. I was uncomfortable with the lies but settled with having left both wives without worry, for now.

The drive north had been a blur of familiar highways and troubled thought. I tried, without success, to bring focus to the last couple days. Over and over, I pushed back my disappointment with Michael, finally accepting it as transference of the anger I felt for allowing myself to become involved. Then, I revisited my own behavior. Why was I so comfortable with the way I had acted? It had been so easy for me to bully Laskowski and Catella, and their goons in the pickup. Just like my handling of Tommy Ton, I had stepped right up and delivered, as if I did that kind of thing every day. Where did that come from?

The answer came quickly. The union's tactics were dangerous for our employees and jeopardized our livelihood and our family's security. Tommy Ton had threatened Michael outright. I put it uneasily to rest, knowing I would do it all over again, if I had to.

Then I struggled with feelings of pending doom for Michael and, in a sense, for myself. Where was this all leading to? Two days ago, we faced a serious situation with Local 714 over an issue that Michael and I had, in some part, created. Months before, as we explored the Employee Stock Ownership Plan, we knew it would require the eventual decertification from the Teamsters Union by our employees. The reality of it was, we had used the ESOP as the vehicle to rid ourselves of Local 714's interference with our business. And when the NLRB ruled against the decertification vote, we strategically stood in the wings while Bobby Moretti led our people away from the union. We had pushed Laskowski and Catella into a corner, leaving them no options. The union had to mount a strong protest against the company's actions. That's what unions do. They're in business to protect their membership, whether the members want it or not. But unions were created to improve the lot of the working man, not to impose their will on the workers. And that's where the issue began and ended for me. There, and in the way Local 714 went about their business.

But now, if I could believe Catella, and I thought I could, the union was walking away, doing the right thing. And as tainted as their motivation was, influenced by the legacy of my grandfather, I accepted the results without misgivings. In fact, almost everything of importance that had happened over the last couple days had somehow involved my last name, including the FBI's assumptions and threats. And what about the FBI?

I pressed the speed dial on my cell.

"Good afternoon, Domanski - I mean, DTC, Samantha speaking."

"Sam, it's Joseph. Please get the Newark office of the FBI on the line and patch me in."

While I waited I fished out Special Agent Dwyer's card from my pocket.

"Okay, Joseph." The line was ringing.

"You can hang up now, Sam."

"Oh, uh, okay. Bye Joseph."

"Bye Sam."

A recorded voice answered. "You have reached the Federal Bureau of . . ."

I punched the zero and waited.

"Federal Bureau of Investigation, can I help you?" A pleasant female voice.

"Yes, I need to speak with the agent in charge of this office."

"And may I ask the nature of your call?"

"Please tell him it's a matter of national security."

"Okaaay, I'll see if he's in, sir. Please hold."

From the tone of her voice, I wondered if she was thinking I was probably some nutcase, calling to report a UFO landing or an assassination conspiracy.

"This is Agent Hamley, can I help you?"

"Perhaps, are you the Agent-in-Charge?"

"No, sir, that would be Special Agent Fred Raymond. But he's unavailable right now. What can I do for you?"

"When will Agent Raymond be available?"

"That depends, sir. You mentioned that you have a concern relating to national security. I can take your information and see that Special Agent Raymond gets it right away."

I realized I wasn't going to get past this agent without giving him something.

"My name is Joseph Napolo. I own DTC Transportation, a trucking company in Edison. Monday afternoon, one of my trucks was hijacked and on Tuesday one of your agents came to my office to interview me. I want to discuss that visit with Agent Raymond."

"How is this a matter of national security, sir?"

"The cargo that was taken was DOD classified."

"Mr. Napolo, can I ask you to be more specific as to what exactly you need to talk to Agent Raymond about?"

"Listen, forget him. What I really need to know is did the FBI actually send an agent to interview me? Can you verify that?"

"Mr. Napolo, didn't you just tell me that one of our agents came to your office?"

"Yes, but his behavior was, I don't know, rude - unusual. I would like to verify that this agent was from your office."

"What's was his name, sir?"

I glanced at the card. "Clifford Dwyer."

"Hold on."

A few seconds later. "Mr. Napolo, I can confirm that there is no Agent Dwyer working out of the Newark office. Did he say where he was from?"

"I have his card, but there's only a pager number on it. Is that unusual?"

"The Bureau doesn't issue calling cards but some agents choose to print their own. Hold on."

Thirty seconds later. "Mr. Napolo, are you sure you have the name right, Clifford Dwyer?"

"He had ID and that's what's on his card."

"Ah . . . hold on, again, please."

More than a minute later. "Mr. Napolo, I can only confirm that no one from the FBI, this office or anywhere else, was sent to interview you. Are you sure he was from the FBI? Impersonating a federal officer is a serious offense."

*Fucking Catella was right.* "I thought so, but I could be wrong. Maybe I should double check with my partner."

"Okay, Mr. Napolo. Anything else I can do for you today?"

"No. Thanks for your help."

Without realizing, I tapped the brakes. The driver behind me leaned on his horn as I slowly drifted onto the shoulder. I came to a stop. I had to think. What the hell's going on? The week started with the Teamsters, and Michael making a deal with Mob for one of our trucks. So what do I do? I play tough guy with the union and a bookie with serious connections. A phony FBI agent comes to our office and threatens us. Then, we go for a sit down with a mob underboss that knew my grandfather. Michael makes a deal with the underboss and I let it happen even though I know it's wrong. That night, our trucks get torched by God knows who. Today, Michael goes to a meeting with a guy that probably killed two men the other night, gets shot at, and is now somewhere with that guy, who the underboss wants dead. But the underboss gets killed. The union backs off. The union guys and the underboss' right hand man want to be my friend. And now, FirsTech, the company whose cargo was hijacked on Monday - whose head of security is mentioned by the guys who shot at Michael, pressures me to come to see them, and I'm driving there with a forty-five in a cigar box under my seat. Where's this all going? Where's the connectivity? There must be a center, something at the core of all this. What am I missing? I have to find a way to get in touch with Michael, to warn him. Maybe . . .

Suddenly, my thinking was interrupted by a thought. I hadn't checked the gun. A few times, as I was growing up, I had taken it out just to look at it, to feel it and point it. But not once had I checked to see if it was loaded.

I reached under the seat and pulled out the cigar box. I opened it on the passenger seat. Holding the pistol by the grip carefully, so not to have my finger near the trigger, I pulled back the slide and a shell ejected against the seatback. I pulled again and again until on the sixth pull the slide locked open. The breach was empty.

As I gathered up the six bullets, I thought again about that chilly night in March of '63 at the curb in front of my parents' house. I would never forget the horror of Mario's head blown apart by a bullet just like the ones I held in my fist. Or the surreal image of my grandfather Carmine hunched over Nico, driving the tire iron into his throat, doing what had to be done to save us from one of these bullets. And, strangely, how the strength of the unbroken pact I had made with my grandfather brought solace to the memory of it all.

But that was a long time ago and things were different now. I tossed the bullets through the passenger window into the woods on the side of the road.

## The Smoke and Gun Club at Bella Collina Livingston Manor, New York

At the front gate, two guards passed mirrors, explosive and chemical sniffing devices over, under, and inside my car while a third, staid yet courteous young man engaged me in pleasant conversation. By the guard's stiff posture, it was apparent that he was wearing body armor and, at one point, I saw a serious looking weapon attached to the inside of his uniform jacket. When the guard asked me if I was in possession of any firearms, I declared the forty-five, which the guard appropriated for "safe keeping", advising me it would be available upon request but under the discretion of the club's range master. He looked at me strangely when I handed him the cigar box.

Once the guards were certain that I was not a car bomber on a mad suicide mission, they instructed to me to proceed to the front entrance were a valet would further assist me. As I drove the Cherokee up the hill, I noticed that the large willow trees and giant concrete planters that alternately bordered the cobblestones were closely spaced to prevent a vehicle from leaving the driveway. I began to speculate why the security measures at the front gate wouldn't have been enough but my attention was quickly diverted.

Ahead of me on the hill, the enormous Federal-style brick mansion loomed. It was a spectacular sight. The evening sun, lying low but bright in the western sky, illuminated one side of the massive white dome that capped the center of the huge building. The towering alabaster columns that supported the large portico cast long thin shadows across the manicured landscaping. Colorful spring plantings burst like fireworks from every shrubbery bed. And a large fountain pool in the center of the circular drive shot a shimmering umbrella of sparkling mountain water at least thirty feet into the air.

I wondered whether it was the magnificent proportions or the overwhelming beauty of this place that was most inspiring. It was, I decided, neither of them alone but the wonder of both together that created the splendor.

I slowed to a near stop when I reached the circular portion of the drive. A black Suburban with darkened windows was parked to the left; ever ready, I imagined, to pull forward and block off the main driveway before disgorging several well-armed guards trained to thwart any number of potential threats. Another subtle yet powerful image.

I drove around under the portico. Four valets, ramrod straight and smartly uniformed in dark purple tunics with gold braided epaulets, matching chauffeur caps, and white gloves, were positioned to receive me.

The one at my door tipped his cap. "Good evening, Mr. Napolo." The front gate must have called ahead. "Welcome to The Smoke and Gun Club at Bella Collina. May we take your bags?"

"Yes, just one in the back."

"Yes, sir. Please leave your keys."

I waited for a ticket but none was offered, so I followed the valet with my bag up the wide marble stairs. When we reached the top step, the double front doors swung open and two men in yet different uniforms - waistcoats, vests, and neck ties - stood at the ready. One of them took my bag from the valet and stepped aside, waiting. The other one, older but tall and fit, spoke.

"Welcome to The Smoke and Gun Club at Bella Collina, Mr. Napolo. My name is David. I am Head of Household Staff. And while you are our guest, seeing that your needs and comforts are consistently provided for is my staff's mission. We are available to you twenty-four hours a day. By pressing the pound sign on any phone throughout the estate, you will be immediately connected to a member of my staff. Mr. Pucci wants you to know that he will be greatly disappointed if at any time during your stay the quality of our service is anything less than exceptional." David leaned in closer. "So please, sir," his tone had softened. "There is no request too large or too, shall I say, *private* that we can not accommodate - whether it's something as simple as a late night snack or, perhaps, another late night *creature* comfort - we are at your disposal, discretely, of course."

David straightened up and continued more brightly, "Carlo will show you to your quarters now, sir. Cocktails and hors d'oeuvres will be served here, in the rotunda, at seven - about thirty minutes from now. Have a nice evening, Mr. Napolo."

"Thank you, David." I smiled politely.

"Do you prefer the elevator or the stairs, sir?" Carlo asked me in a heavy Italian accent.

"The stairs will be fine."

"Yes, sir."

The rotunda was very large, about sixty feet in diameter, I guessed. There seemed to be no ceiling to the space as it soared up through the translucent panels in the dome. The staircase began at the right side of the rotunda and was splayed at the bottom so the first steps were probably fourteen or fifteen feet across, narrowing to about half that width as it wound its way up around the curved white marble wall. As I climbed the marble steps, I noticed the stone carvers' craftsmanship. In relief, a tasteful vine and leaf design decorated the entire length of the wide marble banister. Finely etched designs accented each baluster and the scrollwork along the stone walls. As we climbed past the second floor, I looked down and saw the black and white marble tiles on the floor unfolding geometrically from a white star in the center of the room, almost unnoticeably increasing in size as the pattern curved and expanded to the outer edges. The effect was dizzying as one climbed up and around.

Muffled voices from below drew my eyes to the front door. David and another member of his staff were greeting an arriving guest. David's voice lowered. He was probably into the pimping part of his speech. By the time we reached the third floor landing, I had promised myself to use the elevator for the rest of my stay.

"May I unpack you, sir?" Carlo asked after unlocking my room and handing me the key.

"No, thanks. I'm fine."

Carlo went into the dressing area and then returned to the main room without the bag. He showed me the entertainment center in the massive armoire and gave me brief instructions on the use of the satellite remote and the audio and video equipment, as well as showing me an extensive list of music and videos I could order. Then he took me over to the wet bar and showed me the fully stocked liquor cabinet and refrigerator, explaining that if there was something lacking to call the household staff as David had instructed. Finally, he handed me a device the size of a pager.

"This is a security alarm. Please keep this with you at all times during your stay. If at any time your security is compromised, press this button. Within seven seconds, no matter where you are on the estate, a security team will respond. There are also red lighted buttons on your nightstand, in the bath and dressing area, and throughout this building that also summon security. Do you have any questions, sir?"

"No, not right now. Thank you, Carlo."

I reached out with a five dollar bill but Carlo put his hands up in surrender.

"Thank you anyway, sir. But Mr. Pucci's insists that we never accept tips from his guests. Now, if there's nothing else, I'll wish you a pleasant stay."

"Thanks, again, Carlo." Then looking at the security pager, I said. "Oh, one thing. How will they know where I am if I press this thing."

"Oh, don't worry, they always know where you are, Mr. Napolo." Carlo smiled and closed the door behind him.

# CHAPTER 20

**Stewart International Airport**
**New Windsor, New York**

Michael's hands were bound behind his back with plastic restraints as soon as they had put him inside the van in the Sheraton parking lot. As they slid a black hood over his head, he was told, in very clear terms, to sit quietly until further instructed. After a short ride, they led him across a grass-covered area and into what he would find to be a helicopter. In the dark under the hood, he had no visual perspective as the helicopter lifted and banked forward and to the side. He felt disoriented and queasy so he breathed deeply to control the sensation, but the air exchange under the hood was poor and he became increasingly lightheaded. Thankfully, about thirty minutes later they landed.

On the ground, after the rotors had stopped and the engines were quiet, he felt the helicopter being rolled across a bumpy surface. Then he heard a metallic rumbling sound and other noises he couldn't identify. He looked out the bottom of the hood. It was getting darker and darker, and when the dragging sound stopped, the background noise was muffled. Michael guessed correctly that the helicopter had been moved into a building and the doors had been closed.

Two sets of feet climbed into the helicopter and grabbed his upper arms. "Let's go," one of them said as they jerked him up and led him out of the chopper.

Michael was guided left and right and then right again. At the bottom of a flight of stairs he was told to "Step up . . . up . . . up . . . up . . ." until he reached to top. When he hesitated there, he was roughly tugged along on a wood floor. They held him at a forty-five degree angle as they walked. He decided it was because he was in a corridor too narrow for the three of them to walk abreast. They stopped and he heard a door open. Four paces later across a different, harder floor they turned him around. He heard a ripping sound like duct tape being pulled from the roll.

"We're cutting your hands loose. Don't move."

As soon as the restraints were off, they pushed him down into a chair and bound his forearms and wrists to the arms of the chair with the duct tape. Next his ankles were taped to the chair legs. Lastly, his chest and upper arms were wrapped to the back of the chair.

One of them said, "Sit tight." Both of them chuckled.

Michael heard them walking away. "Wait a minute," he said from under the hood, stopping the footsteps. "I want to call my lawyer."

"Your lawyer?"

"Yes, I . . ." But the sounds of the door closing and the two men laughing on the other side of it cut him short.

Michael had heard a slight echo in the room when they spoke. He listened in the darkness under the hood and heard a slow drip of water. The air was damp and there was a faint smell of urine. Quick footsteps on the wood floor coming toward the door made him turn his head to the sounds. Closer now. The door opened and shut quickly. Two steps and then scuffled to a stop. He sensed someone a few feet in front of him. Then the hood was pulled off his head.

Aaron Lincoln laughed. "You've got hood hair, Mr. Cogan."

Michael blinked slowly to focus. "What the hell is this, Dwyer? Where am I?"

"You don't know where you are?" Lincoln waved a latex-gloved hand. "Look around."

Michael did. It was a bathroom, an old one. There were four large urinals along the wall in front of him covered with brown stains and spider web cracks. They reminded Michael of the ones in his grammar school that went all the way to the floor, large enough for a dwarf to shower in, with a foot pedal for flushing. To his right were four toilet stalls. One door was missing and another hung only by the top hinge. The metal partitions were rusted and pitted, especially inside by the bowls. On the wall to his left, only three of the original four sinks remained. One of the sinks dripped water from its faucet. Plumbing jutted from the wall where the fourth one had been. The mirrors above the sinks were oxidized, cloudy and cracked. The floor and walls were covered with several shades of heavy green ceramic tiles that were also stained and broken in places. There was only one small window high up on the wall between the urinals and the sinks. It had been recently filled in with cement blocks. The only light came from a bare bulb in what remained of the ceiling fixture.

Lincoln waited until Michael's gaze came back to him. "Whadaya think?"

Michael glared at him.

Lincoln shrugged. "Well, what's to like about a smelly old bathroom. In fact, I'd rather die than have to take a shit in one of these stalls. How 'bout you?"

Michael studied Lincoln's face. Joseph was right, he thought, there's something wrong with this guy.

"What are you looking at me like that for? " Lincoln asked.

"Am I under arrest? I want to call my lawyer."

Lincoln grinned, ignoring Michael's question. "You're lookin' at me like you like me. Do you like me? Are you a faggot? One of those guys with a wife and kids that likes to suck dick now and then? Is that why you're lookin' at me like that? You wanna suck my dick? Is that what you want? Huh?"

Michael opened his mouth to speak but he couldn't.

"Well, I'll take that for a yes," Lincoln said as he walked over to the door and locked it.

"What are you doing?" Michael demanded.

"Just making sure that no one interrupts us."

Lincoln moved in very close to Michael. His crotch was only about a foot from Michael's face when he unzipped his fly.

Michael was aghast. "This is fuckin' crazy. I want a lawyer, now!"

Lincoln nodded. "I think most lawyers are cocksuckers, too. But I don't want a lawyer to suck my cock. I want you to."

Lincoln pulled the .22 revolver from behind his back and put the muzzle against Michael's forehead. "Just in case you get any ideas about using your teeth . . ."

Michael closed his eyes and clamped his mouth shut. Could this really be happening? Was this it? The moment of truth. The moment all men talked about with other men at least one time in their lives, usually after a few beers. *What would you do if* . . . Invariably, the answers were, *Fuck that!* Or, *No fucking way, man! They'd have to kill me.* Well, here he was, with a wife and kids to support. What the fuck! This *can't* be happening. God damn it, I'll never gamble again . . .

Michael felt the gun leave his forehead. Did prayers get answered that quickly? Then he heard, "Open wide, sweet lips."

With eyes still closed and his jaws locked, Michael shook his head and braced himself against the unthinkable. But the gun hitting him hard in his left temple took him by surprise and dazed him. His eyes and mouth open involuntarily as his head flopped to the right.

"That's for thinking that *I'm* a faggot," Lincoln said, as he stepped back and zipped up his fly. "I fucking hate faggots. But I guess you wouldn't know that, would you? Hell, you don't know anything about me. You think you do, but you don't. Well, I will tell you that I'm not really an FBI agent, but you might have guessed that by now. In fact, I fuckin' hate them, too. Bunch of paper-pushin' bureaucratic assholes with guns. So now, you're probably wondering, who the fuck is this guy?"

Lincoln leaned over and grabbed Michael's chin to straighten his head. "Look at me."

Michael blinked away the blood from the nasty gash on his temple and looked into Lincoln's eyes. After Lincoln was sure Michael was alert he continued.

"Who am I? I'm your host, the master of ceremonies, runner of the game. And as a gambling man, I'm sure you like games. In fact, I'd be surprised if you didn't especially like *this* game. It's called Maim the Mick."

Lincoln let go of Michael's chin and began to pace the floor in front of him. "Now, you're probably wondering, how do you play this game? Well, the rules are simple, Michael - I can call you Michael, can't I? After all you almost sucked my dick, right? So *Michael,* here are the rules. I ask you questions and you tell me the answers. If I don't like your answers, if I believe that they are in any way untrue or evasive, then I will begin to disfigure you. Care to place a wager? Perhaps a finger or an ear?"

"Why are you doing this?" Michael asked. "We were calling you to make arrangements to give you the crate and whatever the hell's inside it."

"No. You were calling me to *sell* me the crate. Did you really think I was going to pay you a million dollars for something I can get for free?"

Michael nodded.

Lincoln took two deliberate quick steps forward and shot Michael through the back of this left hand.

"Shit!" Michael screamed, more from the shock of it than the pain.

"Still think so?"

"No." Michael groaned, looking in disbelief at bloody hole in his hand.

Lincoln looked down at Michael who had tears in his eyes and shook his head in disgust.

"Oh, grow up," Lincoln taunted. "Jesus, look at you, you've peed in your pants."

Michael didn't have to look. He felt the warmth between his legs. Besides, he couldn't take his eyes off his hand and his blood spreading across the armrest and dripping onto the floor. He tried to move his fingers but it only resulted in more pain. He moaned, a little too loudly, he thought. But nothing in his life had prepared him for this. He was locked in a room with a sadistic maniac and there was nothing he could do about. In the movies, his only frame of reference at the moment, the tough guys usually had some wisecrack ready for times like this. But that was the movies and tough guys didn't wet their pants.

Michael looked up at Lincoln. "Look you've made your point. We don't need to continue this. I'll tell you whatever you want to know. I swear."

Lincoln regarded him for a moment. "I hope so because the game's just about to begin."

"Oh, Jesus."

"Jesus can't help you, unless of course *He* knows the answers to my questions. So let's get started. Are you ready to play?"

Michael bowed his head.

"Okay, first question: Where's the crate?"

Michael looked up and sighed. "Johnny Anelli stole the crate. It was a mistake though. He thought the trailer had shoes in it. He has it. I told him about the million dollars you offered and we were calling you to set it up. But he didn't tell me where the crate is. Frankly, I never even asked. That's the truth."

Lincoln briefly lingered on his response.

"Where is Anelli right now?"

"I told you at the hotel, I don't know. He left me there and told me he'd be in touch. That's all I know."

Lincoln cocked the revolver and pointed it at Michael's face. "This is an important question, so I'm gonna ask you one more time. Where can I find John Anelli?"

Michael looked at the revolver and then at Lincoln. "Please, I don't know. He always contacted me. I didn't even know his last name until I heard it on the news yesterday. I swear, I don't know. And if I did, why wouldn't I tell you? Think about it. You're pointing a gun at me; you've already shot me once, for chrissake. What the fuck, man! You think that right now, I give a shit about him or the goddam crate. If I fuckin' knew *anything*, I'd tell you."

Lincoln paused to study Michael's face. "Does Napolo know where the crate is?"

"No. Leave him out of this. Joseph has *nothing* to do with this. It's all my doing. I got into some trouble over a gambling debt. I owed money to some guys so I made a deal with Anelli to pay them off. I set up the truckload of shoes for him to hijack. But Joseph knew nothing about that. He only tried to help me after the fact."

Lincoln smiled. "So, you want me to believe that Joseph Napolo, grandson of Carmine Napolo, let's his best friend and partner get jammed up by the Napolo Crime Family? Do I look stupid?"

Lincoln moved the gun closer to Michael's face.

"No."

"Good answer. But I asked you two questions."

Michael hesitated.

Lincoln jammed the pistol into Michael' cheek and screamed, "Napolo! Tell me about Napolo!"

"I . . . ah," Michael's voice quivered. "I . . . ah . . . told you . . . Joseph didn't know about this until after . . . *after* the hijacking. Besides, Joseph's not connected . . . to that. *Please* . . . I'm tellin' you the truth . . . I swear to *God*."

Lincoln could smell fear. He knew it well. He had developed a nose for it over the years and come to enjoy the aroma. Early on, he had learned how to create fear. That was the easy part. But the smell came along later, on a sweet breeze that carried him to new heights. And ever since, the desperation and hopelessness of his victims excited something in him. Somehow the common understanding that he alone held their lives in his hands made him feel uncannily more human, brimming with perception, as if gifted with second sight. And isn't that what ultimately separates man from the beasts? The ability to reason and form conclusions, to come to know certain things from cumulative experiences. Yes, to be afraid was beastly. But to truly understand fear is most human. Because fear is a complex emotion that men embraced in different ways. Some men, like Vinny Diamonds, were concerned more with their reaction to being afraid than the reality it presented. Tough guys to the end. Other men responded recklessly, wild with anxiety, tripping from truths to lies and back again, desperately trying to escape the inevitable. In Lincoln's judgement though, Michael Cogan fell into the third and largest group. Those men with other things in their lives that mattered to them, who when absolutely convinced that they're being confronted with the inconceivable horrors of mutilation and death will tell the truth, the whole truth and nothing but the truth, hoping it will save them. But was Michael Cogan truly convinced?

"Bullshit!" Lincoln shouted, stepping back to put the pistol in his belt. "I think it's time to Maim the Mick!"

Lincoln reached to his ankle and came up with a knife.

Michael drew up against the duct tape and screamed, "No! It's not bullshit!"

Lincoln moved in. He grabbed the top of Michael's ear, pulling it down and away from his head. Michael jerked and bucked trying with everything he had to get free, but Lincoln held on and twisted his ear until he stopped. Lincoln raised the knife.

"*Please . . . don't,*" Michael pleaded. "*Please.*"

Lincoln pressed the edge of the blade against the back of Michael's ear in the soft flesh where the cartilage meets the skull. Michael froze and squeezed his eyes tightly closed.

"*Please . . .*" Michael whimpered between rapid breaths. "*Don't do this . . .* I'm begging you . . . I've told you the truth . . . I'll help you . . . I'll do whatever I can . . . whatever you want. Just *please don't* do this."

Lincoln slowly leaned over and whispered into Michael's gnarled ear, "Promise?"

Michael nodded carefully. Lincoln straightened up and let the knife slide away. After a long hard twist, he let the ear go.

Lincoln stepped away and bent to put the knife back in its sheath on his ankle. Then he smoothed his pant leg, stood and tugged at his shirt cuffs, and rolled his head around on his neck several times. When he stopped, his cold gray eyes centered on Michael.

He said, "The game's over, for now. But don't forget your promise because I won't".

Lincoln turned and walked to the door but stopped short. For a few seconds he stood there with his back to Michael. He began to roll his head around again, thinking, *Was Cogan still useful?* Finally, slowly, he turned around, with the revolver in his hand again.

"One more question, Michael. How do you spell chrysanthemum?"

# CHAPTER 21

## The Smoke and Gun Club at Bella Collina
## Livingston Manor, New York

I nursed a Grey Goose on the rocks through the cocktail hour, returning to the bar only for refills of ice to keep my glass full. At the raw bar, Wilson Dennis had introduced me to a couple guys from a firm that supplied gyroscopic components for electronic warfare intercept and countermeasures systems manufactured by FirsTech. After five minutes of dull and uncomfortable small talk, I excused myself and headed over to a tray of jumbo coconut shrimp being passed around by one of the all-male wait staff. There, I eavesdropped on a conversation between a major with Army Command and Control Systems and a naval commander both wearing civilian business suits, as were all the military attendees. Their discussion was centered on the need for "intel platform stabilization" and the "DIA's failure to break the NRO's stranglehold on SATINT policy". Continuing on my way, pretending to be searching out someone in particular, I was stopped by a faithful rendition of a Thelonious Monk composition being played by the trio in the center of the rotunda. For a few minutes, I soaked in the marvel of the friendly acoustics formed by the dome and the round walls. However, to my disappointment, my enjoyment was fleeting, distracted by a nearby conversation about microwave-based digital frequency discriminators. Moving along, I drifted past group after group of men engaged in discussions peppered with acronyms and code names like Firefinder and Shortstop and Lightance. In every case, the talk was animated but centered solely around transportable missile launch systems or weapons guidance components or the status of various unintelligible electromechanical technologies. Of the fifty or so men in the room, I was sure there wasn't one I could have a normal conversation with.

At one point, I had a good chuckle with myself. I thought of the awards to come. *And for excellence in trucking . . .* Well, we did have GPS vehicle locator and engine monitoring technology in all our trucks. Probably wouldn't impress any of these guys, though. Maybe I would mention it, just for laughs.

After a while, I occupied myself by trying to identify the civilian contractors from the officers of various branches of the government and military complex. Generally, the military was closer cropped and in better shape, wearing inexpensive yet fresh-pressed business suits and highly polished shoes. The contractors seemed to range from geeky technos in rumpled sport coats to well-groomed executives in more fashionable serious business attire. The government types, I concluded, ran the gamut from high-end civil servants making the most of the free drinks and fancy snacks, to a couple groups of tight-lipped suits that tended to look around their immediate area before leaning in close to each other when they spoke.

I was focusing on a new group of four men across the rotunda when I noticed one of the men was looking back. When our eyes met, the man smiled kindly and nodded once. He was about my age; probably six feet tall, slim with dark hair and very well dressed. His eyes were dark and penetrating. I thought that he would have been immediately noticed by any women in the room. With that thought, it suddenly struck me there wasn't even *one* woman in attendance to test my theory. The handsome man's gaze lingered on me even as he returned to the conversation. The three other men in the group appeared to be intent on his every word. He was clearly someone they felt favored to be talking with.

I was about to move on when I noticed Wilson Dennis sidling up behind the handsome man to whisper in his ear. Handsome man looked to the ground as he cocked his head to hear Dennis. Then he looked over directly at me again and then back to Dennis to say something. Dennis caught my eye, smiled broadly and waved. Handsome man looked, too, but didn't wave. Then, without taking his eyes off me, he said something to the three men which caused them to step back, allowing Wilson Dennis and handsome man to walk through them toward me. I held my ground as they made their way over, nodding and smiling graciously to other guests along the way.

"Joseph, I want you to meet Nicolas Pucci," Dennis said cheerily as they closed in. "Nicolas, this is Joseph Napolo."

"It's a pleasure to finally meet you, Joseph. I'm very glad you could make it tonight." Nicolas said, extending his hand.

I took his hand. "It's nice to meet you, too. Thank you for inviting me."

We held the grip through an unnaturally long silence that was becoming uncomfortable. But I held on. I didn't want to be the first one to break eye contact. Finally, Nicolas released and said, "Has everything here at the club been to your liking?"

"Absolutely, so far everything's been first class. It's a wonderful place. Quite beautiful," I said, playing to what I guessed Nicolas would want to hear. "I look forward to seeing more of it."

"And you shall. Wilson and I will see to that. We're very proud of the club and its amenities. My uncle oversaw every detail and we go to great lengths to ensure everything we do would meet with this approval."

"Your uncle?" I asked.

"Yes, my late uncle, Joseph Antonelli, was the founder of FirsTech and Bella Collina was his estate. It was as much his passion as his home. Every brick, every piece of stone, every flower and tree, as I said every detail - no matter how minor, he personally attended to."

"Well, by his accomplishments here and, of course, with FirsTech, your uncle must have been a very special man." I continued to play along.

"Yes, he was. But, of course, I would think so. He raised me like a son but more importantly, he was my mentor, my life coach, if you will."

Nicolas paused and waited for a response.

I was sure that Nicolas wanted to tell me more, so I led him on with, "Oh, really?"

"Yes, he taught me early on that a man's life should be lived as if he were creating a masterwork or a fine meal. In fact, when I was a boy, every Sunday he'd sit me in the kitchen with him while he prepared his Sunday meat sauce and he'd talk to me as he stirred and added the spices and meats. He'd lecture me over and over again how every single ingredient had to be the finest available, fresh and ripe, and in the exact proportions for the sauce to be its best. You see, the sauce was his metaphor. He likened it to great art and the grandest achievements in science and engineering, and to all the most valuable things in human history. He taught me that a man needs a recipe for his life; one that accepted no substitutes for the best and allowed no compromise of what you know to be correct. Those Sunday afternoons were my favorite time with him."

Nicolas stopped again. This time he was done, which caught me off guard.

"I ah, had a . . . my grandfather used to make meat sauce, too," I blurted, feeling instantly foolish.

Nicolas smiled and continued, "Yes, well, the only reason I mentioned this is that he brought the same passion and sensibilities to his business, which is why FirsTech is the industry leader it is today. He would never tolerate compromise or second efforts. And though he demanded the best, he was easily able to inspire that level of performance and dedication from everyone he came in contact with. My uncle was someone that you just didn't want to disappoint."

"I'm sorry I never got the opportunity to meet him," I said, as sincerely as possible.

Nicolas and Wilson exchanged thoughtful glances before Nicolas continued more casually.

"So, Joseph, Wilson tells me that he's convinced you to join us at the pistol range in the morning."

"He has. But I hope he's also told you that I'm a rank amateur and that I'll be doing my best just not to embarrass myself."

They laughed.

"I told him there's nothing to it," Wilson said to Nicolas. Then to me. "A short lesson and before you know it we'll have you squeezing off three-inch groupings from 25 meters."

I shrugged. "I take it that's a good thing."

"It's a damn good thing," Wilson confirmed.

"He should know," Nicolas said. "He's been tryin' to get that good his whole life. And that's a long time."

Wilson laughed. "Okay. Okay. Well, we'll see in the morning, won't we?"

"We will, indeed," Nicolas said, grinning. Then to me, "I almost forgot. Congratulations on your award. Have you seen this year's gift?"

"Gift? No."

"Oh, of course, this is your company's first award, your first year here. Well, you should know that we keep it very low key, with regard to the awards. On the table over there under the clock, you'll find DTC's award, really just a small gift of thanks for the excellent service your company's provided to FirsTech. There's also a list of all the honorees displayed for anyone who cares to see and that's the sum of it. I think you'll agree that our businesses provide enough excruciatingly dull moments without any help from us. The last thing we need is to suffer one more inconsequential speech or tiresome ceremony."

"No argument here," I said, honestly. "I've always been a strong opponent of the necessary evils. Frankly, I never understood why they were so necessary."

Nicolas smiled softly and nodded imperceptibly. "I think we're gonna to get along just fine. And that's a good thing, isn't it Wilson?"

"That's outstanding."

*       *       *

Dinner was a buffet set out in the same grand style and in proportion to everything else at Bella Collina. Steam trays, platters, bowls, and carving stations ran for forty feet along a beautifully decorated buffet table against one wall of the dinning hall. A staff of at least fifteen manned the far side of the table, poised to serve the guests as they moved indecisively along, stopping occasionally to select from an unending variety of salads, entrees, and side dishes. There were not only an incredible variety of meats, seafood, and pasta but all were offered in several different preparations. Two-and-a-half pound lobsters were served boiled, stuffed, or broiled, whole or tails. The aged beef cuts were sirloin, porterhouse, filet mignon, or sliced London broil and cooked to order. There was veal Marsala, Sorrentino, scallopini, and thick juicy chops. Stuffed shrimp, garlic shrimp, boiled and peeled shrimp. Numerous hot and cold preparations of clams, mussels, oysters, calamari and scungulli. Homemade pastas in marinara, Alfredo, vodka, and meat sauce with meatballs. Grilled sausages from around the world. There was tuna and salmon and swordfish and grouper and a few more fish that I couldn't identify, served grilled, broiled, blackened or topped with delicate gourmet sauces. Past the entrees, the table was ladened with a couple dozen types of vegetables and potatoes ready to compliment even the most creatively assembled meal. I thought that I would describe the spread to Cathy by likening it to having half a dozen five-star restaurants joined together serving every dish on their menus. Michael would've loved this.

But *that* thought brought me quickly back to reality. No one had asked me about Michael. So even though there was a little room left on my plate, I headed back to my table.

"See anything you like?" Wilson asked as I sat down to his left.

"I don't think a blind man could say he hadn't," I replied quickly.

"Well, enjoy and eat plenty. There's no reason to be delicate here. We're all among friends."

"Wine, Joseph?" Nicolas asked, holding a bottle of red standing on the other side of me.

"Please. Thank you," I said, noting that Nicolas had waited to sit, ensuring that I would be in between Wilson and him.

Nicolas poured and passed the bottle around the table to the three other men sitting with them. When they each had a full glass, Nicolas raised his goblet.

"To old friends," he said. And turning to me, he added, "And to new ones. Salute."

After the toast, introductions were made. Two of the men were "government contract specialists" and the other was "with the Pentagon". I recognized that they were being purposely vague about their work and their employers. When no more was offered, none was asked. And that seemed just fine with everyone.

George from the Pentagon finished his glass of wine and reached for the bottle. "This is excellent Chianti, Nicolas." Then looking at the label, "Brunelleschi. I don't think I've seen this anywhere. I'd loved to know where you get it."

*Brunelleschi?* I looked up from my plate.

"Actually, you can only get it here at the club," Nicolas told him. "We import it from Italy, directly from the winery. It's a small local vineyard, that's been in the same family for hundreds of years."

One of the contract specialists put down his glass. "It's wonderful. How did you come upon it?"

I cocked my head toward Nicolas, pretending to have only a polite interest in the conversation.

"It's an interesting story. My uncle discovered it many years ago, during a trip to Italy. Back then, he traveled frequently to Livorno on business. And since he was born in Naples and immigrated to America as a young boy, he took these opportunities to tour the northern provinces. Eventually, he fell in love with the people and the wines of Tuscany, and he began planning his trips so he could spend time exploring the vineyards in the Chianti Classico District between Siena and Florence. On one of these trips, he met the Brunelleschi family and sampled their Chianti. My uncle told me it was like nothing he had ever tasted before, like his first drink of wine all over again. He was so impressed with the wine that he befriended the family and found that they had fallen on hard times. Apparently, the family was descendant of the great Italian Renaissance Architect, Filippo Brunelleschi. Brunelleschi did most of his work in Florence, his most famous being the magnificent dome for the Cathedral of Florence. Anyway, during the war the vines had been neglected and the annual production was now barely enough to feed the family, let alone fund the restoration of the vineyard. So, my uncle struck a deal with the family patriarch. He became his partner, providing the money to rejuvenate the vines and, therefore, the family's future. In return, he only asked that he and his heirs be exclusively privileged to import their wine to

America. Today, it's a flourishing winery. Still small and family run, but prosperous. Now I purchase the wine from the grandson of the man that made the deal with my uncle."

To the other men at the table, it may have appeared that I was entranced by Nicolas' story. In fact, I was stunned. My grandfather was born in Naples and had also imported Brunelleschi for himself and, as far as I knew, it was not otherwise available. But more chilling was the recollection of my grandfather telling a very similar, if not identical, story about finding the wine. I had learned about the great architect, Brunelleschi, sitting by my mother's stove one Sunday afternoon. Santa Maria del Fiore, the Cathedral's original name, was built a century before Brunelleschi was commissioned to finish the Dome. No one had yet figured out how to construct the massive dome without buttresses, which were forbidden by the city fathers' building code. Brunelleschi had spent two years in Rome with his friend Donatella studying the ancient ruins and, it is believed, that this study, his background in mathematics and his ability to visualize and draft designs in three dimensions afforded him the vision to accomplish this feat. In fact, Brunelleschi is credited with inventing the "vanishing point" concept, using linear perspective in his architectural designs. Donatella was the first Renaissance artist to use the vanishing point in his paintings.

Could this be a coincidence, an old tale told by influential old Italian men about their special wine? No, I thought quickly, this is no coincidence. And if it wasn't, then what was it?

Pucci and Dennis no doubt knew who my grandfather was. The extensive background checks that had been done before his company was cleared to haul FirsTech's classified cargo had surely revealed that I was the grandson of Carmine Napolo. Were they trying to goad me into a discussion about Don Carmine? It wouldn't be the first time that mere strangers' curiosity led them to contrive a way to prod me into a discussion about my infamous grandfather. The Mafia carried a mystique that intrigued all types of people. It could be the guy behind the counter at the dry cleaners or a sophisticated business associate, upon hearing my last name they would usually start with a nervous laugh, *Not the Napolo Family?* I would never deny it. *Yes, he was my grandfather.* Sometimes the questions continued. *What was he like?* I would tell them that I was just a kid we he died and that he was like any other grandfather. *Was he a nice guy?* I would usually end it by saying, *He was a nice grandfather, but he wasn't a nice guy. He was a mobster, and he did all the things that mobster do. Why would you think he was a nice guy?* But not tonight. I was the one on a fishing trip. If Pucci and Dennis were casting they were going to need better bait.

Pentagon George interrupted my thinking. "Your uncle could've made another fortune importing this wine," he said to Nicolas. "Did he ever consider it?"

"No, not to my knowledge. He enjoyed drinking the wine too much to have it ruined by the business of selling it. Besides, the winery's too small to support even one of the major markets in the Unites States. Virtually all of their business is in Italy. It's become a premium wine there, sold only in the finest restaurants and to a few well-heeled private customers on the continent. I've been told that the Pope is partial to the Brunelleschi Reservo and keeps an adequate supply."

"That would be one hell of an endorsement deal," the man they called Sanford said. "An ad man's dream come true. Imagine all the heavenly and divine references we'd be subject to."

The men at the table laughed. I did too, but it was forced. Like my appetite, my sense of humor was fading fast. My grandfather had known a Pope or two in his day, but I didn't think that was common knowledge. I lifted my glass and with a few turns of my wrist, rolled the wine around the inside of the goblet.

"Anything the matter, Joseph?" Nicolas asked.

I shook my head and replied, "No, just the thought of the Pope enjoying this wine reminded me of an old Tom Waite's song. It's a blues song and there's a line that says, *'How do the angels get to sleep when the devil leaves the porch light on?'*"

The men at the table chuckled.

I looked left and right at Nicolas and Wilson. They were both laughing politely, looking like they knew just where the switch to the porch light was located.

\*  \*  \*

"Nicky, me boy." The man spoke loud and thick; his tongue and lips slowed by a combination of too much alcohol and the fat Cuban cigar in his mouth. "Great pahdy," he slurred in a strong South Boston accent as he slapped Nicolas much too hard on the back.

I watched Nicolas spin around and glare hostilely at the man. His disgust was apparent but the large drunken man continued.

"So where're the broads, Nicky? I awdered a redhead for tonight. An' I tol' your man David I wanted a *real* redhead, nawght some two-tone dye jawb, and I'm 'bout ready for some of that right now."

I looked around the large cherry wood paneled cigar room. About twenty of Nicolas' guests had accepted his invitation to join him for a cigar and an after dinner drink. State-of-the-art air purification systems effectively cleansed the air of the thick, sweet smoke from the hand-rolled Cuban leaf being puffed by the overfed men lounging in overstuffed leather chairs and sofas. Others stood in small conversation groups around the room and against the cherry wood bar. A few had wandered out through the tall French doors onto the balcony that overlooked the lighted gardens and fountains that sloped down and then uphill at the back of the estate. Most of the heads in the room were now turned toward the boisterous New Englander and Nicolas.

Frowning, Nicolas took the man by the elbow and guided him toward the doors that lead from the cigar room to the rotunda. I chose a path toward the bar, which would bring me close to the pair. As I came within earshot, I heard Nicolas speaking softly to the drunk. The drunk pulled his arm from Nicolas' grasp and turned angrily. I stopped, close enough to intervene, if necessary.

The drunk pulled the cigar from his mouth. "Don't you patronize me. I'll call ya whateva I gawddam want, *Nicky boy*. You jus' betta rememba who the fuck I am."

I saw Nicolas reach into his pocket as he leaned in close to the man. "I know full well who you are. But tonight, you're a guest at *my* club. You've had too much to drink and your behavior is abhorrent."

With that the drunk tossed the cigar on the floor and stepped menacingly toward Nicolas.

"Fuck you, pretty boy," he said as he cocked his fist.

The doors from the rotunda burst open. Four security men, two with their hands inside their jackets, surrounded Nicolas and the drunk. The leader of the security team gripped the drunkard's right arm just above the elbow with one hand and bent his right hand and fingers back with the other. The drunk bent forwards, wincing in pain, immobilized.

"I think you should retire for the evening," Nicolas said to him. "Oh, and please don't you ever forget who *I* am. My name is Nicolas. That's how I expect to be addressed. Not Nicky or Nick, and certainly not *Nicky Boy*. I don't think that's too much to ask, especially in my own home, is it?"

The drunk sheepishly looked up at Nicolas. "No, I guess nawght."

"Good. Now, these gentlemen will see you to your room where you should spend the rest of the evening relaxing with your redheaded lady."

The quickly sobering man turned back to Nicolas as he was being lead away. "Nicolas, I'm sorry I . . . "

Nicolas cut him short with a quick wave. "Don't worry about it. Go have your fun."

Then Nicolas pulled a ten-inch Churchill from his jacket pocket and placed it in the man's mouth. "For later," he said, with a wink and a smile.

As the security team left with their charge, Nicolas turned around and saw me standing close by.

"Watching my back?" Nicolas asked him.

"Something like that. You never know with some guys and he was a big boy."

Nicolas raised his eyebrows and nodded. "It seems there's one in every crowd, isn't there?"

"Unfortunately, and they can ruin a party."

"Well not this one," Nicolas asserted brightly, throwing his arm around my shoulder. "Come on, let's get a fresh brandy and I'll show you around the club."

Nicolas donned a likeable style that facilitated comfortable conversation and a pleasant sense of familiarity as he led me on the tour. As we walked through the billiards parlor, Nicolas described the four regulation clay tennis courts and the eighteen-hole golf course cut into the sloping hillside out beyond the gardens. Gary Player had designed it for his uncle. Then he led me through the card room, the movie theater and on to the large grill room where, with a teenager's enthusiasm, he showed me the club's extensive collection of the latest electronic games. We took turns in the authentic F-16 flight simulator and decided that we were best to keep our day jobs. The two indoor Bocce courts were next. They were nestled in an elaborate Italian-ornate garden patio with real grass, shrubbery, flowers, and grapevines woven over a trellis, all grown under lights that were politely hidden behind retractable ceiling panels. After the world class gym and the carpeted, oak locker room, we ended up downstairs in the shooting range.

I had never been in a shooting range before, but I was sure that they didn't all look like this. Nicolas had adjusted a dimmer panel so that recessed spotlights dimly lit the space. There were eight individually lighted shooting stalls with shelves and shooting platforms covered in padded plum-colored leather. Each stall was equipped with a color monitor that was linked to eight video cameras, one for each shooter's target. A small panel enabled the shooter to switch between a close up views of his target or to split screen images of the targets of any or all of the other stalls. Nicolas explained that the cameras were equipped with infrared directional and focus controls that automatically tracked the target as it moved along the trolley system back and forth for variable distance shooting, or horizontally for lateral movement shooting practice. The ceiling and walls of the room and each stall were covered with black sound-absorbing foam panels. Thick carpeting on the floor completed the noise dampening. In acoustical engineer's parlance, the room was "dead". Speaking in there was like talking with a heavy wool blanket over your head.

"This is where Wilson and I come to let loose. Millions of dollars in bets that will never be paid have been won and lost down here." Nicolas said after finishing the technical portion of the tour.

"Who's ahead?"

"The ammunition manufacturers."

I chuckled and walked to one of the stalls. I peered into the blackness, unable to see any targets or the end of the room.

"How far are the targets? I can't see a thing."

"We're two stories below ground level," Nicolas said as he approached the stall. "The range was built by first excavating the area and then the back gardens and fountains were built on top. The maximum target distance is just over five hundred yards. Watch."

Nicolas slid out a drawer from below the shooting platform. A keyboard, a small monitor, and another lighted control panel were mounted in the drawer. Nicolas began pressing keys and membrane switches and the range lit up. I was able to see tiny targets at the far end of range.

"Jesus, who the hell can see that let alone hit it?"

"The range is built to handle 50-BMG-caliber rounds with no problem. With a good rifle and scope, say a McMillan or a Remington or even an H&K 93, 500 yards is a drop in the bucket. But if you want it closer you simply toggle forward or enter the distance here and the target moves."

Nicolas hit several buttons and all the lights in the range went dark except for the one illuminating that stall's target. Then he entered 100 on the keypad and the target moved toward them silently like a ghost, stopping exactly one hundred yards out. The camera's electronic sensors kept the target perfectly framed in the television monitor. Only the slight fluttering of the target's corners belied the fact that it was moving to its new position.

"That's a little better," I said.

"We can also change the target automatically."

Nicolas hit several keys and the round target disappeared into the ceiling. Several seconds later it dropped back into position, this time with the type of target that contained a silhouette of man.

"That's cool," I blurted involuntarily.

"That's nothing. Wait'll you see *this*. Follow me."

Nicolas led me to a half-door next to the last stall. We stepped into the range and I looked down, a reaction to what I felt underfoot. The floor covering was a dark brown, dense and short-cropped type of plastic grass, like Astroturf, only very soft and well padded. Nicolas slid open a panel on the wall and took out a wireless keypad about half the size of a normal keyboard.

Beaming, Nicolas said, "*This* is the ultimate remote control for grownup boys. Do you feel like ridding the big city of terrorist? Or is the old West more your style?"

I shrugged. "I've become a fan of country music lately, so let's say the old West."

Nicolas nodded and tapped at the keyboard. When he finished the lighting began to change and I heard the soft purr of electric machinery. Slowly, the entire range came to life. For the first hundred yards or so, the floor heaved up in certain spots creating a rolling landscape replete with cactus, shrubs, and rock formations. Beyond, for over a quarter of mile, parts of one building after another slid out from the walls, dropped from the ceiling and rose from the floor until Main Street in Dodge City circa 1875 was faithfully reproduced, down to the hitching posts and water troughs in front of the saloon and the hotel and other places that were too far away for me to identify. I stood in awe as Nicolas punched a few more keys. The lighting changed to simulate early morning on a sunny summer day.

"I can make any time of day or night. Now, watch about halfway down the street on the right. Disney and George Lucas don't even dream of stuff like this yet."

I saw a man, actually a cowboy, step into the street and begin walking toward them. I could hear faint footsteps and the jingle of spurs.

Nicolas spoke in a loud whisper. "It's state-of-the-art electromagnetic holography married with computer generated animation of digitized human actors. FirsTech has been developing the technology for military applications. It's highly classified stuff. But I own it so I get to play with it."

The figure appeared to be a real person, three-dimensional with thoroughly life-like movement down to the motions of his clothing as he walked. Even the shadowing was true as the cowboy passed under porch roofs and then back into the angled morning sunlight. There was no flicker or translucence like most holographs that I had ever seen. The cowboy stopped and looked toward Nicolas and me. Then he tipped his hat and entered the saloon.

"That's incredible."

"He was a friendly one. Maybe he saw that we were unarmed."

I looked at Nicolas.

"Just kidding. They can't actually see us but the sensors in the floor tell them where we are. If he was a bad guy he may have drawn on us or stepped into the middle of the street for a duel."

"They shoot?"

"Yes, they shoot lasers. Actually, there are tens of thousands of laser ports and sensors throughout the town. A chain of supercomputers randomly creates the good guys and the bad guys. The computers are artificially intelligent and they can mastermind an infinite number of people and games. Of course, the user can enter certain parameters and scenarios that dictate the type of play desired. You can be the good guy or the bad guy. You can fight alone or with real or holographic compadres."

"I still don't understand how it works. Howdoya play?"

"Think of it as the world's most sophisticated laser tag game. If we were playing now, we'd be wearing cowboy clothing and hats studded with tiny wireless sensors. We'd be armed with our choice of authentic period revolvers, rifles, or shotguns. They'd be loaded with live blank ammo and fitted with miniaturized laser shooting devices. When our adversaries decide to shoot at us or visa versa, the computer matches their position with the lasers and sensors behind them. Even if a shot goes wild, the computer tracks it and senses the point of impact. Windows break, horses and innocent bystanders go down, victims cry out from their wounds. The computer even adjusts for accuracy when a man is running as opposed to when he's behind something with a platform to rest his weapon on and improve his aim. It also provides true-to-life directional sound that makes all the shouting and shooting very real. And each holographic person has his own characteristics and personality. There's a lot of them but after a while you actually get to know a few of them. And trust me, the good, the bad, and the ugly are all represented. And there're some real bad actors out there. They rob, pillage, take hostages, shoot unarmed citizens, the works. Watch this, it's a demo program."

Nicolas tapped a few keys and the town magically came to life, the whole quarter-mile strip. The streets and sidewalks filled with people, everyday citizens going about their business, most on foot and a few on horseback. The sounds of a cowboy town in motion filled the room: muffled conversations, friendly shouts across the street, clomping horse hooves, a baby crying in its carriage. Then a man with a shotgun shouts from the roof of the hotel shouts, "Johnson!" A man across the street outside the bank looks up quickly. The man on the roof takes aim and fires, loudly. The man in the street, Johnson, dives to the right just in time. Holographic dirt explodes where the shotgun blast hits the street. Johnson rolls and springs to his feet, firing his six-shooter three times. The man on the roof groans, grabs his chest and falls two stories to the street, landing in a cloud of dust. The townspeople who had ducked and ran screaming for cover slowly rise to their feet and come up from behind wagons and water troughs and out of store front doors to gather around the dead man. Johnson holsters his gun and dusts himself off. Then, suddenly, they were all gone. The street was empty and quiet.

The images and sounds had been as real as a modern movie, but better, three-dimensional, and the gunshots had reverberated in my chest like the boomers on the Fourth of July. I found myself involuntarily taking a deep breath through my nose, half expecting to smell the dirt and the cordite.

"That was unbelievable," I exclaimed, grinning widely.

Nicolas raised his eyebrows again and nodded. "Believe it. And we could've walked down the street and been right in the middle of it all. The military and law enforcement guys that have played this say that it's very close to actual combat. It simulates the stress and fear factors very well."

"This could be a great training tool, for the police or military."

Nicolas nodded. "Exactly, but it's still very expensive. Not yet practical for ordinary domestic law enforcement or mass military training. However, it *is* already being used for classified, very selective, mission-specific training. I'm not at liberty to tell you much more than that, but you can use your imagination. A few years from now, we'll have a more affordable, declassified version. By the way, your DOD classification applies to this little toy. If you weren't cleared to at least secret, I couldn't have shown you this."

"I understand," I said. "Ya know, seeing something like this makes you wonder what else is out there."

Nicolas smiled that devil-who-left-the-porchlight-on-smile. He couldn't have asked for a better segue.

"You wouldn't believe how fast things are coming. Just imagine if we could create these holographs from space, using satellite platforms. We could put holographic armies, naval fleets and aircraft anywhere in the world with the flip of a switch. We could turn a platoon of marines into a holographic battalion. A few hummers, tanks and APC's into a virtual armored division. And, there are loads of civilian applications. Like virtual security, both human and canine, completely indistinguishable from the real thing, down to the dogs' bark."

"What about it's bite?" I said, only partially in jest.

"Mix in some real guards and dogs and would you want to bet on which ones were real?"

"After seeing this, I guess not," I admitted.

"Exactly."

Nicolas hit a key on the remote and Dodge City began to recede into the walls, floor and ceiling. I watched the buildings come apart and fall away until nothing remained in the cavernous space. Then I turned to see Nicolas staring at me with an odd, very serious expression.

"Joseph, this room, like the rest of the estate is electronically shielded and swept at frequent intervals by the most sophisticated electronic devices available, some of which we don't even tell our customers that we've invented, because some of those customers . . . well, let's just say that we need to keep some things for ourselves. Do you understand?"

"So far, but why are you telling me this?" I asked, sensing that the timbre of our conversation had suddenly changed.

"Because you need to know how serious my work is and how serious I am about my work. Because I'm still not sure about you and yet I've decided to take a chance with you, just on gut feel, and that's not too smart. And because you have to know that if you choose to tell anyone about what you've seen here or what we've discussed or what I'm about to tell you, it'll not only violate your secrecy agreement with the DOD, which is a federal offense, but it also may jeopardize other things important to you."

I was taken aback by Nicolas' sudden change in attitude but I shifted gears quickly upon hearing the last few words.

"What other things are you taking about?" I asked firmly.

"Your government contracts, your DOD status, for starters."

"And . . . "

"Let's just leave it at that, for now."

"Let's not," I said. "In fact, let's talk about why you made so sure I came to this party tonight and why I ended up at *your* table sitting between Dennis and you. Then let's talk about why you really brought me down here. Or, how about we talk about . . . ." I was going to say *'making fucking meat sauce and Brunelleschi wine'* but I caught himself. ". . . the hijacking of your classified shipment and why that hasn't been mentioned once tonight."

Nicolas lifted his chin and said, "Okay. Let's talk about that. I was just coming to it anyway. But first, I have to ask you to imagine one more thing."

"Just so there's a point to it."

"Oh there is."

"Go ahead."

Nicolas paused, scratching the back of his neck before he began. "Okay, imagine a known tyrannical enemy of the free world, a supporter of international terrorism with almost unlimited means - say petrodollars, who has been very busy over the last few years buying sophisticated weapons technology illegally on the gray market. This ill-gotten technology is sophisticated enough that he may now have the ability to shoot down an estimated thirty-five or forty percent of every fighter sortie and cruise missile attack launched against him. If that were true, the United States and its UN allies might consider long and hard before they attempted another one of their good-for-the-free-world policing actions like Desert Storm or Kosovo. The potential loss of men and machines would give them great pause. Fortunately, thirty-five or forty percent is worse case and the bad guy knows this. If it's only ten percent, and that's proven early on in a conflict, the good guys would no doubt accept those losses and persevere to an eventual victory. Unfortunately, no one really knows, and that's not good because each day the bad guy gets more of the technology in place, swinging the odds in his favor."

Nicolas raised his eyebrows. "Now imagine that *we* have the technology to equip the nose cones of our jet fighters and cruise missiles with the computer enhanced electromagnetic holography you saw here tonight. What if one cruise missile could replicate itself in flight five or ten fold, creating virtual missiles on parallel paths but in varying altitudes, projections that have both a visual and a magnetic-mass image detectable by radar. A few cruise missiles could be made to look like a few dozen. A sortie of twenty fighters would look like eighty. Even after they figure out the ruse, it would take them years to develop the technology to identify the actual from the virtual threat. Until then, their systems would be overwhelmed with data, real and false. They'd be left no choice but to try to shoot at as many of the targets as possible. Then it's simple math. The odds of a real hit are reduced directly by the number of virtual targets."

"Sounds like star wars meets hall of mirrors," I said, impatiently. "So, where's the connection. What does this have to do with the hijacking?"

Nicolas looked me square in the eyes. "Inside the missing crate is a working first-run production model of something called the Holographic Arial Weapons Image Replicator, HAWIRE for short, or for laymen, the image multiplier I just described to you. Now suppose that there's an ex-intelligence operative gone bad, a very dangerous and resourceful man, that has a very lucrative contract to deliver this device to the bad guys. Suppose he has a looming deadline and that he will stop at nothing to complete his mission. Consider the implications of . . ."

"Wait a minute here," I said, holding up his hands. "This is starting to sound like a trailer for a bad movie - 'Imagine this', 'suppose that', 'consider this'. All we're missing is the ominous music. You pronounced how serious you are and, after this little demonstration, I have no reason to doubt it, but let's stop this histrionic and mysterious language. I can understand the seriousness of the situation without all the drama. Besides, I've been up since three this morning and I'm tired, so let's talk straight."

Nicolas was taken aback. He deliberated briefly and said, "Okay, let's."

"Good," I said. "So far you've told me that FirsTech shipped a very important top secret device on one of my trucks without any special security precautions. Why?"

"Good question," Nicolas conceded. "There's a time-tested theory that supports the hiding in plain sight rationale. So most classified cargo travels around the country in much the same manner as a shipment of breakfast cereal or toys or car parts; on contracted common carriers like DTC. As for security, the trailer was outfitted with GPS locator transmitters and other backup security measures, including two DOD trained and certified FirsTech security agents in a tail car."

This, I thought, might explain Wilson Dennis' cavalier remarks after the hijacking about getting the freight back. "So what happened?" I said.

"Our agents followed the truck when it was diverted to the warehouse in Kearny. While they were setting up their surveillance, they were killed."

"Killed? Jesus. How? We didn't hear anything about *that*."

"They were shot, executed, as they sat in their car."

"What about the other backup measures, the GPS transmitter?"

"I told you we had a dangerous *and* resourceful opponent. It seems he's been able to compromise FirsTech's security group. The GPS transmitter and other equipment built into the shipping crate were apparently sabotaged. Only the equipment fitted into your trailer was operating at the time of the hijacking."

"So," I began to conclude. "This ex-intelligence guy compromised your security and killed your security agents. Why doesn't he have the HAWIRE? Why is he still looking for it? And where do I fit in here, other than as the owner of the truck?"

As he was speaking the words, I was answering my own questions. Johnny Onions had the crate, not this other guy. And, if that was true, maybe Johnny killed the security team. Two more murders added to the list.

"Com'on, Joseph, you know exactly where you fit in," Nicolas huffed. "And you know god damn well why Aaron Lincoln doesn't have the crate, don't you. So, why don't we *both* talk straight?"

My stomach tightened. "Who the hell is Aaron Lincoln?"

"Lincoln's the ex-intelligence guy. And in the interest of straight talking, I'll tell you that he's been responsible for most of the bloodshed over the last couple days. And while he did plan to somehow divert your truck with the HAWIRE on board and sell it to our enemy, his most skillful planning would never have contained a contingency for Michael Cogan to be involved in the hijacking of a truckload of shoes on the same day. This, of course, is not news to you, is it?"

I was feeling the affects of rising well before dawn. My body was tired. And Nicolas' last statement weakened me further. I needed to get off my feet so that I could conserve what remained of the day's energies, to redirect it to this conversation.

"Let's go sit down," I said as I turned away and walked through the opening that led to the other side of the shooting stalls. Nicolas returned the remote controller to its shelf and dimmed the lights before following me over to the leather chairs in the elevated sitting area behind the stalls.

I sank into a deep, soft armchair and let out an involuntary sigh. Nicolas sat across from me. When the squeaks from the rich leather subsided and we were settled, I began to speak but Nicolas held up a hand, stopping me.

"Before you say anything more," he began, "I want to clear the air. I think we're heading in the wrong direction. I'm not your enemy. Quite the opposite, in fact. I should tell you that we know all about Michael's deal to give up the truckload of shoes to repay his gambling debt. And, frankly, we've known all along about Cogan's gambling problem. It surfaced during the background checks we did five years ago. We thought he had it under control, though. But all that isn't important anymore. What's important is your understanding that we have a very serious matter of national and international security on our hands, and that it's in our mutual interest to work together to recover the missing HAWIRE before Lincoln does."

I nodded. "The FBI made it very clear. They gave Michael and me an ultimatum. Return the crate or else."

"The FBI?"

"Yeah, they paid us a visit yesterday."

"A visit?"

"Yes, at our office. Why?"

"What did he look like?"

I squinted. "Why do you say 'he' and not 'they'?"

Nicolas ignored the question and said, "*He* was late forties, early fifties, a little over six feet, thin but fit, with short-cropped graying hair and very unusual blue-gray eyes. Am I right?"

"Yes, exactly. But I'm not so sure he was FBI."

"He wasn't. That was Aaron Lincoln and you're one of the few people who's met him in the last few days that's still alive."

"Whadaya mean?"

Nicolas thought a second. "Lincoln's a cold blooded killer, a trained and experienced assassin. There's a lot of money in this for Lincoln if he can meet his deadline to recover the HAWIRE. He's on a mission. And, well, ah . . . let's just say that you don't want to be an obstacle between Lincoln and the success of his mission. Leave it at that, for now."

I leaned forward and leaned toward Nicolas. "That's the second time, you've said that. So for the second time I'll say, no – let's not. You say you're not my enemy, but exactly what are you?"

"Someone you should trust."

"Oh, I see. Just like that, huh? Ya know, I'm feeling very uncomfortable with this conversation and unless that changes quickly, I'm leaving, tonight. I've had enough of this."

"That wouldn't be a good idea. You need me as much as I need you right now, if not more."

I pushed myself out of the chair. "I don't see it that way. If you know so much, then you've probably figured out that Michael and I are the only ones with a line to the guy who has the HAWIRE. Without me, my cooperation, this guy Lincoln has at least a good a chance finding the thing as you do. And if he does, it's not going to look too good for your company, is it?"

"No, but we'd survive it. On the other hand, I'm not sure that Michael Cogan will."

I sprang forward and stood over Nicolas. "And what the fuck does that mean?"

Nicolas calmly looked up. "We have confirmation that Michael was escorted from the Sheraton Hotel in Woodbridge, NJ by three men that identified themselves as FBI agents. The desk clerk gave a flawless description of Lincoln as the agent in charge. Michael was taken away in a van that was found abandoned in a field that had been recently used as a landing pad for a helicopter. Lincoln has a helicopter. There's almost no chance that Lincoln doesn't have him. I'm sorry."

I uncoiled. "When did this happen?"

"Late this afternoon."

"Shit," I muttered, as I backed up and flopped down into the chair.

Nicolas gave me a few moments, to let it sink in.

Finally, I looked up. "I don't know where the crate is. There's a wiseguy named Johnny Anelli. He took the crate, by accident. He was Michael's, umm, associate in the hijacking scheme and Michael was with him this afternoon. I think they must have been arranging to trade the crate back to Lincoln, who they thought was the FBI. Lincoln had offered a million-dollar reward for its return. Did they get Anelli, too?"

"No. He wasn't with them when they left the hotel."

"Is Anelli alive?"

"For the time being and until we know otherwise, we can only assume that he is."

I exhaled deeply. "Do you know where Michael is? Is he . . . okay?"

"We know that Lincoln operates out of a building at Stewart Airport. It's near Newburgh. We don't know if he has Michael there or, frankly if Michael's okay or not. Again, I'm sorry, but that's all we know right now. Can you get a hold of this Anelli?"

I shook my head. "No. The only thing I have is a pager number for Agent Dwyer, Lincoln's FBI alias. But if we know where Lincoln is, why don't we just call the police or the real FBI and get this thing over with."

"That would like signing your partner's death warrant. Lincoln has never left a witness."

"But . . ."

Nicolas had raised his hand, signaling me to stop. A door at the end of the row of stalls had opened. A short, portly man wearing a brown workshop apron came out carrying a tray, whistling an unrecognizable tune. He stopped short when he saw Nicolas and me sitting in the half-light on the other side of the room.

"Nicolas, that you?" The man called out, squinting over the top of half-frame glasses that rested low on the bridge of his nose.

"Yes, Al it's just me," Nicolas answered. Then in a whisper to me, "It's our gunsmith." Then lower, "Listen, I have an idea that might work. Let me talk it over with Wilson in the morning. If we can come up with something that gives us both what we want, can I count on you?"

"Does the plan include getting Michael back safely?"

"If he's still alive, yes."

I looked into Nicolas' eyes. They were clear and steady.

I nodded and whispered, "Okay."

The gunsmith approached the sitting area. After giving me a knowing and confident glance, Nicolas looked over at him.

"Al, what are you doing here so late?" Nicolas asked.

"I'm getting ready for tomorrow. Last minute stuff, match schedules, guest requirements, weapons checks, stuff like that. You know me, Nicolas, nothing ever feels done. Drives my wife crazy."

"I do know you, Al. You're a perfectionist, and that's a blessing and a curse. Let me introduce you to Joseph Napolo. Joseph meet Al Schmidt, master gunsmith and our range master."

"Nice to meet you." I shook hands with the gunsmith.

"Napolo?" Schmidt asked. "Where do I know that name?"

Here we go, I thought. Almost made it through the day without someone asking, The Napolo *Family*?

But, to my surprise, Schmidt said, "Oh, yeah, the forty-five auto, the Colt 1911. That's yours, right?"

"Yes, that's right," I replied, welcoming the deviation.

"Mr. Dennis asked me to take a look at it, clean it up. How much do you know about your gun?"

"Very little. It's been in the family for some time but it's been in storage for a long time."

Schmidt smiled crookedly. "Well, it shows and it wasn't stored properly. For long term storage it should've been well oiled and in a plastic bag or vacuum packed to seal out moisture. Luckily, Colt made a very durable weapon. There was some rust but it's still in good condition. And it's a rare piece, ya know. I went on the Internet and checked the serial number with Colt. It was manufactured in 1914 for the US Armed Forces, one of the first four thousand Colt made. I got real excited when I learned its vintage, so I broke it down, cleaned everything up, and reassembled it. All original parts, by the way, from the two-tone clip to the hardwood grips. Then, I took the liberty of sightin' it and runnin' twenty-one rounds through it. It performed beautifully. Cosmetically, the gun retains over 95% of the original Parkerized finish. There's some minor sharp edge rounding and holster wear on the front strap and the front of the frame, and unfortunately the muzzle's been threaded, probably fitted for a flash or noise suppressor at one time. Ya know, if it didn't have the threading on the muzzle, it'd be a collector-quality piece. But, ya know, it's still a rare gun and it's in fine working order now. It'll shoot exactly where you point it, every time."

"So all I gotta do is just point it straight and I'm okay?" I said.

Schmidt shrugged. "Sure, just straight and completely steady, with the front sight post settled perfectly into the rear slot and, allowing for windage and distance drop, you'll do just fine."

"Oh, that's all? In that case, maybe I'll just keep it as a collector's item. Pass it on to my sons."

Schmidt held up his forefinger. "Ya know, I did want to ask you about somethin' I found on the grip. I wanna show you. Got a minute?"

I looked to Nicolas who nodded.

"Sure," I said.

The gunsmith placed his tray of ammunition in one of the shooting stalls and hurried through the door into his shop, which adjoined the armory. He returned immediately with my gun cradled carefully on two white gloved fingers to minimize skin oil tranfers.

"Wow," I said. "It looks like a new gun."

Schmidt beamed, obviously proud of his work. Then he turned the pistol upside down and pointed to the bottom of the wood handgrips.

"I don't know how well you'll be able to see it in this light, but on the bottom of the left grip someone took great care to carve tiny letters."

"I never noticed them before," I said, knowing that I hadn't even look at the gun in maybe thirty years.

Schmidt held the gun up. "Can you see them? The letters, 'NP dash NPII dash NPIII'."

As I bent to look, Nicolas shot forward. "Can I see that?" He said, taking the gun from Schmidt.

Nicolas stepped directly under the nearest recessed ceiling light and examined the bottom of the handgrip closely. Then he ran his fingers slowly over the carved letters, back and forth several times. When he stopped, his face was ashen. He had seen a ghost.

Without looking up, he asked me, "Where did you say you got this gun?"

"I don't really know," I lied. "As I said, it's been in the family a long time. Why?"

Nicolas slowly raised his head. His jaw was set hard and he was breathing deeply through his nose. His eyes were moistened.

"This was my father's gun," Nicolas said, softly.

I stiffened and said, "What?"

"*Your* father's gun?" Schmidt asked as if he didn't hear it right the first time.

"Yes! This was my father's. The letters, they're initials. I watched him carve these letters." Then to me. "How did you get this?"

I stared at him as my mind raced. *How did I get this? Oh, let me tell you the story. I picked it up out of the street. It belonged to one of my grandfather's bodyguards, Nico. He dropped it when my grandfather hit him in the head with a tire iron. Nico had already killed the other bodyguard, Mario, with this gun and he was going to kill my grandfather and probably me, too. But my grandfather killed him first. Funny thing, this Nico was actually a relative, a second or third cousin of my grandfather's. Isn't that a nice story? No, I don't think it's your father's gun, unless your father was named . . .*

My mouth was suddenly dry as I answered, "I, ah, I'm really not sure, Nicolas. Are you sure?"

Nicolas nodded. "My father took me into the kitchen one night when I was five or six years old. He had been drinking. I can remember his breath. He showed me this gun, showed me how it worked. He even let me dry fire it several times. He told me how it had been his father's and that someday it would be mine. Then he took out his folding knife and carved our three initials here. NP stands for Nicola Pucci, my grandfather. He passed the gun on to my father, Nicola Pucci the Second, NPII and I'm the Third. When he finished carving he blew off the shavings, pulled me onto his lap, and using the point of the knife to underscore the initials, he said, 'Padre a figlio, padre a figlio.' Father to son, father to son. Then he said to me, 'When you become a man, this gun will pass to you, just like our name, Nico Pucci'. Am I sure?" Nicolas looked into my eyes. "Yes, I'm sure. As sure as I am my name is Nicola Pucci, the third."

I fought to control my reaction to what I had just heard. *Nico, my God! Could Nico, my grandfather's Judas, have been Nicola Pucci? Nicolas's father? How . . .?*

Nicolas and Schmidt were both staring at me, waiting for me.

240

I threw up my hands. "Look, I don't know. Your guess is as good as mine. Maybe he sold it and didn't tell you," I offered, trying to sound credible.

Nicolas straightened up and cleared his throat. "I don't know, maybe. He always carried it with him, though. I assumed he was carrying it when he was killed and it burned with him."

"Burned?" Schmidt winced.

"Yes, he died in a car crash in '63. My uncle told me that the car caught fire and exploded."

"That's horrible. I'm sorry. Why did your father carry a gun?" I asked, feeling quite sure I already knew the answer.

"He worked in private security. Provided personal protection for VIP's." Nicolas said, as he handed the pistol back to Schmidt.

No one spoke.

"Strange coincidence, isn't?" Schmidt finally said to fill the dead air.

But neither Nicolas nor I answered. We were locked in a stare that neither of us wanted to break.

Finally Nicolas said, "Strange? Yes, it is. Wouldn't you agree, Joseph?"

"Very," I agreed, not breaking eye contact.

"Sure is," Schmidt concluded.

Schmidt excused himself, to finish his work. We bid him good night and went upstairs to the rotunda without speaking a word. At the foot of the winding staircase, we shook hands over customary pleasantries and Nicolas' assurance that he would have a plan of action for me to consider when we met for breakfast.

Forgetting my earlier promise to myself about taking the elevator, I started up the stairs and immediately felt the fatigue from a very long day burning in my legs. However, when I sensed Nicolas' eyes on the center of my back I pushed aside the pain and stepped more sprightly, pretending the evening's revelations and implications were not weighing on me. But I could do nothing to push aside the images that were filling my head; vivid recollections of making meat sauce and Brunelleschi wine, and my grandfather; Tommy Ton and Johnny Onions and Vinny Diamonds; poor Michael, and Lincoln, and holographic cruise missiles, the missing crate; Mario's bloody head and Nico lying in the street; and my grandfather.

At the first landing, I glanced over my shoulder. Nicolas was still standing at the foot of the stairs. I turned around and asked, "What did you say your uncle's name was?"

"Antonelli," Nicolas replied.

"Joe Antonelli?"

"*Joseph* Antonelli," Nicolas quickly corrected me. "My uncle had strong feelings about the use of proper name derivatives. He found it disrespectful. Good night, now."

Nicolas turned and walked away, precluding any further questions.

I listened to his footfalls echoing through the rotunda. They were heavy, weary steps.

He holds no truck with coincidences either, I thought.

## The Hilton Hotel
## The Meadowlands in East Rutherford, NJ

When she had approached him in the bar off the lobby, he suspected that she was a hooker. All the makeup and hair and perfume. But that was okay. Johnny Anelli had nothing against hookers. In fact, some of his best relationships had been with prostitutes. Not streetwalkers, mind you, but call girls. And, if you ever asked Johnny what the difference was he'd be happy to tell you. Certainly, the fact that she was working the Hilton showed him something. Good sense, at least. Going in, she would know that the Hilton's customers, or the companies they worked for, could afford the minimum two hundred and twenty-dollar a night room. Generally, they were not the kind of clientele that you had to worry about being locked in a room with, alone and naked. And tonight, thanks to Michael Cogan's cash advance, Johnny Onions was just that, a registered guest of the Hilton Hotel enjoying a late evening cocktail before retiring. So, after a little small talk, Johnny and Charmagne had agreed on a price and walked arm-in-arm to the elevators.

Later, Johnny called to her, "How much time we got left?"

He was lying naked on the king-size bed, face-up on top of the bedspread, smoking a cigarette. Charmagne was in the bathroom with the door locked, peeing and rinsing her mouth out, unable to hear him. Johnny heard the toilet flush and reached for the remote control. The final credits on the pay-TV soft porn he had been watching were rolling. He hit the selector and ordered another feature, number five, Horny Housewives.

Charmagne came out of the bathroom a few minutes later wearing her mini-skirt and clunky, four-inch platform high heels.

"You say somethin', honey?"

"Yeah, how much time we got left? I just ordered another movie for us."

"Well, you enjoy it, baby. I gotta go," Charmagne said, reaching for her bra.

Johnny pushed himself up on one elbow. "Go? I paid for an hour. I got at least thirty, maybe forty minutes left."

"Sorry, baby," Charmagne cooed, taking her shirt from the dresser. "But you got off already. You shoulda held out a little longer. But it ain't your fault, honey, 'cause blow jobs are my specialty. In fact, you did pretty good. Most guys can't last more than a few minutes with me, so consider yourself lucky."

Johnny swung his legs off the bed. "Lucky! Hey, fuck that! I paid for a fuckin' hour, ya hear me. No one said nothin' 'bout getting' my rocks off or not. An hour's an hour, and if I wanna blow my load five fuckin' times in an hour then that's too fuckin' bad for you. So, before you piss me off, take off those clothes and get your ass back in bed."

Charmagne had been watching Johnny's face as it changed during his tirade. This is not your usual Hilton john, she thought. There was something scary about this guy. But there was no way she was going to let him see her fear.

"Willya gimme a nice tip?" She asked him with her hand on her hip, her bra loose on her shoulders.

"Yeah, I'll give ya a tip. Here it is: Cut the crap and get your little titties over here."

"Common, baby, be nice. I don't like it when you talk to me like that. You be nice to me and I'll be *real* nice to you. Okay, baby?"

Johnny looked up at the ceiling and shook his head. "Okay, okay. You stay and show me a real good time, I'll give ya a tip. I got the money, don't worry 'bout that."

"Another hundred?"

"Aw for chrissake, you're takin' all the fun outta it. You're wreckin' the mood here."

"Oh, baby, calm down. It's jus' that . . . well, I do this for a living, ya know."

"Yeah, yeah, yeah, I don't give a fuck. I'll give ya another hundred, just shut the fuck up about it."

"Oh, you're so sweet, baby. I'm gonna rock your world," Charmagne said in her most sultry voice, slipping the bra off her shoulders and tossing it on the dresser.

They looked at each other for a moment. After a few seconds Johnny spread his arms and said, "Come to papa."

"Money first, baby. You should know the rules by now."

"Fuckin' A."

Johnny pushed himself off the bed with a grunt and grabbed his pants off the back of a chair. He fished the fold of bills out of his pocket and peeled off two fifties. He didn't miss that Charmagne's eyes were glued to the wade of money. He made sure that he stuffed the bills back deep into the pocket

243

and folded the pants so that the pocket opening was tucked inside before he put them over the chair again.

Then he held up the two fifties and said, "Come and get 'em, sweet cheeks."

Charmagne smiled and slithered over to him. When she was close enough, Johnny hooked a finger into the top of her skirt and she let him pull her over. Johnny waved the bills in her face and then began to raise them over her head. Her eyes followed the money. Suddenly, he pressed his mouth against hers and forced her lips open with this tongue.

Charmagne recoiled and pulled her head away, but Johnny held on to the front of her skirt. She put her hands on his chest.

"No kissing, baby. I don't kiss."

Johnny snorted a laugh. "You'll blow me but you won't kiss me?"

"That's different."

Johnny wasn't surprised. Hookers rarely kissed.

"Okay, here comes your money."

Johnny ever so slowly began to lower the fifties. Her eyes locked on the bills as if they were presents from heaven. First, he let them caress the hair on the top of her head. Then he dripped them over her forehead. Charmagne went cross-eyed when the money drifted down the bridge of her nose. And when they passed by her mouth she stuck out her tongue and wiggled it seductively, wetting the bills. Below her throat, Johnny took one bill in each hand so he could split the path down her chest and leisurely tease each nipple on the way. Gradually, over her belly, he let the bills converge again and he took them in his right hand, freeing his left to pull open the top of her skirt.

Charmagne was now watching intently as the bills began to disappear down her skirt. Then she felt his fingers tugging at her panties. Her eyes widened and she grabbed his wrist.

"That's enough, baby," she said, touching his chin with her other hand, gently trying to lift his face. "You're making me crazy," she continued, as breathily as she could.

"Just a little more," Johnny said, huskily. "I'm almost there."

"No!"

In one motion, Charmagne shoved his chin up and away, and pulled his hand out of her panties. Johnny stumbled back.

"What the fuck is wrong with you, you crazy bitch?" Johnny said, as he lunged for her.

Charmagne stepped back but not quick enough. Johnny managed to get his fingers back into her skirt. He pulled hard and heard the thin material ripping. Charmagne resisted, which only served to make Johnny pulled harder. The cheap skirt ripped off in his hands. Charmagne lost her balance and fell back onto the bed.

Johnny was on her before she completed her first bounce on the mattress. He pinned her hands above her head and groped down her side until he found the side of her panties on her hip.

Charmagne screamed, "No! Don't, please!"

Johnny sneered at her and ripped off her panties. His hand roamed down the outside of her smooth thigh.

Charmagne began to breathe quickly and deeply. Johnny felt her chest pushing up against his weight with each breath and seeing the wild look in her eyes, he thought, *This is what she wanted. She likes it rough. I'm driving her wild.*

Johnny let his hand round her knee and begin to come up the inside of her thigh. Charmagne gasped and stopped breathing. The look on her face turned to terror as Johnny's hand slid up toward her crotch.

"You love this, don't you, baby." Johnny smiled.

Charmagne whimpered, "Please stop."

"Oh, yeah. Sure baby, I get it. Beg me. Beg me some more."

Charmagne bucked under him, "No! Let me up."

"Sure, you can get up as soon as I get some of *this*."

Johnny's hand shot up and cupped Charmagne's crotch. Charmagne watched the smile on Johnny's face quickly dissolve into a puddle of confusion.

Johnny yanked his hand away from her crotch and rolled off Charmagne. He looked down and then jumped up from the bed.

"A dick! You gotta fuckin' dick! You fuckin' ... "

Johnny didn't know how to finish the sentence so he did what came naturally. He balled up his fist and cocked his arm. But Charmagne was faster. She kicked up hard and caught Johnny in the balls with the toe of her big platforms. Then she rolled over and jumped to her feet on the bed. When Johnny straightened up, she rocked back and lifted her leg. Johnny never saw her foot whip out from under her knee. The sole of the thick, hard platform shoe caught him square in the chin. The last thing he remembered was her - him or whatever, tits bouncing and dick swinging, coming at him with the lamp from the nightstand raised over her head.

When he woke, Johnny looked over at the clock. He closed his right eye to focus. It was 12:45 a.m. He'd been out for over an hour. He lifted his aching head off the pillow. The phone was on the floor. His suitcase has been tossed. He saw his pants had been thrown on the dresser. The pockets were inside out. His Members Only jacket was on the floor. The box of nine-millimeter ammo was lying next to it, empty except for couple rounds dropped on the floor. That fucking freak had his money and his gun. He wanted to scream but he couldn't spit out the pair of socks stuffed in his mouth. And he couldn't pull the socks out of his mouth because his hands, like his feet, were tied to the bedposts with electrical chord. The television was on, loud. He could hear a late-night televangelists preaching about forgiveness.

So there he was. Naked, tied spread-eagle to his bed in the Hilton. His cash was gone. His Beretta was gone, too. And the TV was tuned to a 24-hour Christian station. *That fuckin' mutant motherfucker*, he thought. *Forgiveness! Fuck that! I fuckin' kill it, if I ever see it again.*

But Johnny needed to calm down. Not surprisingly, his head was pounding like there was a jackhammer at work against the inside of his skull. His shoulders and hips were sore from being stretched to the corners of the bed and his big toe had started to bleed again. He took a deep breath and closed his eyes. He decided that all he could do was to figure a way to get to sleep and wait for the chambermaids to come knocking in the morning.

And hope that the maids couldn't read English because Charmagne was a vengeful person.

She had left a sign on the door.

## PLEASE DO NOT DISTURB

## I HAVE THE FLU

## I NEED TO SLEEP IN

# CHAPTER 22

**Thursday Morning**
**Stewart International Airport**
**New Windsor, NY**

Last night, shortly after Lincoln left him, Michael's wounds were expertly field dressed by two men wearing black ski masks. They worked quickly and quietly, cutting him free of the duct tape and leaving an air mattress, a wool blanket, and a dark blue jump suit on the damp floor before locking him in the dark again.

But Michael couldn't get Lincoln out of his head. He had looked into Lincoln's eyes and repeated, "Chrysanthemum?"

"Yes, spell chrysanthemum."

Lincoln's light gray eyes had dilated to black holes that seemed to suck the air from Michael's lungs. He felt the chill of something dark and dreadful. He looked down at the floor, searching for that mysterious space that floats between our eyes and what we're looking at; that dull, hazy place where minds focus and thoughts form.

"Chrysanthemum," Michael began, still looking down. "C-H-R-Y-S-A-N-T-H-E-M-U-M, chrysanthemum."

Lincoln lowered the pistol and cocked his head. "Catholic school?"

"What?"

"You went to Catholic School, right?"

Michael nodded.

Lincoln shrugged and turned off the light as he left the room.

The sounds of the helicopter gaining speed and then fading into the distance brought Michael back to his new reality. After confirming there was no way he was getting out through the locked door, he slipped off his wet pants, pulled on the jump suit, and settled for being dry and relieved to think that maybe they had left for the night. But about two hours later the helicopter returned. Only after a long time listening for sounds outside his door, and despite the throbbing pain in his left hand, Michael fell asleep to the steady drip of rusty water from one of the old faucets.

His sleep was fitful, though. He suffered through a series of awful nightmares that cruelly twisted the recent events and people in his life into frightening vignettes. One after another, they played out evilly and hopelessly until out of sheer desperation he woke, again and again, more than once wishing that the light switch was in his side of the door.

Of course, the worst one kept recurring. In it, his wife and children watched at first helplessly and then, to his horror, indifferently as Lincoln mutilated him. When he called out to them, to apologize and beg their forgiveness, to promise them it would be okay, or to tell them to run away, they refused to hear him. Worse still, the horrendous pain and disfigurement he was suffering had no impact on them. It was as if he, or perhaps they, had ceased to be human, unable to either love or hate. With each unmerciful recurrence, the scene continued to unfold until finally it became dreadfully apparent that his family had lost all perception of him. And he them, because they were Lincoln's family now.

After each nightmare, falling back to sleep had been a restive and exhausting endeavor. The gunshot wound in his left hand was intensely painful. When he could settle into a position that allowed him to keep his hand and arm perfectly still, the pain would subside to a pronounced throb. But as soon as the physical ache receded, his mental anguish brought a suffering from which there seemed no relief. His mind loosed a raging river of white-water consciousness that angrily tumbled together the fear for his personal well being with throes of acute guilt and the pending loss of all things he loved. What had he let himself become? Why was he repeatedly unable to control himself until it was too late? How could he explain all this to Ilene and his children? And what if he didn't survive these unthinkable circumstances and was spending his last hours as a pitiless victim of his own greed and weakness? His family would be forever burdened with his shameful legacy.

He envisioned Ilene alone, confused, and distraught over the memory of him. His children's faces, saddened and disturbed, hovered in his thoughts and haunted him. The wretchedness of it all made him nauseous. Once, he had to crawl over and vomited into one of the urinals.

At the lowest point, he resorted to making absolute and fervent promises to change his life, if only he could have the chance. At first, he hesitated to make these vows to anyone in particular, like God, because Michael had never been religious about anything except for gambling. Sure, he was doing his duty as a good Irish Catholic raising his children in the One True Church. Michael had been given the same opportunity but he, like a lot of us boomers, eventually decided that organized religion was not a modern notion. He had come to believe that religion's and perhaps even God's perpetuation only served to fill the mysterious voids that could not yet be reasonably explained away by science or mathematics or technology.

But this night, this awful night, dark and crowded with horror and doubt, these neoteric sensibilities fell away like rotting flesh from the bone.

So before the tears of sorrow had stopped pooling in his eyes, and after he swore to be a changed and better man, to live his life satisfied with moderate pursuits, to find wonderment and peace in the little moments, he closed his eyes and prayed, "Please, God."

Nevertheless, the drip of the faucet didn't stop and his hand continued to throb. God helps those who help themselves, he remembered and crawled along the damp tile floor toward the leaky sink.

Michael sat under the leaky basin and groped along the wall until he found the pipes leading to the faucets. Halfway up the pipes he found spigot handles for the hot and cold water. He tried to turn the hot water handle but it was already tightly closed. The cold water handle rotated a quarter turn before stopping. Michael listened for the leak and heard that it was unabated. He reached for the cold water handle again and twisted it hard, grunting as he leaned his weight on his left elbow to keep his injured hand off the floor. Suddenly the handle gave way. Michael lost his balance and flopped onto his side.

Michael's breath hissed from between his teeth as he fought the pain from smacking his wounded hand against the floor. He rolled over on his back and waited for the throbbing to subside. As his breathing became less labored, he heard the faucet drip once. He waited. A whole minute passed before the next drop hit the sink. He felt himself tensing but quickly uncoiled, realizing that while it was not fixed it was better, and right now he'd take the small victory.

Better still, clutched in his right fist was the round spigot handle. The stem had broken off and three inches of it protruded from the center of the handle. Michael held it close to his face and in the dim light from under the door he examined the rusted steel spike that jutted out from between his fingers. He gripped the handle and poked the stem lightly against his thigh. He decided it would hurt if any real force were applied. Then he tightened his fist, clenched his jaw, and punched the ceramic wall tile under the sink.

The spike easily pierced the thick tile and sharp ceramic chips exploded off the wall, stinging his face.

Michael rolled out from under the sink and stood. Assuming a boxer's stance, balanced forward on the balls of his feet, he jabbed the air several times with his spiked fist, testing different punches against unseen but not unknown opponents. Satisfied that he could inflict serious damage with one or two quick strikes, he laid back on the air mattress.

He listened. The faucet dripped again. His hand hurt like hell. He had no idea what time it was or when they'd be coming for him again, but he smiled at the darkness as he slipped his weapon into his pocket.

## The Smoke and Gun Club at Bella Collina

Cathy had called my room at six a.m. I could tell from her first words that she was upset.

"Joseph, why haven't you been answering your cell phone?" She had said as soon as I answered. "I've been trying to reach you all night." Her voice was tired and weighted with tension.

"It doesn't work here. What's wrong?"

"Why doesn't your phone work?"

"The building's shielded."

"Why? What do you mean?"

"Honey, it's a security thing. They block cell phones. Forget about that - what's wrong?"

"The FBI was here last night."

I sat up. "The FBI was at our house?"

"Yes, at our house. What's going on, Joseph? Are you in trouble? They scared me, and the kids."

My spine snapped up straight. "The kids? They talked to kids?"

"No, but they could tell something serious was going on."

"Tell me what happened." I was on my feet.

"They asked a lot of questions about you and where you were. They told me it was very important that they talk to you and that you better call them as soon as possible. Joseph, what's going on?"

"It's probably nothing, Cath. Just something to do with the hijacking. But tell me exactly what they said. It's important."

"Well, one of them, the older one, did all the talking. He was a real creep."

"What did he look like, Cath?"

"What difference does that make?"

"Humor me. Was he tall and thin, late forties-fifty, with short graying hair and unusual, light gray eyes? Was his name Dwyer?"

"Yes, how did you know?"

My chest tightened and I squeezed the phone in my fist.

"Joseph?"

I caught my breath. "Yeah, I'm here. What did he tell you?"

"He didn't tell me much, just that he needed to know where you were and when you were coming home. He said it was a matter of life and death. He wanted to wait for you until I told him that you were gone for the night. Then he acted like he didn't believe me. That's when he scared me"

"Scared you?" I struggled to stay calm. "Whadaya mean? What'd he do?"

"He got mad and acted very threatening. He raised his voice and kept coming toward me until I was backed up against the wall in the foyer and then he continued to question me over and over again about where you were and when you'd be home. That's when the kids came to the top on the stairs and saw him."

"That son of bitch!" I was pacing, tethered to the nightstand by the phone cord.

"Joseph, what's happening and where's Michael? Is he with you? The switchboard at the club told Ilene he wasn't there."

"He already left, for golf," I lied.

"At six in the morning? Why did they tell Ilene he wasn't there?"

"How the hell would I know, Cath."

"Don't you dare be short with me. I don't deserve it. You two guys have been acting strange all week. There are all these problems at the company, the union, the hijacking, the fire, and you go off on short notice to this dinner where no one can get in touch with you all night. Ilene hasn't heard from Michael since he left the house yesterday morning, for God's sake. Your children are worried about you. I'm concerned and frankly a little scared, and all you're doing is answering my questions with more questions. It's not fair and it's not like you. I want to know what's going on."

I knew she was right. I hadn't given Cathy or the boys much thought in the last twenty-four hours and little else since Monday. But Cathy wasn't complaining about the long hours away from home. She understood that running a business occasionally required me to shift my focus, devoting the time and energy I would normally spend with the family to the company. That was part of the deal, part of the joint decision we had made when we decided to partner with Michael and Ilene to buy Domanski Truck Lines. For weeks before we made our offer, the risks and rewards were carefully considered. We identified the sacrifices and compromises that would have

251

to be made and, except for the inevitable rough spots, things had worked out very well. Our income had grown steadily and, with the business nearly debt-free, the future was looking stronger than ever. Even the partnership between the two families had worked out well. The four of us had remained good friends, drawn closer still by celebrating the good and weathering the bad times together. Even the ugly matter of Michael's gambling seemed to strengthen the bond between us. Right from the start, it had been the four of us, all for one and one for all. Michael and I ran the business but Cathy and Ilene had always been equal partners.

Moreover, and above all that, I had always closely guarded what my father had said to me more that once. Probably in reaction to what his father had done for a living, he would say, 'If you can't discuss your business with your wife, then you should find a new business'. Up to this point, I had never needed to be reminded.

But this was different. This was not my business. This was something new and I was unsure of the rules and less certain of the consequences. So, for now Cathy would have to trust me, as much as I could trust myself.

"I'm sorry, Cath," I said, as gently as I could. "You're right. I'm a little worn out from all the nonsense this week. I guess I should fill you in, best I can."

"I would appreciate that. Are we in trouble?"

I sighed loudly. "Yes, maybe. This hijacking may get blown outta proportion. The FBI thinks that because of my last name, I might have had something to do with it."

"Oh God, Joseph! Are you serious?" Cathy paused. "You didn't, did you?"

I thought for a second. "No, *I* didn't."

"Then they'll find that out and everything will be fine. Right?"

"I hope so."

"You're not telling me everything, are you?"

"No, and I can't tell you anything more right now. I know this is asking a lot, but you're just gonna have to trust me. Trust that I haven't done anything wrong and that I'm gonna do everything I can to protect you and the boys."

"Protect us? From what?"

"From bad news . . ." and *bad people,* I thought not to add.

"Joseph, I can't . . . "

"Cathy, please I'll try to tell you more tonight or tomorrow. I promise I won't let you down. Now if that Agent Dwyer calls, tell him I'll contact him today. If he comes by the house again, call the police. Tell Chief Reed to come right over and stay with you until Dwyer leaves. You don't have to talk to him and I don't want you alone with him. Understand?"

"Yes . . . "

"Good. Now, just tell Ilene that Michael's out of touch 'till later today, playing golf and a luncheon afterwards, and that I'll try to get him to call her later."

"Where is Michael really?"

I thought for a moment. "Let's just say he's probably not playing golf."

Cathy sighed. "In the middle of all this he's off gambling somewhere, isn't he?"

"Could be," I said, wishing it were true.

"Ilene will kill him if she finds out."

"Honey, I have to go."

"Be careful, Joseph. I love you."

"I love you, too. Kiss the kids for me."

Less that an later, I sat in the grill room sipping a second cup of coffee, watching Nicolas Pucci and Wilson Dennis work the room of men finishing their breakfasts. They moved separately from table to table, standing or taking an empty chair just long enough for brief conversation that was often animated and frequently punctuated with the distinctive guffaws indicative of man-talk. Judging by the descriptive hand motions accompanying the different conversations, I guessed the discussions ranged from golf shots to skeet shots to the size of a woman's breasts. Clearly, there was no business being done over breakfast.

As the men at the tables began to wander off to their tee times and tennis rackets, cue sticks and shotguns, Nicolas made a point of catching my eye. We exchanged confirming glances and Nicolas headed to the table where Wilson Dennis was engaged. Placing his hand on Wilson's back, Nicolas whispered something into his ear, which caused Wilson to nod and finish his conversation with a wide grin. They made their way over to my table still smiling.

"Good morning, Joseph. Did you sleep well?" Wilson asked.

"I had a very long day yesterday so, yes, I slept like a log," I answered flatly.

"Outstanding," Wilson said, beaming.

"That's good," Nicolas said and then added, "Because I think this could be another long day."

I placed my coffee cup on the saucer and concentrated on slowly folding my napkin. When I was done, I looked up at them and said, "Then we better get started."

Nicolas led us down to the shooting range where three adjacent stalls had been lighted and prepped. Al Schmidt met us carrying a wood tray that held three handguns and dozen loaded clips. The reconditioned Colt .45 was in the center of the tray.

"Good morning, gentlemen," Schmidt said with a slight bow and a big smile.

Wilson greeted him. "Morning, Al. Howya doin' today?"

Schmidt shrugged. "When you're married to my wife, you lie and say things like 'I'm doin' fine'."

Nicolas shook his head and said, "You know Joseph, we've met Al's wife and she's a lovely woman. A real classy lady. So don't believe a word he says. He's a lucky guy and he knows it."

Schmidt shrugged again. "You single guys got a lot to learn. That's all I can say. You married, Joseph?"

"Yes, I am."

"Ya know what I'm talkin' about then, doncha?"

"I think so, Al," I agreed, hoping to end the discussion.

Schmidt winked at me and said, "Okay then, I'll get you guys set up."

Wilson said to him, "Once you're through, Al, why doncha head up to the grill room for some breakfast."

Schmidt nodded, acknowledging that he understood that he was to make himself scarce until the match was over.

Schmidt quickly went about his business of placing the handguns and clips in the three stalls. He came back and told us that he had left more loaded clips and extra ammunition for each of their guns on his workbench, should they decide to have a second match. Then he wished us all 'good shooting' and headed for the door.

When Schmidt was out of earshot, I turned to Nicolas and said, "I was under the impression that we were gonna have a serious discussion this morning."

"And we are," Nicolas confirmed, somewhat annoyed.

Wilson leaned in and spoke in a low, serious tone. "Joseph, you need to understand that there are too many people at the club today that would wonder why the two of us are having a private meeting with *you* and not them, frankly. So we're gonna stick with our plan and have our match. Besides, there's no better place in this building to talk than down here. The shooting headsets and lip mikes operate on a closed wire system that's local to this room and absolutely secure."

Wilson walked over to one of the lighted stalls, slid out the keypad and tapped several keys. When he was done, opera music filled the room.

Wilson came back to where they we standing. "That's Pavoratti singing the part of Rodolfo in La Boheme. Do you like opera, Joseph?"

"I've never really given it a chance. So I'll have to say that I'm not sure if I do or not."

"Wilson and I enjoy shooting to opera," Nicolas said. "Personally, I think it's because the intellectual requirements and the emotional impact of shooting and opera are very similar. Both can powerful experiences but only the best is controlled and precise enough to arouse a truly passionate response."

Wilson cocked his head and pursed his lips. "My, my, Nicolas - well said. Outstanding." Then to me. "And, of course, there is the added benefit of the music masking our conversation. But if the opera is distracting for you, the headsets have electronic noise-cancellation technology built in. The technology somehow reads the sound waves of the ambient noise, the opera and gunshots in the case, and then instantly creates the exact opposite sound waves, which completely cancels the noise. You can shoot in total silence or adjust the cancellation or volume of specific ambient noises or have the music of your choice direct in your headset. So you can cancel the opera and still hear your shots, which I would recommend as an integral element of the shooting experience. Like Nicolas, I enjoy the mix of opera and gunshots. But no matter what you select, our conversation through the lip mikes will automatically adjust the volume down to background levels when we're talking to each other. Com'on, I'll get you set up."

Wilson led me to the center stall and where he helped me adjust my headset and lip mike. Wilson tapped a membrane switch on the keypad and the muffled music I was hearing through the ear covers disappeared into the purest silence I had ever experienced. If the totally deaf hear absolutely nothing than this is it, I thought. Perfect and pure quiet. It was unsettlingly.

Then I heard someone clear his throat. "Joseph? Nicolas?" Wilson's voice

"I'm here, Wilson." Nicolas' voice.

"Joseph?" Wilson again.

"Yes, I'm here," I answered and looked around.

Wilson Dennis and Nicolas Pucci were in the stalls on either side of me. I stepped back to see them readying their pistols, inserting clips and snapping the slides on their autoloaders closed. Nicolas sensed me behind him and turned around.

"Do you need some help getting started?" Nicolas asked me.

I frowned. "Frankly, in view of the fact that this guy Lincoln kidnapped my partner yesterday and then went to my home last night, where he terrorized my wife and children, the last thing I want to do right now is to join in a light-hearted shooting match with you two. Right now, I want to talk about getting that fuckin' madman away from my family and outta my life. I

255

wanna get my partner back to his family, and I wanna hear what you two have to say about gettin' that done, *today.*" Then turning to Wilson. "And, I don't really give a damn about what other people here might think. That's not my problem."

Nicolas and Wilson exchanged looks.

"Tell me what happened last night, with your family," Wilson said, removing his headset and looking more serious than I had ever seen him.

"He posed as FBI Agent Dwyer again and interrogated my wife as to my whereabouts. He made threatening comments and nearly assaulted my wife." I slowly shifted his gaze from Wilson to Nicolas. "My *children* witnessed it."

"I'm sorry." Nicolas said without hesitation.

"That cowardly son of a bitch," Wilson muttered, mostly to himself.

I sensed honesty in the spontaneity of their responses and seized the opportunity. "Okay, now that we're all outraged and sorry, I wanna hear what we're gonna do about it. And if I don't like what I hear, I'm gonna take care of this my way."

Nicolas was removing his headset as he spoke. "Wilson, leave the music on."

Nicolas started to move toward the elevated observation area where there was a cluster of leather furniture around a heavy mahogany coffee table. I took off my headset and hurried to take the chair in the middle of the setting. I had been to enough meetings to understand the value of positioning.

Nicolas looked at Wilson and nodded once. Wilson turned to me and began, "Okay, Nicolas and I met late last night and then again early this morning. We considered several options to achieve our mutual objectives, which we defined, as three-fold. One, to keep the HAWIRE from falling into the wrong hands. Two, safely return Michael Cogan to his family. And three, to neutralize Lincoln."

I looked at Nicolas. "Neutralize?"

"Yes." Nicolas replied.

"What does that mean?"

"It means that we do whatever it takes to make him a non-issue."

I smirked. "A '*non-issue*'? Are you serious?"

Wilson put his hand up. "Let's not get stuck on this. Why don't you let him finish and then you can ask all the questions you want."

I sat back in surrender. The leather cushions sighed.

Wilson continued. "As I was saying, we considered several alternatives, carefully weighing the risks and the probability of success. Unfortunately, no matter how hard we tried, we couldn't find a credible alternative that didn't require you to play a pivotal role. Can we count on you, Joseph?"

"Depends on what you want me to do *and* if the plan includes the safe return of Michael as the top priority."

"It does, if he's still alive, but the plan's not foolproof. You need to understand that nothing like this is, especially when you're dealing with a guy like Lincoln because he's, ah, . . ."

"I know," I said glancing at Nicolas, ". . . dangerous and resourceful."

Wilson shrugged and nodded.

"Okay," I said. "So, what do you want me to do?"

Wilson slid to edge of his seat. "First, it's important for you know that we're making compromises. Ideally, our plan would have called for the return of the original missing HAWIRE. But having to rely on locating this character John Anelli and then securing his, ah . . . cooperation, well, that was a variable we couldn't quantify. So we developed a game plan that doesn't require us to get the HAWIRE back *first*. This plan has the greatest chance of getting Cogan back safely and allows us to set a trap for Lincoln. If he's off the streets, or somehow *neutralized*, then we've satisfied the concerns of all parties, including you. Afterwards we can concentrate on locating Anelli and the original HAWIRE. We're going to use a substitute HAWIRE, a working replacement that will be indistinguishable from the original. It'll be identical, down to the shipping crate with the disabled security and GPS transmitter."

"What are you going to do with *that*?"

"It's our bait. Lincoln bait."

"Keep going." I urged.

"You told Nicolas that you have Lincoln's pager number, so you're gonna page Lincoln. When he calls you back, you're going to tell him that you have the HAWIRE and that you'll trade it for two million dollars and Michael Cogan."

"His original offer was only one million."

"Yeah, well now you're raising the stakes. Remember, Lincoln thinks that you're involved in the hijacking, that you were gonna profit off the original scheme. Well, now *you're* pissed off. He drew first blood, so to speak. He kidnapped your partner. He went to your home and fucked with your family. But *you* still have what *he* wants, what he *needs*, and now he's gonna pay more for it. He fucked with you, now you're fucking with him. That's it - end of story."

I shook my head. "So you believe this guy's gonna just capitulate and agree to this? What if this just pisses him off? I don't need him doin' somethin' crazy. For chrissake, we're talkin' about my friend and my family here. He knows where I live."

Nicolas showed me his palms. "Whoa, slow down. Give us some credit. Listen to rest of the plan. Then ask all the questions you want."

I thought for a moment. "Alright."

Wilson started again. "We know Lincoln as well as anybody can. We considered his personality and motivations and then calculated his reactions to every step and potential misstep of this plan. And while nothing can be guaranteed, we're gonna do everything in our power to ensure nothing goes wrong. And if it does, there'll be a contingency. Now, if he balks at the two million, you're gonna tell him to go fuck himself. Lincoln will then use Michael and/or your family or some other threat in an attempt to offset you. Whatever he says, you'll tell him that if anything happens to Michael or your family, you'll see that he never gets the HAWIRE. Believe me, he'll deal with you. There's a *whole* lot of money in this for Lincoln if he delivers the HAWIRE to the bad guys. And if he doesn't, the consequences for a guy like Lincoln are devastating. All he has is his reputation to trade on and in his business you're only as good as your last fuckup. Sure, he'll be pissed, but he'll deal. He has no choice. Better still, the more pissed off he is, the more likely it is that he'll make a mistake. And remember, Lincoln and the HAWIRE aren't going anywhere after you meet him. We've taken care of that."

I raised his eyebrows. "And what exactly does *that* mean?"

"Lincoln can not and will not be allowed to get away with the HAWIRE. It's bait, but think of it as a very expensive lure. One that we will not part with. We're gonna have a special team that's trained in counter-terrorism assault and hostage rescue tactics. They'll provide air and ground coverage of your meeting with Lincoln. This unit is highly trained to observe and analyze dynamic operations. They're trained and authorized to make split-second decisions based on situational developments. This allows them to pursue the mission's objectives without waiting for directives from command and control. Their mission is to record the transaction on videotape and, once the incriminating actions are recorded, they'll swoop in and secure the area. But, should something start going south at any time during the meet, they'll revert to their primary objective, which is protection for Michael and you."

Wilson sat back. The leather creaked.

Nicolas turned toward me. "Any questions so far?"

I cradled my face in my left hand. "Where's this meeting with Lincoln supposed to take place?"

Wilson cleared his throat. "About thirty-five miles south of here there's the Ramapo rest stop on the Thruway near Sloatsburg. Next to the rest area, hidden by a large wooded berm, there's a DOT maintenance yard that's unmanned after about eight o'clock in the morning. Some of the crews come back about eleven thirty for lunch, but after one until around three-thirty there's no one around. It's a typical maintenance yard. Road equipment, personal cars, crew shack, repair garage, salt and sand silos, and one way in and out. All that means plenty of concealment for our tactical team. The wooded hills that overlook the yard are ideal for spotters and snipers. You'll insist on meeting Lincoln there at two o'clock in front of the salt silo. That'll give us time to get our men into position and time enough to clean up afterwards before the road crews come in for the night."

"Suppose he won't meet me there?"

"That's not an option," Nicolas huffed. "You've got to be in control of this. You've got to understand and *believe* that. It's the only way you're gonna be able to convince him that you're demands are non-negotiable. If you sound weak or hesitant at all, he's gonna eat you alive. *You* are controlling this transaction, from start to finish. If you don't, if Lincoln takes control at any point, we're gonna have problems. Can you handle this?"

For a long thirty seconds, I stared at the bronze replica of Remington's *Cowboy* that sat in the center of the mahogany table. My thoughts went to Jimmy Merchanti's description of the armed men whose mission to capture or kill Michael and Johnny Anelli the day before had failed. "This, ah, team, how do you know they're good enough to protect Michael and I? Who are they."

Wilson sat up. "They're the best. A special quick response tactical unit culled from elite commando forces - the FBI Hostage Rescue Team, Secret Service, SEALS, Delta Force, and God knows where else. If these guys can't do it, it can't be done."

I narrowed my eyes. "And tell me how *you* guys have access to this *team*."

"Certain well-placed friends of ours in the intelligence community are contributing these tactical resources," Wilson said. "They do this quite willingly, even agreeing to let you and Michael walk away as protected confidential informants, knowing they'll earn commendations for thwarting this threat to our national security. Of course, it doesn't hurt that the mission will also lead to the capture or demise of Aaron Lincoln, one of their wayward angels. As a matter of pride, these people would prefer to be the ones to clip his wings, so to speak."

"And Michael and I walk away? No repercussions? No further involvement? No nothing?"

Nicolas nodded. "Correct. You go home, back to your lives, business as usual - like nothing ever happened."

I turned to Wilson. "Now let's hear the downside?"

"The downside is that something goes wrong - something that the team can't control. Say Lincoln spots the trap, flares off, and eludes all our resources. Not likely, but anything's possible. Then he's on the loose and we'll need to protect you and your family until we find him."

"What about Michael?"

"If he's still alive and Lincoln suspects you crossed him, odds are he'll be dead before dinner time. Hard fact, but I think we wanna be talkin' turkey here."

I nodded and sat back in the noisy leather. I picked a tiny ball of lint off my sleeve and as I rolled it between my thumb and forefinger, I was drawn inexorably to a single, overpowering notion: *This is absolutely fucking crazy!*

"I'm sorry, gentlemen," I chuckled. "But I have to ask. Are you serious? Do you really think I'm gonna get involved in something like this, simply on your say so? Forgive me, but that's . . . absolutely fucking crazy. Look at it from my perspective. I don't travel in your circles. All I know is what I see on the TV - the History Channel, Discovery, stuff like that. I've watched the programs and know that the FBI handles domestic terrorism and espionage. Why aren't I talking to *them* instead of you? And why aren't you or they sending this special unit, this ah, dream team of yours to Lincoln's place at the airport. It doesn't make sense. And even if I was talking to the FBI, I'd want some assurances, in writing, that Michael and I would be protected, immunity or whatever. I wouldn't take *their* word for it. Why should I take yours? Maybe I'm missing something here."

I paused, waiting a few seconds for one of them to jump in. They didn't. "Sorry, but as it stands, I don't want any part of this. Frankly, I think it's best if I just go to the FBI and take my chances."

I watched as Nicolas and Wilson stared at each other over the Remington; a cowboy tossed in his saddle, frozen in bronze with his crop raised high in one hand, the reins in his other are stretched taut as his horse rears, perhaps spooked by a rattlesnake.

Finally, Wilson turned away, closed his eyes and steepled his fingers across the bridge of his nose, his thumbs supporting his chin.

The leather chirped as Nicolas shifted and squared his shoulders to me. "Do you like history?"

"What?"

"You said you watched the History Channel. How well do you know your history? What do you know about the Normandie?"

"The invasion of Normandy?"

"No, the *S.S. Normandie*, the cruise ship that had been converted to a troop carrier during World War Two. It blew up in New York Harbor in 1942."

"Nicolas . . . "

"Humor me. There's more you should know before you make your decision."

I shrugged. "Okay."

"In 1942, Naval Intelligence wasn't quite the formidable organization it is today. Even so, they suspected, quite correctly in fact, that the explosion on the *Normandie* was an act of sabotage. More importantly, it was a very public dramatization of the vulnerability of our home ports. The country's worst fears had been confirmed. The War had reached our shores. And, Naval Intelligence needed a quick fix.

"In 1942 there was another organization that was considerably more formidable than it is today. It was known as the Mafia, the Cosa Nostra, or the Mob. At that time, Salvatore Lucania, whom history knows as Charles "Lucky" Luciano, was the undisputed Capo di tutti Capi even though he had been imprisoned since the mid thirties. Problem was, Charlie Lucky had a penchant for call girls. Truth is, it was as much a pass time as a business for him. Either way, it got him in trouble. He was serving a 30 to 50 year sentence for compulsory prostitution, which was the only charge Thomas Dewey could make stick. But by that time, his criminal empire was truly vast, touching every rung of society's ladder, from the political elite to the longshoremen and other unions."

I shifted in the noisy leather.

Nicolas mistook my fidgeting for impatience and conveyed his own. "This is a long story. Get comfortable."

When I had settled Nicolas continued. "After a brief and frustrating investigation on the waterfront, Naval Intelligence met with Luciano at Clinton Prison, in Dannemora, New York. The Navy knew his syndicate controlled the longshoremen and, therefore, the entire waterfront community. Appealing to Lucky's patriotic spirit, they were able to get his help in tightening security on the piers in the greater New York area and presumably throughout the country. Remarkably, there wasn't a single instance of sabotage anywhere in the country for the rest of the War.

"Later in the War, Luciano's again contributed to the war effort. He used his contacts on Sicily and in Italy to provide information to the American Armed Forces about enemy positions and troop strengths prior to the Allied invasions."

I sighed loudly. "I saw that episode, too."

"I would have guessed you had. If so, you certainly noticed that your grandfather was mentioned repeatedly in the second half."

Wilson straightened and glared at Nicolas. Nicolas pretended not to notice.

I used those few seconds to adjust to a blast of heat that surge through my body. I calmed myself and said, "Your point?"

"No point." Nicolas remained steady. "Just wanted to be sure I had your attention."

Slowly, as if I was moving through axle grease, I leaned forward toward Nicolas. "Go on."

Nicolas leaned back and folded his hands in his lap. "These incidences are commonly portrayed as interesting but minor footnotes in the history of organized crime. However, and I don't say this casually, they were actually the beginning of a long and deep relationship between the Mafia and the United States government, specifically the intelligence community.

"You see, Luciano and his close associates, your grandfather among them, were the architects of a grand plan that required their sphere of influence to reach beyond the local law enforcement, politicians, and judges they had had in their pockets for years. They needed good friends around the country and in Washington to further their new international enterprises, primarily drug trafficking and money laundering that would fuel the expansion of their control over a variety of legitimate businesses. But the War and Luciano's imprisonment had slowed their progress.

"What the History Channel didn't tell you, because they don't know, is that while sitting in jail in 1942, Luciano saw an opportunity to advance this plan and, at the same time, get himself released from prison. Luciano himself gave the orders from his cell. Explosives were pilfered from the Brooklyn Navy Yard and used to blow up the *Normandie*. Early in the investigation of the incident, Luciano's contacts within the NYPD suggested to Naval Intelligence that they seek Luciano's assistance. After the war, in 1946, a federal judge commuted Luciano's sentence and he was deported to Rome, where he continued his reign as the Boss of all Bosses.

"Luciano moved to Cuba in 1947, to be closer to America and in the process he established a beachhead on the island. Although the Cuban government deported him only months later under pressure from our government, he freely returned there many times over the years to meet with his loyal associates still operating in America. Luciano and the American Mafia quickly endeared themselves to the Batista government, which allowed them to control several luxury resorts and casinos that were highly profitable in their own right but also ideal for laundering the huge profits being generated by their empire.

"But the fifties, as you know, was the last but brilliant hurray for the Luciano generation of the Mafia. Under strong management and with few challenges from law enforcement, their empire became a vast consortium of legal and illegal enterprises, including their holdings in Las Vegas. The drug trade flourished largely on the backs of the black inner city population. This, of course, was still a time when the African American was barely a member of society. To infest their ghetto neighborhoods with narcotics was not an issue for most of Luciano's organization and, apparently, not for most of the law enforcement community either. Your grandfather, by the way, did not hold this view. However, as a practical man, he didn't oppose it either.

"So, how did the Mafia escape the attention it deserved during the fifties? Well, it was a prosperous, almost magical time in America. The Mafia fed off the American dream and capitalized on the distractions of The Cold War and the Communist hysteria that consumed the country. And, of course, they did it the old fashion way, too. By owning the right people, doing the right favors, and evolving their master plan to the point where J. Edgar Hoover publicly declared in 1959 that there was no such thing as the Mafia in America.

"But that wasn't even a close second to the greatest thing that happened in 1959. Far from it, because in 1959, John Fitzgerald Kennedy announced his candidacy for the 1960 presidential election and then proceeded to win the Democratic nomination. So when his father, Joe Kennedy, sought out his former bootlegging associates for their help in electing his son, Luciano's organization was on the verge of realizing their ultimate dream, a good friend in the Oval Office. And while no price would have been too much for this connection, the cost was actually quite reasonable. They provided money, of course, disguised as legitimate campaign contributions, and the avenues for cash to flow through on their way to the campaign's coffers. But, most importantly, they delivered millions of votes from the organized labor unions they controlled. It was, however, literally too good to be true.

"Almost immediately after taking office there were problems with Camelot. First, Kennedy and his brother, Robert, approved a top-secret plan to invade Cuba and topple the Communist Castro regime. Luciano's organization had lost all their holdings in Cuba and so they too had an interest in eliminating Castro. They had, in fact, already worked with the CIA in several failed assassination attempts. So, when the CIA needed funding and underground channels to get the funds and weapons to the private army they were training, they turned again to their Italian friends. Of course, you know the results of the Bay of Pigs invasion and that the Kennedys refused to send the air support that would have changed the outcome of the battle.

"This was the Kennedys' first of several affronts to the CIA and the Mafia. The others came in rapid succession over the next two years. The Kennedy administration continued to reign in the CIA and the FBI, limiting their power and controlling their scope. The CIA was forced to answer to Congress for the first time. Hoover was coerced into using his FBI to participate in the enforcement of the federal equal rights agenda as well open investigations of Jimmy Hoffa, organized labor and their ties with organized crime. The same legal and illegal organizations that had delivered the Kennedys the White House were now being investigated and prosecuted.

"About the same time, Luciano died of heart failure in Naples and Joe Kennedy suffered a debilitating stroke in Hyannisport. While the Mafia in America struggled over new leadership, the Kennedys became even more emboldened now that they were out from under their father's iron hand. Soon, Joe Valachi was on live television telling the Senate Investigating Committee about the American Mafia and exposing secrets that had been kept by generations of Mafioso. They had come so close, only to be betrayed like they have never been betrayed before. No doubt, Luciano was twisting in his grave.

"But this was still the early sixties, '63 to be exact. The Mafia was still a very powerful force, one that you didn't fuck with no matter who you were. The next fall three assassins supplied by the French Mob, drug trafficking associates of the Luciano's American Mafia, flew into Mexico City. They crossed quietly into Texas in mid-November and stayed at a safe house in Dallas until the morning of the twenty-second, when they packed their belongings and headed to Dealey Plaza. After the assassination, what they call 'good friends' helped them make their way to Chicago and then into Canada. Other good friends in New Orleans, Dallas, and Washington had seen to it that everything was in order for Oswald to take the fall. Make no mistake, none of it would have been possible without the cooperation of the CIA, their man Lee Harvey, the FBI, the Secret Service, the Dallas Police and a variety of other good friends, including Marcello in New Orleans and good ole Jack Ruby.

"After Dallas, the association between the Mafia and the CIA and other intelligence organizations continued to grow and prosper, all having sprung from Charlie Lucky's crazy jailhouse plan. It took many forms. In the sixties, there were the funding channels for clandestine CIA operations in South and Central America and the, ah, *cancellation* of Robert Kennedy's presidential bid in sixty-eight. During Viet Nam, the financial and logistical support of CIA operations and front businesses in Southeast Asia was facilitated by drug and weapons trading that continued into the seventies and early eighties. You remember the disastrous yet very profitable Iran-Contra guns-for-money escapade? Well there were dozens and dozens of other covert operations around the world where secret money or illegal or quasi-legal trade was required. The alliance was strategic and always profitable."

I leaned forward, about to speak.

Nicolas held up his hand. "I know I've been going on for some time here and you're wondering what this has to do with what we've talking about. But I had to lay the groundwork for what I'm about to tell you . . ."

Nicolas paused and looked at Wilson. Wilson shook his head and closed his eyes as he turned away.

Nicholas looked me square in the eyes. He said, "I know all this because your grandfather, Carmine Napolo, was my uncle."

"*What?*"

"Your grandfather was my uncle."

I smirked. "Oh, really. I know all my cousins and you're not one of them."

"Well, that's right. He wasn't a blood uncle, but he raised me and that's what I called him."

I chuckled, shaking my head. "Nicolas, don't be ridiculous. My grandfather died in 1963. I had dinner with him every Sunday, including the Sunday before he was killed. He couldn't have raised you."

"He could have if he didn't die in 1963 and then changed his name to Joseph Antonelli. He told me that he had picked the name Joseph because of his father and you. He thought you were special and he cherished the Sunday afternoons he spent with you in your mother's kitchen. He loved you very much. He never got over having to leave you and your family."

"Oh, please. Stop it," I said. "This is nonsense. My grandfather was burned to death, beyond recognition. They planted a bomb in his car, for chrissake. I went to his funeral."

Nicolas smiled warmly, appearing empathetic. Then he leaned in over the table, pulled his wallet from his back pocket and took several photographs out. Wilson stood and walked silently away, not toward anything, just away, making small circles, his head down and his hands stuffed in his pockets.

As Nicolas laid out the pictures for me to see, he said, "Burned beyond recognition? Do you recognize anyone in these?"

I glanced down at the photographs. The same bearded man appeared in all three pictures, although he aged considerably from the first to the last. With the man in each photograph was Nicolas Pucci as a boy, a teen, and then a young man.

I was ready to explode, to let Nicolas know that I had had enough, to ask him what the hell he was doing, when the eyes of the bearded man in the first picture drew me in. I reached for the photo and held it up close.

"It's him," Nicolas said. "That's your grandfather."

I could feel Nicolas watching me. Wilson stopped in his tracks and waited.

I studied the image. The nose was different, narrower, and the beard hid the mouth and chin. But the shape of the head, the hairline and forehead were right and the eyes - the smiling eyes, were unmistakable. I picked up the other pictures and observed the eyes growing older, the hair thinning, and the beard going completely gray. The longer I looked the more sure I was. The smiling, bearded man with his arm proudly around Nicolas Pucci's young shoulders was indeed my grandfather.

I stacked the photographs and placed them back on the table. I sat back, not wanting to say anything just yet, unable to find any words.

Before I could look up, Nicolas said, "The man who was killed in your grandfather's car that night was my father, Nico Pucci. He was the Don's bodyguard. I'm sure you knew him. He was always with your grandfather, every Sunday for sure. I know, because I was alone a lot on Sunday's after my mother died."

I stood up and walked around behind my chair. I gripped the leather at the top of the chair back and leaned my weight forward. My gaze drifted to the stack of photographs. But the visions flashing in my mind's eye were blinding me. *There was my grandfather, the infamous Don Carmine, stirring the meat sauce. His eyes, the eyes in the pictures, tired but relaxed and happy, glistening as he talks to the boy at his side. Perhaps he is describing the smallest details of Michelangelo Buonarroti's Pieta, telling how the Master of the High Renaissance had included in the sculpture a self-portrait in the figure supporting Christ from behind.* Was the boy he was talking to me or Nicolas, or both of us? *Then, there was Nicolas Pucci pouring the Brunelleschi Chianti and telling the wine's story at the table the night before. The same story I had heard told.* It couldn't be true, could it? *Now, Nicolas scolding the drunk from Boston for calling him Nicky Boy, and Nicolas at the bottom of the staircase telling him that his uncle insisted upon being called Joseph.* Could it be? If it was, what did it mean? *Finally, Nico, lying dead in the street and Pop Pop Carmine sitting in his Chrysler touching the first two fingers of his right hand to his lips and moving them slowly to my lips. "We must never tell another man what happened here tonight. Never."* His fingers to his lips.

I looked up. "What was wrong with my grandfather's hand," I said remembering Tommy Ton's challenge to me.

Nicolas grinned. "There was nothing wrong with his *hand*." He held up his right index finger. "This finger was bent at the last joint, though."

I straightened up and stepped back from the chair. I could feel Nicolas and Wilson staring at me, waiting. I walked to the left a few paces and then back, and then to the right and back again. But I couldn't evade them. I turned and walked the five or six feet to the wall behind me where I stood facing the wall with my hands clasped behind me. I looked up at the ceiling. There was no where else to go.

I returned to my chair, sat back and crossed my legs. I motioned to the empty chair at my right. "Sit down, Wilson," I said.

When the leather under Wilson had quieted, I turned to Nicolas and said, "Okay, now supposing all this is true, tell me what happened after my grandfather *didn't* die and what this all means for me, here today."

Nicolas' dark eyes twinkled. "Well, after my father was killed and everyone assumed it was your grandfather, the Don seized the opportunity to make his break - to get out of the life he had grown wary of. You see, he had sensed the beginning of the end of the old ways. Luciano was gone and the Families were feuding over control of the syndicate. There were betrayals from within and without. He feared that these forces of instability had irrevocably damaged their Thing. Then Valachi's testimony, his breaking of his vow of Omerta, confirmed something that had been deeply troubling him. He had been growing increasingly disturbed by the new generation of Mafioso coming up under him. For the most part, they had been born and raised in America. He felt they lacked the deep cultural influences and values of the old world, the old ways. They had been *taught* not *bred* to be men of honor, and it was becoming increasingly obvious to him that they had failed to learn that honor was above all else. Combine that with the fast money that the drug trade was generating - even the street level soldiers were earning big . . . well, he saw that mix of weakness and greed as a very destructive force.

"America was changing, too. And while no one could have foreseen the changes about to come in the late sixties, by '63 your grandfather knew that nothing would ever be the same. He wanted no part of this new order or disorder, as he saw it. And, of course, he was absolutely correct. Nothing was ever the same again for the Mafia in America. The twenty years of phenomenal growth and stability under Luciano, the rock-solid empire that he and your grandfather and their peers had built steadily crumbled from that point forward.

"Then, although it was years later, came the coup de grace. The wrecking ball. A combination of the RICO Act, the Latino, oriental and Russian Mobs, but more importantly, one goodfella after another turning and entering the witness protection program and then writing their books and screenplays. It seemed that after the Godfather movies there was suddenly a place and time for every wiseguys' fifteen minutes of fame. Your grandfather's premonition was absolutely on target. It saddened him 'till the day he died.

"Anyway, at the time of my father's death, your grandfather secretly owned the controlling interest in a small electronics firm called FirsTech. At that time, FirsTech was a CIA front company that produced electronic surveillance and counter-surveillance equipment. It's only customers were the CIA and other intelligence agencies that the CIA chose to share in the top-secret technologies. With the help of the agency, FirsTech had been quietly recruiting the top engineering and technical talent from around the country and the world. FirsTech's product offerings soon grew beyond those that were specifically requested by the agency, until my uncle could foresee a day that FirsTech could be the leading supplier of high tech intelligence and defense systems. Of course, his good friends in the intelligence community ensured the successful growth of FirsTech, knowing that they could rely on FirsTech for far more than superior technical products.

"So, that night when my father's body was mistaken for your grandfather's, the Don used his agency contacts to disappear, to see that Carmine Napolo was dead and gone forever. He gathered his mistress, Marie Antonelli, and took her name. She became my Aunt Marie."

"Where did you come into this?" I asked.

"He had me brought to him that night."

"Why?"

"Because . . . well I guess I'm actually am a distant cousin of yours, fourth or fifth maybe. My grandfather and your grandfather were second or third cousins in the old country. Your grandfather knew I had been orphaned by the death of my father and he did the honorable thing. He took me in and raised me. I was seven years old.

"Anyway, the three of us moved here to Bella Collina. The construction of FirsTech World Headquarters in Liberty began immediately thereafter with Joseph Antonelli at the helm as Chairman and CEO. He held those positions until the day he died."

"When did he die?"

"In May of '95. Congestive heart failure. He lived to see you grow up and own your own company. And to give you business."

"He was alive when we started doing business with FirsTech?"

"He's *why* you started doing business with FirsTech, and the DOD and many other companies that are now and will remain loyal customers of yours. Did you think your little piss-ant trucking company was that special? How do you account for your rapid growth and unfettered expansion into the defense contracting community? Good luck?"

"How about good service," I said.

Nicolas shrugged.

We sat quietly for a long moment. In the background, Jose Perez was singing *Questro a Quella* from Verdi's Rigoletto. I realized that I had not really heard the opera music since sitting down. I let myself listen. It was beautiful. I wondered if it had been playing the whole time.

"Do you have any questions?" Wilson asked.

"Questions?" I snickered. "Are you kidding?"

"Well, I have one," Nicolas said. "Does this change your position? Are you ready to come on board?"

"On board?"

"With our plan."

"To save your company's ass?"

Nicolas straightened and clenched his jaw. "How about your partner's ass. And remember this is your grandfather's company. Doesn't that mean anything to you?"

"As far as I'm concerned my grandfather died in 1963. He ceased to exist for me after that and nothing I've heard here changes that for me. He left my family and me behind, and all we got left with was his bad name."

"But I've told you the whole story. He had no choice."

"Well, good for him and for you, I guess. What am I supposed to do with what you've told me. Feel good? Feel obligated? Tell the world and change history?"

"Frankly, there's nothing you can do with what I've told you. There's no way any of it can be proved. If you told anyone, they'd think you were crazy. I was hoping, though, that you'd like to know that your grandfather went on to do some good things, that he used his genius and power to make significant contributions to our nation. That he was a patriot."

"A *patriot*? Participating in the Kennedy assassinations and in the illegal activities of the CIA and, God knows what else? That's your idea of patriotism?"

Nicolas narrowed his eyes. "In the overall, yes."

"Well, not mine. And, while your stories have been very interesting, I think it's all bullshit – stories any good researcher could've come up with, pictures that were probably altered. With your resources and contacts, God knows what else is going on here. So, the answer to your question is, no. I'm not on board. I have a family. And there's no way I'm meeting this guy Lincoln in a deserted maintenance yard."

"We recognize it's dangerous," Wilson said. "You'll need to be armed and trained how to use your weapon. We'll take care of that here, this morning. And remember, our team will be in place. They'll protect you."

"You can't guarantee that and you know it."

"Fuck this!" Nicolas shouted. "Here's what I *can* guarantee. If you think you can walk outta here and go to the FBI, you haven't heard a word I said. Because if you do, I promise to use all my influence to see that you are implicated as one of the conspirators in the plan to sell the HAWIRE to an enemy of our country. Once the scheme and your involvement is made public, which I will also guarantee, Lincoln will disappear but not before extracting some type of payback from you or your family, and not before adding Michael to this week's body count. Now, I'm tired of fuckin' talkin'. We've presented you with a viable option, a plan that works for both of us. We're going to extraordinary lengths to protect you during and after the meeting. We're doing this because of who you are, because your grandfather would have wanted it this way. But, you're really pushin' it and I've had enough of your bullshit, wise-ass comments. So, I want your goddam answer, now." Pointing at me. "But before you say anything, you better think about who you're fucking with here. Make no mistake about it, my uncle taught me well. Push me further and Lincoln'll be the least of your fuckin' problems."

I straightened. "Well, that certainly sounded like someone raised by my grandfather."

Nicolas shook his head in disgust and glared at Wilson.

I looked down at my hands folded in my lap. I already knew what I had to do but I waited a moment, hoping that something would come to me; something that I could use to change all this, to make it go away. Nothing did. Except that I had to try to get Michael back to his family. But there was a tremendous risk involved and the only potential reward, other than Michael's safety, was that I would not be blamed for something that I didn't do. There needed to be more balance. I thought for another moment.

"I'll go along with your plan on the following conditions. I want your legal department to prepare an agreement that will be sent to my attorney before I go to the meeting with Lincoln. This agreement will clearly state that Michael and I have had no involvement with the hijacking of the HAWIRE and that we became involved at your request to assist your efforts to recover it. It will state that we volunteered to do this out of patriotic duty as good citizens of this country. In addition, for the protection of our families, I want a little insurance policy, underwritten by FirsTech. This separate agreement will state that if either Michael or I or any members of our families are harmed or killed under any suspicious circumstances, accidental or not, at any time over the next twenty years, FirsTech will promise to pay each of our families ten million dollars."

"Ten million!" Nicolas huffed. "How did you come up with that figure?"

"It's a nice round number, enough to ensure our survivors live very comfortably. Hopefully, it's enough to ensure that you'll want us all to remain very healthy. And be sure you understand it's ten million *each*. So it's actually twenty million, if anything happens to any one of us."

Nicolas lifted his eyebrows. "Anything else?"

"Yes," I said, getting comfortable with making it up as I went. "I want both agreements to have a confidentiality clause that stipulates that the funds will be immediately released to us if any part of either agreement is made known to anyone. It will be written to survive FirsTech and both of you. It also will stipulate that the funds will be released against the terms and conditions of the agreement on the unilateral determination of my attorney and that his determination can not be contested by FirsTech or any other party. And, the twenty million gets wired to my attorney's interest bearing escrow account by noon today. If after twenty years nothing has happened, the principle is returned to you and we, or our heirs, keep the interest."

Nicolas frowned. "Noon today may not be possible."

"Oh, I think someone like you, with all your *good friends,* can manage it."

I watched as Nicolas' quick glance to Wilson was returned with a nod.

"Okay, we agree," Nicolas said. "But what if Michael's already dead? That's a possibility, you know."

"Then you pay Michael's family ten million now and the other ten stays in escrow."

Nicolas shook his head. "We'll only pay five plus the ten. There's no fault if he's already dead."

"Seven point five plus the ten."

Nicolas eyed me. "Okay, you have a deal. I'll call our Chief Counsel."

"One more thing."

"More?"

"Just a question. Do you know how my grandfather injured his finger?"

Nicolas looked over at Wilson. Wilson shrugged.

Nicolas shook his head. "I don't know. He never mentioned it."

"You never asked?"

"No."

I looked down at my own index finger and recalled the night my grandfather had reached for the flapping piece of paper in the fan. I was only four or five at the time, but I remembered my grandfather wrapping a dishtowel around his bloody finger and how he had apologized for yelling '*Son of a bitch!*' on his way out the door to the emergency room. After that night, every time there was a lesson to be punctuated, my grandfather would hold up his crooked finger and say, 'Hey, you want your finger to look like this? This is what God does to you if don't do the right thing'. I recalled my mother wincing each time my grandfather wagged the ugly finger in someone's face. But no matter how angry my grandfather was, sooner or later everyone, young and old, would ask him how his finger became so disjointed. One Sunday evening, I witnessed my grandfather angrily poking his finger at one of the mysterious after dinner visitors. After the man recovered from his scolding, even he found the temerity to ask the Don what had happened to his finger. My grandfather told him. He never hesitated to tell anyone, or to laugh at his own carelessness. How was it that these two guys, one of them he supposedly raised, never heard that story?

"Okay, let's page Lincoln," I said into my lap. Looking up, I continued, "Then I want you guys to teach me how to shoot."

# CHAPTER 23

## Stewart International Airport
## New Windsor, NY

Aaron Lincoln had just finished his daily morning regiment when his pager beeped. Precisely one hour earlier he had begun exactly thirty-five minutes of physical conditioning, an intense combination of aerobic and strength training, followed by a light breakfast consisting of a liter of spring water and fresh fruit, usually one grapefruit and a single banana, for which he allowed exactly six minutes. The remaining nineteen minutes were reserved for his bowel movement, a shave, a quick shower, and dressing. These three activities were lumped together to allow for the variable time element of his bowel movement, which was the only task in the hour that he would not put a clock on. He had come to realize that no matter how he adjusted his diet and the timing of his consumption, there were other factors that exerted control over his digestive system. Stress, fatigue, and the current status of his general physical health all wreaked havoc with his fiat to quickly and completely evacuate his bowels each morning.

Today had been one of those days. On the toilet, he searched for the cause of today's loose yet stubborn stool. He sensed no new ailment lurking within. No headache or stuffiness or respiratory congestion that might be signaling the start of a cold or flu. There was no tenderness in his throat or abdominal region. His back and neck had felt fine during his exercising. And he had masturbated, quickly and neatly, the night before because it was the third of the month and he did that on odd numbered days, so it couldn't be that either. He decided the stress of the approaching deadline for delivery of the HAWIRE was the probable cause.

But this morning's extended time on the crapper had caused him further distress. Completing his ritual on schedule had become difficult, if not impossible. He contemplated skipping shaving but at the last minute decided he would shave in the shower to save time. It did and he was fully dressed with almost a full minute to spare before the allotted hour expired. For Aaron Lincoln, all's well that ends well, so he approached his desk and the beeping pager with a spring in his step and a smile on his face.

The tiny LED screen on the pager showed a ten-digit number, with an unusual area code that was probably a cell phone. But before he would return the call, Lincoln wanted to know the caller and his location. The pager was linked to sophisticated software in his laptop that enabled him to trace any call, from any phone, except satellite. Lincoln clicked on the phone icon. The results were instantaneous but confusing. The cell phone number belonged to Joseph Napolo but the window that normally listed the location of the call, triangulated longitude and latitude reference points that were converted into street addresses, was obviously malfunctioning. It listed addresses in thirty-four states, from New Hampshire to Nebraska to California. As Lincoln scrolled through the list, his bowels tightened. Every address was in a town named Lincoln.

He clicked again on the phone icon and let the software rerun. The results were the same. Lincoln, California; Lincoln, New Hampshire; Lincoln, Nebraska - Lincoln, Lincoln, Lincoln . . .

He sat back staring at the screen, letting his breath flow in and out his nostrils, as he fought to bring his breathing and heart rate under control. Perhaps he had underestimated Joseph Napolo. Or, perhaps Napolo wasn't acting alone. Well, okay, if they wanted to play games . . .

On his satellite phone, Lincoln dialed the number on the pager. I answered after the first ring.

"Agent Dwyer?"

"Is this Joseph Napolo?" Lincoln answered.

"Yes. Agent Dwyer?"

"Cute little trick. One of these days you'll have to tell me how it works."

"What are you talking about?"

"You know god damn well what I'm talking about. Do you really think you're in a position to be playing games with me?"

"Look, I have no idea what you're talking about but I know you have Michael Cogan and that's why I'm calling. I want to meet you - today. I have what you want and you have what I want. This can be real quick and easy. But I want this over with, today."

"And what do you have for me?"

"I have the green metal crate that was on my truck. I'm prepared to trade you the crate for Michael and two million dollars."

"Two million?" Lincoln chuckled. "My offer was for one. But that offer's withdrawn. Now that I have your partner, I think that's all I need."

"Well, you're wrong. You see, I've checked with the FBI and they don't know anything about an Agent Clifford Dwyer. They don't even know that the hijacking involved a classified shipment. So, it's clear that you're not who you say you are. And, it's also clear that you don't know enough about me. Because if you did, you'd know that I'm not gonna negotiate with you. My terms are firm: Michael Cogan and two million dollars cash or I take the crate to the real FBI, today."

"Oh really. And what do you think will happen to Michael Cogan?"

"If anything happens to Michael or anyone else that I know, I'll take the crate to the FBI *and* show them the security tape I have of you in our office. After I tell them a slightly altered version of what's happened over the last couple days, you'll be wanted for espionage and murder."

Lincoln winced. *Security tape! Damn it!* "And what do you think will happen to *you* if you do that?"

"I know what won't happen for you. You won't have the crate and somehow I think that's very important to you."

Lincoln hesitated. "Awright. I want that tape, though. Bring the tape and the crate and you'll get Cogan back. Any funny stuff, any copies of that tape, and I promise you that you'll end up like the rest of your *goombahs* did this week."

I let the words sink in. "If you mean the mob killings, they weren't my *compare.*"

"Yeah, whatever you say. They're dead just the same."

I cupped the mouthpiece on the phone. My heart was pounding against my breastplate and I was short of breath. *This guy did that? He killed Vinny Diamonds?* I gulped several deep breaths.

"I'll bring the tape but I want Michael *and* the two million."

I heard a rusting sound as if Lincoln had covered the mouthpiece. Then I heard short, clipped, muffled curses. I'm certain that he wanted to reach through the phone, grab me by the throat, and then laugh in my face as he crushed my trachea. But that would have to wait.

After a few moments, he came back. In a relaxed voice, he said, "Okay, Mr. Napolo, you have a deal. Now let's get this over with. You seem to have thought this through, so let's hear what you have in mind."

## DTC Transportation
## Edison, New Jersey

The auxiliary telephone bell on the wall of the garage was ringing. It was loud so it could be heard over the din of the air compressors and power tools and radios that reverberated through the cavernous tuck shop.

"Shop," Ripton answered.

"Ripton?"

"Yeah, who's this?"

"Moretti."

"Hey, man, what's up?"

"I need a rig. Joseph called from FirsTech, needs a special pickup this morning. Whadaya got left?"

"We finished the brake job on twenty-four. I just got back from the road test a few minutes ago. You can have her in about twenty minutes; I need to bleed off some air and recheck the fluids. But tell whoever's gonna make the run that the brakes are new and they're set a little high."

"I'm gonna take it. I'll let you know if they need adjusting."

"I thought you were off the road for a while."

"Nah, I'm fine. Besides I hate sittin' around."

"If you say so. What size box you gonna need, forty-eight or fifty-three?"

"Forty-eight'll do," Moretti said. "It's only one piece."

"Okay, gimme twenty minutes or so. I'll have Ricky grab a trailer and run it around front for ya."

"Thanks, Rip."

## Waverly Place Arms
## Greenwich Village, New York City

Fabrizio Benedetto lived in the tradition of the most successful and long-lived Mafia Dons. By fashioning a quiet life, shunning the outward signs of wealth and power, and insisting upon the same loyalty to tradition from his captains and soldiers, the Napolo Family had survived and prospered into the new millennium. Miraculously, not one Napolo Family associate had yet to cooperate with the authorities and enter the witness protection program. Many attributed this to Benedetto's unflinching enforcement of the traditional codes of conduct. A closer look would reveal his uncanny ability for staying one step ahead of frustrated investigators, allowing the Napolo

Family to escape all but the most trifling prosecutorial efforts. As a result, the Family was also able to evade the ruinous media attention salaciously reserved for organized crime trials.

And so it was, until the sensational events of the last couple days.

"Not too good, this morning," the sturdy day nurse, Mrs. Wilkins, said as she ripped apart the Velcro fastening to remove the blood pressure cuff from Fabrizio Benedetto's arm. "And you look tired. You should rest."

The Don looked at her with the special contempt he saved for all his medical caretakers. Mrs. Wilkins knew the look and often took the opportunity to remind him that it wasn't her presence that had made him sick but the reverse series of events that required it. However, she knew that today was not the day to initiate a round of spirited persiflage.

"Do you read the newspapers, Mrs. Wilkins?" He asked without looking at her.

"When I get the chance." Her back to him, wrapping the rubber tubing around the rolled pressure cuff.

"You watch TV or listen to the radio?"

"Yes, of course," said Mrs. Wilkins, turning around.

"Then you know that friends of mine were killed yesterday. Some of them I've known since they were young boys." Glancing up at her. "Do you really think that I can rest?" Catching her eyes. "Do you think I will?"

Mrs. Wilkins looked down at her patient. She knew all too well of his reputation but had become familiar with him as just another old man, failing from age, bad lungs, and weak heart muscles, bound to his wheelchair for mobility, lest a few dozen steps sap the day's strength from him. But now, as she listened to his voice and looked past his tired, watery eyes she sensed the capacities of a younger and stronger man. A man of serious intent. A man capable of the things she had heard.

"I understand, but I still think you should rest."

Fabrizio Benedetto shook his head at her persistence. "I have to go to the park. I need you to take me there. Will that make you afraid?"

"Should I be?"

"Maybe."

"Are *you*?"

"A little."

"Then why are you going."

"Because I have to. I have no choice. But my men will be watching and they'll protect us, if they have to."

"I'm just a fat old lady. Why would anyone want to hurt me?"

Benedetto's eyes twinkled. "I could give them plenty of reasons."

Mrs. Wilkins laughed.

Benedetto became serious again. "The newspapers and TV will be waiting for me downstairs. That will help to make it safer. But they'll be asking questions and taking my picture and you'll be on the front page with me. Does that bother you?"

Mrs. Wilkins shrugged. "My grandchildren will probably think it's cool or phat or whatever they say now. But why are you going out? Why are you letting them do this?"

"I need to show my enemies and my friends that I am not afraid, that I will not hide, that I am still strong. I need to carry on, like I am expected to." Looking away. "And I need to meet someone in the elevator, to talk in private, when we come back."

"Okay, Mr. Benedetto, let's go for a walk. I'll get a blanket for your lap."

"No. Just my brown jacket, please. We'll leave the wheelchair in the lobby."

## The Smoke and Gun Club at Bella Collina Livingston Manor, New York

"It's called the Weaver stance," Wilson said. "It's taught to every police recruit on his first day at the pistol range." Tapping my elbows. "Loosen up a little. Your elbows are too straight and they have to point more outwards, less down. Form an elongated triangle shape with your elbows - chin and pistol as the long points."

I brought my hands closer to my face and raised my elbows.

Wilson stepped back. "That's it. Now spread your feet and keep your weight evenly distributed. Good. Aim at that target on the left."

I swung the pistol left.

Wilson shook his head. "No. Look at your elbows. See you've compromised the triangle shape. The triangle must stay rigid. To change your aim, you turn or bend at the waist, your shoulders stay with the triangle, they only move as part of it. Watch."

Wilson raised his right hand formed like a pistol and braced it from below with his left. He bounced on the balls of his feet to test his balance before settling back onto his heels into a picture-perfect stance. Then he swung his pistol left and right, up and down, moving forward and back, and side to side, the whole time maintaining the triangle, executing the dance with the balance and agility of a man half his age.

"Now you try it, live. Lock and load." Wilson said.

I fed the seven-round magazine into the Colt 1911 and pulled back the slide to chamber the first round. Wilson had already given me brief but thorough instructions on the features and safe handling of the gun. I kept the muzzle pointed down range and checked the safety. It was on. I laid the gun on the leather-covered shelf and pulled on his headset. When I had adjusted the lip mike, I put on a pair of yellow-tinted shooting glasses that both eliminated the glare off the targets and somehow sharpen the focus.

"Next time put your headset and glasses on *before* you lock and load."

I had heard Wilson in his headset and glanced over his shoulder. Wilson stood behind and slightly to right of me, his headset and shooting glasses in place. I nodded at him.

"Okay, then. Let's get started. Pick up your weapon and assume your stance. I want you to take three shots as fast as you can at the center target. Now the muzzle's gonna pop up from the recoil. You'll need to maintain control of the gun and your target. As soon as the muzzle jumps, quickly but steadily lower the gun back onto the target. Use your left hand to create a solid platform and to firmly control your descent. Resettle your sights as you're coming back down on target. Keep your triangle at all times. As soon as you've reacquired the target, squeeze off the next round. Watch me."

Wilson pantomimed the sequence with his finger gun.

"Your turn. Do you want some music? I've got Verdi's Aida on."

"Sure, in the background might be nice."

I listened to the music. It was soaring and dramatic. I motioned for Wilson to turn it down a bit. When the volume was right, I signaled thumbs up.

"I'm gonna stay over your shoulder here and watch your form." Wilson said above the music in the headset.

I picked up the Colt and looked toward the target. Wilson had set the target, a life-size outline of a man, at ten yards. I didn't question the distance, but if I had Wilson would have told me that most real-life gunplay takes place at close quarters, well within twenty or thirty feet. He might have also told me that I was about to get a crash course in combat pistol techniques and that the better I did here, the more chance I had of surviving the meeting with Lincoln

I settled into my stance and formed my triangle. I maneuvered the front sight blade into the slot of the rear sight and aimed at the black circle at center of the target's chest. When the front blade was centered in the rear slot and its tip was level with the top of the slot, I squeezed the trigger. The pistol jumped in my hand. The noise was deafening. The force of recoil and the loudness of the report surprised me. I held the gun pointed down range but didn't take a second shot.

Before I could look back at Wilson, I heard from him. "More than you expected? I set your headset to allow the gunshot to come through at natural volume. I wanted you to feel and hear it. The last thing you need is to be surprised at the wrong time. Now let's try again. Three quick shots. I'm leaving the headset alone to simulate live combat shooting."

I turned back to the target and repeated the ritual, taking my time to get it right. The front blade slid into the slot and I fired. This time I was ready. I kept control of the recoil, brought the muzzle down on target and fired again, and again. The music volume seemed to creep up with each shot.

As I lowered the gun to the table, Wilson barked in my ears. "Target on left. Bring 'em down!"

A man-target burst out of the darkness about ten yards out to the left. I reformed the triangle, swung my shoulders and fired. *Boom! Boom!*

"Target far right!"

I spun right to see a target lit up no more than fifteen away.

*Boom!*

I pulled the trigger again but it wouldn't move. I looked at the gun. The slide had locked open. The clip was empty. The music faded to background.

Wilson tapped my on the shoulder. "Let's see who lived."

Wilson reached passed me and tapped a couple membrane keys on the console. The targets floated toward the stall.

"Well, the first guy didn't walk away. Your first shot was a little high, that one in the neck, under the chin. But it probably would've taken out his spine and brain stem – could have nearly taken the head off a small person. The three-shot volley got you one kill shot in the chest. The one in the hip would've knocked him down, but the lower left torso would've probably passed right through 'em without hitting a major organ or doing any serious damage."

Wilson pulled the left target toward us. "Whoa. Both shots center chest. Dead man here. Let's see man number three." Wilson reached for it. "Clean miss." Turning to me. "You're dead - he killed you when you ran out of bullets. Did you count your shots?"

"No."

"Well, you've got seven rounds in that old Colt. You've gotta learn to count 'em and be ready to reload. Let's try it again. This time you're gonna have to reload. You're gonna have eight or ten targets and three clips. I won't announce them so heads up. Shoot to kill. Head shots are kills. Body shots are maybes, especially if they're wearing body armor." Pausing to look directly at me. "I know Lincoln does"

I acknowledged his last comment with a slight nod. "What's with the music? It was awfully loud when I was shooting."

"That was on purpose. You've got to learn to filter out the diversions. Loud music. Gunshots. Traffic. Innocent bystanders in the kill zone. They're all distractions that can get you killed. You need to train to block them out, to tunnel in and stay focused. Ready to go again?"

I nodded and reached for the Colt.

Wilson reached across and pointed toward the Colt. "On second thought, let's give this antique a rest."

Wilson turned away and then back, producing a highly polished maple wood box from the next stall. He opened the top. "Use these."

Inside were two unusual-looking pistols and five magazines, all snugly cradled in formed foam padding covered with a maroon velveteen material. Wilson took out the larger pistol and handed it to me.

"That's a ten millimeter Glock 20. It's the sidearm of choice for a lot of law enforcement and special ops forces. Personally, I think Glock makes the most reliable handguns in the world. Some might argue that Heckler & Koch's autoloaders are number one, but not by me. You know you can shoot that Glock under water. Hell, you can take it out of the water, bury it in sand, pull it out and run a clip through it without any affect. It's an *outstanding* piece. I think you'll like it. It's a lot lighter than your .45 and easier to handle. It weighs less than a pound but the recoil is minimized by a mechanical reduction system. It's got Trijicon night sights and a mini laser aimer. Wherever the little red dot is when you pull the trigger that's where your bullet's going. If you don't jerk your shot, it'll happen every time." Reaching into the wood case. "And this is his little brother."

Wilson held a similar looking but much smaller autoloader.

"This is the Glock 29, the subcompact version of the 20. This'll be your backup piece. It's also chambered for ten millimeter but it'll fit anywhere - your pocket, your ankle, or in a hideout holster inside your pants. The nice thing is that after you finish its small seven-round clip it'll feed the same high-capacity magazines as his big brother. This way you only need to carry one type of spare magazines. For now, let's get some practice in with the 20 and the laser aimer. Oh, and these high-capacity magazines hold fifteen rounds." With a smile. "Can you count to fifteen?"

"I'll manage."

"Good." Wilson pointed at the Glock in my hand. "That's the safety and this is the mag release. Here's the laser switch. There's no external hammer like your .45. It's double action so after you chamber the first round you just pull the trigger. Okay?"

I nodded.

"Alright then, switch on the laser and lock and load. There's a lot of bad guys out there."

## Waverly Place Arms
## Greenwich Village, New York City

The reporters and cameramen were still shouting questions and rolling video tape over the shoulders of the NYPD and several well-dressed Family men as Fabrizio Benedetto and Mrs. Wilkins walked back into the relative quiet and security of the lobby. Benedetto was exhausted and grateful that his wheel chair was only a few more steps away, around the corner by the elevators, out of sight of the media. Mrs. Wilkins went ahead to steady the chair for him. He eased into it with a loud sigh.

"Here," she said, handing him the clear plastic mouthpiece connected to the small oxygen tank strapped to his chair.

Benedetto shot her a look but quickly realized his contempt was misdirected and he placed the device over his mouth and nose without protest.

"Take a few good breaths before we get into the elevator," she said, choosing to ignore his irritation.

The Don obeyed and almost immediately began to feel the affects of the pure oxygen. After a few moments he signaled for her to press the elevator button. Inside the elevator, Mrs. Wilkins took a key and inserted it into the control panel on the wall. The key allowed them access to the penthouse on the restricted fourteenth floor. Without it you couldn't get to the fifth floor either, but very few people knew this because no one lived on the fifth floor. Benedetto continued to breathe the oxygen as they rode up.

When the doors opened, Benedetto handed her the mouthpiece. "You go on in. I'm meeting someone on another floor. I'll be back up in a little while."

"You're exhausted. You should . . ."

Benedetto raised his hand and cut her short. Mrs. Wilkins shook her head and turned off the oxygen. She backed out of the elevator as he reached for the control panel. He felt her glare as the elevator doors closed. He pushed the button to reopen the doors. She was still standing there; feet planted at shoulder width and arms entwined across her matronly breasts.

Benedetto looked up at her. "Thank you, Mrs. Wilkins."

"You're welcome, Mr. Benedetto."

He winked devilishly as the doors closed again. She rolled her eyes in response.

Benedetto rode down to the eighth floor. When the doors opened Jimmy Merchanti was standing in the opening. Benedetto waved him into the elevator with a slight pull of his right fingers.

"Lobby, please," Benedetto said into the air as he pressed the buttons for the lobby, and the fifth floor.

They rode in silence and left the elevator on the fifth floor. They proceeded quietly to apartment number 511. Once inside the sparsely furnished living room, Merchanti followed a series of hand signals from Benedetto; locking the door, pushing his wheel chair close to the television, sitting in a chair next to Benedetto, and handing him the remote control from the armrest.

Benedetto pressed the power button and CNN blinked onto the screen. The volume was much louder than it needed to be, but he didn't turn it down.

The pretty morning anchorwoman was speaking.

"*. . . FBI sources have confirmed that a faction of the Brooklyn-based Russian Mafia is the bureau's primary suspect for yesterday's bold mid-day massacre of nine members of the Napolo Crime Family. The confirmation was obtained following the identification of the tenth victim of the slaying as Russian mobster Igor Steponovich. FBI sources told CNN that Steponovich, whose street name was Johnny Steps, was an enforcer for the Russian mob.*

*Yesterday's death toll has secured The May Massacre a place in history as this country's worst mob-related mass slaying since the infamous St. Valentine's Day Massacre. Over seventy years ago, on February 14th 1929, seven members of the Bugs Moran Gang were machined gunned to death in a Chicago garage. Rival gangster, Al Capone, was allegedly responsible for . . .*"

Benedetto tapped Merchanti's arm and leaned toward him. Merchanti lowered his ear.

"This is all bullshit," Benedetto said. "The Russians did not do this."

Merchanti frowned at the Don and pointed at the television. "But Johnny Steps . . ."

Benedetto raised a hand to silence him. "Listen to me. I can't explain why Johnny Steps was there, but the Russians didn't do this. They will pay the price, but they are not the ones. You understand?"

Jimmy slid to the end of his seat. "Who then? Tell me, and I'll . . ."

"Never mind that, for now. Let the world think it was the Russians. Let the Ivans feel the heat and suffer the losses. Eventually they'll come to us, begging for a truce, and we'll have it on our terms. But for now, you . . . *we* stay away from them. The Ivans are my concern and I alone will see to them."

"But . . . ah," Merchanti almost addressed the Don by name but, remembering the rule, caught himself. No one ever used names here. Even though the whole fifth floor was electronically swept every day for surveillance devices, the technology was changing so quickly you never knew who might be listening.

"With all respect, how can we do nothing? How can you ask me to stand aside? Nine good men are gone. They were my friends and I . . ."

"Basta, smettela!" *Stop, enough!* said the Don, narrowing his cloudy eyes. "I have a more important thing for you to do for me - something only you can accomplish. But you must listen to me and forget about the Russians. To be the boss of this Family you must learn that seeking revenge is like picking fruit. You are young and so hungry for revenge that you want to grab the lowest hanging piece, to eat quickly and stop the hunger. But that's the act of a desperate, starving man. Sure, you may no longer be hungry but there was no enjoyment in eating it. You have to step back and look at the whole tree, see all the fruit until you find the right one, the one that is most ripe and juicy. Then, you climb up, slowly so you don't shake the branches, and take it. Then, when you eat your belly is full *and* your mouth smiles from its sweet taste."

Merchanti had listened closely, knowing every word was important and that the message wouldn't be repeated. Had he heard correctly? *'The boss of this Family'*?

"I understand," Merchanti said. "But I . . ."

Benedetto raised a hand again and nodded to the television. The front of the Waverly Place Arms was pictured above the anchorwoman's left shoulder.

". . . *and now we have a live report on this developing story. Vance Horgdal is in New York City's Greenwich Village, only a few blocks from the murder scene. Vance?*"

"*Diane, behind me is the Waverly Place Arms, home of the alleged Napolo Crime Family Boss Fabrizio Benedetto. Just a few minutes ago, the aged Don casually strolled out the front door and walked a block and a half east to Washington Square Park, where he and a female companion sat on a bench feeding pigeons. After about ten minutes, they returned to this apartment building. Along the way, Benedetto waved and smiled at neighborhood folks, stopping on two occasions for a friendly chat. The Don's steady gait and easy demeanor belied all the rumors of his failing health and he showed no signs of concern over yesterday's murders. We reporters were kept at a distance by a squad of New York's Finest and a handful of what can only be described as large, well-dressed men obviously in the employ of Benedetto. At one point, I was able to ask the Don about yesterday's massacre.*"

The videotape image of Benedetto walking arm-in-arm with Mrs. Wilkins filled the screen. Off camera the reporter's voice shouted.

"*Mr. Benedetto, some are saying that yesterday's murders were a bold first strike by the Russian Mob in a bid for control of organized crime in this city and beyond. How will you react to this challenge?*"

The camera went in tight on Benedetto.

The Don frowned. *"Like any New Yorker, such horrible violence only a few blocks from my home causes me great concern. It is a regrettable incident for our city and for the victims and their families."*

The reporter persisted. *"Will there be a war to settle the score?"*

Benedetto looked puzzled. *"I am a retired businessman who enjoys watching the Yankees and feeding the pigeons. Wars are waged by politicians and generals, not old men."*

The camera went back to the reporter. *"So there you have it, Diane, the most powerful Mob boss in the country . . ."*

Benedetto tapped Merchanti's arm. Merchanti leaned to him.

Benedetto whispered. "You know Joseph Napolo." It wasn't a question.

Merchanti nodded without showing his surprise.

"His grandfather was like a father to me. He was a great man. He sacrificed his life for this Thing of Ours. And he made this Family what it is today. Make no mistake, he is why we have survived and retained our position of power to this day."

Merchanti had heard it all before but he respectfully nodded again.

"Many years ago, I made a promise to him - a promise that certain circumstances will now force me to break. But I think that I'd be forgiven. A good friend of ours has told me that his grandson is in trouble. And his troubles may be related to our . . . problem. I think that Don Carmine himself would do as I've decided. Either way, I'm an old man and I won't have to live long with my infidelity."

The Don's breathing suddenly became labored and quick. He closed his eyes and fought the panic that would exacerbate the attack.

Merchanti averted his glance and listened to the little gasps of air, one tiny pant at a time. He waited while the intervals between lengthened and the breathing deepened. Not too much longer, he thought.

The Don was thinking the same thing. Not too much longer. One of these days he would not be able to recover on his own. Lately, he had found himself hoping that Mrs. Wilkins or one of her counterparts weren't around when it happened. He was getting too tired for all this.

*" . . . one hour from now, at eleven a.m. eastern time, Special Agent-in-Charge Robert Groves of the FBI's New York Field Office and New York City Police Commissioner Vincent Campbell have scheduled a joint news conference to update the public on the investigation into yesterday's Mob-related slayings in lower Manhattan. CNN has also just learned that early this morning a joint NYPD and FBI task force conducted a series of raids on known Russian Mob hangouts in the Brighton Beach section of Brooklyn. During one of the raids a gun battle erupted, leaving two suspects dead and three wounded, including*

*an FBI agent. It is assumed that the details of the raids will be the focus of today's . . ."*

"Do you need some water?" Merchanti asked when the redness began to fade from Benedetto's face.

Benedetto shook his head slightly and said, hoarsely, "No."

Benedetto cleared his throat and spit into a handkerchief. "I am a sick, old man. I need to make my plans. Vinny is gone. This Family needs a new Underboss, someone young and strong and smart." Turning to Merchanti. "I'm moving you up." Leaning forward and looking firmly into Merchanti's eyes. "Do I have your pledge of loyalty?"

Merchanti fought back a grin that was threatening to spread across his face. "Yes. I pledge my life to you and I am honored to do so."

Benedetto held his glance for a moment before sitting back again. "Are there four or five good men left that are loyal to you? Men that will follow you without question, without hesitation? Men that you will need to trust with your life?"

Merchanti thought a moment. "Yes."

"Do you know how to contact Joseph Napolo?"

"Yes."

"Good. Now, I want you to tell me what you know about this thing in Jersey with Joseph Napolo, and then I have a story to pass on to you. It's a story about the great Don Carmine and a good friend of ours who called me today. A man named McBride."

# CHAPTER 24

## The Smoke and Gun Club at Bella Collina
## Livingston Manor, New York

Unbeknownst to Wilson Dennis and me, Nicolas Pucci had returned to the range and sat quietly in the near dark of the elevated observation area behind the shooting stalls. He had been watching us for about twenty minutes, enjoying the opera and the smell of the cordite.

Nicolas took particular interest in the improvement of my shooting skills with each new set of targets. He watched me intently absorb Wilson's brief but expert lessons between each set. The teacher and the student had connected. It was time to break it up.

I had just finished an intense round. Thirty-two furious shots at thirteen targets that had appeared at random, often two or three at a time, high and low, sometimes moving toward me or at angles, and always representing an imagined threat that made my heart race like a down-shifted Cummins diesel rounding a step and dangerous curve.

As soon as I lowered the Glock, Nicolas descended from the shadows, clapping his hands. "Very nice shooting. I'm impressed."

Wilson and I turned around. I tilted my head toward Wilson. "I've got a great instructor."

"He's got a lot of natural ability," said Wilson. "His scores have been outstanding, especially for a novice. Hell, a lot of guys I know who've been shooting for years would be very happy with hits like this."

Nicolas glanced at the targets and nodded agreeably, recognizing that Wilson's instruction had focused on close-order combat and not match pistol distance and accuracy. I was being trained to survive a firefight.

Nicolas squared his shoulders to me. "The arrangements we agreed to are being completed."

"I talked to my lawyer earlier," I said. "He's expecting a call from your guy."

"That happened. In fact, they've already exchanged email versions and we've signed the final documents. They're being hand-delivered to your attorney. Our chopper should be setting down in Jersey right about now. As soon your attorney hands our man the executed agreements, the funds will be transferred. You should be able to confirm everything's done by eleven thirty or quarter to twelve."

The reality of the situation began to descend on me. In about three hours I would be in a very dangerous situation, one that could have severe legal and personal consequences no matter what precautions had been taken. Cathy might never forgive me if something went wrong. And, if it went right, I would have a secret to keep from her for the rest of my life. My stomach began to feel hollow and a bit nauseous. I removed my headset and glasses and gulped a mouthful of air.

Nicolas and Wilson exchanged glances. They had both witnessed the color draining from my face.

"Are you okay?" Wilson asked.

"I'm fine," I lied, again. It was getting too easy. "Just a little dry. I could use a soda or some juice. Let's take a break. I wanna to go up and pack, maybe get something to eat before I have to go."

"Okay," Nicolas said. "If you wanna rest for a while, you can order up whatever you want to your room." Nicolas looked at my face again. "You probably should rest awhile. We need you to be ready for this thing."

"I think I'll do that. But don't worry, I'll be ready."

Wilson glanced at his watch. "Good. Then let's meet down here at twelve thirty. Your truck should be here, loaded, and ready to roll by twelve forty-five, but we're gonna need a few minutes to get you wired and into some body armor. Do you have a jacket or a windbreaker with you to hide the holsters?"

"Holsters?"

"Yeah, holsters," Wilson said. "We're making you a gift of this set of Glocks. We're having them and your .45 registered in your name. We're also arranging to get you a concealed carry permit for you to leave here with. Our contacts will backdate the paperwork and make it look like you got DOD approval several years ago due to your DOD clearance to handle highly classified cargo."

I took a deep breath and ran my fingers through my hair. "Okay, I'll see you here at twelve thirty, but I don't own a windbreaker."

*    *    *

Back in my room, I ordered a tuna on rye with a Diet Coke and packed while I waited for it to be delivered. I checked my cell phone but there was no service. Whatever they did to make it work for me to call Lincoln had been disabled. I used the phone on the desk to call my office. No important messages except perhaps the two calls from Albert Catella.

I called our lawyer, Sam Meltzer, again and spent the next twenty minutes explaining to him the details he needed to know. Michael and I had been referred to Sam when we were arranging for the purchase of Domanski Trucking. He had been our attorney ever since and had become a good golf friend. Sam listened intently, feverishly taking notes, occasionally interrupting with a question or with an 'Oh, my God!' I kept the conversation on track, avoiding unnecessary details and any of Sam's questions that probed too deeply. In the end, Sam had a firm grasp on the situation and was fully prepared to handle the legal and financial side of the FirsTech agreement.

Then I dialed my cell phone's voice mailbox. There was a message, probably from Cathy.

"Joseph, page me as soon as you get this message. It's very important."

It wasn't a woman voice. I played the message again to try to recognize the voice. Why don't people leave their names? Was it their ignorance or their arrogance? The next replay I got it. This caller was just being careful. It was Jimmy Merchanti.

I erased the message. The last thing I needed right now was Merchanti and his agenda. Regardless, there was no way I was going to use the phone in the room to contact him. I dialed my home.

"Napolo residence." It was little Mickey.

"Hey, Mick it's dad. What are you doin' home today?"

"I have a tummy ache. Mommy said I didn't have to go to school today."

"A tummy ache? Did you eat some worms or bugs?"

"No daddy. That's usgusting."

"Usgusting? You mean *dis*gusting?"

"That's what I said, usgusting."

"Oh, sorry, I didn't hear you. Is mommy home?"

"Acourse mommy's home. I'm too little to stay home alone, daddy."

"Oh, that's right. I keep forgetting because you're so big. Can I talk to mommy?"

"Daddy?"

"Yeah, Mick."

"A mean man came and made mommy cry. He made me cry, too. Mommy said you're gonna yell at him and make him cry an' say he's sorry. Are you gonna do that daddy?"

My eyes began to well up. "I'm gonna talk to that man in a little while. I'm gonna yell real loud at him. Okay?"

"Okay."

"Can I talk to mommy now?"

"Okay. Daddy?"

"Yeah, Mick."

"When are you coming home?"

"I think I'll be home tonight."

"Okay, daddy. Bye."

I listened to the phone clatter to the floor and Mickey yelling for his mother. While I waited, I wiped my eyes.

"Hi, how are you?" Cathy was out of breath from running to the phone.

"Everything's fine. Mickey's sick?"

"He said he had an upset stomach this morning. Poor guy had a couple nightmares last night and climbed in our bed about one. I think last night scared him and he just wanted to stay home with me."

"He sounds better."

"He is. He's fine."

"Good." I took a breath. "Cathy, everything's okay but I need you to do something and I don't have the time to get into a long discussion over it. It's *very* important and I need you to trust me. Now I know this is asking a lot, but I need you to be ready to leave the house as soon as Joseph and Robbie get off the school bus today. Pack a few days' worth of clothes and go to the place we stayed at during the Nor'easter in '92."

"You mean the . . ."

"Yes, just off the exit. Don't say the name."

"But . . ."

"*Please*, just listen to me for a minute."

"Okay."

"On the way there, stop at the bank and take out a couple thousand dollars. Pay cash for everything. I *don't* want you to use the credit cards *at all*. Call Ilene and tell her to do the same thing. Do whatever you have to do to get her to do it. Don't use your real names to register. Use your college roommate's name. Have Ilene use her sister's married name. If you don't hear from me by five o'clock, call Sam Meltzer. He'll know what to do."

290

"Sam Meltzer the lawyer?"

"Yes, his number's in the blue address book under the phone."

"Joseph, you're scaring me."

"I know. I'm sorry. Honey, everything's gonna be all right. I just don't want you or the kids, or Ilene, to have to be involved in this thing."

"We can handle it. We've been through it all with you two guys."

"Cath, this is different. You can't help."

"Just tell me what's going on then."

"I can't do that. Not now. I just need you to trust me and do this. I need to focus on what I have to do without worrying about you and the kids."

"Tell me why we have to leave our home. You can't just ask me to leave without some kind of explanation."

I rubbed my forehead and began to speak very slowly. "I love you, Cath, but this is not up for discussion. I don't have time. Now, as the mother of my children, I'm asking you to do this for me, unconditionally. Please, take my children and go to . . . that place. Make Ilene do the same thing. I know you can. Will you do that for me?"

"Oh, God." Cathy's voice quivered. She had heard my tone.

"Will you do this for me, Cath?"

"You're scaring the shit out of me!"

"I need you to promise me you'll do this. Please."

"If you tell me, promise me, that everything will be okay - that *you'll* be okay, and that I'm gonna see you soon, I will." She was on the verge of crying.

I squeezed my eyes tight and pursed my lips.

"Promise me, Joseph."

I couldn't.

"I love you, Cath."

"Oh, God, Joseph." She broke and sobbed loudly.

"Will you do it, Cath?"

"Yes." She sniffled and cleared her throat. "Of course."

There was a long silence. Finally I said, "Cath? Remember the night you said you never wanted to see me again and I stood outside your parents' house until your father called the police?"

"Yeah," Cathy chuckled between her sniffles.

"And how I came right back after the police chased me away."

"We could hear your broken muffler driving around the block. My dad was so mad at you. So was I, but I made him promise not to call the police again. You stood out there all night."

"Remember what I did the next morning?"

"Of, course. You were so tired and wet. Your voice was cracking." I could hear her smile. "Do it again, now."

I cleared my throat and began to sing in a soft voice.

*"Remember the first time,*
*You said that we were through?*
*And how I cried*
*'Cause I still loved you?*
*Well, I got drunk down at Eddie's Bar,*
*Got chased off by the police car,*
*So baby, please,*
*No heartbreak this time 'round."*

"Go on," Cathy said. "That's not all of it."

"Okay. I'm getting down on one knee." I did. "Cathy, will you marry me?"

"And I said, yes, if you promise never to sing to me again."

"Oh, sorry, I forgot that part."

"Sure ya did."

We both smiled.

"I'll talk to ya later, honey, at the place."

"Okay. I love you. Please be careful."

"I will. I love you, too."

I went into the bathroom and began packing my toiletries. I avoided the mirror above the sink, not wanting to see my red and watery eyes. I finished packing and leaned heavily on the vanity, looking down at the tops of my hands, feeling drained and empty as if my organs had dissolved leaving me hollow inside. I sucked in a deep breath as if it would fill the void. What the hell was I doing here?

I slowly raised my head and looked at my reflection. The image was murky and I began to blink away the wetness in my eyes. I thought about Cathy and the boys, and Michael and his family, and how hard we had worked to make good lives for ourselves. And, how little Mickey had said *usgusitng*, like Joseph Jr.'s *mcscuse me*, and Robbie's *Hammerham Lincoln*. These were the little things that I tucked away and securely bundled with the other precious moments that I retrieved whenever I needed to smile and to feel their warmth.

And, there was another reason I clung to these special memories. Some time ago, I secretly began storing video clips and photographs and school work in a digital scrapbook for each of them. I had decided that I would take the microphone at each of their weddings and send them off with a special tribute. In front of the wedding guests and their beautiful brides, I was going to narrate a video of their cutest, most embarrassing and most poignant moments. I so looked forward to it that it had motivated me to quit smoking seven years earlier. The thought of it helped to ease the painful reality of them growing up so quickly.

Nothing was going to alter those plans. Nothing was going to deprive me of those little moments that made for a big, full life.

Then like August rainwater from a late afternoon thunderstorm steaming off the soft, hot blacktop in the truck yard, the haze slowly lifted. In the mirror, my eyes were clear now. My lips were pressed firmly together and the flesh over my jowls had drawn tight as my jaw muscles twitched and my nostrils flared. But my breathing was even and controlled. And my mind was right.

# CHAPTER 25
## The Seasons Diner
## Woodbridge, NJ

"Why doncha take off those fuckin' sunglasses? You're inside for Chrissake," said Albert, Alley Cat, Catella.

Johnny Onions looked around and over his shoulder, then one more time to his left before he took them off.

Catella made a face. "Jesus Christ, you look like shit. What the fuck happened to you?"

"Never mind that. You gonna help me or what?"

"Hey, she hasn't even brought our coffee yet. What the fuck's wrong with you. You forget how to act civil?"

"Albert . . ."

Catella put his hand up. "Here she comes."

The waitress clunked down thick ceramic cups and saucers in front of them. "Who gets the decaf?"

"Me," Catella said.

The waitress poured their coffee and took their orders. Cheeseburger deluxe for Johnny and liverwurst on rye with mayo and onions for Catella. Johnny lit a cigarette and tossed the match on the floor. The waitress noticed and screwed up her face.

"I'll be right back with an ashtray," she said and left, stuffing the order pad into her apron.

"What's with the decaf?" Johnny asked when she was out of earshot.

"Doctor said too much caffeine was givin' me the heart palations. I can only have one, maybe two cups in the morning now."

"You mean heart *palpitations?*"

"Yeah."

The waitress cruised by the table and slid an ashtray under Johnny's cigarette without missing a step.

Catella pointed a finger at Johnny. "You look like shit. You should think about seeing a doctor, too."

"I've had a rough couple days. I fell in the shower the other night, hit my head and ripped the fuckin' nail off my big toe."

Catella cringed. "Oh shit, that must've fuckin' hurt like hell."

"Fuckin' A right. Still does and my goddam head, too."

"You takin' anything?"

"I'm eatin' Tylenol like candy."

"I think I heard that's bad for your stomach?"

Johnny shrugged and looked around. "Okay, had enough small talk? Is it civil enough for ya yet?"

Catella exhaled and fluttered his lips. "Awright, Johnny." He leaned over his coffee. "I called Napolo but he's not in the office. They don't expect him back until this afternoon."

"Fuck!" Johnny said between clenched teeth. "What about the other things?'

"I got a couple hundred here for ya. Best I can do right now."

Johnny nodded. "And the other thing?"

"We gotta talk about that."

"What talk?"

"Hey, I'm out here in the middle a Jersey. I'm in a meetin' when you call. You gimme two hours notice. Besides, I don' know how good an idea it is for me anyway. I got a good thing goin' here, Johnny; sixty-seven grand a year, new Town Car, gas, insurance, and I already got Laskowski keepin' both eyes on me."

"Ouffa," Johnny sighed.

Catella looked down at the table. "And maybe it's this thing with Napolo, too." Looking up. "It ain't right, not no more. What's done is done, but, ah . . . ya know who he is, right?"

"Yeah. So what? He ain't shit. He's nobody."

"So, there should be some respect. For the old man, if nothin' else. It ain't right, Johnny. Not knowin' before, well okay. But now that I know what I know, I'm tellin ya it ain't fuckin' right. Hey, ya know those two guys got some real fuckin' trouble now."

"Nothin' they didn't earn. 'Specially that Cogan."

"Cogan maybe. You said the Feds pick 'im up?"

"Yeah, but he's got some kinda deal goin' with 'em. They're gonna pay 'im a couple hundred grand if he returns the crate that was on the truck. My cut's a hundred large. But his problem is, I'm the one knows where the crate is and there's no way *I* can go near the Feds."

"A couple hundred grand? Com'on, Johnny, that's bullshit."

"What bullshit?"

"There's no fuckin' way the Feds are payin' that kinda money. Didja ever think you might be gettin' set up?"

Johnny sat back and let his eyes drift up and away while he thought a moment. Then he shook his head and looked back at Catella. "Nah, I don't think so. When the Feds were takin' him, he coulda told 'em I was down the hall at the ice machine."

Catella shrugged. "How doya know they were FBI? There was an incident with our pickets and an FBI guy at DTC, so I did some checking. I'm not so sure the guy that visited Cogan was FBI."

"Look, I only know what Cogan tol' me and I don't think he was lyin'. We spent some time together. I watched him. He wanted this thing happen as much as I did."

"I don't know, man," Catella said, shaking his head. "I still think it's bullshit. And even if - you can't trust the fuckin' Feds. What, you think they're above lyin' to Cogan?"

"Look, I ain't here askin' for advice. I'm askin' for a favor. Ya gonna help me or what?"

"Johnny, we go way back, you and me. We done each other a lot of favors over the years and we can't forget that. So, yeah, I'm gonna help ya. But, I'm also gonna tell ya what I think. Listen or not, up to you."

Johnny rolled his eyes. "So I listen and then you get me what I need?"

"Yeah."

"Okay, go ahead." Johnny sat back and crossed his arms.

Catella exhaled. "Fuck it. Never mind."

"No, no, no. Go ahead, I know you'll feel better."

"No. Fuck it."

"Com'on, Alley. I know you. You gotta have the last word or you don't feel right. So, go ahead, I'm listenin'."

Catella stared at Johnny. "Okay." Leaning over the table. "There's things goin' on here with all this that ain't right. There's too much stuff happenin' that can't be explained."

"Like what?"

Whispering. "Like if you didn't whack those guys in your apartment, who did? Like if I don't know who torched Napolo's trucks, then who did it? And, like no one who knows anything believes for a minute that the fuckin'

Ivans would have the balls to move on Benedetto. So if they didn't, then who took out Vinny Diamonds and all those guys?"

"So whadaya sayin'? I did all that?"

"'Thefuck, you're missin' the point. All I'm sayin' is, doesn't it make ya think about what's goin' here? Aren't you the least bit curious?"

"Curious? Yeah. I'd like to know who fuckin' whacked all those guys so I could thank him. Fucker did me a big favor." Johnny sipped his coffee. "So, I listened, ya gonna get me the gun or what?"

Catella sat back. "You are unfuckingbelievable." Catella paused for deep breath. "But no more phone calls. Meet me at that go-go joint on Dowd Avenue near the airport about six."

"Ya mean that place Good Lookers?"

"Yeah, the one with the boob nipples in the O's on the sign."

"Awright, but you keep tryin' Napolo. Ya know what I need. And look, if I pull this thing off, I got twenty grand for ya."

"You pull this thing off and I'll kiss your ass at the tunnel entrance at rush hour. And make that thirty grand."

"Twenty-five."

"Deal."

The waitress appeared with their lunch. "Who gets the cheeseburger?"

Johnny pointed to the space in front of him. "Here."

As the waitress slid Catella's sandwich over to him Johnny said, "Hey, honey, this is s'posed to be deluxe. Where's the lettuce, tomato and mayo?"

"You didn't order a deluxe." Whipping out her pad. "Says right here, cheeseburger and fries."

Johnny pointed at himself. "You telling me what I ordered?" Pointing at the waitress. "I'm tellin' you I ordered a deluxe. So take this away and bring me a deluxe."

The waitress was about to challenge him again but something in his beat-up face, the steady eyes under the droopy lids, told her to let it go. "I'll bring ya the lettuce, tomato, and mayo," she said.

"Bring me a *deluxe,* for chrissake."

"*Sir,* a deluxe is what you have except with lettuce and tomato and mayonnaise."

"Are you shittin' me? Dollar fifty more for vegetables and mayo?"

"And fries."

"Then why'd ya write fries down if it was included?"

The waitress straightened and subconsciously pushed her order pad deeper into her apron pocket. "I didn't."

"Lemme see," Johnny said reaching for her.

"No," she said twisting away.

Johnny squinted at Catella who was shaking his head as he took a bite of his sandwich. "Now she's fuckin' lyin' to me," Johnny said to him. Then to the waitress. "You gonna admit you're lyin' and bring me a fuckin' deluxe or what?"

The waitress pursed her lips. Then she said, "I'm gonna take that away and bring it back with lettuce, tomato, and mayo on the side because that's a cheeseburger deluxe. No matter what you say, that's a deluxe."

"Ya know what, lady, you're ruinin' my fuckin' appetite. So just shut the fuck up and bring me a goddam cheeseburger deluxe."

"You're an *awful* man," she said before she stomped off.

Johnny held out his palms to Catella. "I need this shit?"

Catella shook his head and continued chewing his liverwurst.

## Stewart International Airport
## New Windsor, NY

Lincoln had heard the chopper returning and went downstairs to greet his crew. They were returning from a reconnaissance mission, a fly-over of the DOT maintenance yard where he would be meeting me later. Lincoln waited for the rotors to slow and the dust to settle before he walked onto the tarmac.

The pilot, Randell, followed by the crew chief walked over to where Lincoln stood.

"We topped off the tanks and test-fired the minigun over the mountains," Randell began. "Everything's fine. In fact, she's running especially smooth today. Low humidity and very light winds. We scanned . . ."

Lincoln cut him off with a wave of his hand. "Inside. Don't talk out here."

Lincoln led them into the building where he knew he would be safe from long-range parabolic listening devices.

"Okay, go ahead," Lincoln said.

Randell spoke. "We did a high altitude IR scan over the entire site, including the surrounding area for about 2000 yards out. We ran the scan through the computer and the only thing that looked suspicious turned out to be a couple of deer in the woods to the southwest. No signs of any other unusual activity. I've got it on CD if you want to check it out."

Lincoln shook his head. "No, we're gonna scan again before we go in anyway. You guys go get changed. Black jumpsuits, body armor, no ID's, sidearms and a couple H&K's. Rig 'em quiet and bring plenty of extra magazines. Billy and DK left in the truck about half an hour ago. They'll be waiting at the rest stop until we call 'em. We're leavin' in fifteen."

"We takin' the guy upstairs with us?"

"Yeah, we have to. His partner thinks I'm gonna trade him for the hardware."

"Okay, so we're gonna load the crate on the truck and then what are we gonna do with the bodies?"

"We'll load 'em in the chopper and drop 'em in the mountains."

"Sounds like a plan, boss. We'll bring a couple plastic tarps. See ya in fifteen."

## The New York Thruway - Southbound Near Sloatsburg, NY

I was having a hard time getting comfortable. I had been adjusting the electronic driver's seat controls every few minutes since I left The Smoke and Gun Club. I tapped the recline switch again. A little better. Not much, though. I wished for a cigarette, as if that's all it would take to settle me down. I took a deep breath; my method of pushing back the urges to smoke that still crept up on me even after all these years. I took another breath and tugged at the front of my shirt. It was bunching up around my neck. Face it, I thought, there was no way I'm going to feel comfortable. After all, I was driving to a meeting with an international assassin that would be abruptly interrupted by a heavily armed elite SWAT team.

And if that wasn't reason enough for my discomfort, Wilson Dennis and two FirsTech security men had strapped me into Kevlar body armor that held my torso rigid and tall like some sort of orthopedic corset. They then helped me into a top-of-the-line Bianchi shoulder holster rig. The Glock 20 hung under my left arm. Under my right, two fifteen round clips were slung in quick-retrieval sleeves. The smaller Glock 29 was tucked into a small holster that clipped to my waistband and hung inside my pants at the small of my back. I had three more loaded magazines in the pockets of the jacket they had provided. Tiny GPS tracking transmitters were sewn into the left cuff of my pants and the waistband of my boxer shorts. There were also two others that they didn't tell me about, one in the pocket flap of the jacket and another under the rear bumper of my Cherokee. They had also told me about the voice transmitter in the collar of my jacket but didn't mention the one inside the cab of my Jeep. Nor did they tell me that four miniature video cameras and sensitive microphones were hidden in the roof rack of the Jeep. The wide-angle lens on the cameras would provide 360-degree coverage and the microphones could detect a whisper at fifty yards. Whatever was about to happen in the maintenance yard was going to be watched in real-time living color via encrypted satellite relay to a secured room off Nicolas Pucci's private study at Bella Collina.

In my pocket was a leather fold that held two photo ID cards. One card identified me as Joseph Napolo, Security Consultant, FirsTech Security Group. The Department of Defense's Special Investigations Division issued the second card. Among other things, the card authorized me to carry concealed weapons. The Colt 1911 was next to me on the passenger seat inside a soft pistol case with four loaded clips. Wilson reminded me to unzip it, lock, load, and slide the handgrip free before I got out of the Jeep, just in case. I was definitely suited up. And, like the first time I put on a football uniform years ago, with the shoulder and body pads, jock and cup, my new cleats and helmet, I felt stiff and awkward. I wondered if the feeling would go away like it used to as soon as the kick-off whistle blew.

I took another deep, cigarette-withdrawal breath and focused on the back of the DTC trailer I was following. The mud flap behind the right rear wheels was missing a bolt or two and it was whipping to the side. I hated seeing that. In my mind, a loose mud flap or a broken running light spoke volumes about the type of company that was running that equipment. Little things got peoples' attention and it was the little things in our business, the details, that were important. And, if the mud flap was loose, it meant the trailer had not been into the shop lately and that there were bound to be other little things in need of maintenance. I would have to remember to tell Bobby to have the trailer PM'd.

I shook my head. It was funny how your mind worked. Mud flaps and trailer maintenance at a time like this? It probably was a good defense mechanism. I had made my peace with my decision to do this thing. I had done what I could to protect and financially provide for our families in case of worst events. I certainly didn't need any last minute second thoughts that might weaken my resolve or soften my focus. The matter of Bobby Moretti driving the truck had been troublesome enough.

I had assumed that I would be going alone, driving the rig to the meeting. I was surprised to see Moretti driving at all with his injuries. That was explained away by my last-minute call for a truck this morning. There were no other drivers available by that time. Thursday was always a busy day. Freight that had to deliver before the weekend had to move on Thursday. Truckers were routinely pressed to make up for dispatchers' oversights, production delays, or salesmen's late orders. And, as the last link in the supply chain, no matter what happened before the cargo was loaded on the truck, the trucker would be the one chastised as the weak link if the delivery was late. So, on Thursday, DTC's trucks often went out under capacity to ensure the aggressive schedule of pickup and delivery appointments was met without compromise. This meant more drivers and trucks were needed to carry the same tonnage as most other days of the week. Bobby had simply shrugged and reminded me what day it was. That, and proclaim his fitness by cursing doctors for their insulated view of the world.

"Fuckin' doctors," Moretti had begun the rant, curling his fingers around an imaginary penis and stroking his hand back and forth. "I'm fine, Joseph. Looks worse than it is. You know these fuckin' doctors. They think nothin' of tellin' ya to take ten days off. Like no one else in the world has to work for a living. Sure if ya make the kind of money they do, ten days off's no big deal. Ya know it's got somethin' to do with malpractice. I'm s'posed to stay home and go broke so they don't get sued, right? Fuckin' doctors, fuck them."

But that alone had not gotten Bobby in the truck to drive to the meeting. When I began to explain to Moretti that he would have to wait back at FirsTech, Wilson pulled me aside and convinced me that Moretti would be safe and that having the Cherokee available for a quick getaway might be a good idea, one that I couldn't argue with.

Moretti was told that Michael had been kidnapped, that the ransom was the crate, and that a SWAT team was going to make the arrest. And before they finished explaining the best case and worst case scenarios for him to consider, Moretti insisted upon going.

"I've heard enough. I'm going, Joseph," he had said. "I wanna be there when they get this fuck."

So while Moretti was fitted with body armor, Wilson posed as a government agent and swore him to secrecy. I thought that the adlibbed oath contained enough references to "national interests" and "enemies of the state" and "acts of treason" and "punishable under federal law" to sound both legally binding and genuinely foreboding. By the look on Moretti's face, so did he.

I had initially insisted that Moretti would stay in the cab of the truck, out of harms way, and only leave the cab if I decided we should make a break in the Jeep. Moretti and Wilson argued that another witness might help control the situation and that Moretti should get out of the truck, unlock the trailer doors, and then stay visible but behind me, to watch my flanks and rear.

"I got the eyes of an eagle," Moretti had said. "They're a little swollen, but I can still see good. And don't worry. I spent thirteen months in Nam. Got my ass home in one piece by knowing when to duck. I'll be watching both our sixes."

In the end, I relented. I knew I could trust Moretti. Besides, Wilson and Moretti were making good arguments and neither of them was about to be convinced otherwise. But now, a few miles from the meeting, I was wondering if I was just afraid and maybe agreeing to have Moretti come along had a lot to do with that. And what if they had been totally forthcoming about the kind of person Lincoln was, would Moretti have volunteered so readily? And then again, maybe worrying about Moretti was another thing I didn't need; somebody else that I would have to consider in that split second I would have if things started going badly. Someone else that might get hurt.

Then the right turn blinker on the tail of the trailer began to flash. I checked my watch. It was fourteen minutes to two. My stomach fluttered and my bowels constricted as I followed Moretti's rig onto the exit ramp for the DOT maintenance yard.

## Bella Collina
## Livingston Manor, New York

"You can't let this happen! I won't allow it!" Wilson was standing, leaning on his fists over Nicolas' desk.

Nicolas sprang to his feet. "Sit down, Wilson! Who do you think you're talking to?"

Wilson held his ground. "I know goddam well *who* I'm talking to. The same guy I talked into taking the training wheels off his first bike. Remember?"

Nicolas began to say something but didn't.

"Remember!" Wilson persisted.

Nicolas sighed and sat back down. "Yeah, I remember."

Wilson pushed himself up and walked over to the wet bar. He poured spring water into a glass and drank it slowly.

When he finished he turned and said, "We've gone too far with this, Nicolas. All that stuff about his grandfather . . . it got you nowhere. The stories, the wine, the *photographs* - Christ, you even had Schmidt carve those initials in the grips of his gun, didn't you? What were you thinking? *Forty* years later this guy's gonna feel some sense of duty to the memory of his gangster grandfather." Wilson shook his head. "And after all that, you still had to resort to threatening him to get him to cooperate. You called this one wrong. And now you want to send him to meet Lincoln without any backup?"

"Right or wrong, after all that we have to send him to Lincoln without backup. We're sending in the one observer and that's it."

"He's a civilian for chrissake. Haven't there been enough dead bodies this week? We are what we are, but there used to be rules."

"Rules? Com'on Wilson. You of all people."

"No." Pointing his finger at Nicolas. "You're wrong. And the old man would've told you the same thing. This is wrong. We created this . . . he didn't. Christ, the guy's got a family."

"Is that why you were tryin' so hard to teach him to shoot? Do you really think a two-hour lesson's gonna prepare him to go up against someone like Lincoln? Or have you just gone soft in your old age? Maybe tryin' to clear your conscience?"

"I told you last night and this morning before breakfast how I felt about this, the way I wanted to handle it. You chose to do it your way. So don't you worry about *my* conscience."

"Fuck you. You have gone soft. This isn't about you and me or Joseph Napolo or Michael Cogan. It's about the mission. Remember the mission, Wilson? What about that?"

"Yeah, sure, the mission." Wilson looked away for a moment. "And two or three billion in contracts."

"That's right, Wilson. We get to make a lot of money *and* do good things. What's wrong with that? Where's the downside?"

Wilson looked at Nicolas in disbelief. "Good things?"

"Yeah, good things - for our country and for the free world."

"Well, God bless America."

## New York State DOT Maintenance Yard Ramapo, NY

Moretti had parked the idling tractor-trailer about fifty yards in front of the salt silo. I pulled up next to him. Moretti climbed down out of the cab and walked over to the Cherokee.

"So, now what?" Moretti asked, leaning into the open window.

I shrugged. "We wait, I guess."

Moretti looked across at the pistol case on the passenger seat. "Is that what I think it is?"

"Yeah, get in."

Moretti climbed in and slid the pistol out of the case. "An old .45. You expectin' some real trouble?"

"I don't know, Bobby. Maybe. Better safe than sorry."

"I guess a little insurance never hurts."

I thought a moment and then opened my jacket and showed Moretti the Glock under my arm.

"This is mine. That's yours, if you want it. I assume they taught you how to use one in the army."

Moretti nodded. "I carried a cheap snub nose .38 in the bush for back-up. Traded a guy an AK-47 that I took off a dead gook. But, yeah, I know how to use this."

Moretti pulled back the slide and looked into the breach and down the barrel. "Nice and clean." Then he snapped the slide closed and aimed the .45 at the salt silo. "I could back you up real nice with this beast."

I watched Moretti dry-fire the pistol and then pull the slide back into the locked open position again. Moretti reached for a loaded magazine.

"You don't have to do this, Bobby. It's not your deal. It wouldn't be a problem if you took a walk over that hill and waited in the rest stop - sit in the Burger King and have a cup a coffee."

Moretti slapped the clip home, released the slide, and lowered the hammer with his thumb. Turning to me with a crooked smile, he said, "Fuck that." He thumped the Kevlar vest under his shirt with his knuckles. "I'm all dressed up and ready to rock 'n' roll."

I nodded as Moretti stuffed the three remaining loaded magazines in his jacket pocket. "Okay, but let the SWAT team do their job. We use these in self defense only."

"Sure, no problem."

As Moretti stuffed the .45 into his waistband at the small of his back under his jacket, I took the Glock out from under my arm and fed in one of the clips from my pocket. Before I returned the Glock to the holster, I switched on the laser aimer, just like Wilson had told me.

I turned to Moretti. "Let's get out and wait. This vest is killing me."

*    *    *

As Lincoln's Bell Long Ranger settled into a hover at 1200 feet, Lincoln tapped at the on-board computer's keyboard and waited for the screen to change. He turned and looked at Michael Cogan who was buckled into the seat to his right. Michael's hands were in his lap, bound with plastic restraints. His head was covered with a black hood.

Lincoln reached over and pulled the hood off Michael's head. Michael blinked to adjust to the daylight.

"Look at you. You look like shit, Cogan," Lincoln said shaking his head. "You need a shave, a shower, and a good shampooing. Personal hygiene's important, ya know? But I guess that's the least of your problems, isn't it?" Turning back to the computer. "Now we're gonna see if your friend has tried to fuck with me."

"Whadaya mean?"

"You'll see. Here it comes."

Michael watched the screen jump and flood with color. After a few moments, he was able to establish that it was an aerial view of several buildings and what appeared to be a tractor-trailer and a smaller vehicle parked in front of one of the two larger structures. The images were splotched with different primary colors as if a five-year-old had painted them.

Lincoln leaned into the screen and pointed at two small red blotches between the two vehicles. "One of these is probably your friend, Napolo. The other one must be the truck driver."

"What is this?" Michael asked.

"An infrared spectrum analysis," Lincoln answered, ever eager to tout his technical gadgetry. "Anything red or orange is hot. Then it goes greens to blues for cooler surfaces."

Michael saw that the hoods of the vehicles were deepest reds. Varying hues of red and orange spread across the rest of the vehicles. The blacktop surface of the yard and the roofs of the buildings were shades of lighter orange, and the surrounding vegetation was a mix of greens and blues.

Lincoln ran a finger across the screen over the area around the yard. Then he moved the mouse, clicked and dragged a square over a portion of the green/blue. He tapped the keyboard and the square enlarged, filling the screen. Lincoln leaned in again and examined the screen. After a few seconds, he touched the keys that returned the screen to the full view. Lincoln repeated the process six or seven times, each time selecting a different portion of the screen to enlarge and examine.

When he had completed inspecting the blue/green portion, he drew squares around each of the four buildings and the two vehicles. Once they were each enlarged, he ran a filter program that took about ten seconds to cycle. He explained to Michael that the filter program enhanced the analysis to allow temperature-specific hot points to be viewed through the roofs. The filter Lincoln was using sought out items ranging in temperature from 96 to 103 degrees Fahrenheit. If a human being, or any other object in that temperature range, was inside any of the buildings or vehicles, they would appear red and circled in white, separate and distinct from any other color or image on the screen. Only two circles appeared. They were between the two vehicles. Bobby Moretti and me.

Lincoln turned to Michael.

"You're lucky. Your partner used his head. But just in case . . ."

Lincoln stroked the keyboard and a window popped open in the upper left corner of the screen. In the window was the icon for the six-barreled minigun slung under the nose of the Bell Long Ranger, disguised as an electronic instrumentation pod. Lincoln dragged the sighting icon over and dropped the sights on one of the circles. He repeated the process for the other circle.

"What did you just do?" Michael asked.

"The minigun is now locked on those infrared signatures. If anything happens I don't like, Napolo and whoever he's with will be ripped to pieces. And, at sixty rounds a second, most of the pieces they find will fit into sandwich bags."

Michael cringed and let his bound hands wander over the spigot handle still in his pocket. While Lincoln had been concentrating on the screen, he had been using his fingers to turn the handle so that it was now properly positioned in his pocket, round handle near the top with the three-inch rusty spike pointed down. Unfortunately, the seatbelt was restricting his arms and he couldn't get his hands around to take it out of his pocket. But as soon as the seatbelt was undone . . .

"Randell," Lincoln said loudly into his lip mike, making Michael jump and move his hands away from his pocket. "Call Billy and DK. Tell 'em we got a green LZ and to drive over and wait for instructions. I've got the minigun sighted and locked. I'll release it back to you when we're on the ground. I'm switching to video. Take us down to 300 feet and hold. Keep your eyes open for any activity."

*       *       *

On the ground, Moretti and I heard the helicopter at the same time. We both looked up.

"That could be him," I said into the air.

The sound of a truck approaching on the far side of the semi drew our attention. A white truck, a Mitsubishi Fuso twenty-two foot cab-over straight job, pulled around behind us and stopped about fifteen yards from the rear of the trailer. Two men got out of the truck and stood by their open doors. Their black jeans and bulky black flak jackets gave them away. They were not New York State DOT employees.

I called over to them. "Where's Dwyer?"

Neither of them answered.

Louder this time. "Where's Dwyer?"

My cell phone rang in my back pocket. The two men glanced at each other through the open doors of their truck. I looked at Moretti and began to reach for my phone. As soon as my arm began to move, the two men reached inside the truck. Moretti grabbed my arm.

"They've got weapons on the seats," Moretti whispered barely moving his lips.

I saw what was happening and raised both palms in surrender. Then I smiled at the men and whispered to Moretti, "Be cool. Michael and the guy are probably in the chopper."

I called to the men again. "My phone's ringing."

One of the men, the smaller one, nodded and motioned with his hand.

I slowly reached for the phone and looked at the display. Private caller. I tapped a key and the phone went silent. I tossed it through the window of the Cherokee into the front seat.

I let my hands fall to his sides. The men at the truck did the same. Then the smaller one on the passenger side put his hand to his ear, obviously listening to an earpiece.

"We wanna see the merchandise," the one who had been listening called out.

"I wanna see my partner and the money, first," I shouted back.

The listener tugged at his collar and spoke into it. He cocked his head, listening again.

"The man says we gotta see the crate and then he brings down your partner."

"Okay," I said to the listener. "Stay where you are and we'll open the doors. The crate's on the tail."

The listener pointed at the trailer. "Okay, go ahead."

Moretti and I walked to the back doors of the DTC trailer. I stood to the side while Moretti began unlocking the swing doors. As Moretti worked the latches with his back to Lincoln's men, he whispered loud enough for only me to hear.

"Fold your arms across your chest with your right hand near the butt of that gun under your arm. When I swing the doors open, I'll go to the other side, you stay there. Use the door for cover if anything happens. Shoot for the legs first, our guns are no good against those flak jackets."

When the latches were open, Moretti let his right hand drop to his side, closer to the Colt under his jacket, and swung the heavy nine-foot doors open, pushing the right door towards me so I could grab it and walk it over until it was perpendicular to the trailer. Moretti did the same with the left door. There was now about twenty feet separating us. Moretti liked the advantage of having triangulated our field of fire, with the enemy at the apex.

The listener and his bigger partner took a step toward the open truck.

"Hold it!" I yelled and pointed to the listener. "Only you come forward and with your hands up."

As soon as I said it, I thought it sounded stupid. . . . *with your hands up! Could you sound any more like an amateur?* My thoughts were cut short.

"You," Moretti shouted, pointing at the bigger guy. "Step away from that truck."

The bigger guy looked at the listener but didn't move.

"You heard 'im," I said. "Take five giant steps to the left."

*Giant steps? Too much time with the kids.*

The listener raised his hands and nodded to his partner who shrugged in a no-big-deal way before he sidestepped away from the truck.

"Okay," I said. "Now you, come on over here."

The listener walked to the back of the DTC trailer and peered inside. The green metal crate sat about ten feet inside the trailer over the rear axle.

"Satisfied?" I asked.

"It's a green metal crate, all right. But what's inside?"

"You'll see as soon as I see my partner and the money."

"I need to put my hands down so I can contact the man."

"Okay," I said as I opened my jacket, revealing the Glock under his arm. "But be cool."

"Don't sweat it."

The listener pulled up his collar and spoke. "The crate's on the truck but he won't let me inside until he sees his partner, and the money."

The listener listened for a few seconds and then turned to me. "The man's coming down."

The sound of the helicopter rotors became louder. Moretti raised his voice above the noise. "Okay, you," talking to the listener. "Take a few steps back and sit down with your legs crossed." Then louder to the bigger guy. "You, too, get your big ass over here and sit with your legs crossed, like a good little Indian."

The big guy sauntered up to Moretti and leaned close. "Hey, fuck you, man."

"Fuck me?" Moretti stepped back and whipped out the .45 from behind his back, pointing it at the big guy's face. "No, fuck you! Now sit down, asshole. Both of youse fuck faces, make like Indians."

The big guy looked directly down the barrel of the Colt and smirked at Moretti.

"Okay, we'll see," he said, grinning as he sat down and crossed his legs.

I wondered if Moretti's move with the gun hadn't escalated the situation, but I couldn't argue with success. We had gained control. So far, we had the advantage. Moretti and his military experience were turning out to be quite valuable. Right now, I was very glad that I hadn't insisted on coming alone.

The prop wash from the helicopter's rotors was now whipping our hair and swirling debris and loose dirt around the yard.

"We should search these guys," I yelled to Moretti.

"No time," Moretti shouted back. "He's landing behind us. I'll watch these guys. You go." Then for affect. "These guys try anything, I'm gonna blow their fuckin' heads off. So be ready."

I turned around and squinted to see through the dust cloud. The Bell Long Ranger was touching down, settling onto its skids very close to the front of the DTC truck and my Cherokee. I glanced up at the rotor blades. Another six or eight feet, they would have been over the hood of the truck and the roof of the Jeep. Another fifteen feet, they would have ripped into the front of the trailer. Then I realized what was happening. The helicopter was blocking both vehicles. The Mitsubishi Fuso truck was blocking the back of the tractor-trailer. Moretti was occupied in the rear with the two goons, out of sight. And I was out front, alone, with the helicopter with at least three bad guys on board. Suddenly, our advantage seemed fleeting, at best.

I folded his arms across my chest again and wrapped my hand around the grip of the Glock. I fingered the safety, struggling to remember which position was off. I guessed and flipped the selector.

As the rotors of the Bell Long Ranger settled into an idle-speed spin, Lincoln slid the back door open and stepped out under the slowing turning blades. A chill crept up my spine as Lincoln began to walk toward me.

There was something unearthly about the way Lincoln moved. Something with the way his head turned on his neck and how his light gray eyes didn't need to squint or blink away the dust. How he didn't stoop and run under the spinning rotors as I had seen on television and the movies. Instead, he casually strolled over, seeming to be impervious to the whipping prop wash as if he was encased in a magical protective bubble, his sort-cropped hair remaining unruffled. Only the slight rippling of the sleeves and pant legs of his tight-fitting fight suit made him seem part of this world. He stopped ten paces in front of me, close enough to converse without shouting above the low whine of helicopter's idling turbines.

"So, Mr. Napolo, we meet again."

"Where's Michael?"

"In the chopper," Lincoln said jerking his head backward. "In the back seat."

I stepped sideways and looked, keeping my arms crossed and my hand on the Glock. Michael saw me and raised his cuffed hands in a wave.

"Get 'im out," I said to Lincoln.

"First things first." Pointing at my crossed arms. "Your body language tells me one of two things; you're either unreceptive to me or perhaps you've got a gun under your jacket."

"Maybe both."

"Either way, it's quite offensive. So, if it's a gun, please pull it out *slowly* and throw it under your truck."

I shook my head. "I don't think so."

"Oh, please, now you're insulting me. See that pod under the nose of the chopper pointed directly at you. Inside it there's a 7.62-millimeter minigun. It shoots 4000 rounds per minute. My crew chief's waiting for my signal. I step to the right and you turn into hamburger. So, let's cut the fuckin' bullshit. Throw your gun under the truck and tell your man to come over here and do the same."

I thought about the code words that Wilson had given me: *Time to go.* All I had to do was say those words and the cavalry would come swooping in. Snipers would open up on threatening targets. Flash grenades would explode. Moretti and I would roll under the trucks. And the SWAT team would race in and clean up with silenced small arms fire.

But it wasn't time to go, yet. First, I needed to get Michael out of the helicopter and Lincoln's hand in the cookie jar.

"Okay," I sighed. "I'm gonna take out my gun and put it under the truck."

"Do it *slowly*."

I took out the Glock and placed it on the ground. With my right foot, I slid it under the Cherokee.

"Good boy. Now call your guy. Tell him to bring my men around."

"Bobby," I called.

From behind the truck. "Yeah."

"Bring those guys over here."

"Why?"

"Change of plans."

"I don't think . . ."

"Bobby, listen to me. I need you to put your gun down and bring those guys around. Please do it now."

"Okay, boss."

The big guy used only his legs to push himself up on his feet. He grinned at Moretti. "Now who's the asshole, fuck face?"

Moretti lowered the Colt and shrugged, "We'll see."

The listener laughed. "Yeah, we sure will."

Lincoln's men came around from the back of the trailer followed by Moretti.

Lincoln's face lit up when he saw Moretti. "Well look who's here. My good friend with the punching bag face. This is a very pleasant surprise. I've been thinking about you since those Teamsters trashed my car."

Moretti grinned. "I figured that'd give you sumthin' to remember me by."

Lincoln's face went cold. "Throw your gun under the Jeep."

I looked back. "Go ahead, Bobby. Do what he says."

Moretti glared at Lincoln and tossed the .45 under the Cherokee.

"Still think you know me?" Lincoln asked Moretti.

Moretti nodded. "It'll come to me."

"DK," Lincoln said to the big guy. "See if you can jog his memory."

The big guy moved like a machine, a very quick machine, swinging around, arms and legs blurring through the air. When the brief martial arts ballet was over, Moretti was slumped against the rear wheels of the DTC tractor, barely conscious after the ferocious kick to the side of his face.

I tensed and became aware of the smaller Glock pressing against my back. I looked at Lincoln and at Michael, and at the crew chief in the open cockpit window and at the minigun. There was nothing I could do for Moretti, right now.

I swung back to Lincoln. "Let's get this over with."

"Good idea," Lincoln said. "Billy get the tools and open the crate."

"Bring Michael out," I said.

Lincoln smiled. "Sure, I'll get him."

Lincoln walked back under the slowly spinning rotors and reached into the doorway. Billy, the listener, got a duffel bag from the cab of the Mitsubishi Fuso and climbed into the trailer. The big guy, DK, stood to the side of me.

I watched Michael, hands bound, struggling to keep his balance as he stepped out of the helicopter. There was a thick bandage on his left hand and the deep cut on the swollen bruise above his left eye. Michael's hair was matted from sleep and dried blood. Lincoln led him over by the elbow.

"Michael, are you okay?"

Michael nodded, fear and anxiety tightening his face. "I'm okay, man. Sorry about this."

"What happened to your hand?"

"This guy shot me."

I jerked toward Lincoln. "You *shot* him? Why?"

Lincoln shrugged and smiled. "Because I felt like it."

I raised my chin and clenched my jaw. The big guy shuffled a little, preparing to thwart any move I might make.

"Relax, Joseph," Michael said. "It's not too bad. Let it go."

Lincoln turned to Michael. "Not too bad? How's this feel?"

Lincoln grabbed Michael's bandaged hand and squeezed hard. Michael groaned and hunched over, pinching his eyes tight against the pain.

I coiled my arms. "You fuck!"

I began to move toward Lincoln but the big guy grabbed my right shoulder and turned me. I spun around, ready, but the big guy was set to strike, knees bent, left arm up and right fist cocked and loaded.

"Joseph, don't!" Michael gasped between breaths. "These guys are crazy. Just give them what they what. Do what they say."

I slowly broke contact with the big guy and turned back to Lincoln.

"Where's the money? I want to see it, now."

"Hey, hey, hey, don't get pushy. I'm not one of your greasy wop errand boys. In fact, I've done the Feds a favor this week and thinned your ranks a little. In fact, I think you're probably gonna have to hold a recruiting drive. There are quite a few openings. Let's see," Lincoln looked up, feigning deep thought. "You're gonna need a couple new fat slobs and seven or eight more ginzos with very poor taste in fashion. First name Tony's a plus but Vinny, Sal, Dominick, or Paulie will do just fine. A stupid nickname is helpful but, if unavailable, one will be provided for you."

Lincoln belly laughed. I glared at him.

"Oh, what's a matter, Joey? No sense of humor? Even at a time like this a little levity is good for the soul. Hell, they say laughter can even cure cancer. You believe that?"

"*You* killed those men?"

Lincoln shrugged again and was about to answer when his eyes drifted from me to a point over my shoulder. I turned and saw Billy coming from behind the trailer.

"We got a problem, boss," Billy said, when he joined the group. "The serial number doesn't match."

"Are you sure?" Lincoln asked.

"It's off by one digit. We're lookin' for the last five digits AQ1101. This one's AQ1102."

Lincoln closed his eyes and shook his head slowly. Then his lids snapped open like they were spring-loaded and he pulled Michael roughly to him. Lincoln pressed the muzzle of his Glock against Michael's temple.

"Wand those two," he said to his men.

Billy tossed DK a device from the toolbox. It had a black handle with an oblong loop of metal on one end. He switched it on and bent to Moretti, who was still dazed. He passed the loop over Moretti's body, arms, and legs. DK stood and shook his head. Then he stepped up to me and stopped the wand at my neck, showing the tiny flashing red lights to Lincoln. He continued down my body, stopping each time the red lights lit up, at my pocket, my waistband and my pant cuff.

Lincoln clenched his teeth and grunted, "Fuck!"

Lincoln made scissors motions with his fingers. DK pulled a large folding knife from his pocket and flipped open the blade.

"Time to go," I said, a little too loud.

"Go? You're not going anywhere," Lincoln said and nodded at DK.

I saw Michael's eyes widen. I turned and saw DK bringing the knife up toward my neck. I tensed and pulled away but DK grabbed my collar and yanked my back, holding me firmly. I braced myself and tightened my biceps. I wasn't going to just stand there and let this guy stab me.

But DK's grip loosened and he began to feel along the collar of my jacket until he found the small lump. He sliced into the material and ripped out the transmitter. He showed the tiny device to Lincoln before he crushed it under his boot. I hoped that my message had been heard.

Next, to my surprise, DK cut off the flap on my jacket pocket, found the transmitter and put it under his heel. When the wand reached my waist, I thought about the Glock still clipped to my belt against my back.

"I'll do it," I said, pulling the waistband of my boxer shorts out of his pants.

DK felt along the elastic until he found it. He used his knife and boot again. When he bent to my pant cuff, I imagined kicking him in the face, but the thought quickly passed. DK was a large, muscular man with a long, sharp knife and there was little doubt that Lincoln's reaction would be a bullet in the head for Michael. Besides, the rescue operation might only be seconds away.

After the transmitter had been cut from my cuff and destroyed, Lincoln lowered his pistol and stuck it under Michael's chin.

"What kind of game do you think you're running, Napolo? Who's on the other end of those transmitters."

"Let's just say that Michael and I have a lot of good friends, Mr. *Lincoln*."

Lincoln grinned broadly and let his head loll to the left. Then, using the muzzle of his pistol, he turned Michael's face to him. Looking into Michael's eyes, he said to me, "If you know my name then you know my reputation. So why don't you tell your friend that I won't hesitate to blow his fuckin' head off if you don't tell me who you're transmitting to."

I looked up at the spinning rotors, creating an opportunity to glance around, hoping to catch a glimpse of the assault team beginning their attack. I detected no movement. They were either very stealthy or waiting for something. Maybe Lincoln was too close to Michael for a clean shot. Perhaps Lincoln's gun under Michael's chin presented too great a risk. Or, were they waiting until they had the clear evidence they wanted, no matter what the apparent danger was?

"Okay," I said. "You made your point. My men over in the rest stop were monitoring the transmitters. They have the videotape from the terminal. The plan was for me to signal them to bring the tape when I saw the money."

Lincoln squinted at me. "Why don't I believe you?"

313

I shrugged. "I don't know."

"Where'd you get the set-up?"

"We bought it - at the spy store."

Lincoln looked at his two men and chuckled. "Isn't that great. They sell this stuff at the malls now. All you need is a MasterCard and you're in the spy business." Then to me. "Where'd you get the item on the truck? Who you working with?"

"That's another shipment from FirsTech we got yesterday. We had to use it because we couldn't get to the original one on time. What's the difference? It's the same thing."

Lincoln squinted at me and shook his head. Then he removed the Glock from under Michael's chin and waved it in my face as he spoke. "So lemme get this straight. You come here today, somehow knowing who I am, with dummy merchandise and a half-assed plan to rip me off. Did you really think you were gonna pull this off? Are you that stupid?"

"What's so stupid about it? I still haven't seen the money. Maybe you thought you'd rip me off? Maybe I was just being careful?"

"Careful? You might just get yourself and your friends killed being careful. Did you consider that?"

"Sure. But I don't think you'll do that. Because if you do, you'll never get the original crate or the tape and you'll never know if the one on the truck is real or not - not until you take it somewhere and test it. Besides, you don't know who I've talked to and what they'll do with that information if we're harmed or killed."

Lincoln laughed. "You watch too many movies, Joey. In the movies, the guy who's me cares about that stuff. I don't. I'm a ghost. I'm untouchable. The movie rules don't apply to me. Because I'll not only waste you and your fuckin' friends but then I might go visit your wives and kids, and who knows what I'll do to them. One thing for sure, you'll never know, but you'll die wondering. Either way, afterwards I become invisible again and I'm gone. Somewhere else, living my life, going on and on, doing the things I do over and over again, never once - not for a fuckin' New York second - thinking again about you or your family. So let's cut the bullshit." Grabbing Michael again and putting the muzzle of the Glock against his temple. "Where's the fucking crate?"

"It's safe. Where's the money?"

Lincoln eyes flashed. "You got some balls, Napolo."

"No, I've just got the crate. And I know how badly you want it."

"Fuck you," Lincoln said as he reached over and twisted Michael's hand again. Michael screamed and doubled over. Tears welled in his eyes.

I made use of the moment, furtively scanning the periphery for signs of the assault. *Why weren't they coming?* Lincoln's gun had been down long enough. A marksman could have taken him out. They noise of the helicopter's idling turbines would have masked the early sounds of the team rushing in. A perfect opportunity had been lost. *Where were they? What would it take?*

Lincoln shoved Michael toward the one called Billy. "Put him back in the chopper."

"What a minute," I said. "I agree. Let's cut the crap and finish this."

"Too, late. I saw the way you're looking around. We've been here too long already. But you're right; I want that crate and the tape. So here's the deal. We'll call today the dress rehearsal. You need more practice. So you page me in two hours. I'll tell you where and when you're gonna deliver the crate and the tape. You try any more cute tricks like today and everybody dies. Understand?"

I nodded. "Yeah, but why don't we just plan on meeting here tomorrow, same time."

"No."

"Why?"

"Because I don't want to."

"Well, frankly, I'm comfortable here and as far as Michael goes, well he got me into this shit in the first place. I certainly don't want to see anything happen to him, but I'm not puttin' myself or my family's lives on the line for him either. So, if you want the crate, you meet me here tomorrow with the money. If not, well that's up to you."

Lincoln stared at me for a long ten seconds. "Okay, have it your way. Just don't forget what I told you about fuckin' with me. Tomorrow's no rehearsal. Real life, or death. You understand me."

"Yeah."

"By the way, you know what's in the crate?"

"No idea. Some kind of military hardware."

Lincoln rotated his head. "And why don't I believe you?"

I shrugged. "I don't know."

Lincoln looked over at Moretti who was alert, sitting with his back against the rear tandem wheel of the truck. He was pressing the sleeve of his jacket against his upper lip. Moretti saw Lincoln looking at him and straightened his back against the tire, letting his arm fall into his lap. His upper lip was badly split. The slice was deep and swollen, leaving a bloody inverted V-shaped gap in his mustache.

"Ouch, that's gonna need a few stitches." Lincoln said to Moretti. "Does it hurt?"

"Fuck you."

Lincoln shrugged. "Anything else you wanna get off your chest before I go?"

"Yeah, I remember you now."

Lincoln walked over and stood above him. "Oh, really?"

"Knew all the time actually."

Lincoln reached into his jacket and pulled out the silenced .22. He pointed at Moretti's face. "I doubt it. But just in case . . ." Over his shoulder to me. "Hey, Joey, you a good speller?"

Moretti and I both took notice of the new gun and exchanged worried glances.

"I asked you a question, Napolo. Are you a good speller?"

"Why?"

"Because if you can't spell chrysanthemum, I'm gonna waste this wise-assed motherfucker. That's why."

Moretti looked back and forth between Lincoln and me.

"Spell chrysanthemum. Do it now." Lincoln said, still staring at Moretti.

"Are you serious?"

"Technically, that's a wrong answer. But since this is a rehearsal of sorts, I'll give you one more chance." Cocking the revolver. "Spell chrysanthemum, Joey."

Moretti looked up at me. *Do it!* His eyes commanded.

I began, "C-H-R-Y-S-A-N-T-H . . ." *Fuck*, I wasn't sure, is it *E or I? E or I?* Moretti shrugged. He wasn't either. I let the word repeat in my head. I took deep breath.

"E-M-U-M." I finished quickly and closed his eyes.

"Correct." Lincoln turned to me. "College boy?"

"Yeah, I went to college."

Turning back to Moretti. "Oh, then you've got to spell two words. How about . . . rhododendron?"

I took a breath and exhaled loudly. "Rhododendron. R-H-O-D . . . O . . . D-E-N . . . D-R-O-N."

"Very good, college boy."

Lincoln pointed the muzzle of the .22 at the sky and thumbed the hammer back down. Looking at Moretti. "Too bad. But I'm a man of my word." Facing me again with the pistol pointed at my chest. "I hope you are, too. Or else . . ." he said, stretching his arm and pressing the tip of the silencer against my nose. "Bang, everybody's dead."

I looked over the top of the gun, into Lincoln's eyes. They were gray and cold and limitless like a flat winter sky. I peered deeper, searching for a spark of humanity lurking within, seeking a remnant of conscience buried somewhere there in the dust of the dead. But there was none. No soul, just a hollowed out human being, carved away by too much evil, unbalanced by even an ounce of goodness.

Oddly, I was suddenly calmed. The stress of the last twenty-four hours seemed to lift away. I felt the corners of my mouth curl up in an equally peculiar smile. My fear of what would happen next had just been replaced with the certainty of what I would never let happen again.

Reaching up with the tip of my finger, I pushed the barrel of the pistol away from my nose and said to Lincoln, "You're a real asshole."

Lincoln laughed and turned to his men. "Let's go."

I watched Lincoln's men climb into the Mitsubishi Fuso and then swung around to see Lincoln board the helicopter, sliding the door closed behind him. The helicopter's turbines whined louder and the rotor blade tips lifted as they picked up speed. I turned my back to the rotor wash and offered a hand to help Moretti to his feet. The Mitsubishi Fuso was already exiting the yard, heading onto the southbound lanes of the thruway. When I turned back to the chopper it was inside a whirlwind of dust. I squinted up at the rotors spinning so close to the front of our Freightliner. Just a few yards more and they would be ripping into the air foil on top of the cab and just beyond that they would tear into the front of the trailer. Then the Bell Long Ranger lifted gently off the ground, tilted forward, and skimmed the surface before it lifted again, higher and faster this time. I followed it up and around, and as it banked north I saw Michael in the window looking down at me.

I began to raise my arm to wave to Michael but I hesitated and stopped myself. I didn't know how to send the proper signals; that Ilene and the kids were okay, and that because good men will sometimes do bad things, everything would soon be right again.

317

# CHAPTER 26
## Bella Collina
## Livingston Manor, New York

Wilson Dennis and Nicolas Pucci had sat silently watching the encounter at the maintenance yard on the monitors in Nicolas' private study. When Lincoln's helicopter lifted off, Wilson swiveled his chair toward Nicolas and stared. Nicolas removed his steepled fingers from between his eyebrows and let them intertwine to form a platform for his chin. His eyes drifted down to the carpet.

The ringing tone from Wilson's cell phone broke the silence.

"It's him, isn't it?" Nicolas said, looking up at one of the monitors that showed me with my cell phone to my ear.

"This should be interesting," Wilson deadpanned as he pressed the speaker button on the phone.

"This is Wilson Dennis."

"You mind tellin' me what the fuck happened to your *team*? Where the fuck were they? Waiting for us to get killed, for chrissake?"

"We didn't get the evidence we needed. We needed to witness the exchange and Lincoln taking possession. You knew the rules."

"Fuck the rules. Our protection was supposed to be top priority. That asshole had a gun to our heads several times. Tell your men to come out and show themselves. I wanna see them. I wanna see where they are."

"I can't communicate with them."

"Bullshit! You had transmitters all over me and you expect me to believe that? Tell them to come out, *now*."

"I can't do that. Lincoln might still be in the area. We can't risk him seeing them. It could jeopardize your meeting tomorrow."

Nicolas shot Wilson a look. Wilson caught it and returned a puzzled shrug. Nicolas shook his head.

"Lincoln's long gone. I wanna see them . . . just one of 'em."

"I won't do that. It's too dangerous."

"Won't or can't? Maybe there's no one out there."

Wilson paused. "Why don't you come back here and we'll talk."

"*Talk?* My family, my friend and his family are in serious danger. What do you think I want to talk to you about? Maybe some more fuckin' stories about my grandfather . . . shit that any good researcher could find out? Frankly, Wilson, I can't believe what's goin' on here or that I can trust anything you say."

"Believe that I'm on your side, Joseph. Don't ever forget that."

"Right now, that scares the shit outta me. So, now I'm gonna handle this my way. To hell with you and Pucci and your goddam HAWIRE."

Nicolas leaned to the phone.

"Joseph, Nicolas here. Don't be stupid. You're outta your league."

"That's no longer your concern."

"What about our deal. There's twenty million for you and your partner at stake."

"Our deal? That's laughable."

"Look Joseph, we need the original HAWIRE and you know how to get it. Lincoln's scheduled to deliver it to the Lufthansa air cargo terminal at Newark Airport tomorrow by five o'clock. That's why he's pushing so hard. And if you haven't figured it out by now, this is a sting operation. Lincoln was supposed to take the first shipment and deliver it to Lufthansa. We were gonna take him down at the airport along with his contacts there. Obviously, that plan went out the window when Anelli took the wrong trailer. Now you're involved whether you like it or not."

"You're wrong. I'm no longer involved. As of right now, I'm out of this as far as you're concerned. And don't you get it? I don't care about the money. This was never about money. It's all about Michael and our families, and getting our lives back. And you just demonstrated that you don't give a shit about us. So I want this over with between us. Bobby's got to get to a hospital and then he'll return the crate on the truck to you. After that we're fuckin' done."

"I don't think so," Nicolas said clenching his jaw. "We've got today's meeting on tape - video tape. With a little creative editing, it could be very incriminating for you. You know I won't hesitate to use it. So you're not done 'till I say so. And now that we know that Lincoln has the serial number of the first HAWIRE, that's the one that has to get to Lufthansa by five tomorrow. If and when that happens, the tape gets destroyed, your confidential informant status is intact, and, as a gesture of our appreciation, you can have the money - all of it will get released to you immediately. If it doesn't happen, the tape will be another piece of damning evidence that I'll see is used against you and your partner. So, if it's your family you're concerned about, start thinking how they'll fare while you're serving a life sentence in federal prison for espionage and treason."

I pressed the cell phone against my thigh and cursed under my breath. I paced to the left and right and then turned unwittingly back at the cameras in the roof rack. I brought the cell phone back to my ear.

I said, "If the crate gets to Lufthansa by five tomorrow then this is over?"

Wilson nodded at Nicolas.

"Over, and you're a rich man," Nicolas said.

"Then send my attorney an addendum to the agreement that states exactly that; if the crate gets to Lufthansa by five tomorrow, the money gets released immediately."

"We'll need proof of delivery before the money is released."

"How the hell am I gonna get a P.O.D. to you? I'm not gonna be deliverin' the damn the thing."

"Lincoln knows how to make the delivery," Wilson said. "The contact at the Lufthansa cargo terminal is a guy on the receiving dock named Rudy. But Rudy doesn't know Lincoln. He's just looking for the crate - it doesn't matter who delivers it. Just see that the crate gets tendered to Rudy. That'll do it. You understand?"

"No other stipulations?"

"No."

"Okay. Get that into the Addendum - the delivery to Rudy."

"Consider it done."

"I'll be calling my attorney in two hours to check. By the way, Wilson, how did you know about tomorrow's meeting?"

"We were listening - the transmitters, remember?"

"The four transmitters hidden in my clothes?"

"Yes."

"Oh, that's funny. They were all found and destroyed before we discussed the meeting. There must be another one. Where is it?"

Nicolas shook his head at Wilson.

"I think you're mistaken," Wilson said. "There are no other transmitters."

"And the cameras?"

"My men . . ."

"Right, your men. Just get that addendum to my attorney and I'll take care of my end. Good-bye *gentlemen.*"

I hung up and dropped the cell phone. I put my heel to it and stomped it into the gravel next to the broken transmitters.

Moretti asked, "Whada we doin' now, boss?"

"You're goin' to the hospital and getting that lip looked at. I'm afraid Lincoln was right, you're gonna need a few stitches. Head into Newburgh. There's gotta be a hospital there. Then I need you to return that damn crate back to FirsTech and head home. Get some rest."

"What about tomorrow?"

"I don't know yet."

"I want in, boss. No matter what, I wanna be there."

"Why? I almost got you killed today, Bobby."

"Fuck those assholes. I don't know what you have in mind for tomorrow, but I know I'd like a shot at some good ol' fashion payback."

I eyed him for a long moment and nodded. "I'll call you later. I need to get some different clothes and something else to drive."

Nicolas swiveled his chair toward Wilson. "We're gonna lose him if he changes vehicles."

"He'll be back there tomorrow at two. It's the only chance he has of getting his partner back. And he knows the crate has to get to the airport. I think we're okay."

Nicolas took a deep breath and sat back in his chair. "You fucked up, Wilson. You confused the sequence of events and tipped him off. It's not like you. Should I be worried?"

Wilson put his hands up. "An honest mistake. Nobody's perfect."

"You used to be."

"I used to be a lot of things."

## Hertz Car Rentals
## Newark Liberty International Airport
## Newark, New Jersey

"What time tomorrow will you be returning the car, Mr. Napolo?" A pleasant African-American woman in a Hertz uniform asked.

"About five o'clock."

Click-click-click. Long nails on the keyboard.

"Do you want the insurance coverage?"

"Yes, hundred percent coverage, no deductible."

Click-click. Click.

"Do you want to buy the gas or return the car full?"

"I'll buy the gas."

Click. Click-click. Click.

The printer under the counter tap-tapped and the woman tore off the contract. "Please initial here and here for the gas and the insurance, and down here for the cell phone, and sign here at the bottom. Do you need any directions?"

"No, thank you."

I signed the form and waited for the woman to separate the parts and stuff my copy into the folder.

"It's the black Lincoln Town Car in space number seventeen. The keys are in the car."

"Thank you."

"Mr. Napolo, do you know you have a tag on your sleeve?"

I looked at my sleeves. There was a Macy's tag hanging from the left cuff of my new jacket. It was dark blue, light weight with lots of pockets and Velcro and zippers.

"New jacket," I said, as I tore the tag off.

"Give it here," she said, palm up on the counter.

"Thanks."

"Oh, that's okay. I know how it is. One time, I went on this blind date and I had tags hangin' out the back of my dress all night. I was so embarrassed. I thought that man would never call me again."

I made a face, hoping to look sympathetic, trying to make a getaway, but found myself asking, "So, did he?"

"Oh, yes he did. He's my husband now. Ya know, he never did mention those tags. Maybe he never saw 'em."

"Maybe. Have a good day."

"You, too, Mr. Napolo."

I found the Town Car in space seventeen. Before I got in, I checked my shirt and pants for tags. I had bought a complete set of clothes including underwear, socks and shoes, at the Macy's in the Paramus Mall on my way down from New York. To the saleslady's surprise, I changed in the dressing room, carrying my old clothes out in the bag. They were now locked in my Jeep with the Kevlar vest, the holsters, and everything else that had once been at The Smoke and Gun Club except for the two Glocks, the Colt 1911, and the extra loaded clips I was carrying in the Macy's bag.

I exited the Hertz lot mentally retracing my steps, checking that I had taken every precaution possible. All the things that could have been electronically bugged by Wilson and Pucci were in the Cherokee sitting in the Hertz lot. I had used my credit card at Macy's and to rent the car. But the trail would stop at Hertz. Even if they were able to check what I rented, black Lincoln Town Cars were the vehicles of choice for hundreds of livery and limousine companies in the metro New York area. At any one time, there were probably a couple thousand of them cruising the streets of Manhattan and all the highways, bridges, and tunnels around the city and the three major airports.

I had picked up three rolls of quarters at the bank in the mall to use in the payphones along my route. In case payphones weren't convenient, I had the rented a cell phone from Hertz.

Cathy had been my first call. I called her from the bank of payphones just past the Paramus toll plaza on the Parkway as soon as I had left the mall. After explaining I would not be seeing them until tomorrow, I told her she had to change hotels. The one they were staying at was in a cluster of mid-range national chains. I told her to move to the one in the southwest corner. The fear in her voice was mixed with impatience and growing anger. I did my best to calm her down but failed miserably. She handed the phone to Joseph Jr. in frustration.

I talked to my three boys and pumped quarter after quarter into the phone, not wanting the call to end. Finally, when I had said good-bye to each of them, I asked Cathy to please bear with me for one more day. I promised her it would be over tomorrow night, knowing that I was leaving her angry, afraid and alone, and with the difficult task of explaining to the kids and Ilene why they had to switch hotels. More difficult, I knew, would be her believing my promise that by tomorrow night everything would be back to normal. I finished the call, knowing that this was one of those times, that no matter how hard you tried there was nothing more you could do or say.

I took a few deep breaths to push away a strong nicotine craving that had crept up on me. Then I pumped a few more quarters into the phone and dialed the office. Samantha read off a list of twelve or fifteen messages. I gave her follow-up instructions after each of them except for two. The calls from Albert Catella and "Jimmy from New York" I would handle myself.

I had Sam transfer me into the dispatch office. Carlos, the head dispatcher, always had at least a couple calls on hold waiting for him. He took my call immediately. Carlos' job required him to be expert in brief yet effective conversations. His report was succinct. Busy but no major problems. The Teamster's picket line was down to six well-behaved men. He put me on hold.

Janie Steple had followed my call into dispatch. She had an important message and picked up the extension. The Newark office of the National Labor Relations Board had called. Local 714 had withdrawn their unfair labor practice charge and would no longer oppose a decertification vote.

The NLRB was wondering if Monday would be a convenient day to hold the balloting. I told Janie the sooner the better and to get back to them to arrange it for Monday.

Next I called my cell phone's voice mailbox. Five messages. Three were inconsequential. The other two were a second set of urgent pleadings for callbacks from Albert Catella and "Jimmy from New York". I had decided to postpone the calls until I was rid of the Cherokee and any potential electronic surveillance.

The Town Car was a big change from the Cherokee. It drove like a boat, just quieter. I looked at my watch. It was four forty-eight as I steered the Town Car into the Marriott Hotel on the airport property. Taking advantage of the car's for-hire appearance, I parked near the entrance and found the bank of payphones off the lobby.

I dialed the pager number Jimmy Merchanti had given me. After tapping in the number of the payphone to Jimmy's pager, I moved to the next phone and called Catella at Local 714.

Catella picked up quickly. "Joseph, I'm glad ya called."

"Albert, I'm returning your call and, ah, thanks for backing off the NLRB. They're gonna allow a vote on Monday."

"No problem. But, I need a favor - for a friend of mine. I need to talk ta ya, in private."

"I need a favor, too, Albert."

"When can we talk? It needs to be soon, though."

"Me, too," I said. "Soon, I mean. Tonight."

"Okay, where and when?"

"I'm not sure yet, I need to make a call first.

"Where are ya now?"

"At the airport. But I'm not sure where I'll be later."

"Can ya call me back at six, then. I'll give ya a number but you have ta call from a payphone."

"Okay, shoot."

I jotted the number on the jacket of the car rental contract.

"Joseph, please call me. It's very important. If the number's busy, just call right back. It's a payphone."

"I'll call exactly at six."

"Great. Talk to ya later."

I moved over to the payphone that I had used to page Jimmy Merchanti. I picked up a discarded copy of USA Today on the table across from the payphones. The large two-line headline on the front page read, *Mob War Bloodies New York.* I scanned the article. Russian mobsters were turning up dead all over the city. So far, seventeen bodies had been found, eleven of them in the Brighton Beach section of Brooklyn. Residents of Brighton Beach, many of whom are Russian immigrants, told of their concern for the safety of their families and were staying off the streets whenever possible. Area merchants complained of a fifty percent drop in business and were calling for stepped up efforts to halt the violence. The mayor expressed frustration with the lawlessness and was pledging all his resources to bring the perpetrators to justice. The joint organized crime task force had no comment when asked if they had any suspects in the killings of the Russians. Notably, no members of the Napolo Crime Family or any other Italian mobsters had been victims since the slayings at the Taverna Reggia.

I was turning to the inside page where the story continued when the payphone rang.

I answered, "Hello?"

"Is this Joseph?"

"Yes."

"It's me, Jimmy. Where have I called? Can you talk?"

"A little. I'm in a hotel lobby, on a payphone."

"Good. Is everything okay with you?"

"Yes and no. You?"

"Same as you. How about your partner?"

"Not too good, right now."

"How bad?"

"Could be a lot better but nothing final yet."

"Hmm," Jimmy grunted. "Maybe I can help."

"Maybe. I need to talk to you. I have some information you should hear."

"Where are you? Can ya get into the city?"

"Aren't they watching you. I don't need that right now."

"I'm sure they're lookin' but they'll only see me if I want them to. We know how to play. Trust me, no one will see you. Besides, I really need ya to come into the city - to meet with someone."

"Who?"

"Can't say."

"Well then I don't have time for meetings. But I do have a proposition for you. One I think you'll be very interested in after I tell you what I learned."

"Anything you have to tell me he'll have to hear anyway. It's important that you accept his invitation. For both of us."

"Tell me who it is then."

"I can't say his name. It's not allowed. Ya understand?"

I remembered reading something about that. "I think so but I don't think it's a good idea."

"This person can help you with your problem. He knows you're in trouble and he just wants to help."

"Why?"

"Think about it, will ya?"

I did. "Money, love, sex, or power? Those are usually the reasons people do things. Which is it?"

"Well, at his age, it ain't sex, but the other three may qualify."

I looked at my watch. "Okay, but it's got to be soon."

"How long will it take you to get to the Village?"

"It's rush hour, so half an hour - maybe forty-five."

"Okay. So, you're gonna meet me at a place on Christopher Street between Waverly and Greenwich. There'll be a parking space for you around the block at the corner of West Eighth and Fifth. There'll be a guy there in a dark blue Caddy holdin' a space for ya on the southwest corner of West Eighth. When he sees ya, he'll pull out, you pull in. Whadarya drivin'?"

"A new black Lincoln Town Car."

"Nice."

"It's a rental."

"Hey, we can arrange something."

"Never mind that."

"Okay. After ya park, look for another guy, an older guy, on the corner wearing a light green jacket and black pants. Follow him through the alleys. Stay behind him so it don't look like you're following 'im. He'll walk past the back loading dock of City Linens. I'll meet you out back there. Okay?"

"Okay. See ya in a while."

I hung up and looked at my watch again. It was just five o'clock. I dialed the number for Teamster Local 714.

Catella came on the line.

"Albert, Joseph again. I won't be able to call you at six. How 'bout we meet somewhere later, about ten?"

"Where?"

"I don't know. I need a hotel or motel that takes cash and won't ask for a credit card. Any suggestions?"

"Sure. The Oasis on Route 1 in Jersey City. No one will bother ya there. It's got a lounge, too."

"Sounds okay. Can you get a hold of your friend from Perth Amboy?"

"Ya mean my friend who knows your partner?"

"Uh huh."

"Yeah, I think so."

326

"Can you bring him with you tonight?"

"Probably."

"It's important."

"I can make it happen. In fact, he wanted me to give you a message. Now he can give it to you himself."

"Good. Ten o'clock okay for you, at the Oasis, in the lounge?"

"Yeah, sure. Ten o'clock in the lounge."

## City Linens
## Greenwich Village, New York City

Two white sixteen-foot step vans were backed up to the outdoor loading platform in the alley behind City Linens. Jimmy Merchanti was standing just inside the personnel door on the truck docks. He was wearing a white cap and matching white coveralls with the blue City Linens logo embroidered over his right breast. "Stanley" was stitched in the blue-bordered oval patch. He waved me over and disappeared inside the doorway. I glanced down the alley. It was deserted. The old man in the green jacket I'd been following was nowhere to be seen.

I climbed the steps to the loading platform. Outside the open door Merchanti had entered, I could smell the strong odors of bleach and detergent. I stepped inside where the air was warmer and the smells stronger. I could hear the low rumbling noise from the large commercial laundry equipment and steam hissing from the pressing machines. I looked around, waiting for my eyes to adjust to the darker interior.

I heard the door close behind me and turned to see Jimmy Merchanti holding out a pair of City Linens white coveralls to me.

"Put these on. He's waiting for us."

I took them from him and said, "Nice to see you, too . . . *Stanley?*"

Merchanti looked down at his patch and smiled. "Funny, but the man doesn't like to be kept waiting. So slip those on . . ." Holding up the shoulders of coveralls in my hands and looking at the patch. " . . . *Leo.*"

I stepped into the coveralls and zipped up the front. I looked down. The pant legs were short. I tugged them down.

"You look fine. Put this on and let's go," Merchanti said, handing me a white City Linens cap.

I followed him down the loading dock and into the back of the step van. The driver had the engine started before Merchanti had closed the rear doors of the truck. We sat on a wood bench that had been bolted to the inside wall. After a left turn on Christopher Street and another quick left onto Waverly Place, we pulled into the gated service entrance to the Waverly Place Arms.

The driver reached out the window and pressed the button on the speaker box.

He said to the grill on the box, "City Linens."

The gates opened. We drove around back where the driveway dipped below street level and waited for the overhead door to finish opening. Once inside the underground service garage, the door closed behind us and the driver parked head-in to the loading area.

Merchanti wheeled a laundry cart brimming with folded linens to the rear doors. The doors swung open and the driver helped Merchanti lower the laundry cart to the ground.

"Wait in the van for us," Merchanti said to the driver. Then he looked over at me. "Let's go Leo."

I joined Merchanti on the ground and waited while he closed the van's door, leaving the driver inside sitting on the bench shuffling a deck of cards.

"You push. I'll pull," Merchanti said to me as he grabbed the front of the laundry cart.

Merchanti led us through a neat and very clean rubbish room with several metal chutes in the ceiling that fed a trash compactor and two large bins for recyclables. The air was densely scented with a sickly sweet floral deodorizer. The smell made me wonder about chrysanthemums and rhododendrons.

Further down the hall, past an area of locked storage closets was the service elevator. Merchanti pushed the laundry cart against the wall and began unzipping his coveralls.

"Take those off and put them in here," Merchanti said, throwing his cap into the laundry cart.

I complied and followed Merchanti into the elevator. Merchanti put his finger to his lips to warn me not to speak. Then he took a key from his pocket and inserted into the control panel. The doors closed and Merchanti pressed the button for the fifth floor. We spent the ride straightening our clothes and finger combing our hair, checking our reflections in the shiny steel control panels.

When the doors opened on the fifth floor, Merchanti again put his finger to his lips and leaned out into the hallway. Merchanti looked left and right. He waved to someone down the hall and then motioned for me to follow him. I stepped into the hallway and saw two men heading back into an apartment at the end of the hall. One of them was carrying a 12-gauge pump shotgun with a pistol grip and the other had a silenced automatic machine pistol, enough firepower to turn the narrow hall into a bloody kill zone.

At the door to apartment 511, I heard a loud television. Merchanti knocked once, paused and knocked two more times. He turned to face the end of the hall.

Inside 511, Fabrizio Benedetto heard the knocks and switched the television to channel 3. The screen split into quadrants; four views from the closed circuit cameras in the hallway and elevators. In the lower left picture, Merchanti was standing outside the door facing the camera. Benedetto switched back to MSNBC, rolled his wheel chair to the door, unlocked the deadbolt, and rolled the chair back to give the door room to open.

Merchanti led me inside and locked the door behind us. Benedetto made a slight gestured with his hand and Merchanti wheeled him over to his place in front of the television. I waited by the door, taking in the sparsely furnished living room until Benedetto looked over at me and patted the arm of the chair next to him. I crossed the room and sat. Merchanti took a seat across from us.

Benedetto cleared his throat and extended his right hand to me. It was a boney hand and the flesh was loose and cool, but the grip was firm. Benedetto covered my hand with his left and guided our hands down onto the arm of his wheelchair. Benedetto looked down at our clasped hands.

"I remember the last time I was with your grandfather like it was yesterday. He took my hand in his just like this and kissed me good-bye." Benedetto looked into my face. "You have his eyes, the lids, and his mouth. Do you remember him? You were just a boy when he died."

"Yes, of course, we spent most Sundays together."

Benedetto nodded. "I came to your father's house on several occasions."

"I remember men coming to see him after dinner."

"What else do you remember? What do you know about him?"

"I remember him as my grandfather. The rest I mostly learned from books and TV, some from my father."

"Do you know he wanted to protect you from his business and his life? Do you understand that he went to his death with my word that I would use all my power to ensure that his family never got involved?"

"I knew that he never wanted my father to be involved. That's why he made him go to dental school."

Benedetto chuckled but quickly lost his breath and began coughing and gasping for air. He let my hand go and gripped the arms of the wheel chair. Merchanti shifted forward, hesitating, not wanting to offer his assistance too soon and risk embarrassing the Don. The fit continued uncomfortably long. Merchanti exchanged glances with me and got to his feet.

"Should I get you the oxygen, Don Fabrizio?"

Benedetto waved him off. Merchanti slowly stepped back and felt his way back into his chair not taking his eyes off of Benedetto, watching the old man struggle until the spasms subsided.

"Sorry," Benedetto continued slowly after gathering his breath. "I was just remembering how your grandfather used say, 'Imagine, my son a dentist, wearing those funny shoes.' Then he'd laugh. But we all knew how proud he was. There was no way he could hide it. Once he said to me, 'Think how nice it would be to spend your life fixing people's smiles.' He wouldn't let any of us go to him to get our teeth fixed, though. Only the judges and policemen and other important friends could go. And they did. He was a good dentist, I hear. How is your father?"

"He's well. He's retired."

"Good for him."

Benedetto's gaze drifted to the television. The MSNBC pundit was summarizing the day's Wall Street activity. Benedetto shook his head.

"Do you play the market, Joseph?"

"No, not really. I have some investments, but they're conservative, long-term."

"I play. I even trade on-line. My caretaker's son taught me how to use the computer. My doctor doesn't like it, though. Says it gets me too upset. Says it's gonna kill me. Imagine that . . ." Benedetto raised his eyebrows and smirked, ". . . after all these years."

I let the old man's charm work on me. I smiled.

Benedetto glanced at the television again briefly and then slowly swung back to me. Then in a tone that melted the smile on my face, he said, "You know would break your grandfather's heart to see you sitting here with me. And for me, it means I have broken my vow to him and that breaks *my* heart. You must understand that I do this only because I believe he would do the same if he were here. Even so, this is a serious matter for me; one that leaves me with great conflict. So I must ask you, why?"

"Why? Why am I here?"

Benedetto's watery eyes flashed with anger. "Don't play games with me! I'm too old and tired for that. You are here because I wanted you here!" He coughed several times. "Now tell me why you've let your grandfather down like this? Why have you become involved in such a mess?"

I sat up, feeling like I'd been slapped in the face. And then it hit me. I looked at Merchanti who was frowning, clearing playing to Benedetto. I swung back to Benedetto, my eyes pinched.

"With all due respect, Mr. Benedetto, to hell with my grandfather. If it weren't for him, and guys like him and the two of you, frankly, my family wouldn't be hiding from a psychopath, my friend wouldn't be his hostage and maybe his next victim, and I wouldn't need to be here. So don't talk to me about broken hearts and letting people down. I know all about that. And let's be clear, I'm here because *I* decided to come here. I'm here because I think we can help each other. And, another thing, if my grandfather was so worried about his family getting involved, then why'd he invite his business into my mother's living room every Sunday night? Why did he invite you there? Don't go to the dentist's office but it's okay to come to his home. Truth is, Mr. Benedetto, while I'm sure what you're saying is true, in the end, my grandfather always did what was best for *him*. So, I'm not in the least concerned what he would think or that he'd be broken hearted. I worry what my father and mother and my wife and children would think if they knew I was here, and what it would do to them. So, let's get down to business. The sooner I can get outta here the better, for both of us. Right?"

Benedetto didn't flinch. He sat staring back at me and then calmly brought his palms together and folded his hands in front of him.

"You look more like him when you're angry," he said.

Benedetto's moist eyes roamed over my face. Then he looked away and said, "So, okay, how can you help me?"

"I know who killed Vinny Venezio and his men. He also probably killed the two men in Hackensack."

Merchanti stiffened. "Who?"

Benedetto put his hand up to silence Merchanti. Benedetto smiled at me, "And for this information you want what from me?"

"Nothing. I just want you to have your revenge - but on my terms, my way. And, I want some answers."

"Answers?"

"Yes, about my grandfather."

Benedetto looked up at the ceiling when he spoke. "Tell me who you think did this to our men?"

"I will. But first I have some questions."

Benedetto turned back to me and shrugged. "Questions are harmless. It's the answers . . . Go ahead, ask your questions."

"How and when did my grandfather die?"

Benedetto look puzzled. "Every schoolboy with even a minor interest knows that."

"Tell me anyway."

Benedetto looked at Merchanti before he answered. "He died a couple blocks from here on a Saturday night in March 1963. Alfonso Baressi was responsible for the car bomb that killed him."

"Are you sure?"

Benedetto's hands fell into his lap. "Am I sure it was Baressi?"

"No, how do you know it was my grandfather that died that night? Are you sure it was him?"

Benedetto searched my face. "I saw his body. He was badly burned but I could recognize his shoes and jewelry, his rings and watch, and his overcoat, the cashmere. It was custom made for him. And they found his fedora across the street. It was also one of a kind. The papers made a big deal of how far the explosion had blown it." Benedetto looked me in the eyes. "And I saw his teeth."

"They identified him by his teeth?"

"Officially, I don't know. But *I* did. You can recognize a man's teeth. Ask your father."

I sat back in my chair and looked at the floor. After a moment, I said, "Okay. What do you know about a company called FirsTech?"

Benedetto thought a moment and looked over a Merchanti. Merchanti hunched his shoulders and put his palms up in surrender. Benedetto pursed his lips and shook his head. "Why?"

I had watched the interaction between them and detected no dishonesty in their reactions. I said, "No reason. Just that it was their freight that was stolen off my truck."

"Aah, FirsTech. I didn't know the name but I know the problem. Do you know the problem?"

"If you're referring to the fact that it's classified military equipment, yes."

"That's what it is. That's not the problem, though."

"What do you mean?" I asked.

Benedetto looked over at Merchanti. "Get the phone."

Merchanti walked into the bedroom and returned with a portable phone with a thick antenna that was bent at a forty-five degree angle. I recognized it as a satellite phone from some movie I had seen. Merchanti handed the phone to Benedetto.

"This is a special phone. A special man gave it to me several years ago so I wouldn't have to go out to payphones any more to talk to him. His name is McBride. Have you heard of him?"

I shook my head.

"Mr. McBride is very old and dear friend of ours. He was a very special friend of your grandfather's. I have never met him and probably never will. It wouldn't be good for us to be seen together. Yet we have done each other many favors over the years. The type of favors that no one else could for the other. You see, we live in two very different worlds yet often we find ourselves walking the same streets, so to speak. One of the reasons I had you come here today was so you could speak with Mr. McBride. He wants you to know what the real problem is with this FirsTech thing."

I looked at the phone and felt my stomach flutter. Did I really want to hear this? Could I afford not to?

I took a deep breath. "Okay." I held out my hand for the phone.

Benedetto pressed four buttons and handed the phone to me. In the earpiece I heard a long tone, then a slow but steady *tick, tick, tick.*

"This is McBride." The voice was electronically altered and suffered from digital reconstruction.

"This is . . ." I paused and looked at Benedetto.

McBride interrupted. "The phone is secure, but I know who you are, you don't have to say. I was hoping you'd call. I guess you've met my old friend and he's told you a little about me."

"Very little. So let's say that I have no idea who you are, why we're talkin', or why I should believe anything you're gonna tell me."

"Fair enough," McBride said. He paused for a moment. "Your grandfather had a disfigured right index finger. He nearly lost the tip at the last knuckle when he tried to remove a piece of paper from the metal blades of an electric table fan."

"Common knowledge."

"He always put a beef bouillon cube in his meat sauce. It was the secret part of his recipe."

"Good, but . . ."

"He told me he would never forgive himself for having let you see him use a tire iron to kill his body guard, Nico, in front of your parent's house."

I sucked in a mouthful air and shot glances at Merchanti and Benedetto as if somehow they could have heard what was said. They hadn't, but they both registered the shock on my face.

I heard the electronic voice in the distance. The phone was in my hand on the armrest. I returned it to my ear.

"What?" I said into the phone.

"Do I have your attention?"

"How did you . . ."

I considered my own question. The only way McBride could have learned that was from his grandfather. So, my grandfather had told an old friend. Obviously they were close, but so what.

I recovered. " . . . You have my attention, for whatever that's worth."

"I thought that might do it," the electronic voice chuckled. "You need to know that Nicolas Pucci and Wilson Dennis are not your enemies, but they are not telling you the truth about the HAWIRE."

*He knows the name of it! But nothing should surprise me now.*

"You should also know that they are not bad people but they will stop at nothing to get their job done. You must see that the HAWIRE gets to

Newark Airport at five tomorrow. It's a critical milestone in the final stages of an eighteen-month plan. Your failure will have far-reaching ramifications for our government and our allies all over the world. I know that sounds a bit dramatic but I don't know any other way to say it."

I huffed. "Well you'd better find one, because it's the same rhetoric that Pucci and Dennis have been feeding me and frankly I'm tired of it."

"Okay. You have DOD clearance, not to this level but high enough to get you in serious trouble if any of this gets out, so here it is. FirsTech was commissioned by the, ah, government, we'll say, to develop the HAWIRE. It was supposed to do exactly what you were told it would. The problem is, it doesn't work. Not yet anyway. Probably needs at least another year of development. Unfortunately, we - the United States, our allies, and the rest of the free world – may not have another year.

"The entire free world recognizes that states like Iraq, Iran, Syria, Yemen, and so on, have supported and continue to support international terrorism. We need to stop them, if not outright punish them. If we don't, the West continues to be subject to their growing hatred of us, their threat of withholding their oil supplies, and their sponsorship of terror.

"Iraq and Saddam Hussein are at the top of the list. That's well known. What's not so well known is that our old friend Saddam and a few of his friends have been very busy since the Gulf War, especially since Iraq's ouster of the UN weapons inspection teams. Along with rebuilding and strengthening conventional forces, he has been amassing weapons of mass destruction - chemical, biological, and, we think, some degree of nuclear capability. We also think he has been quietly procuring ex-Soviet and North Korean missile delivery system expertise and hardware that could threaten the entire gulf region, and maybe well beyond. To make matters worse, our in-country intelligence has recently released an updated personality profile that characterized Saddam's mental state as increasingly unstable, delusional, and at times, psychopathic. Instead of the years softening his stance, his private rants against the United States and our allies have become more frequent and emboldened, often maniacally referring to the destruction of the son of the devil, the son of the first George Bush. We believe his threats may eventually materialize into some form of Jihad-like, suicidal offensive action that could have disastrous consequences for the Gulf region.

"Meanwhile, aside from his support of terrorism, living conditions for the Iraqi people continue to decline. Due to the embargoes, inadequate food and medical supplies have severely deteriorated the quality of life for most citizens. Infant mortality rates are among the worst in the world. In some regions of the country, death from treatable injuries and curable disease is as bad as in some tribal third-world countries. Because of this, there are already rumblings that the UN may soon seek the United States' support to loosen the terms of the trade embargo for humanitarian reasons as part of a deal with Saddam to allow UN weapons inspectors back in. That would put us between the proverbial rock and a hard place. If we agree to the lifting of certain embargoed items, Saddam can continue his hide and seek games with his weapons and claim victory. If we don't, best case we stand to be criticized as human rights hypocrites. Worst case, we could lose strategically important allies in the Gulf and harden the heretofore hands-off positions of major states like Russia and China. It's a lose - lose for us. Frankly, we could give a shit about weapons inspections any more. We know all we need to know. We know he has them. But, the other Arab states – our friends and enemies alike – would never support an attack against Iraq or another terrorist state without some hard, verifiable proof. We don't have that – just our intelligence and that's not enough. And, we need to retain any goodwill we have in that region.

"The good news is that our intelligence has become better over the years. We think we now know where Saddam is eighty-four percent of the time. If we subject that eighty-four percent to regression probability analysis and apply a redundancy formula, our chances of finding him are dramatically improved. That means at any given moment we have almost a ninety-five percent chance of dropping a five thousand pound laser-guided bunker busting bomb right on his head. An event that, according to secret polls and other information sources, would not be considered a tragedy by the general citizenry of Iraq or any other country in the modern world. Obviously, without Saddam around and a more moderate and friendly government in place, we would be freed up to cooperate with the UN and the Gulf region would have a far better chance of stabilizing in our favor. Of course, in the process we would seek out and destroy every terrorist and dismantle their support systems.

"However, without clear and present justification, the United States can not consider an action that, for all intents and purposes, is an assassination. So, the question was, not only how do we get Saddam to make the first move, but how do we lure him out on our terms? How do we prevent ground incursions against Kuwait or unprovoked missile attacks against Israel or our other allies in the region? The answer is to give him a reason to think he could win an air war against us. Give him a false sense of security that would goad him into saving his ground troops and his limited warhead-carrying missile inventory until he had defeated, or at least, depleted our local fighter-bomber presence. The answer to the answer is the HAWIRE."

McBride paused, maybe for affect, maybe to catch his breath. I didn't care which; I wasn't ready to react.

McBride cleared his throat. "Are you still there?"

"I'm here. Go on."

"The HAWIRE currently appears to function correctly. But, the magnetic mass and visual signatures of the holographic replicas are not without some subtle deficiencies. In the hands of skilled technicians, which Sadam has plenty of, the HAWIRE's fighter and missile replications can be reverse-engineered and distinguished by programming radar filters to look for the weaknesses in the images. If our enemy thinks he has the ability to identify the actual target, with the advances he has made in his anti-aircraft and anti-missile defense systems, we're confident he'll risk a provocation - maybe move on a neighbor state friendly with us. He's smart enough to know that if we suffer air loses of twenty to forty percent, it would be politically disastrous for the current administration. And, if he assumed he could take out enough of our units early in the air war and slow down our response to his offensive, it would give him the time he needed to safely and successfully deploy his troops and new missiles."

"No one in their right mind would think he could eventually win this war?" I scoffed.

"That assumes these assholes were ever in their right minds. Total victory's not important to these guys. Remember Saddam claimed victory after the first Gulf War. What's important to these types is not what sane men call victory. Simply strengthening their own position at home may be enough. If he thinks he can humiliate the United States and our allies by flexing his muscles, dropping a few warheads loaded with chemical or biological weapons, maybe a nuke or two, into a couple nearby states friendly with us, and then get out with his own ass and with acceptable retaliatory loses at home, that's probably good enough for him. What he doesn't know is that any shooting war's gonna be a very short one. Combat models predict that we'll take out most of their command and control sites and defensive systems in the first day. Day two, we'll take out over ninety-three percent of their facilities that make and store weapons of mass destruction. All the while, we'll be hunting the leaders. By day three, the models say we'll have found them all. With them dead, the war will be over within the next twenty-four hours, no question. With such a clean and decisive victory over such an egregious tyrannical state that had the balls to someday attack - perhaps with nuclear weapons, a peace-loving democratic nation, a member of the free world's economic community, we'll have every peacenik lining up behind us, cheering us on as we continue to eradicate the earth of tyrants and terror."

"Wow," I said. "This is unbelievable. So, it's that simple? This HAWIRE's goes from Newark, New Jersey to the Middle East or God-knows-where, and then on to free all the world's oppressed masses and win peace on earth." It wasn't really a question.

"Since you choose to be flip and over-simplified, in a word, yes. For over a year, the enemy's been fed information about the HAWIRE and its deployment with our forces. He thinks that we now have HAWIRE capability in the region, but that we won't use it and risk its exposure unless there's an all-out war. He's paid millions so far for the information and has contracted with operatives to buy the unit you have from Lincoln."

"Hey, slow down. Let's be clear, for the record, that I don't have this thing and never did."

"But you can get to it. We know that, and we know what you've arranged with Lincoln for tomorrow. We also know that this has become a serious problem for you, personally. Please understand that no one ever intended that to happen. This was supposed to be a controlled event, with Lincoln as the unsuspecting pawn in the plan."

"Lincoln? The unsuspecting pawn? Whose bright idea was that?"

"Hard as it may be for you to believe, Lincoln was a perfect choice. He lends absolute credibility to the whole scenario. And, as the word pawn implies, we planned and controlled all his movements until this week when the hijacking went wrong. Our first move was seeing that he was offered a large amount of money from an arms broker with a history of acting as a go-between in deals that circumvent arms embargoes and restricted items regulations. Lincoln's job was relatively easy: steal the HAWIRE and deliver it to Lufthansa at Newark. The second move was getting him retained by FirsTech as a security consultant. That was easy because it's Lincoln's legit cover business and because FirsTech was a major player in the plan. Infiltrating and infecting FirsTech's security was the next step. He could do that as part of his consultancy contract to test their security readiness. Then he simply had to plan and execute the hijacking of your truck and deliver the HAWIRE to the airport as scheduled. We made that easy, too. No one else was supposed to or needed to get involved. Certainly, no one was meant to get hurt."

I chuckled. "No one was supposed to get hurt? Are you serious? You're planning a war for chrissake."

"Please, Joseph, now's not the time for liberal school-boy rhetoric. We're all adults here and there's a lot of grown up issues at stake."

"The only *issues* I care about are the ones that affect me and my partner and our families. Frankly, the rest of this stuff is more that I needed to know and not anything I want to be involved with."

"It's too late for that. Your partner saw to that."

"No, your friends sitting here next to me saw to that. Them and their friends and the world they come from."

"That's a little harsh coming from you, isn't it? Aren't you the same guy who used his grandfather's name to make a deal with Vinny Venezio? The same guy who shook down FirsTech for twenty million dollars?"

*Who is this guy,* I thought. *And what doesn't he know?* I quickly put the thought behind me. My head was filled with enough mystery.

"Put whatever spin on this that you want, Mr. McBride or whoever you are. Bottom line is that Monday morning I was Joseph Napolo; husband, father, businessman, and assistant Little League coach. Three days later, I'm here. And don't try to tell me that any of this is my doing. Maybe I learned a lot more that I wanted to about certain things this week. And maybe some of that has to do with my last name. And I supposed some things are changed forever because of what's happened this week, but it won't change me or my family. I refuse to let that happen. So, if you're thinking that what you just told me is going to make any difference or change anything I've come here for today, you're wrong. It was a good story, and for all I know that's all it is because it's the third story I've heard about the HAWIRE in the last twenty-four hours. Hell, you could be just some guy sitting in the apartment down the hall. So, good luck, Mr. McBride. I'll do whatever I can to get the HAWIRE to Lufthansa at five tomorrow. But it'll be for my reasons and nothing to do with anything else. After that, I don't care what happens to it."

"If you do that, you'll be a hero - unsung like most of the real heroes, but a hero nonetheless."

"If my wife and kids and parents can't know about it, then it doesn't exist for me. So save your medals and your speeches."

"Well, as I understand it, you'll be a rich man if you succeed. They'll all be able to know that."

I exhaled loudly. "Is there anything you don't know, Mr. McBride?"

"Information is power and I'm a very powerful man. But I'm old now, remember I knew your grandfather, and I won't be around forever, so you can take comfort in the fact that the information we discussed - all of it - will go with me. I'm not your enemy, Joseph."

Something in McBride's voice had changed. It softened as he had spoken the last few sentences. "Can I believe that? I'd like to."

"Yes, my boy, you can," McBride said, sounding fatherly. "Just do your best to get that HAWIRE to the airport on time. My power has its limits. Do you understand?"

"I think so."

"Good. Then good-bye and good luck with the team."

"The team?"

"The Little League team."

The phone went dead and I handed it to Merchanti.

Benedetto raised his head. "So?"

"So, . . .?"

"So, who do you think killed my men?"

I looked back and forth at Benedetto and Merchanti. "He's goes by the name of Lincoln, Aaron Lincoln."

Benedetto smiled. "I know."

Merchanti shot Benedetto a look. "You know?"

"Yes, Mr. McBride told me."

*McBride.* I rolled my eyes and let them come to rest on Benedetto's face. "Do you want Lincoln?"

"Yes."

"I can arrange that, but it has to be done my way."

"What's your way?"

"I need help with something and, for a couple a reasons, you're the best person to help me. The interesting part is that by helping me, you get Lincoln, *and* you collect two million dollars in the process, like a payment for helping me. This way it's just business between us and, when it's over, we're done with each other. We walk away like it never happened, like we never met. We never speak of this arrangement. We never contact each other again. As I said, like it never happened. Do you agree?"

Benedetto shrugged. "Why not?"

"I have another condition. You must share the money, twenty-five percent goes to this guy John Anelli. And you must promise to let him walk away with it."

Benedetto shrugged again. "I have nothing against Johnny Anelli? Do you Jimmy?"

Merchanti shook his head. "Vinny did, but that's over now."

Benedetto put his palms out. "But tell me, why should I share my money with Anelli?"

"I think he still has the, ah, merchandise that I need to deliver tomorrow. I'll need his cooperation to get this done. And, I think he may have saved my partner's life."

"Then you should pay him."

I shook my head. "I said it has to be my way."

Benedetto squinted at me, studying my face again. Then the corners of his mouth curled up and he nodded, "Okay, your way. Tell us."

# CHAPTER 27

## The Oasis Motel
## Jersey City, New Jersey

I placed the K Mart and Macy's bags on the bed in my room. The night desk clerk hadn't looked twice at the shopping bags. I assumed that most guests of the Oasis Motel probably checked in with less luggage, if any at all. The young couple at the desk ahead of me was carrying only a six-pack of beer and a brown paper bag that clanked when they nuzzled each other while the clerk turned to take their room key off the pegboard.

In my room, I dumped the contents of the K Mart bag onto the bed. Toiletries, socks, underwear, a shirt, and VHS videotape. I pulled all the tags off the clothes and unwrapped the videotape. The three pistols and extra clips were in the Macy's bag. I wrapped the Colt 1911, the bigger Glock 20, and the extra clips in a towel from the bathroom. I put the wrapped guns back in the Macy's bag and stuffed it underneath the dresser.

I hefted the compact Glock 29 and slipped it into the right pocket of my jacket. It fit perfectly and rested nicely so that the grip was readily accessible. I practiced pulling it out quickly several times and then checked myself in the full-length mirror on the back of the bathroom door. Satisfied no one could see that the gun was in my pocket, I put the two remaining magazines loaded with 10-millimeter rounds in my left jacket pocket.

I checked my watch. It was twenty minutes to ten. I looked at myself in the mirror again. There was no telltale bulging but I could feel the weight in my pockets. Turning again, I faced the mirror and searched myself up and down several times. Finally my reflection looked me in the squarely in the eyes. I shook my head and thought, *What the hell am I doing?*

I pulled the Glock out of my pocket and ejected the clip. I thumbed out the rounds and jostled them in my fist for a few seconds. Then I fed the empty clip back into the handgrip and put the unloaded Glock back in my pocket. I put the loose bullets and the two spare clips from my pocket in the bag under the dresser. I left the room without looking in the mirror again.

The lounge was at the west end of the motel, on the other side of the office. The structures were connected but a grass island separated the parking lots. On a pole at the curb there was a large sign with a neon setting-sun and palm tree. Several of the neon letters were no longer lit so it read, *ake a Bre k at the Oasis, Co ktails & old Beer.* There were half a dozen cars in the lot but I didn't see Catella's Lincoln.

Inside, the Oasis was anything but refreshing. It smelled of stale beer and cigarettes. The lighting was minimal but colorful, red and green. There was a ratty looking thatched roof over the bar. Four men, each alone, sat underneath the roof on worn-out bamboo stools. Behind the bar a few dozen soiled stuffed toy parrots and other tropical-looking birds were perched among the dusty bottles and cloudy glasses. Several of the birds wore eyeglasses or sunglasses that were no doubt left behind by lightheaded patrons. Others had cigarettes dangling from their beaks. One was hanging by its neck from a plastic six-pack holder. Another had a corkscrew through its head. One had no head at all. Tacked to the walls were faded and curling unframed travel posters of island beaches with grass huts and watery sunsets and surfboarders in places far away from Jersey City. They said things like *Hawaii, your Pacific Paradise* and *Jamaica is for Lovers.* Frank Sinatra was playing on the jukebox.

I took a seat at a corner table that had a view of the front door. I wondered if there was a waitress and if anyone there knew that an oasis was a place in the desert, or if that really mattered in a place like Jersey City, New Jersey.

After a few minutes and no sign of a waitress, I went up to the bar.

"I'll have an old beer," I said, smiling at the old barmaid.

"A what?"

"An old beer, like the sign says."

"What sign?"

"Outside. The lights out, it says old beer instead of cold beer."

"Oh, I get it. So what kinda beer ya want? And don' ask me what we got. It's on the sign behind me."

I looked at the handwritten sign. "No Amstel Light?"

The barmaid puffed and shook her head. "Can you read? Is that on the sign?"

"Okay, gimme a Coors Light."

The barmaid plunked the bottle in front of me. "That's two fifty."

I peeled off three singles. "You need a little Jimmy Buffet in here."

"Little Jimmy who?"

"Jimmy Buffet. He sings . . ."

The barmaid had already turned her back to me and was pressing the keys on the cash register.

"Keep the change," I said at her back and turned to walk to the table.

Two men were coming through the door. I recognized Alley Cat Catella and pointed to the table in the corner. Catella headed to me and the other man, Anelli, I presumed, walked to the table. He had a slight limp.

Catella extended his right hand. "Howya doon?"

I shook his hand. "Fine. You?"

"Eh. We'll see. We gotta talk. Lemme get us some drinks." Pointing at my beer. "You okay?"

"Yeah. I'll meetya at the table."

Johnny Onions Anelli was sitting in my seat and was lighting a cigarette. In the flame of lighter, I glimpsed a weary man.

Johnny looked up. "You Napolo?"

I put my index finger to my lips. "Never mind that for now. Let's wait for the other guy."

I sat and took a pull off my beer. Anelli was staring at me when I placed the bottle on the table. I stared back until Johnny Onions looked away.

Catella arrived seconds later with a beer and what looked like a Manhattan for Johnny.

"You two introduce yourselves?" Catella asked as he sat.

"We were waiting for you," I said.

"Okay, this is . . ."

"Wait." I cut him off. "I wanna check you guys before we talk."

"Check us?" Johnny asked.

"Yeah, for wires and stuff like that."

"Whathefuck's with this?" Johnny growled. "Maybe we should be checking you."

I looked back and forth between Catella and Anelli. "Well, maybe that's not a bad idea. Let's check each other."

Catella looked at Johnny. "Seems fair."

Johnny huffed and let his hands slap the tabletop. "Ouffa!"

"How doya wanna do this?" Catella said to me.

"In the men's room," I said. "You and I'll go first."

Johnny waved a hand toward the men's room. "Don't get too touchy-feely in there. They got another name for that."

"What's that?" Catella asked as he stood.

"Faggot."

As soon as the men's room door closed, Catella started. "Hey, I apologize for him. He's a little, ah, on edge, with all that's goin' on. You can understand, right?"

"I know he's your friend, but he's a little creep, Albert. That's all there is to it. So let's get this over with. But I've gotta warn ya, I'm not wired but I do have a gun in my jacket pocket."

"A gun? For what?"

"Like you said, with all that's goin' on, you can understand, right?"

Catella raised his eyebrows. "Just didn't figure you for the gun type."

"I'm not."

"Well, Johnny is and he's got one, too."

"I coulda guessed that. So, he shouldn't have any problem with mine."

Catella cocked his head. "Let's not tell him, okay? He might make a big deal of it."

"Whatever you say, Albert. Who's goin' first?"

Catella made a face, his lips turned down at the corners, and he held up his arms. "Be my guest."

I patted Catella down and then let him do the same to me. Catella hesitated when he felt the weight in my jacket pocket. Then he gripped the Glock through the jacket, feeling the shape of the gun.

"I'll tell Johnny you're clean so he don't have to know about the gun. It might be an issue."

I shrugged. "Okay, send him in."

Johnny sauntered into the men's room. When the door closed he leaned against it and took out a large revolver, maybe a .357 magnum. He pointed it at me and said, "Jus' so ya know, I got it." He held it in his hand as he stretched out his arms for the search.

I patted his torso and legs and said, "Turn around."

Johnny obliged. When his face was to the door, I pulled the small Glock out of my pocket. I pushed Johnny's face against the door with my left forearm and pressed the muzzle of the Glock into Johnny's cheek.

"Jus' so ya know I got it," I said. "Now stay like that and gimme yours."

"Fuck!" Johnny cursed.

I reached over and took the revolver. I slipped it in my pocket and ran my hand over Johnny's back.

"You gonna take that thing outta my face now?"

"In a second. First we need to understand each other."

"Whadaya talkin' about?"

I brought my lips within a few inches of Johnny's ear. "Listen very closely. I'm gonna offer you guys a deal tonight, a very profitable deal. But before that, we're gonna agree on a somethin' here, a little private contract just between you and me. Now the terms of this contract are pretty simple. After tonight, you're gonna agree to stay away from me, my partner, and anyone we know for the rest of your life. We, in turn, agree to stay away from you. If you agree to this right now, I've arranged for you to walk away from everything that's happened this week, with no repercussions, from *anyone* – in New Jersey, New York, anyone anywhere. If that happens, then we'll all live happily ever after. If it doesn't, or if you break our contract, all bets are off, and I'll see that you never bother anyone ever again. Do you think we can proceed under those conditions?"

"You threatenin' me?"

"Yes, absolutely. I've made a lot of new friends this week. Some of them would be very capable of doing me this favor. Remember, as one of my new friends said to me a couple days ago, all *my* contracts have a grandfather clause. Ya know what I mean?"

Johnny closed his eyes and nodded. "Yeah, sure."

I pushed the muzzle of the Glock harder into Johnny's cheek. "Doesn't sound like you believe it."

"Yeah, okay, I guess I do."

I leaned on the gun. "You guess?"

Johnny grunted. "Okay, I get your drift."

I eased up the pressure on the Glock.

Johnny wiggled his cheek and said, "So, what's this deal you're talkin' about."

"I'll tell ya at the table, after I hear you say you agree to this, ah, contract."

Johnny exhaled. "Ouffa! Awright, I agree."

"Good. I'm glad we understand each other."

"Yeah, right."

I stepped away and Johnny turned around. He reached for the pack of cigarettes in his shirt pocket and slipped one between his lips. Looking at the Glock in my hand, he said, "Well, well. Who'd a thought?"

I ignored him and took out Johnny's revolver. I opened the cylinder and dumped the cartridges into my hand. I handed the empty gun back to Johnny and put the bullets in my pocket. I waived the Glock toward the door. "Let's go back to the table."

Catella looked up as we approached. He saw Johnny's pained expression. "Everything okay?"

Johnny said, "Yeah, sure, everything's just fine, fuckin' beautiful."

I sat between the two of them and took a long drink of beer. I put the bottle down hard. "So, boys, doya know that today's your lucky day?"

Catella and Anelli looked at each other.

Johnny Onions said, "Whadaya mean?"

I looked at Johnny's worn face. "Well, *you* certainly can't get by on just your good looks any more, so I assume this meeting was, in one way or another, about money. And if I'm right, which I'm sure I am, then this is your lucky day."

"How lucky?" Johnny asked.

"Five hundred thousand and a free pass guaranteed by Fabrizio Benedetto, if you still have the crate."

Johnny looked again at Catella then back at me. "I'm still listenin'."

"I thought so. You still have it?"

"Maybe."

I leaned my face in close to him and scowled. "Look, these are fucking simple yes or no questions. I don't want to spend any more time with you than I have to. So say, yes or no, and if yes, can you get it tomorrow?"

"Yes."

"To both?"

"Yeah."

I leaned back smiled. "Then we're in business, gentlemen."

## Stewart International Airport
## New Windsor, New York

Lincoln's pager woke him and he rolled over to look at the clock next to the .50 caliber Desert Eagle on the bed stand. It was eleven ten, which meant he had been asleep for over an hour. He grabbed the pager and silenced the alarm. He didn't recognize the number on the back-lit LCD panel.

Using his night-vision in the windowless room, he located the shower sandals he had placed on the floor beside the bed. Carefully, so his bare feet wouldn't touch the floor, he slipped his toes into the straps. On the way to his office, he pulled on a pair of sweatpants and a T-shirt. It was cool in the old brick building and he didn't want to risk a chill.

In his office, Lincoln sat at his computer and traced the number that had called his pager. After a few seconds the address appeared. It was a pay phone on Route 9 in Elizabeth, NJ. He powered up his satellite phone and dialed the number.

"Hello." I answered.

"Who's this?" Lincoln asked.

"I'm calling about our meeting tomorrow. Does that help?"

"Whathefuck you paging me for at this hour?"

"I just want to be sure that we are straight on some things."

"Oh? And what's that?"

"The money. The two million."

"What about it?"

"Nothing happens tomorrow until I see the money and my partner in good health."

"Explain."

"Until I see the money and my partner, my truck with the crate on it will be in the rest stop. If everything's to my liking, I'll call the driver and tell 'im to drive over. Then we make the exchange"

Lincoln grinned. "Okay, so your truck's gonna wait in the rest stop until I come and show you the money?"

"And my partner."

"Sounds reasonable. Now you listen to me. The only people I wanna see there tomorrow are you and the truck driver. I want that videotape, and the crate better be the right one, the right serial number."

"That's no problem. I'm all set on my end."

"Well, there better be no fuckin' problems, 'cause if there is you and your partner are gonna die in that maintenance yard. Then, maybe I'll pay a visit to your families. Is Cogan's wife as pretty as yours?"

I gnashed my teeth and struggled to keep my voice calm. "I don't like it when you bring my family into this, Mr. Lincoln."

"Then do the right thing tomorrow, Mr. Napolo."

"Oh, I will, Mr. Lincoln, you can count on it."

# CHAPTER 28

### Friday Morning
### The Airport Marriott Hotel
### Newark International Airport

I had slept well in spite of the saggy mattress at the Oasis. Thursday had been a long, tough day and, after the meeting with Catella and Anelli, I was exhausted. However, I knew that fatigue alone wasn't going to be enough. There would be an endless series of second-guesses and what-ifs and questions, moral and otherwise, flashing through my head as I lay in bed trying to fall asleep. It would've been like watching a television that you couldn't turn away from with the channel changer jammed wide open. So to be sure I'd be able to get the sleep I needed, I had returned to the room with a double Christian Brothers brandy. It did the trick. I woke without the alarm at six-forty, feeling rested and ready.

It was now a little before eight. I had ordered a breakfast sandwich to go at McDonalds on the way to the airport Marriott and stood sipping a large coffee at the bank of pay phones off the lobby. I dropped a few quarters into the phone and dialed my office.

"DTC." It was Samantha sounding sleepy.

"Sam, it's Joseph. You okay?"

"Oh, yeah. Just a little tired. I was out last night and my car broke down. By the time I got home it was late."

"Sorry. Is your car okay?"

"No, they had to tow it, but the state trooper who came was really cute. I think he might call me."

"Oh, well, good luck with that, Sam."

"Thanks. Are ya coming in today? Everyone's asking about you and Michael."

"Everyone who?"

"Ya know, everyone here."

"Well, no, neither of us will be in today. We have appointments. Just take messages or put 'em through to our voice mail. We'll check in as time permits but probably not until much later this afternoon. Is Bobby Moretti in?"

"Yeah, I think he's in dispatch. I'll switch ya over there."

"Thanks, Sam, and good luck with the trooper."

Moretti picked up on the first ring. "Dispatch."

"Bobby it's me."

"Hey, boss, where are you?"

"On the turnpike. How's your lip?"

"Twelve stitches, four inside, eight out. The worst part is they had to shave my mustache. I've had that thing since February sixth, nineteen seventy. Started growing it the day I was discharged. I'm gettin' a lot of double-takes and a few choice words from my co-workers."

I chuckled. "I can't picture you without it."

"Well, you'll see it soon enough. We're still on for today, right?"

"Yeah, it's still on, but are you still sure about this? I'll understand if you've had second thoughts."

"Yeah, well I've had plenty a second thoughts only none of 'em involve me not bein' there today."

"You're sure? You know this is gonna be dangerous."

"After yesterday, you couldn't keep me away even if you fired me. You gotta know how bad I want another shot at those assholes."

"Okay. I guess you know I really need your help and that I can't tell you how much this means to me. If everything goes as planned, I got a big bonus waitin' for you."

"Fuggedaboudit. So what's goin' on?"

"First, I need you to get four of our rigs up to the rest area next to that maintenance yard by noon. They need to be empty with padlocks on the trailer doors. Have Ripton meet our drivers up there with the van and bring them home. Tell him you'll meet them there to get their keys. Then I need you to go over to Eastern Truck Lease and rent a rig. Ask for Donny. Tell 'im I sent you and that we need one of the old high-cube forty-foot ocean containers he has in the yard. Tell 'im we need it to haul some scrap so we need something heavy, and one that he doesn't mind getting' a little banged up. Okay?"

"Yeah, sure, but it's pretty busy here today. I dunno if I can get four of our empties up there by noon."

"Bobby, it's gotta happen. Tell Carlos to broker the loads, move things around, or give the damn freight away, I don't care. I need those fuckin' empties up there. Understand?"

"Got it, boss. What else?"

"Don't wear your vest from yesterday?"

"Don't wear it? Why?"

"They may have been bugged by FirsTech."

"You serious?"

"I'm not sure, but I don't want any uninvited audiences for today's show."

"Show, huh? Whadaya got planned, boss?"

The money dropped inside the phone and a tone interrupted their conversation.

"We only have a few seconds, Bobby, so take care of those things and meet me at Vince Lombardi with the rental as soon as you can."

"Okay, gimme about two hours."

The phone went dead.

I fed four more quarters into the phone and called our lawyer's office. Sam Meltzer came on the line after only few seconds.

"Joseph, what the hell, you okay?"

"I'm fine, Sam. Is everything done? Have we finalized the second agreement?"

"Yes, everything's taken care of. The money's sitting in my account waiting for the proof of delivery from Lufthansa cargo."

"Delivery to a guy named Rudy at Lufthansa, right?"

"Yeah, Rudy at Lufthansa. As soon as FirsTech confirms delivery, the money gets released to you. It seemed a little loose so I put a six o'clock deadline on it. Then I got on a conference call with this guy Rudy and the FirsTech's attorney to confirm it all. Everything seems to be all set but these guys make me nervous. With everything that's going on and the potential ramifications, everything moved very quickly. These guys, I dunno, they ah . . . They were almost too accommodating, too assured."

"Well, I'm sure they know exactly what they're doin'."

"I'm sure. But how 'bout you, Joseph? Do you know what you're doin'?"

I sighed. "I dunno, Sam. Are you certain the papers fully exonerate Michael and me?"

"Yes, they're clear enough. Pretty good stuff actually. They paint you guys as real heroes, going way beyond the call of ordinary citizens, but they're only 'papers', as you say. And if there's ever any hard physical evidence that contradicts them, you can wipe your ass with these contracts 'cause that's all they'll be good for. How much do you trust these guys?"

"Not much, especially if the crate doesn't get to the airport later."

"You want my advice?"

"No, Sam. I've made up my mind. I know what I've gotta do and your advice would be too sobering for me right now. There's a lot to this that I can't tell you. And none of it would make you feel any better, probably worse, so let's just leave it as it is."

"Leave it where? Me thinking that you're fuckin' outta your mind and headed for big trouble?"

"Yeah, and me trusting you to take care of things for me in case something happens."

"No problem. I've contacted a top firm in Newark to handle your defense."

"Thanks, but I meant if the worst happens."

There was a pause. "You have my word as an attorney and your friend. I'll see that Cathy, Ilene and the kids are set for life."

"Thank you, Sam. I need you to start thinking about something else."

"What's that?"

"If everything goes in our favor, I want to donate the money to a good charity, maybe one that cares for orphaned or disadvantaged kids. Can you do some research for me?"

"Well, yeah, but are you sure about this? Twenty million's a lot a money. Why not give them ten and keep ten or maybe set up an annuity. That way you can keep the principal, it'll throw off a million a year or so, and you'll still have legacy money for your heirs."

"Sam, I can't really think too much about it now, I just know that I can't keep the money. That makes me . . . well, I don't know what it makes me, but I'm not gonna keep it."

"I recommend you hang on to it until this thing is definitely settled in your favor. Serious charges may arise out of this. Federal charges. Your legal bill could cost you every cent of it."

"I know. We'll discuss it next week. In the interim, please check out those charities for me, okay?"

"Okay, Joseph, whatever you say. Now you forget about this part of it and concentrate on watchin' your ass today. And remember, at any time, you can change your mind and we'll figure a way outta this thing for you guys."

"I don't think that's possible at this point"

"You know I don't - can't, as your attorney, agree with what you're doing."

"Understood. This is against your advice."

"Okay, but I can still wish you luck. And call me, good or bad, as soon as you can."

"I will. Thanks, again, Sam."

I hung up feeling comfortable that my friend Sam would be there, for as long as he was needed, even if Michael and I weren't around. Cathy and the kids would be fine. They would be financially secure. Their lives would go on without me; sadly, and forever questioning, but they would go on. And I could trust Sam to make sure they knew the truth, whatever that ended up being.

I dialed the hotel to talk to Cathy and the kids but got the voice mail in their room. They were probably at breakfast or, if I knew my boys, in the game room pumping quarters into the machines or in the indoor pool. After the tone, I said, "Hey, guys, just calling to tell you I miss you all and that I love you. I'll call you later this afternoon and see ya tonight. Wait for me at the hotel."

I paused, wanting to say more, afraid to say too much. "Boys take care of your mother. All of you take care of each other and be good. Love you all. Bye-bye."

I hung up and took a deep breath. Maybe it was better that I hadn't been able to reach them. Knowing that it might be the last time that I ever talked to them would've been too much. Maybe I should just take a quick ride down the Parkway and see them, hug them and kiss them. If I hurried . . .

No, better to just to hold them in my thoughts. I closed my eyes tight and pressed my two index fingers against my eyelids to squeeze out the moisture. I cleared my throat and walked away from the phones, through the lobby and out to the Town Car.

As I put the key into the door lock, a well-dressed elderly woman standing on the curb next to her luggage called to me.

"Excuse me," she said, waving her arm. "Are you here for someone or are you alone?"

"Alone?"

"Yes, well I mean, can I hire you for a ride?"

I looked at the Town Car and then, still thinking about my family, smiled at her. "No, sorry, I'm never alone."

# CHAPTER 29
## Bella Collina
## Livingston Manor, New York

"It's just about show time," Nicolas said, as Wilson closed the heavy door to the private study. "I was wondering where you were,"

Wilson sat down next to him in the leather executive chair at the console. He smiled weakly and said, "I've been taking care of some last minute details."

"Oh?"

"Among other things there was a guy, Lincoln's man I'm sure, with a Vaime SSR in the foothills over looking the maintenance yard."

"A Vaime what?"

"SSR - for Silenced Sniper Rifle. Special forces stuff. SAS uses them. A very effective lightweight rifle. Quiet as a mouse."

"And . . .?"

"And one of my men has it now. He's lying on top of Lincoln's guy so Lincoln will see only one heat signature from the air."

"And Lincoln's guy doesn't mind being a mattress."

Wilson ignored Nicolas' attempt to lighten the mood. "No, not any more."

"What if Lincoln calls his man. I'm sure they had comm."

"He'll get no answer. Sometime those things don't work."

Nicolas closed his eyes and rubbed his forehead with his hand. He finished slowly by massaging his eyelids. He blinked his eyes as he began to speak.

"Wilson, something's happened between us over the last couple days." His fingers dallied a toggle switch on the console. "We seem to have . . . drifted. We always discussed even the most minor alterations to our plans, *before* they were executed. What happened to that? What's changed?"

"What's changed?" Wilson shook his head. "You asking me that question is the very reason I didn't consult you. I didn't have time to argue the merits with you. You're too focused, Nicolas. And I guess that's why you can be so successful in this game. You have the ability to set everything in black or white. Good or bad for the project, the mission, no matter what the cost - as long as it's profitable, of course. Maybe I am getting old and soft, but I don't think so. I think I'm just being true to the spirit of your uncle. The old ways aren't the bad ways, ya know. They did get us to where we are today."

"Oh, for Chrissake, Wilson," Nicolas huffed. "This has got nothing to do with the fuckin' *old ways*. This has to do with you thinking I'm a goddam monster. That I don't give a shit what happens to Napolo and his partner. Well, fuck you - I do give a shit. That's why I agreed to have our man there. One man. Not two. But of course, who knows if I would have agreed to the second man, I wasn't asked, was I?"

"Well, would you have agreed?"

"No, the risk of exposure is too great. As it is, Lincoln may find out. He's a smart fucker. You don't know what he had arranged with his man."

"I think we can guess what he had arranged. So I'll take that chance. It's better than the alternative."

Nicolas shook his head and looked off to one side. "Do we at least get some video-com from your man?"

Wilson nodded. "He's wearing a camera. It's on his headband though. We may not get much."

"So what's his job?"

"You mean besides taking out Lincoln's man who could've easily put a couple steel-jacketed rounds through the heads of the guys on our side?"

"Yes, does he have any other orders?"

"Yeah, he was instructed to ensure that we live up to our part of the bargain . . . you remember, we told Napolo that his protection was our top priority."

Nicolas glared at Wilson. "But *not* at the risk of compromising the mission, right?"

Wilson exhaled loudly and shook his head.

"Right, Wilson? I wanna hear you say it."

"Of course not, Nicolas. That would be unthinkable."

Nicolas stared at Wilson, who stared back.

Finally, it was Nicolas who turned away toward the console. "What channel's your man's video coming through?"

"They told me it would be on six."

"Let's see what's going on. It's almost two."

## New York State DOT Maintenance Yard Ramapo, NY

I pulled into the yard and put the Town Car in park, letting it idle. I lowered all the windows to let the fresh spring breeze blow through the car. I checked my watch. It was ten minutes before two. The radio was on but it was low. The singer was gravel-voiced, and the lyrics poured out like a thick mix of sand and glue. The music began to gather strength as the singer reached down deep to bring up the power for the chorus. I turned up the volume.

*What made you so pretty?*
*And how'd you get so tough?*
*One too many lovers, girl,*
*One's usually enough.*

*But tonight this block feels like Heaven,*
*Cause I've been with an angel all day,*
*Whoa, let's get off of these streets girl,*
*We knew it was comin' some day.*

I remember wondering if that country song would be the last music I listened to in this life. It felt wrong. It should be Bruce, Tom Waits, the Stones, or Dylan. I reached for the tuning knob but the rented cell phone rang and I clicked off the radio.

"This is Joseph."

"Boss, it's me." It was Moretti. "The Alley Cat's been here and gone. He brought the four drivers for our trucks. He said to tell ya that everything else is set and ready to roll on your signal. Catella also said to tell ya he's leaving to meet the other guy for the Newark thing, whatever that means."

"Good. Didja make the call to Donny?"

"Yeah, I told 'im I left the rig running while I ran in to get a cup a coffee at a dinner on Route 9 in Newark and when I came out it was gone. He was gonna call the cops. I told him I couldn't wait around 'cause I had to get a cab home 'cause I had the runs."

"What'd he say?"

"He was pretty pissed that I wasn't gonna hang around for the police report. I'm sure you're gonna get a call."

"Yeah, well we're both insured."

"I hope some nosey trooper doesn't see the rig sittin' here with me in it. That's gonna be fuckin' hard to explain."

"Well, we only got a few minutes more."

"Those two assholes in the white Fuso cruised by a couple a times, lookin' real hard at our four trucks."

I sensed something and glanced in the rear view mirror. "Speaking of assholes, here they come now. The Mitsubishi's pullin' into the yard. I'll call ya back when it's time."

"Good luck, boss."

"You, too, Bobby."

*     *     *

Lincoln turned to Michael and spoke through the lip mike that was connected through the Bell Long Ranger's intercom system to the headsets they wore.

"Your friend's fuckin' with me. Brings four of your trucks to the rest stop and now this."

"What?" Michael asked.

"This," Lincoln said, pointing to a red smudge on the computer screen. "Looks like a man lying in the brush."

Lincoln's fingers tapped at the keyboard and the monitor changed to black and white. Michael recognized the infrared reverse imaging from the television news war footage. He watched as Lincoln moved the cursor to form a box around the man lying in the hill next to the maintenance yard. Lincoln double clicked the mouse and the area inside the box enlarged, filling the screen.

"And that . . . ," Lincoln said, rubbing his finder across the screen, " . . . is a rifle. Your friend's turned out to be a bit more resourceful than I anticipated. Oh, well . . ."

Lincoln reached behind his seat and came up with a silenced Heckler & Koch MP5 submachine gun. As he cocked the weapon he turned to Michael and said, "Quite often my disappointment in others results in someone dying. And right now I'm *very* disappointed with your partner."

*     *     *

355

Nicolas Pucci and Wilson Dennis were watching the video being broadcast from their man's headband. They saw the tall grass in the foreground begin to wave softly. At first, it appeared as if a gentle wind had caressed the hillside. But then the grass began to whip violently back and forth and then flatten against the ground. The picture on the monitor jerked up toward the sky and then rolled and twisted and rolled over again. The light gray belly of Lincoln's helicopter filled the screen.

"Fuck!" Wilson shouted.

The man on the ground was lying on his back and they watched his rifle come into view as he lifted it to take aim at the Bell Long Ranger. But as the rifle was coming up, they saw Lincoln lean out of the chopper and look down his right arm over the H&K in his hand. The muzzle of submachine gun flashed as Lincoln fired it on full auto.

"Shit!" Nicolas screamed as he slammed against the back of his chair.

The big monitor blinked and then filled with static before going completely black.

\* \* \*

I had watched Lincoln's helicopter approach the area slowly and then veer off to hover over the sloping hill at the south side of the yard. I didn't comprehend the significance of the maneuver until the Bell Long Ranger dropped quickly to less than fifty feet off the ground and I saw Lincoln in the doorway with the gun in his hand. I recognized that the tiny glints spitting out of the side of the gun were the spent shell casings ejecting from the H&K and that the puffs of dry dirt rising from the ground were the few rounds that had not ripped into Merchanti's sharpshooter.

I pressed the redial button on the cell phone. "Bobby, I think Lincoln just shot our back-up man. Do you still wanna go through with this? It's not too late to call it off."

"Son of a bitch! Is that what's goin' on? I couldn't tell from here. It looked like he was gonna land over there."

"Nope. He's comin' around again. Yes or no, Bobby? We gotta decide now."

"We can't just leave."

"As long as Michael's up there with him, *I* can't. But you can."

"No fuckin' way. Let's do it - just like we planned."

"Okay, here he comes. I'll call ya back."

"I'll be ready."

"Thanks, Bobby."

"Fuggedaboudit. But check your weapons. Lock and load, safeties off."

I took out the two Glocks. They were loaded, rounds chambered. I moved the safety switch to the fire position on both guns and returned the compact Glock 29 to my left jacket pocket. Then I activated the laser aimer on the bigger Glock 20 and pointed the pistol at the floor in front of the passenger seat. The bright red laser dot seemed to bore a hole in the black carpeting. With my left hand cradling my right, I steadied my grip and slid the red dot over to a speck of lint on the far corner of the floor mat. I exhaled and the dot settled over the lint. I breathed slowly and evenly. The red dot didn't waver. It centered the lint like drop of blood.

I looked up when gravel and dirt swirling in the rotor wash began pelting the hood and windshield of the Town Car. Lincoln's Bell Long Ranger was setting down about forty feet in front of me. I watched the helicopter land and rotor blades slow to an idle spin. When Lincoln slid the chopper door open, I lowered the window and opened the car door. I noticed that the pod under the helicopter's nose was aimed in my direction.

Lincoln stepped onto the yard and began walking toward me with the H&K subgun still dangling from his right hand. I slid from the driver's seat and knelt behind the car door. I knew the car door wouldn't stop most modern ammunition and certainly not the minigun, but it made me feel protected. I brought up the Glock and rested it on top of the door.

Lincoln stopped and looked down at his chest. He watched the red laser dot rising from his sternum up to his throat. When he could no longer see the dot because it had come to rest on his face, he looked up and grinned at me.

"New wheels?" Lincoln said, motioning at the Town Car. "Real Mafioso mobile."

I didn't answer.

"Oh, no small talk today? Okay then let's get down to business. Put up your weapon or I'll tell my two men behind you and my crew chief controlling the minigun to open up on you," Lincoln said, still smiling.

"If you want the crate, you'll tell your crew chief to aim that thing in the other direction and your two men to come around and stand behind you. And put that gun down while you're at it."

Lincoln chuckled and shook his head. "Suppose I just kill you and go take the crate."

"Good luck. I lied. It's not on any of my trucks and there's probably two dozen other rigs over there. So whadaya gonna do?"

Lincoln looked over the berm at the rest stop. When he turned back to me, he wasn't smiling anymore.

357

"Your men on the hill are dead, ya know?"

I didn't respond. When I talked it muddled my aim. I concentrated on my target. The red dot roamed over the bridge of Lincoln's nose.

"It's true, both of 'em are dead," Lincoln said.

*Both?* I thought. *Merchanti said he was going to put one of his guys, a former Army Ranger, in the hills.*

"I wanna hear you give those orders to your men, *now!*" I shouted.

Lincoln made a face and said, "Or what?"

I squinted and steadied the red dot. *If it's literally the last thing I do, there's no fuckin' way I'm gonna let Lincoln survive me,* I thought. *This ends here. He doesn't win. He doesn't live on to terrorize my family or anyone else.*

"Cum'on now, Mr. Napolo," Lincoln said calmly. "If I move my head just a little, you'll miss and then you're dead. But that won't get either of us what we came here for, will it? So let's start over. I'll do what you want, but then the truck with the crate comes over here. All right?"

"Do what I said. Then we'll discuss what happens next."

Lincoln exhaled dramatically and signaled to the men standing in front of the Mitsubishi Fuso. Then he spoke into his collar and the pod under the nose of the chopper rotated around until it was pointed in the opposite direction.

"Put your gun on the ground and kick it away," I called out as the two men walked past Lincoln.

Lincoln did as he was told. "Okay. Now what, Mr. Napolo?"

"Tell your men to get Michael outta the helicopter and have him bring me the money."

Lincoln shook his head. "First you put your gun away then I'll get him out. But you don't get him until I see the crate."

I expected the push back. I stood slowly and put the Glock in my pocket. "Okay, get Michael and the money."

The two men, the same ones from yesterday, went inside the chopper. When they emerged, one had Michael by the elbow and the other was carrying two large black bags. Michael's hands where bound in front of him and he limped slightly. He walked with his head down until they had cleared the tips of the slowly spinning rotor blades and stood next to Lincoln. When Michael looked up, I saw the sorrow and fear etched in his face. Even though, Michael managed a thin smile and bent his right hand up at the wrist in a feeble wave.

It was a pitiful site. Michael's face was cut, bruised, and swollen. He had obviously been beaten since I had last seen him. The bandage on his hand was blood-soaked and his stance was hobbled. I looked into Michael's sad eyes and winked.

I said to Michael. "Remember Philadelphia, pal, in South Philly that night in your *Move ova Nova?*"

Michael cocked his head and began to recall the images. We were seniors in college. We had been out drinking, bar hopping after their last exam of the first semester. The bars were closed, we were drunk, and Michael had gotten us lost in South Philly. I got out of the car to ask a group of black kids for directions. There were six or seven of them. Michael couldn't hear what was said, but he saw me getting punched and going down. Without a moment's hesitation, Michael put the old Chevy Nova in reverse and slammed his foot to the floor. The tires squealed and the Nova jumped the curb, up onto the sidewalk toward the scuffle, taking out a trash can and the bus stop bench. The black kids scattered and I dove into the car. As we sped away, I said, 'You almost ran me over. You're a real asshole.' Michael smiling and said, 'Yeah, I know.' We laughed all the way home.

Michael nodded. "Yeah, that was fun."

"I'd like to do that again," I said, without expression.

Michael shrugged and said, wondering, "Sure, me too."

I let my stare linger on Michael. Michael's eyebrows arched, silently questioning, sensing a signal, but failing to make the connection.

Lincoln was looking back and forth between us and wondering, too. *What's this about?*

"Awright, enough of this shit," Lincoln said. "Let's get on with this. I wanna see the crate."

I shifted my attention to Lincoln. "Show Michael the money."

"Show me the crate and the video tape."

"The money first or no crate. The video tape's in the car."

Lincoln turned to Billy, the smaller one, and said, "Fuck it, show 'im the money."

Billy dropped the two bags in front of Michael and unzipped them. Michael peered inside and his eyes went wide. He reached his bound hands into one of the bags and moved the bundles of one hundred-dollar bills around. "Shit, there's a whole lot of money in there, Joseph."

"Two million. It's all there," Lincoln said.

"I'll take your word for it," I said. "Now tell 'im to bring it over here and put it in the back seat. Then I'll call the truck over."

Lincoln hesitated and eyed me. After a few seconds, he said, "DK, you do it, but get the video tape."

DK picked up the bags and began walking toward the car. I remembered how the big man had moved when he almost took Bobby's head off.

"Passenger side, big guy. The tape's on the front seat."

DK nodded and smiled an I'm-gonna-get-ya-anyway smile. I angled my body so I could keep both Lincoln and DK in my field of vision. DK tossed the heavy bags into the back seat, grabbed the tape, and slammed the door closed. He stood by the door, glaring at me.

I turned to Lincoln. "Tell Arnold here to go back over there."

Lincoln nodded to DK, who obeyed but kept his eyes glued to me while he walked back to where the smaller one, Billy, was standing.

"Okay, Napolo, your turn," Lincoln said. "The crate?"

I took the cell phone out of my pocket and pressed redial without taking my eyes off Lincoln and his men.

"Okay, come on over," I said into the phone.

Lincoln said, "I hope this is the real thing. I'd hate to be disappointed again."

"You won't be."

"Let's hope not. For your families' sake."

Michael's head snapped toward Lincoln. "What the fuck does that mean?"

"Ask your friend."

Michael looked at me. "Tell me!"

"Special Agent Dwyer here paid a visit to Cathy the other night. Scared her and the kids. He's threatened to harm our families if this doesn't go well today."

Michael balled his good fist and snarled at Lincoln. "You motherfucker!"

Lincoln's head snapped up in mock surprise. "Such language, Mr. Cogan. They didn't teach you *that* in Catholic school did they?"

"Fuck you."

"Oh, my. And you didn't even hear the best part. Tell him, Mr. Napolo."

"Tell him what?"

"That if I'm disappointed a few minutes from now, first I'm gonna kill you both and then I'm gonna go spend some time with your wives." To Michael, grinning. "Is your wife as pretty as Mrs. Napolo?"

Michael glared at Lincoln. His hands moved to the outside of his right pocket and felt the spigot handle through the thin material. The sound of the truck entering the yard made them both look away.

I turned my head toward the truck and watched the rented Freightliner swing in a wide turn until it stopped facing the opposite direction, with the tail end of the old ocean container facing us.

"What's he doin'," Lincoln called to me.

"He's gonna back in so you can open the doors and inspect the crate."

The Freightliner's engine revved and a burst of black exhaust blew out of the vertical chrome pipe behind the cab. It moved backwards slowly, at first. Moretti was straightening the rig out, putting it on a track directly toward Lincoln that would take it past me on the left. Lincoln glanced confidently at his men. I interpreted it as a get-ready signal. *Get ready, all right,* I thought.

The Freightliner's engine continued to groan louder and louder. Lincoln looked at the tail of the trailer and watched it approaching with increasing speed. He frowned and rocked to one side, shifting his weight to one foot and putting his hands on his hips. He looked quickly at me and then back at the rear doors of the container, as it continued to gather more speed, closing fast. Lincoln straightened his back and let his hands fall to his side.

I stared at Michael, trying to catch his eye but he was too busy watching the approaching truck. I waited until Michael realized something wasn't right. The truck was going too fast. It wasn't slowing down. Michael smiled at me and nodded imperceptibly, mouthing the word *'Philadelphia'*. Then he slipped his hand into his pocket and palmed the spigot handle.

The big diesel engine was screaming now. Bobby Moretti had it red-lined. Lincoln's hand went inside his jacket. His eyes shot to me and over to his men who were moving away. He twisted around to see the cockpit of the Bell Long Ranger. The crew chief's eyes were wide and his mouth was open. He was screaming at the pilot. The Bell Long Ranger was in the truck's path.

The Freightliner accelerated past the Mitsubishi Fuso. Lincoln grabbed Michael by the collar and stepped behind him. He had a new Desert Eagle .50 caliber in his hand, loosely pointed at Michael's head.

The Bell Long Ranger's turbine whined loudly and the rotor blade tips began to rise as the blades spun faster and faster, desperately trying to create enough lift to get the bird off the ground. Out of the corner of his eye, Lincoln saw his two men running away from the helicopter. He squinted up at the rotors through swirling dust and then at the back of the approaching trailer. He made a quick calculation and began running, pulling Michael along by the collar.

As the tail of the container sped past the Town Car toward the Bell Long Ranger, I dove across the front seat and rolled onto the floor, face down, covering my head. Just then, the air brakes on the Freightliner unleashed a horrific hiss and the braking tires roared against the loose gravel in the yard. Lincoln looked back over his shoulder at the bellowing monster. Before he dove to the ground, pulling Michael down on top him, he caught a glimpse of Bobby Moretti in the cab of the truck, standing on the brakes, laughing his ass off.

The first tip of one of the chopper's rotor blades nicked the tail of the steel ocean container just as the Bell Long Ranger's skids were beginning to lift off the ground. But even with its brakes locked and tires smoking, the Freightliner was moving too fast. The following rotors tore into the steel container and were sheared off one by one. A dangling rotor blade whipped through the glass of the cockpit and sliced through the crew chief's torso like a filet knife, killing him instantly. The impact of the successive rotors began to spin the tail of the chopper around just as the back doors of the container slammed into the mid-section of the helicopter.

The tremendous force of the impact easily crushed the Bell Long Ranger's light frame. The momentum of the skidding Freightliner carried the helicopter along against the torn-up rear section of the container, smashing it into the supports of the arched opening of the sand silo. The wreckage finally came to rest wedged into the silo's archway.

After hearing the howling and screeching from the rig's seized tires followed by the deafening crashing and crunching of metal on metal, I hunched lower on the floor of the car. I winced at the incredible noises and hoped Michael had gotten far enough away. When it was quiet, I pushed myself up onto the seat and took out the Glock. I checked to see that the laser aimer was still on and then peered over the dashboard.

I glanced quickly at the Bell Long Ranger. It was destroyed. The container had caught it dead center, at the side doors. The cockpit jutted out to the right of the container inside the silo. I could see the tail rotor sticking up over the far side of the container, folded and bent up by the violent collision. I slid off the seat and knelt behind the open driver's door. I scanned the lot for signs of Michael or Lincoln or the other two. Debris from the helicopter and the container was strewn over the yard. Nothing was moving except dark smoke that was beginning to rise from the wreckage inside the silo.

Suddenly, I was lifted to my feet. The Glock was wrenched from my hand and dropped to the ground. Billy and DK had me by the upper arms and were dragging me away from the car like a rag doll. I struggled, but the big man came around with a forearm that caught me across the brow.

In the darkness that followed, I saw little specks of light and heard someone yell from behind, "Hey, youse two fuck faces remember me?"

I felt myself being spun around.

"What, you assholes don't recognize me?" It was Moretti's voice. "Shave an' a haircut, two bits."

I felt the grips on my arms loosen and I dropped to the ground. I pushed up on my elbows and in my clearing vision I saw Moretti standing with his fists on his hips, grinning.

"You move, you die," Moretti said calmly.

"Fuck you!" the big man said, taking a step and going for a pistol inside his jacket.

The smaller one was still reaching behind his back when Moretti's hands rose quickly yet smoothly from his hips, a silenced Heckler & Koch .45 in each hand. Moretti's .45's coughed twice, spitting two quick shots from each of the suppressed autoloaders. The smaller one, Billy, took two rounds in the face and flopped backwards, dead before he hit the ground. DK spun around. A bullet had hit him in the collarbone and exited his upper back. Another had blown away most of his lower right jaw. The big man fell to one knee and teetered, facing me. Part of his jaw bone and teeth were hanging from a torn piece of cheek flesh, leaving a gaping hole that horribly exposed his tongue and the roof of his mouth. I was unable to mask my revulsion as we caught each other's eyes. Another thump from one of Moretti's automatics and the side of DK's head exploded. I heard the empty brass shell casing bouncing on the gravel followed by Moretti saying, "No, fuck you".

I looked at Moretti and barely recognized him. The bruises and the stitches, the shave and the military haircut all contributed to a new lean, hard-edged look, but there was something else about him. He walked toward me, pistols up and ready, scanning the yard for Lincoln, moving like a man trained to be the hunter or the hunted, whatever the situation called for, to do whatever had to be done.

*Who is this guy?* I thought. I saw Moretti's eyes lock onto something behind him over the hood of the car. Moretti swung his pistols.

I heard two thunderous shots. It was Lincoln's big .50 caliber Desert Eagle. Moretti's arms flew out. The two H&K .45's sailed away as he slammed back onto the gravel. He didn't move.

I turned to see Lincoln standing behind Michael in front of the Town Car with the Desert Eagle pointed at Michael's temple. I scrambled back to the open door and picked up the Glock.

"Forget it, Napolo," Lincoln shouted. "You're both gonna die now. And you'll die knowin' that I'm gonna blow your children's faces off and then fuck your wives until they beg me to kill them."

Lincoln pointed the Desert Eagle at me behind the door. The huge .50 caliber slugs would tear through the car door like it was made of cardboard. I fumbled the Glock as I tried to bring it up.

"Remember me now?" Moretti shouted, breathing heavily. "Without the mustache?" He coughed.

Lincoln looked up. Moretti was up on one elbow, with my old .45 in the other hand pointed at Lincoln.

Lincoln's mouth opened to speak but his shock muted him. Moretti tapped his chest with his fist. It clanged.

"Half-inch diamond plate, you asshole. Just like we put under our asses in the Hueys."

Lincoln's eyes narrowed, then widened in recognition. "Pleiku, SOG, right?"

"Yeah, November sixty-nine. You were one sick motherfucker even back then."

"Fuck you. I shoulda wasted all you pussies that night."

"Guess you should've."

Moretti quickly aimed the old Colt and fired. I heard a groan from behind. I turned and saw the helicopter pilot falling backwards, with a dark hole above his left eye, an H&K submachine gun skidding away from him.

Lincoln recognized the split-second distraction as an opportunity, but Moretti anticipated it and was already rolling away when the Desert Eagle fired. The fat .50 caliber round went through Moretti's thigh muscle. Lincoln's second shot hit him in the lower back. Moretti lay face down, not moving.

Lincoln swung his gun back to me but I had also seized the moment and had aimed the Glock, using the open door as a support. The bright laser beam from the Glock's aimer flashed in Lincoln's eyes. Lincoln looked at the red glow coming from under the muzzle of the gun and knew the aimer was on his face. He smiled wickedly and jerked his head behind Michael's.

"Uh-oh, missed me," he said in a singsong voice.

After a couple seconds, Lincoln came out from behind Michael and I reacquired my target.

"Shoot him, Joseph!" Michael said firmly. "Shoot the motherfucker."

Lincoln moved his head quickly again.

"Missed me again." Lilting this time.

Lincoln popped his head up over Michael's left shoulder, waited and ducked behind Michael.

"Made ya miss."

He popped up again over Michael's right shoulder and after a second ducked again. He repeated it over and over again, sometimes alternating the left and right shoulder, sometimes not, varying the time he exposed himself, each time taunting, "Made ya miss."

I struggled to get the laser on Lincoln as he bobbed his head, trying unsuccessfully to anticipate his next move. More than once the red dot floated dangerously across Michael's face.

I squeezed my eyes to clear my vision and took a deep breath. I took aim in the space three inches over Michael's left shoulder and waited.

"Never gonna get me . . . never gonna get me . . ." Lincoln was playground singing now. "Never gonna get me . . ."

Suddenly, the singing stopped. Michael felt Lincoln's hand press firmly down on his shoulder. He heard gravel crunching and sensed Lincoln was about to make a move. Michael tightened his grip on the spigot handle in his fist. The rusted three-inch stem protruded from between his fingers. Michael wrapped his damaged left hand around his right wrist and tightened his biceps.

Lincoln increased the pressure on Michael's shoulder and growled, "Say good bye, Mr. Napolo."

Michael drew a deep breath, ducked his shoulder and grunted as he drove his right elbow back into Lincoln's ribs. But Lincoln had felt Michael moving and was stepping back when the elbow crashed into his lower ribcage. The short distance he had moved lessened the blow, but Lincoln was still off balance when Michael spun around and swung up from his waist. Michael's fist hit Lincoln in the upper neck, driving the jagged spigot stem up into the soft flesh under his jaw. Using the palm of his hand, Michael shoved the spigot handle in as far as he could, pushing the rusted stem through the lower plate of Lincoln's jaw until it was sticking through the floor of his mouth. Lincoln stumbled away, gagging and pulling at the round metal handle that was now flush against his left jawbone.

"SHOOT HIM!" Michael screamed. "SHOOT HIM NOW!"

I took aim at Lincoln who was standing, breathing heavily, head bent to one side and bleeding from the mouth. He was clutching the spigot handle under his jaw with his left hand, holding the Desert Eagle against is thigh in his right. Lincoln's face telegraphed his pain as he looked at me.

"Do it!" Michael pleaded.

I held the laser dot steady on the bridge of Lincoln's nose.

"Drop your gun," I called to Lincoln.

"For chrissake, Joseph! He was gonna kill our families, remember?"

"Drop it, now!" I shouted.

"Whathefuck Joseph? Shoot him! Do it! Fucking shoot him!"

I struggled to keep my aim steady. The laser dot roamed Lincoln face. I watched Lincoln's eyes go back and forth between Michael and me.

Michael yelled, "SHOOT THE MOTHERFUCKER!"

"DROP IT!" I screamed.

Lincoln let the Desert Eagle fall out of his hand and straightened up, best he could.

"Oh fuck," Michael groaned.

Lincoln began to chuckle but the pain brought him up short. He spit out a mouth full of blood.

"What's the matter Napolo?" Lincoln's speech was slurred from the jagged edge of the stem pushing up against his tongue. "Got a little too much of your mommy's blood in your veins?" Deep breathes that splattered blood on the exhale. "Can't even shoot someone who's gonna fuck your wife and kill your kids?"

I stood and walked toward Lincoln, my arms up in the Weaver configuration. I stopped a few feet away with the gun pointed at Lincoln's face. All the muscles in my arms were flexed and taut as if it would take all my strength to pull the trigger.

"He's fuckin' psycho," Michael said. "Do it. What does it matter now?"

Lincoln stared at me. I squinted over the sights of the pistol and envisioned his head disappearing in the nanosecond after I pulled the trigger.

I felt my muscles loosen. It did matter.

Lincoln smirked with one side of his face. "He's not gonna shoot me, are ya Napolo? Ya can't do it, can ya?"

I relaxed my grip and pointed the muzzle of the Glock up toward the sky.

Lincoln turned to Michael. "Told ya." Then to me. "Your grandfather must be flippin' around in his grave seeing what a pussy his grandson turned out to be."

I shook my head. "I don't think so. You're just a nasty piece of shit, Mr. Lincoln, or whoever you are, and I don't think he'd want me to dirty my hands on someone like you."

"You're letting him go?" Michael asked, incredulously. "After what he did to Moretti and me? After he said that about our kids, you're gonna let him go?"

I didn't answer. Instead I looked skyward toward the sounds of an approaching helicopter. It was coming in fast from the north.

Lincoln looked up, too. "Well, that's no one I know, so I'll be going now," he said. Then to me, "Keys in the car?"

I nodded.

"No fuckin' way!" Michael said, as he started toward Lincoln.

I stepped in front of Michael, grabbed his shoulders, and spun him around so I could keep my gun pointed at Lincoln. Michael struggled but I held him and moved my face in close. "Stop it, Michael! We're not murderers." Then when we had locked eyes, I moved closer and whispered, so only Michael could hear, "Do you think I would ever let anything happen to our families? Do you think I haven't taken care of that?"

Michael's eyes searched my face. I drilled into him with my eyes and whispered, "Do you?"

I felt Michael's body droop. I put my arms around him. Then I raised the Glock behind Michael's back and pointed it at Lincoln.

"Get the fuck outta here before I change my mind."

Lincoln put his hands up. "Just wanted to remember you two guys just like that. See I knew you were a faggot, Cogan."

Michael broke away from me. "Fuck you."

Lincoln shrugged and despite the excruciating pain in his jaw and mouth, he laughed, "Sorry, not today."

Lincoln walked to the Town Car. "A Lincoln for Lincoln. Very thoughtful, Napolo."

Michael spun toward me. "What about the money?"

I scowled at him. Michael kicked at the gravel and turned away.

Lincoln closed the door and started the engine. "Don't suppose you wanna tell me where the crate is?" he said through the open window.

I snapped up my arms and pointed the Glock at him.

Lincoln grinned painfully and spit out another mouthful of blood. Then he wiped his lips with the back of his hand, made a gun with his fingers and pointed it at me. He pretended to fire the gun and winked as he drove away.

As the helicopter began its final decent, Michael and I hurried over to Moretti. I slowed and dropped back a couple paces to press a speed dial key on the rented cell phone. I let it ring twice before hanging up.

I knelt with Michael by Moretti. He was lying in a pool of blood but he was breathing. We rolled him over and called his name.

Moretti moaned, "Yeah, . . . stop . . . the bleeding."

One bullet had gone through his side and another through his thigh. I took off my belt and tied it off tight above the wound in the leg. Then I stripped off my jacket and emptied the pockets, letting the guns, magazines, and cell phone scatter on the gravel. I tried ripping the heavy material but failed. Moretti held up a knife in a bloody hand. I began cutting the jacket to bandage his wounds.

"Did you just call 911?" Michael asked.

"No, something else."

"Jesus, cut me loose and I'll call."

I used Moretti's knife on the plastic restraints. Michael turned and reached for the phone. He stopped when he saw the men's shoes.

"Don't make that call. We'll take care of him."

I turned to the familiar voice. It was Wilson Dennis. Two paramedics pushed me aside and threw open their orange case. I sat back and looked up at Wilson and the three men in black combat gear moving to surround us. They quickly positioned themselves, backs to us, sweeping the full 360 degrees around us with their automatic weapons. I noticed there were no markings across their backs and thought back to Merchanti's description of the SWAT teams that had raided the iron works.

"Where's Lincoln?" Wilson asked. "Is he dead?" Motioning to the wreckage.

"No, he left in the car," I said.

"Is the crate on the trailer?"

"No, that's being taken care of separately."

"You came here without the crate?"

I nodded.

Wilson shook his head and made circular motion above his shoulder with his right hand. "Recon and cover," he said, and the three armed men broke away, weapons at ready position.

"Is he gonna be all right?" Michael asked the paramedics.

One of them nodded. "Yeah, he'll be fine. We can stabilize him here but he's gonna need more."

"There's a surgical team standing by at Bella Collina," Wilson interjected. "As soon as you're ready, get 'im in the chopper."

"No, let's just get him to the nearest trauma center," I said. "We'll accept the ride in your helicopter but we don't need any more of your help."

Wilson shook his head. "Our medical team is highly qualified. They're trained and equipped for this type of trauma - better than most hospitals around here. Besides, he's our man, and we don't need any local cops called in on this. That's mandatory for all gunshot wounds."

"Whadaya mean, *your* man?" I said.

Wilson nodded. "His name's Capuano, not Moretti. He's been our deep cover man inside your operation."

I sprang to my feet. "What?" I said, realizing that this certainly explained a few things.

Wilson put a hand up. "Oh, calm down, Joseph. He was put there to protect both our interests. And from the looks of things here, I'd say that today he did just that, didn't he?"

I turned to Michael who said, "Unfuckingbelievable . . ."

I looked down at Moretti or whoever he was. The paramedics had slid a body board under him and were preparing to lift him on to a stretcher.

I held out the palms of my hands. "Bobby?"

Capuano smiled at me and nodded sheepishly. "Don't be mad at me, boss. Jus' doin' my job . . . watching your six."

"And Pucci's, too, right?"

"Yeah, well . . . but no more. I'm gettin' too old for this shit." Turning to Wilson. "I hereby quit."

"We'll talk later, when you're feeling better," Wilson said.

"No we won't. I'm done." To Michael and me. "You got any openings? I kinda liked working for you guys."

Michael rolled his eyes. The paramedics lifted Capuano onto the stretcher.

I put a hand out to the man I knew as Moretti. "Thanks, for everything . . . Bobby, if that's your name."

Capuano clasped my hand. "No problem. How 'bout that job."

I smiled and shrugged. "I dunno. Let us think about it, okay?"

Capuano nodded as they carried him away. Over his shoulder, he said, "Hey, my name really is Bobby."

Wilson's SWAT team returned to his side. They had collected all the weapons, ammunition, and spent shell casings.

The lead man spoke. "Four dead. We put them all in the wreckage, in blankets."

Wilson looked at Michael and me. "The blankets are coated with white phosphorous and other high-heat reactants. When we ignite them they'll burn at almost 4500 degrees. The wreckage will incinerate and the superheat will reduce the bodies to ash. No one needs to know what really happened here if we move fast. Agree?"

I looked at Michael. He nodded.

"We agree," I said.

Wilson took the Glock and the old Colt .45 along with the extra clips from one of his man. He held them out to me. "Here, these are yours."

"I don't need them any more."

"If Lincoln slips through our net, he'll come for you someday. You should know that."

I shook my head. "I've made my own arrangements. So, no thanks. No more guns. Why doncha give that .45 to Pucci. He seemed to think it was his anyway."

"You should re-think this," Wilson said.

Michael leaned in. "Joseph, maybe we should . . ."

"No, no more guns."

Wilson stared at me a moment and then handed the pistols and clips back to his man. "We all need to go now," he said.

Wilson's lead man handed me a pair of keys. "I took these off one of those guys. They look like they go to that truck over there."

"You two get going," Wilson said to Michael and me. "We'll remotely detonate the wreckage from the air after you're on your way." Then to me. "Is everything else taken care of? Will you be meeting the contract deadline?"

"Yes."

"Outstanding."

Wilson turned and headed toward the helicopter, which had begun to rev its turbines. As Wilson was about to duck under the spinning rotor blades he turned and shouted, "Get the hell outta here. Talk to ya next week."

Then he smiled and waved as if we had just finished a friendly round of golf.

*　　*　　*

Lincoln was driving the speed limit on Interstate 87, a few minutes south of the maintenance yard, just past the tandem drop yard where rigs hauling two trailers had to drop one before they proceeded further down the interstate toward the city and other restricted roadways. He had already formulated his plan, though. He knew that he had to get the spigot stem out of his jaw, but chances were that the extrication would result in much more bleeding. As it was, the blood pooling in his mouth was causing him difficulty breathing, requiring him to frequently tilt his head forward and drain his mouth onto the floor between his legs. And, if after he removed the rusty spike the bleeding became much worse, he would have to jump off the highway around White Plains to find a hospital for some emergency treatment. These were the immediate concerns. Once dealt with he could refocus on the task at hand; getting to the airport where he needed to do some damage control. After that, he would again deal with the matter of the crate.

*Napolo. Stupid fuck,* he thought. *He should have listened to Cogan. Thank God he didn't, but he should have.*

He slowly twisted the spigot handle with one hand and drove with the other. The pain was excruciating. Every tug, every movement of his head, shot needles of pain through his neck and face, and made his eyes water. But this was the only way. He could explain some freak accident to the ER nurse. Maybe he had taken the day off to do some work around the house and had tripped and fallen onto the screwdriver he was holding. Sounded good. Certainly better that having to explain the spigot handle under his jaw. Besides, the only sure way to reduce the pain was to remove the metal spike. He had to keep at it. But, each time he turned the handle and pulled there was a sucking sound, a sickly sloshing sucking sound that made him hesitate.

*Fucking Cogan,* he thought. *Who'd thought he had any balls? He'll shit the next time he sees me. I'll get Napolo and him at the same time, just so Cogan can say he was right. And Napolo will die knowing that his failed moment of truth cost him the lives of everybody he loves.*

Lincoln pulled into the far right lane behind a slow moving tractor-trailer and dipped his head forward to vacate the blood from his mouth. He had to get this done. He pulled within four car lengths of the rear of the tractor-trailer and slowed to match its speed. He began to regulate his breathing, taking shallow but long breaths through his nose, letting his vision tunnel onto the rear door handles of the trailer in front of him. The rhythm of his breathing soon fell in pace with his heartbeats and he began to decrease the pace of one with the other. A few more minutes he would be in the place he needed to be, somewhere that was both deep inside and, at the same time, well outside his damaged body. A place, where for the few moments he needed, he would be free from pain, free from all that his body was, free to yank out the rusted spigot stem.

Suddenly, the tail lights on the trailer lit up and the distance between the Town Car and trailer closed up fast. Lincoln whipped the wheel to the left, nearly clipping the corner of the trailer as he veered into the center lane. But another truck was right there. He braked and began to pull left again for the fast lane but another big rig was right there, hemming him in. He looked to his right. Another truck! He tapped the brakes to slow down and heard from behind a long low blast from an airhorn. *Fuck!* The menacing front grill of a big Peterbilt filled his rearview mirror.

Lincoln was no longer anywhere that even remotely resembled a transcendental state. He was smack in the middle of a brand new reality; stuck inside a rolling metal cage of tractors and trailers. Ahead of him, three rigs were traveling side-by-side across the three lanes. To his right and left, two more were keeping him penned in from the side. And in the rear, three trucks sealed off the lanes behind him.

He leaned forward and let the blood fall from his mouth onto his lap. When he looked up, the trucks in front of him had decreased their speed. He tapped the brakes but it wasn't enough. The trucks were continuing to slow down.

Lincoln heard the *kasheesh-kasheesh-kasheesh* of air brakes all around him. He brought his foot down harder on the brake pedal to keep from rear-ending the trailer in front of him. The Peterbilt behind him closed the gap between them as the cube of steel rolled to stop.

Lincoln closed his eyes and put a hand up to his jaw. The jolting and twisting of his head had brought on a whole new level of pain. He opened his eyes when he heard the rear door of the trailer in front of him rolling up. He began to reach around for the nine-millimeter tucked in the small of his back but it was too late.

Jimmy Merchanti was standing in the back of the trailer with several of his men. They had a Remington 12-gauge pump and a couple of AK 47's pointed down at Lincoln. Other armed men quickly appeared on both sides of the car, their guns all aimed at Lincoln. Lincoln put his hands on the top of the steering wheel, closed his eyes, and let his head droop to the left, blood spilling from his mouth.

Two men yanked Lincoln from the car and patted him down. They found the Glock nine, a small 380 automatic strapped to his ankle, and the silenced .22 revolver in his jacket pocket, but they missed the knife in the sleeve of his jacket. Two other men grabbed the bags of money from the back seat and tossed them up into the trailer with Merchanti. Lincoln was hustled to the rear of the trailer. Merchanti stared down at him.

"So you're the motherfucker who thinks he can kill my friends and live? Well look at you now."

Lincoln stared back defiantly.

Merchanti huffed. "What, the garden tool got your tongue?" To his men. "Get him up here."

Two of Merchanti's men on the ground shoved Lincoln against the trailer. Two others inside the trailer reached down. One of them grabbed the shoulder of Lincoln's jacket. The other said, "Look, this fuckin' guy even comes with his own handle." And then he grabbed the spigot handle and pulled Lincoln up into the trailer.

Lincoln screams were muffled when the door of the trailer rolled down behind him. The men on the ground scattered into the other trucks. The big rigs began to move. The Peterbilt rolled forward and began to push the Town Car. With its wheels locked, the Town Car shuttered along the pavement and began angling toward the shoulder. The Peterbilt followed its track until it had pushed it off the highway onto the grass the shoulder. The whole event was over in less than two minutes. The Interstate was clear again and traffic was flowing.

\*     \*     \*

When the traffic had slowed on I-87, I hoped that the cause was Merchanti executing his part of the plan. When the three lanes came to a complete stop, I smiled to myself, knowing that it would be over soon. I drove on the shoulder to the ramp for the tandem yard where I found a bank of pay phones. After calls to our families, I called Hertz and reported the Town Car had been stolen in a carjacking at the Ramapo rest area. Then I dialed Sam Meltzer.

"You okay?" Sam asked as soon as he picked up the phone.

"Everything's fine. Worse part's over."

"And Michael?"

"He's here with me."

"Thank God. Now we wait 'till five."

"That's why I called. I don't have my cell phone and I've got to get Michael to the hospital - he has an injured hand, so I'll contact you. Please wait for my call."

"Of course. What happened to Michael's hand? Is he okay?"

"He'll live, but it may be awhile before he swings any clubs."

"Too bad. I owe him a few bucks and my game's been pretty good lately."

"Well, I don't think he's gonna be takin' any more bets."

"Oh yeah, sorry, never mind. Forget I mentioned it."

When I hung up, Michael tapped me on the shoulder and pointed north. Thick black smoke was rising from the maintenance yard. Neither of us said a word as we climbed back into the Mitsubishi Fuso.

The traffic was moving again when we pulled back onto I-87. After a few minutes, I saw the black Town Car up ahead angled across the shoulder. I waited for a good feeling to come over me. It never came.

"There's the car!" Michael pointed. "Looks like he was rear-ended."

"Don't worry about it. He's not in it."

"How do you know?"

"I just know. I'll tell ya later - it's a very long story."

"Where is he then?"

"On his way to Hell, I hope."

Michael looked at me. "Whathefuck does that means?"

I didn't respond. There was too much to tell and I was too tired to tell it. Michael would just have to wait.

After a minute Michael said, "Jus' gimme a little hint, will ya? At least tell me what you're thinking."

I looked over at him. "I was just thinking that you're a real asshole."

Michael chuckled. "Well, yeah, I know that. Tell me something new, will ya?"

\*     \*     \*

Lincoln figured that they had been traveling for about thirty minutes. The trailer was empty except for Merchanti and three of his men, standing in a circle, holding on to garment hanging ropes that were strung along the ceiling. The lack of weight on board made for a bumpy and jarring ride, and to Lincoln they looked like subway straphangers, bouncing and swaying in unison as they discussed the logistics of disposing of him.

"How long we gonna ride in the back of this fuckin' trailer? This is bad on my knees."

"Yeah, these fuckin' ropes are rippin' up my hands."

"Man, you better switch off. You get too many calluses you'll fuckin' rip your dick to shreds, all that jerkin' off you do."

"Hey, fuck you!"

Laughter.

"Not too much longer," Merchanti said. "In fact, we're probably gettin' close. I got a City Linens van parked at the rest stop near Spring Valley. We'll put him in a laundry cart and take him down to Bergen."

"Bergen? To Marty's?"

Merchanti nodded. "Yeah, the old man arranged it."

"Whoa, that Marty's a crazy fuck, ya know. He's got his basement all set up with this table and all kinds a saws and nasty lookin' medieval shit. Tol' me he got the idea from the end of that movie Braveheart - ya know, when Mel Gibson's stretched out on that table gettin' cut up. He's even got this drain in the floor so he can hose the place down."

"Shit, he's got a stretcher like that?"

"Fuck no, you idiot, just a table with drainage grooves - like big carving board."

"Jesus . . ."

"Oh, yeah, he's fuckin' nuts."

There was a brief silence while they shook their heads in contemplation of the horror about to come.

"So how ya wanna do this, Jimmy?"

"When we stop, just whack him a couple times with the sap and use some duct tape to make sure he stays quiet. The old man wants him awake when we start cutting 'im up."

Lincoln was slumped against the inside wall of the trailer, listening. He had used a biorhythmic meditation technique to recover from the incredible pain of having been lifted up by the spigot handle and then pummeled into near unconsciousness. Remarkably, something good had come of this rough treatment. The rusty stem had been loosened and pulled out a bit. The tip was no longer protruding through the floor of his mouth and he had been using the tip of his tongue to apply pressure to the hole in his mouth, which had drastically reduced the bleeding. Better yet, the stem was now loose enough to pull out with one hard tug.

Lincoln felt the truck slowing down. He continued to feign a dazed, barely conscious state as he slid the razor-sharp steel blade out of the sleeve of his jacket. Then, while the truck swung through the curve on the exit ramp, and Merchanti and his crew held onto the ropes with both hands, tilting as one, looking like their feet were nailed to floor, Lincoln took a deep breath and gripped the spigot handle.

# Later that afternoon . . .

## The Lufthansa Air Cargo Terminal
## Newark International Airport

Albert Catella pulled the twenty-foot rented Ryder truck over to the curb just outside the guardhouse at the entrance to the Lufthansa cargo terminal. Johnny Onions was in the passenger seat. Catella waited until the thundering from a jetliner taking off above them had rolled away.

"Sign says to have your delivery order ready and that all cargo is subject to inspection. You got a delivery order?" Catella asked.

"No one said nothin' about no delivery order."

"Well, now what the fuck do we do? It's almost five and ya know they're gonna wanna inspect us."

"Whathefuck do I know? Napolo jus' said ta ask for a guy called Rudy. That's all he tol'me."

Catella slapped the steering wheel. "Fuckin' great. I don't need this shit, Johnny. I got a good thing goin' at 714. Believe me, this kinda shit I don't need."

Johnny threw his hands up. "Ouffa, how many times I gotta hear how good you got it? Sounds to me like all this job did was turn you into a big fuckin' pussy. Ya had ta trade in your balls on the first day, or what?"

"Hey, fuck you, man. Maybe when you *get* your first fuckin' job we'll talk about my job. Until then, I don't wanna hear your shit. Ya understand?"

"Yeah, yeah." Johnny glanced up. "Hey, who's this fuckin' guy?"

Catella looked through the windshield and saw a tall, lean man dressed all in white walking toward them. He was hanging on to the ends of a white towel that was wrapped around his neck.

"Be cool," Catella said. "I'll handle this."

The man smiled as he approached Catella's window. When Catella rolled the window down, the guy with the towel peered inside. When he bent further into the window, the towel shifted and Catella noticed a bandage covering a nasty bruise under his jaw. His icy gray eyes squinted across at Johnny Onions. He said, "My name's Rudy. Can I help you?"

Johnny smirked at Catella. Then he said to the guy with the towel, "You're just the guy we're lookin' for."

"I thought so. You guys can get out. I'll take it in from here and meet you by the white van over there in about ten minutes."

# CHAPTER 30

**Saturday Morning**
**The Sunset Suites Hotel**
**Tinton Falls, New Jersey**

I was lying in bed listening to Cathy humming in the shower. Our children had gone to the indoor pool with Ilene and the two Cogan kids. I closed my eyes to recapture the smiles on their small faces when I had appeared at the door the night before. I smiled thinking about the big hugs from those little arms. They squeezed me at three different places along my body, according to their ages. Cathy's hug wouldn't let go and left tears on my shoulder. I promised myself that I would make it up to her. I got a good start as soon as the kids left the room this morning. I could tell by her humming.

I put my hands behind my head and smiled at the ceiling. My cell phone hadn't rung once since Michael and I left the maintenance yard and, as far as I was concerned, no news was goods news. No calls from Merchanti or Catella meant that they had each done what was planned, what was necessary, and that they had been successful. Sam Meltzer had call last night to confirm that Rudy at Lufthansa had received the delivery on time. Michael's wound had been stabilized at the emergency room. He was probably going to need to see a hand surgeon but the ER doctor deemed most of the damage repairable. Even the gunshot wound report had fit nicely inside the carjacking story we invented for the loss of the Lincoln Town Car. Maybe I had actually pulled it off. Time would tell, but so far . . .

I reached for the remote control and flipped through the channels. I landed on CNN and watched the end of a financial report. The stock markets had finished another lackluster week. The economy was still sluggish. I really didn't care. It was just nice to be watching something normal, even boring. Something that ordinary people would be watching. People who had worked hard all week, relaxing with their Saturday morning coffee before they went about their ordinary weekends. The kind of people I had been happy to be. Was I still? Had the things I'd done changed that?

I heard the shower curtain jingle along the rod. Cathy was still humming. I tried to place the song. I couldn't, but I heard the words in my head.

*I may never be no rich man in this world,*
*But I'm feelin' quite Rockefeller-like,*
*Since I met you girl . . .*

I smiled, again. The burning tree hadn't fallen in my forest, near my family, on my life. The things of this week would only live in me and, as these things do in time, they would recede into the part of me that kept all the secrets of my life. They would stay in that place, where only I could find them, occasionally creeping out to disturb a night's sleep, but always ready to remind me of the unholy side of myself.

There were several quick but muted taps on the door. Little fists wrapped in towels. Cathy came out from the bathroom and opened the door. We were all together again.

The Napolo family, my family, dressed and packed. We were going home. Joseph Jr. had a Little League game at eleven and Mickey's T-Ball game was at one. Robbie played soccer but his game was on Sunday. I still hadn't put down any lime or fertilizer yet this season. I hoped to squeeze that in, too. I wondered if Cathy had made any other plans for us. I hoped so. I wanted a very full, ordinary weekend.

As we were making our final inspection of the room, checking the under the beds and in the bathroom and closet to be sure that we were leaving nothing behind, I heard the ominous music that CNN was playing for the May Massacre segue. In a couple seconds the anchor would be launching into an update on the Mob War in New York and the Napolo Crime Family would be prominently featured. I scrambled for the remote and pressed the mute button. Someday, when they were older, before they heard it in the schoolyard, I would tell my children about their great-grandfather. Someday, maybe soon, but certainly not today.

I ushered them all quickly into the hall and looked back into the room one more time. On the television, an old black and white photograph of my grandfather wearing tinted glasses was floating above the CNN anchor's shoulder. I closed the door and took my family home.

*   *   *

In the next room, a young man sat on the edge of the bed glued to CNN's reporting of the May Massacre. He had slept off a night of serious drinking and casual sex with a woman he had met in a bar in Red Bank. She left sometime before he woke. No note. No phone number. No nothing. *Fuck her*, he had thought to himself and then laughed because he had.

When the CNN music came on, he had turned up the volume and skittered to the end of the bed to accommodate his hangover eyes. The anchor had just handed off to a reporter live at the scene.

*". . . found early this morning by a trucker who saw what has turned out to be the blood of five men dripping from the back of a trailer parked here in the Spring Valley, New York rest area on Interstate 87. The concerned trucker contacted the New York State Police who discovered what's being described as a gruesome multiple murder. Unconfirmed law enforcement sources on the scene are saying that the murders appear to be related to the New York organized crime war that has dominated this week's news. The same source indicated the victims were brutally slashed to death and that at least two of them were known members of the Napolo Crime Family. In fact, an unidentified investigator was overheard saying that James "Jimmy Boy" Merchanti, a possible successor to the ailing Napolo Family boss, Fabrizio Benedetto, was among the dead. The same unidentified source told us that investigators are looking for answers to a particularly grisly question. What was the significance of the garden spigot handle found imbedded in Jimmy Boy Merchanti's eye? Could this be a secret underworld message sent by rival Russian Mobsters and, if so, what does it mean?*

*"Back to the studio . . ."*

## The Airport Inn Motel
## Newark, New Jersey

*What's that motherfucker doin' in there?* Johnny Onions thought. *Even a good shit, shower and shave don't take that long.* He wanted to yell something to this guy; something like 'Whathefuck ya doin' in there?' But he couldn't. The duct tape was too tight across his mouth.

Catella looked over at Johnny in disgust and then down at the duct tape around his own arms and legs. He had a few thoughts of his own: *I can't fuckin' believe I let him get me into this shit. The whole goddam night taped to this chair, listening to that asshole Rudy snoring. Fucker wouldn't even let us go to*

378

*the bathroom. Peed my pants, twice, for chrissake. Keeps promisin' us the money's comin' in the morning. And what if it doesn't? What're we gonna do about it? What can we do? Not a fuckin' thing, that's what. Jesus, what the fuck was I thinkin'? Took me twenty-five years to get my life squared away. One fuckin' phone call from this asshole Johnny and it's all fucked. I shoulda never . . .*

The bathroom door opened. The tall, thin guy called Rudy came out looking much different. He appeared to have gained about thirty pounds, mostly in the chest and belly. His short, spiked graying hair had been dyed dark brown and combed flat. He now had a matching brown beard that covered the bandage under his left jaw. He was wearing a blue blazer over a yellow cotton golf shirt, khaki pants, and a pair of shiny brown tassel loafers.

Catella and Johnny stared at him in disbelief. They watched him as he stood in front of the full-length mirror, slipping on a pair of wire-framed glasses and taking a passport from his jacket pocket. He looked down at the photo on the passport and then studied himself in the mirror through the contact lenses that had changed the color of his eyes from cold steel gray to warm brown. After adjusting the glasses and pressing at the sides of his new beard, the corners of his mouth turned up. The transformation was complete. The hard-assed guy with the two guns that had duct taped them to the chairs now looked every bit to be a middle-aged professional dressed for a casual Saturday afternoon at the clubhouse.

He slowly turned around to face his two hostages. "Sorry to keep you guys waiting so long. Thank you for your patience. As you can see, these things take a little time." His voice was different, too. Soft and calming. Quite pleasant, in fact.

He came closer and ripped the duct tape off their mouths, Johnny's first.

"You wanna tell us what the fuck's goin' on?" Johnny demanded. "When's the money gettin' here? And *who* the fuck *are* you?"

"Oh my, how rude of me. You can call me Dr. Ansbach, now. Good ole Rudy had to go. As far as the money . . . well, I lied. I already have the money and I'm keeping it, all for me."

Catella looked at the floor and shook his head.

Johnny said, "Whathefuck! This is bullshit! We had a deal, you motherfucker!"

The doctor was pulling on a pair of latex gloves. "Please, I'm a cardiologist, a well-respected surgeon." He held up his gloved hands and wiggled his fingers. "I don't appreciate that language."

"Go fuck yourself," Johnny said.

The doctor was busy pushing the latex down between his fingers. He switched to the other hand as he said, "I can understand your disappointment with the way this has turned out for you, but you can be thankful for a couple things."

Catella looked up. "What's that?"

"Well, happily for you, I have to be going soon. You see, I have a flight to catch. I'm going to the Middle East. I have to see an associate there. Emergency heart surgery, of sorts."

Johnny groaned, "Aw for chrissake."

Catella ignored him. "You said *a couple* a things."

"Oh, yes. Luckily, my knife is very sharp." The good doctor held up a double-edged steel blade.

Catella's mouth fell open. Johnny's head snapped up.

"Hey, what're ya gonna do here?" Johnny asked. "You keep the fuckin' money. It's okay. Have a nice trip, ya know. We don't need no trouble here."

"Oh, no trouble at all," the doctor said. "I'll just need one of you guys to spell chrysanthemum for me."

The Alley Cat and Johnny Onions both looked up at him in disbelief, raising their chins, exposing their necks.

"*What?*" Catella asked.

The doctor raised the knife. "Sorry, wrong answer."

# EPILOGUE

**Seven Months Later . . .**
**November 2001**
**DTC Transportation**
**The Terminal Building**

I checked my watch, again, for the fifth or sixth time that morning. Nine forty. It was almost time. I hurried back to my office and locked the door. Michael was on his way to the bank. We were finalizing the financing for our new state-of-the-art trucking terminal and distribution center in Virginia. Our DOD business was booming. We needed a presence closer to our largest customer, the United States government. Michael wouldn't be back for about forty minutes. Plenty of time.

I turned on the television and flipped the channels until I found *The Day Show*. The affable fat black guy was working the crowd in the street outside the studio. There was a baby from California and a set of middle-aged blonde twins from Minnesota who where celebrating their fortieth birthdays in the Big Apple. They giggled when they told the affable fat black guy that they left their husbands home with the kids. The affable fat black guy made a cute remark and a funny face, as he handed the show back to the handsome fit white guy back inside the studio.

The handsome fit white guy told the camera that coming up would be a special report on America's War on Terror. There were new developments in the Middle East that signaled unprecedented aggressive actions taken against US warplanes patrolling the no-fly zones in Iraq. But first, the bubbly thin Asian woman had another story about the continuing generosity of the American people since 9/11. The camera cut to the bubbly thin Asian woman.

*"Fletcher, you really need to tell me where you got that tie. I just love it. I want it."*

Off camera the handsome fit white guy yelled, *"Well, you can't have it."*

The affable fat black guy chimed in, *"'Cause he borrowed it from his daddy."*

Laughter from the stage crew.

*"Oh, you guys . . . Well, I'm here with Attorney Sam Meltzer who represents a businessman from New Jersey who has decided to do something quite special for the families of victims of terrorism. Mr. Meltzer can you tell us what your client has done?"*

*"Sure, my client, who wishes to remain anonymous, has funded an annuity worth almost twenty million dollars to seed a foundation called, The Grandchildren Fund. The purpose of the foundation is quite simple: to provide grants to the immediate relatives of victims of terrorism, no matter whether they were civilians, police, firefighters, or other first respondents, or military personnel killed or disabled in action,. The grants will allow the children of the victims to be able to spend more time with their grandparents."*

*"What a nice idea. Can you tell us more about it?"*

*"Certainly. You know that in America today we live in a very mobile society, and many families are separated geographically, sometimes thousand of miles apart. Grandparents are often retirees living on a fixed income, finding it difficult - if not impossible, to afford to see their families as often as they would like. And with the victims' families left with one parent and in many cases reduced incomes, they are hard pressed to find the extra money for travel to the grandparents. The foundation will review applications and give selected families the means to see that these children can spend as much time as possible with their grandparents."*

*"What a sweet idea. How will it work?"*

*"The foundation will consider applications for funding of frequent and regular travel by either the grandchildren or the grandparents to each other, for as long as the grandparents live. Or, applicants can apply for relocation grants that would pay all the costs of relocating the grandparents to be near the grandchildren or visa versa."*

*"Oh, this makes me wanna cry. How much money can one family expect to receive."*

*"There's no limit really. Whatever it takes to bring the family together."*

*"What a special and generous person your client must be. Why did he decide to do this? Was there something or someone special in his life that inspired this wonderful idea."*

*"Well, he's had some good business luck that he wanted to share somehow, but more than that, he feels very strongly about children having all the time they can with their grandparents. All but one of his grandparents, his paternal grandfather, had died before he was born or when he was an infant. My client's often said to me that he wishes that he had had more time with his grandparents, the grandfather he knew, especially. As a young boy, he had a very special relationship with this grandfather. The memories of him are among his most cherished. He often wonders how things might have been if he had had the chance to know him better, if his grandfather had lived a little longer . . ."*

# PROLOGUE - CONTINUED

**Saturday Night, March 1963**
**Greenwich Village, New York City**

A man stood in the shadows at the corner at the end of the alley with his hands in the pockets of his raincoat. The collar of his trench coat was pulled up around his neck to his chin and his fedora sat low over his brow, more to conceal his features than to deflect the steady but light drizzle. He was intently observing two men down the alley as they moved quickly and quietly, in and around the light blue Chrysler Imperial. The alley behind the apartment building was very dark. They had arranged for several of the streetlights to be broken the night before and Mother Nature had also cooperated by providing an overcast, moonless night.

Finally, one of the men stepped into the middle of the deserted alley and, after checking in both directions and up into the windows of the building, he joined the second man at the trunk of the car. They opened the trunk and the two of them bent over, busily tinkering with the contents. A minute later, they lifted out the body. One of them held the dead man propped up on the bumper, leaning it against the large pointed tail fin. The other took a full-length camel cashmere overcoat out of the trunk. They both struggled with the corpse but finally got its arms through the sleeves of the coat. Then they carried the body around the car and placed in the driver's seat. When they finished positioning the dead man behind the wheel, they pushed a fedora onto his head and closed the car door. They signaled to the man on the corner before they casually walked away, disappearing in the darkness at the other end of the alley.

The man on the corner turned and walked across the street towards a long dark Cadillac limousine parked in the middle of the block. The rear door swung open for him as he got closer. Inside he moved to the seat across from the three people waiting for him and sat with his back to the driver's compartment. Once seated, he tapped twice on the partition behind his head and the limousine began rolling slowly to the red traffic light at the corner.

Facing him in the rear bench seat were a man and a woman, both beyond middle age, with a boy between them that might have been their grandson. No one spoke as they sat waiting for the light to change. Then, just as the light turned green and the car began to move, the sound of a tremendous explosion and breaking glass erupted behind them. The woman and the boy spun around to look out the rear window. The entrance to alley glowed orange. The limousine accelerated up the avenue. The older man didn't look back.

After a few blocks the younger man spoke. "Well, Don Carmine, you look pretty good for someone that was just blown up in his car and burned beyond recognition."

The older man leaned forward. "Mr. McBride, that is the last time you or anyone else will call me by that name. Carmine Napolo is dead. *No one* must ever know otherwise. My name is now Joseph Antonelli. I am a successful businessman. This is my wife Marie and this is our nephew Nicolas. He's an orphan and we'll be raising him in our new home, upstate in the mountains."

"Of course," McBride said somberly. "And to prove it, we have created a lifetime of records for your new identities. Let me assure you, *nothing* has been left to chance."

"But my name is Nicolino, not Nicolas," the boy protested to his new uncle.

Carmine smiled and looked kindly at the boy. Then in a gentle voice he said, "I knew your father and your grandfather. They were both named Nico, which is short for Nicola, the name Nicolas in America. Nicolino? Well, that's a good name for a young boy from Italy. It is not a good name for a young *man* in America. And it's not a name that other men will respect. So, from this day on you will be called Nicolas - not Nick or Nicky - Nicolas. Nicolas Pucci. It's a good name, don't you think?"

The boy nodded.

"Good." Then turning to McBride. "It's late and we have a long ride. I believe we'll all be asleep before too long. So Mr. McBride, or should I say Mr. *Dennis,* could you tell us about our new home. Is everything as I have asked?"

Wilson Dennis smiled warmly. "Yes, Mr. *Antonelli*. Everything is just as you planned. Your estate is quite beautiful. The grounds and views are outstanding."

"Good. Thank you, Mr. Dennis. Now we can close our eyes, thinking of all the new and wonderful things ahead of us." Then to the boy. "Nicolas, rest your head on your Aunt Marie's shoulder and dream of your new life on our Bella Collina."

Made in the USA
Lexington, KY
09 February 2017